The Only High I Need

Need

Darcy's Story

RIA TOCSIN

DEDICATION

This book is dedicated to all those still fighting through their addiction, to the survivors of addiction, of abuse, of despair and wounds unseen. This is for you. You are not alone.

Know that your courage to endure and rebuild, is proof that brokenness can still become beauty.

Your survival is your strength, and your story matters.

May these pages remind you that even shattered hearts can still beat with hope.

CONTENTS

DISCLAIMER

Before we go any further, I feel that as a responsible narrator (who you may call Lady Jane) I need to let you know that this story is not necessarily for the faint of heart, nor is it suitable for you to read to your five-year old child as a bedtime story – definitely not recommended! It contains language that you may find vulgar, unpalatable and downright colourful, for want of a better description. There are also references to some very sensitive issues, such as suicide, assault, self-harm, sexual conduct and, of course, the main one being drug and alcohol abuse.

Although I have tried to talk about the issues and topics as compassionately as possible, there is some dark humour that may not be for some. However, this is Darcy's story, and she has been through a lot! It is based on truth; these things actually happened to Darcy.

To all intents and purposes though, this is just a story, so let's continue to keep it that way, in case the nasty little 'vultures' start hissing and grunting, as they recognise similarities to themselves, in some of the characters featured in this story. Did you know that vultures do not have a vocal syrinx like other birds and cannot therefore create complex sounds (if only that were true of the 'vultures' in Darcy's story, eh? But it's very fitting for the point I am ineptly trying to make!) If you're reading this story and you can see some similarities to yourself in the way some of these characters behave, then sort it out mate. #justsayin.

ACKNOWLEDGMENTS

I would like to thank the wonderful J.K. Rowling. Her style of writing and storytelling helped me through some very lonely childhood moments, right through to adulthood. I would read her books over and over again. When I decided to put pen to paper, one of my first thoughts was how I wanted to capture my audience in a way that Harry, Hermione and Ron captured me. Her books taught me that there is magic in the world and that you should cling to those magical moments when the shit hits the fan. Even if Darcy was disappointed that she had thought she'd found her 'knight in shining armour' in Finn, only to realise that he actually ended up being an idiot manchild, wrapped in tin foil. She could look on the bright side though – she could always reuse the tin foil to sharpen her scissors (or in this case her pen).

Which brings me to my second acknowledgement. I'd like to thank Mr Ricky Gervais. His stand-up comedy is next level funny, raw and real. He has definitely shaped my sense of humour and witty comebacks! I am, of course, a genius of my own making. That much has to be acknowledgement in itself, and if I'm acknowledging things, I may as well thank the mother, who brought this particular genius into the world! However, the likes of Derek and After Life have been a huge influence in trying to portray Darcy's story of addiction, recovery and mental health struggles, in a way that talks about serious issues, with just that right balance of humour, to enable my readers to feel Darcy's story, as if it were their own.

A quick acknowledgement for the real-life inspiration

behind some of the characters in this book – I certainly couldn't have done it without you cunts. Without you, Darcy's story would have gone unheard. And let's face it – that would have been a disservice to the world in general!

I'd like to thank my sister-in-law for giving me my first Chromebook. Fair enough, it cost me £40, however, it gave me the ability to write whenever the mood took me and to create the first real thing (besides my children) that I can be proud of. Plus, she's always been by my side. So, thank you, from the bottom of my heart.

I'd like to thank Google for helping me when I have struggled to find the right words for certain characters. The word 'skank' for example, was such a befitting word. I am grateful to now have a clearer understanding of what the word means. It has helped me during personal times of turmoil and jubilation, when I've been in one of those mischievous moods, to add more 'oomph' and punch to my words. The thesaurus and been a goddamned godsend, so cheers!

1. WELCOME TO DARCY'S LIFE

Darcy didn't know what she had done wrong. Why? What had sparked his glacial attitude now? Yesterday, when she left him, so that she could pick her mother up from the train station, her husband, Finn, had been sleeping off yet another drink and drug-fuelled day. She was already mentally, emotionally and physically shattered by his antics; she had endured so much from him, and now he had turned cold towards her for no apparent reason.

She was driving home at full speed on the motorway, going over everything in her head. Why? Why had he changed up on her again? Why was she letting him do this to her, yet again!? They no longer lived together but she felt so trapped by everything she felt for him. For a split second, she wanted it to all go away; to end it all; just to feel released by the agony of loving him. She gripped the steering wheel, ready to swerve herself and the car straight into the central reservation, before something stopped her. What? She didn't know. Maybe it was the will to keep fighting that halted her self-destruct and she came to her senses.

The next morning, she didn't feel any better. He remained cold and despondent, even after she poured her heart out to him (by text). She received nothing but short, stunted replies from him. Her mind went to the place she had been fighting against for months. Life felt like too much.

She picked up the folder that had been given to her by the rehabilitation centre for drugs and alcohol, almost three years previously, and searched through it for a blank sheet of paper, with the intention of writing her family a "goodbye" note. What happened next, ladies and gentlemen, you will just have to wait and see. I will say, that for now, she has yet to make a real effort to find a fucking pen (although, if I could, I'd be telling her to write a final "fuck off" to HIM and that bitch Helga). Darcy is a force to be reckoned with, let me tell ya. She didn't need him and that fucking woman destroying any more of her already fragile mind, she just needed to get her head around the fact that Finn was no good for her. Never again would it work out between them and even if it could, she deserved better.

So much had happened over the last few years. The world had moved on and so had she. She was a completely different woman from the shaking, shivering mess that entered through the doors of rehab, nearly three years ago. However, she felt trapped in time. She had acquired yet another husband and was now on her third. They say, 'third time lucky' and all that jazz, well I'm here to tell ya, it's not true! Especially not when you have acquired them from the forbidden pink pound shop of all things fluffy. That's Darcy's comical way of saying she met the silly bastard in rehab. Now, she was dealing with, what can only be described as a car crash of a marriage. All she could do was stand frozen to the spot and pretend to herself that she hadn't seen it coming from the very start. But hey-ho, at least she still had her sobriety, right?

Trying to cope with a relapse is not an easy feat, especially when the relapse isn't your burden to bear. Darcy sat and pondered her life's choices, seriously wondering what the hell she had done to deserve all that had happened to her in the last six months, when Finn's relapse started. However, if she was thinking about it and if she was being completely honest with herself, it had been rocky seas from the start, which had ended in a tsunami of absolute destruction. She was lost for words at just how foolish she had been. Alas, when will she learn? (Well, I say she was lost for words, but this is Darcy we're talking about ladies and gentlemen, so, of course, that much is just a figure of speech. She can talk for England, if given half the chance, as she is about to prove with the help of me, myself and I).

Being a recovering addict and alcoholic herself had given her the ability to see through the eyes of an addict, so it had left her annoyingly empathetic to her husband Finn's plight. He had 'fallen off of the wagon', no, that's wrong, he'd jumped off the wagon and had landed somewhere in Youbastardtown and, in the process of taking a metaphorical sledgehammer to his life, had almost dragged her down with him. However, she had clung on to her sobriety for dear life, for fear that she wouldn't make it out alive, if she risked going down that rabbit hole again.

She had already allowed herself to falter in the past, and if she allowed herself to fall again, she feared there would be no coming back. So, of course, out of sheer spite (let's not forget about that) by staying sober and not allowing certain hateful 'skanklings' the satisfaction of seeing her broken, she was able to say (rather proudly I might add) that for another day at least, she had beaten her addiction and the haters. (There are certain characters in this tale that thrive on seeing others fail. You will be able to spot them a mile off, by the outlandishly childish names they have been given).

In the process of her husband drinking himself into a stupor, he had managed to drag her through hell and back emotionally and she was hanging on by the tiniest of threads. He had taken to testing her resolve on a regular basis, tugging away at it merrily, like it was his toy. Even after everything, she still clung onto the hope that the man she loved would pull his head out of his backside (ha-ha, who am I kidding? Let's quit the formalities, shall we, and just say, "arse") long enough to see what she and countless others saw in him. When he wasn't being such a twit (to put it politely, we won't go into the other, not so gentle names she had in her head for him – let's ease you in gently) he was one of the kindest and most loving men you could ever hope to meet, but he was also selfish, impulsive and had the craziest ex-baby-mamma imaginable. This statement isn't used lightly or picked out of thin air, willy nilly; as the story unfolds, you lovely readers can make your own judgment.

Finn had a dark, horrible side, that you would never believe belonged to the same person. He was like Jekyll and Hyde and all things in between. The only way to cope with all the stress and strain to her heart, and to her brain, was to start writing her story. The names of the people you will be introduced to have been changed for reasons that will soon be explained. We (Darcy and I) have had a little fun naming some of the characters, as a way of venting frustrations, in a non-confrontational, non-violent, albeit slightly childish manner. They have not been plucked from outer space; everything has been thought through meticulously. If not to entertain you, then for personal satisfaction and fun. Also, it's the little things in life that sometimes give us the most pleasure. A little light-hearted fun never hurt anyone, right? If you see either Darcy or me, walking around with a black eye, then you can guess that some people didn't see the funny side. So, to playfully involve the audience, during our attempts to keep some of the harrowing topics we are going to speak about, as light-hearted as we can, with something so serious, let's "BOO!" the characters with the stupid names together, shall we? Here goes....

Darcy started talking in the third person, at the risk of the nasty little goblins, who were adamant in trying to silence her. There were things, certain truths that she had spoken, that were not well received by the ears of the guilty parties. When the news that there was going to be a book written was announced by Finn James Fibberington (the name speaks for itself. Calling him a liar would be factually correct; however, we are trying to keep it light and airy) Helga Satansspawnington (the clue is in the name; she's a nasty piece of work) was shocked, appalled and even outraged, that her antics and bad behaviour may be called out for the world to see. How dare Darcy write a book! This, of course, was unacceptable, considering Helga had worked so hard to cause as much chaos as humanly possible, without taking any accountability. For every action there is a consequence, and this particular book and story is inconsequential, because for arguments sake, this is just a story....

The main character is Darcy Charlotte Fibberington. She is the wife of Finn. This alter-ego has taken a keen interest in talking in the third person and was created to protect herself from some of the hateful people (characters) from the real world in which she actually resides, some of which will be less than flattered at what is revealed as the story unfolds.

However, this is a 'story'. For arguments sake, and to all intents and purposes, that's all it is. You lovely readers need to know nothing more, than you are about to be taken on a journey of self-discovery, adventure, intrigue and scandal. Is this a true story? Are these people real? That's for you to decide. Certainly, some of the far-off planets and make-believe places many of the characters reside, makes for a real intergalactic mind hump (I would have said fuck, but I'm easing you in gently). The threats of being sued for telling the truth, naming and shaming, if you will, have become all too much for Darcy to bear. Helga had already taken too much; she'd tried to smear Darcy's name and drag it through the mud; to make her life a living hell and attempt to steal her husband, Finn. However, we are not quite there yet. I feel the story cannot be told with the true justice it deserves, without first going back to a blissful time, when all Helga was, was Finn's bloody problem.

So, "Cooee, Helga! Hi - yes you. Please forgive me. I say this with as much kindness and sincerity as I can possibly muster. Please crawl back under the rock from whence you came. Your time will come – trust me."

You lovely readers will have the misfortune to be introduced to her later, as the story unfolds. Her role in this particular part of the tale is minimal, but she is like a slow burning stink, that seeps into your clothes. For now, at least, she is insignificant and affords no relevance to Darcy, me or to you.

I feel that further explanation is needed. There is so much more to Darcy's story than meets the eye. I have started at the end really. But every story has to have a beginning, right? How did she get herself into this little twisted pickle, of marrying such a 'peck-a-tron'? (Basically, a nicer way of saying a total dickhead). To get to this point, we firstly need to go back to a time when Darcy felt no hope, no joy and no will to go on. Back to a time when Darcy was married to Thwaite, a completely different lowly swordsman (nicer than calling him a wanker, right?) Writing down the whole story began as a rant (I don't know if you can tell?) about how rubbish she was feeling at the time, and it developed into something that she feels is now greater than herself.

She was once in Finn's shoes, destroying her own life by drinking herself into oblivion. Some people find it hard to believe because of how far she's come, and how much inner strength she's found through it all. But there was once a time, when she wasn't all sweetness and light, nor was she always the shining beacon of positivity and hope for the future, you see before you today. No, she was a mess. I say all this, knowing her life is still far from perfect, as is she, but she has to reluctantly admit, even to herself (which she always finds difficult) that she has come a long way, trodden through the depths of despair and dragged herself through addiction, only just making it out of the other side by the skin of her teeth. She's suffered loss, endured physical, mental, sexual and financial abuse, from people who once vowed to love and protect her. (That's a fact!! There's a cupboard full of wedding dresses and marriage certificates to prove it). How she got to that point in her life, is a whole other story, which will be finding its way onto bookshelves in the future.

In turn, she has let her children down massively through her addiction and selfish choices. They are actually a credit to themselves; she is so proud of the amazing humans they have become, considering the mother they were given. They deserved so much more. However, they've still managed to hold it together and to not follow in her destructive wake. The acknowledgement of this has tortured her in ways that can't be explained.

This is Darcy's story. Addiction and abuse are killers, and they can take anyone in their grasp, gripping you hard before you even know it's there. It lurks in the darkness. They stem from so many things it's hard to know when they could rear their ugly heads and difficult to know what to look out for. There's a fine line, that once crossed, leads to self-loathing, lying, cheating and not only hurting other people, but also yourself. Can anyone honestly put their hands up and say that they've ever made a good choice under the influence of one thing or another? If you can, then congratulations, because it rarely works out that way. You're lucky. For many people, being under the influence of mainly alcohol, or it could be any mind-altering substance – cocaine, heroin, amphetamine, ketamine… the list is endless – is never a pretty experience.

Have you ever found yourself waking up in the morning, after a night on the town, and thinking, *What the hell did I get up to last night? What did I do? Oh God, the shame!* Most of us, if not all, can relate. This isn't just Darcy's story then, everyone's been there, just in different degrees of severity, ranging from a simple, "Oh, no!" right through to the, "What the fuck!!!" Her story tells you about a woman who has fought the demons and emerged at the other end, battered by life, but with a passion for sharing her story. Not for fame and fortune (however nice that would be) but as a way of understanding herself a little better, and a way to get things off her chest, without a murder charge (joking). Seriously though, what was the pivotal point? Where did it all go wrong? By sharing her story, she hopes to help others understand, not only what it's like to live through, but what it must've been like for the victims she left in her wake. As already mentioned, her selfish actions not only affected her children, but also her family, friends and partners. This happens to so many of us. At one point or another in your life, everyone goes through hardships, tragedy or a trauma, which can seem hard to come back or to break free from. All she asks of you, is to look at the similarities and not the differences in what she's saying and to make no judgement. You never know, one day you may need the kindness and compassion that can come from the most unexpected of sources. A small smile or a random act of kindness from a stranger, can sometimes make the difference between night and day to somebody's life.

We are going to attempt to uncover revelations and epiphanies galore, but please forgive the scattiness and sometimes repetitive language. Darcy is a complicated old soul whose thoughts and feelings are sometimes seen as bizarre behaviours, not only to you, but also to herself. Why she does some of the things she does, is occasionally, completely beyond even her own explanation. I can almost guarantee you won't be bored. However, I include a small disclaimer. It is the responsibility of the reader to allow themselves to laugh, smile and sometimes cry along the way.

The road ahead has been a bumpy one for Darcy, who has had to overcome idiots, piss-takers and 'cockwombles' (the definition of a 'cockwomble' is later explained as the plot thickens) and mainly her own fears, of discovering who she is and acknowledging that it's ok to make mistakes; that she is still worthy of love. She is close to accepting that life is full of people who like to trick you into the idea that you don't deserve to be treated respectfully, and that says more about them than it does about you. She is now well on the way to accepting her own shortfalls and embracing her sober life and thriving for it.

This particular journey starts with rehab, where she met him, Finn. It's the start of one journey but it's far from the end. All I can say is strap yourselves in, ladies and gentlemen. Have your tissues at the ready (and no, this is not that kind of book, for you filthy minded folk) and enjoy the ride. In all seriousness folks, I hope you enjoy the read.

2. THE FIRST WEEK

So, ladies and gentlemen. Darcy and I are going to take you down memory lane. Along the journey, there are some pretty big bumps that have the potential to send you into an orbit of your own rumination. Don't be surprised if you have to climb over some pretty hefty personal topics, which may just stir something within you. When you stare into Darcy's soul, you may just find parts of yourself staring back. Just know that Darcy and I (Lady Jane) have got your back. I forewarn you – this is not going to be easy. Some parts don't make for a pleasant read. There is so much to cover. You never know, by embarking on this journey together, we could possibly discover the meaning of life? Wouldn't that be 'fandabidozi'? (A Scottish expression meaning fabulous or brilliant, if you've never heard the term before). However, it's highly doubtful. Darcy is not the font of all knowledge; she is just as confused and messed up by life as the next person, and that's ok. She has learnt that: as long as you are trying to be a better version of yourself today than you were yesterday, then it's ok to make mistakes. It's human nature after all. Out of all the mess, there is always hope. Even when you feel hopeless. Someone or something comes along in your life at the right time and sweeps you off your feet, winding you to the point of being breathless.

Those are just a few words of inspiration for you all, before smashing all your hopes and dreams to pieces. By telling you that life is actually a series of massive disappointments, then, at the end of the long road that is life, death is waiting for you, with its whips and chains, and all you can do is hope it's a swift and painless one, or a little light spanking…if you're into that sort of thing!

Here we go – Darcy was beaten in more ways than one when she walked through the doors of the rehabilitation centre. She felt scared and alone; she knew her family were all rallying around her for support, cheering her on from the sidelines but what did they know? She felt misunderstood. She knew that the probability of returning home and reconciling with her husband, Thwaite Hallux (it's a play on words for referring to someone as a 'twat'! An English, vulgar, slang word that's less than complimentary, in case we have any readers that haven't heard the word before. The dictionary definition is a stupid or obnoxious person and 'hallux' is the medical term for a big toe. Ha-ha! Who knew? And very fitting). She was highly doubtful, if she was entirely honest with herself, *fuck him*, she thought, with mixed emotions. She was drunk, pissed, sozzled, under the influence (whatever you like to call it).

The morning that she was due to go into rehab (or 'prison' as she fondly named it) she had drunk enough booze to wipe out a small army. If this was to be the last time she was allowed to have a drink, then she was going to do it in style. I say 'style' loosely because she looked far from stylish or glamorous, with the makeup she'd worn the night before, smeared down her face from the salty tears that had fallen from her bloodshot eyes, during the car ride over to the place that was going to be her new home for the next three months. Thwaite was nowhere in sight. In fact, Darcy couldn't recollect where he was (the bastard). All she knew was that he wasn't there to support her in getting her life back together, after the seven years of alcohol and drug abuse. Bearing in mind that this was the same drug and alcohol abuse that he hadn't had any problem taking part in, I might add. He was always there for the 'good times' but called her a disgrace when it all went tits up and she was shivering and shaking in a pile of her own vomit, crying about the mess she had made of her life. A life that was once filled with party times and plastic happiness, was replaced by lying, cheating and drinking alone. In fact, he'd encouraged the 'good times' to roll on and on and on, even after Darcy's mother, Angela (her absolute angel, hence the name, although like most mothers, Angela 'did her head in' at times. With honesty and hindsight, though, it may have been due to her mother telling her things she simply didn't want to hear, like a few home truths, for example. She even dared to say, "No," once in a while as well! #howverydareshe). Sorry…even after Angela had warned him about Darcy's history with alcohol. His attitude was: "She's a grown woman, she can make her own decisions," all while plying her with alcohol and reintroducing her to cocaine, a drug she had only dabbled with in her younger years. Before that 'big toe' came into her life and destroyed it, she had been abstinent for four years. The realisation of all that sent her into a 'BOOM' head-blagger moment (which was her way of saying she felt indignant, hard done by and everything else in between (bastard!) *Well, he is a 'big toe' and all,* she thought, chuckling idiotically, as she remembered the time when her daughter, Brie, had taken the mickey out of her choice in men, commenting that Thwaite looked like a massive, big toe. (Ha-ha-ha, he totally does!)

"What were you thinking, marrying that one Mum?" Brie would say on a regular basis. Her nephews called him, 'Baldilocks and the three hairs'. Now she came to think of it, nobody really liked him. And neither did she right now. The nonsensical laughter was followed by an, 'Oh, poor me!' moment (ya know, like ya do. She's very dramatic at times) and she started to cry.

"I'm such a mess. Everyone hates me," she sobbed. But there was no point. She was doing and saying everything she could to try to prolong the moment she walked through the doors. She wanted to change; she didn't want to be like this anymore. But she was scared.

Her sister-in-law, Rhianna, and her mum, Angela, had gone with her that morning to support her. They were trying to talk Darcy down from the edge of her own despair and to reassure her that it was going to be alright. *Who am I without my toxic little friend* (alcohol) *to keep me company?* She thought to herself, feeling nothing but a swirling whirlpool of all the mess she had created for herself. What was she going to do when the fake confidence that drink gave her, was stripped away? What was she going to do with herself?

"FUCK my life, I can't do this," she said, slurring her words, while perched on the wall outside the rehab centre, puffing away on her cigarette and swaying dangerously, looking utterly pathetic and forlorn. Looking back, it was so sad; the emotions were so strong. It was one of the biggest moments in her life. Everything was going through her head. It felt like such a long time to be away from everyone. *They will all be busy getting on with their lives, forgetting that I even exist!* (Coz' that's what her irrational brain did. It was so inspirational at times, NOT. I'm talking to the general public when I say this: As if you're not already feeling like utter pants, your brain cheers you on by making you feel even worse, doesn't it? Why does that happen? God only knows but anyway…back to what I was saying…). She would have to go it alone and actually be herself for a change. But who was she? How did she do that after years of putting on masks, to hide herself away from the opinionated world? It was such a frightening prospect. There was nothing more for it, she downed the rest of the bottle of wine in one go and braced herself for what she knew was coming.

"Come on Darcy," said Angela. She was trying to be as gentle as possible with her approach, but she was losing patience (you couldn't really blame her).

She'd had a full morning of Darcy shouting at her, "It's all your fault. You're the reason I'm like this. I hate you…," and all the other horrible stuff people say when they are drunk, scared and don't really mean it. However, she could be filled with horrible vindictiveness, especially when she wanted to hurt someone's feelings and make them feel guilty for something that wasn't their fault. It was easier for her to take it out on the one person she loved most in the world. It was easier than blaming herself. Angela was the only person in the entire world, who had never left her side, and there were times when Darcy truly 'took the piss' out of her mother's patience, goodwill and support. (I know! At this point, Darcy was a cow. Don't worry, spoiler alert!! She does eventually sort her shit out, I promise.)

There were no more excuses. She had exhausted her alcohol supply and smoked all the cigarettes she could handle without throwing up. Rhianna was now taking the reins on the situation. She could see Angela was becoming frustrated and emotional, with the torrent of abuse she was receiving from her daughter. "Right, come on now, it's time. You got this girl," she said, trying her best to exert a supportive yet authoritative tone. Darcy simply looked at her, as if she didn't know what she was talking about and muttered under her breath, something about nobody understanding her. As they took her suitcase out of the car, she turned on her heel, as if to run away, but instead, doubled back, ran toward the building and banged on the door of the place that was going to change her life. It was as if in that moment, she embraced it; she wanted it. The fear was so real but if she didn't do it, she knew she was eventually going to drink herself into an early grave.

It was all a bit hazy; she was as 'drunk as a skunk'. So, I feel obligated as the narrator to take over this part of the story telling. I have conducted interviews with the relevant parties, to aid me in giving you as much detail as possible (joking, however, it did sound awfully formal of me, didn't it?) So, the staff (workers) at the rehab centre welcomed her. To say that she was being her overdramatic, flouncy self, would be an understatement. When all else failed and there was nothing left, humour was her only cover up. Plus, she had no filter when she was drunk, so she said whatever was on her mind. She had a very unique way of expressing herself, to say the least. Rhianna did say at a later date however, that she wasn't rude, but it must've been rather awkward to watch her making an absolute 'tit' of herself. It was things along the lines of: instead of saying, "Hello," (like a normal person) she came out with, "So, I take it you lot are my jailers for the next three months then? Is this the part where you 'clap me in irons'?" (I know, that was a shit example, but it was one of those times when you had to be there to witness the absurdity).

Wherever Darcy goes, her comical personality shines through. So, when she was asked some of her induction questions, some of the answers she gave were hilarious. The two staff members who were in the room with her couldn't help but laugh, they tried to maintain their professionalism, but they were only human after all. What could they do but laugh when they were in the presence of her comedic genius? Angela, however, didn't see the funny side of her daughter acting the drunken fool (she very rarely ever did – the killjoy). Darcy was treating everything like a joke, to mask what she was really feeling, which was fear, pain and knowing she was going to be on her own, without a drop of alcohol to mask anything. So, Angela left them to it. After she said a tearful goodbye to her daughter (which Darcy did not appreciate at all; she treated her mother with contempt, which looking back, is not something she is proud of). Angela left her in the room that was going to be the setting for her daughter to detoxify the poison out of her body. Angela glanced back tearfully before leaving, which Darcy refused to acknowledge.

At the peak of her addiction, she was drinking two bottles of whiskey a day, and more if she could get away with it. Alcoholism makes you so sneaky. She took to lying about how much she was actually drinking by hiding the evidence around the house. (Top tip for anyone who has any boots in their wardrobe – stick a wine or spirit bottle down the neck of the boot and it will stand upright, like they do when on display in a shop – to those of you who don't like to organise your wardrobes, just throw the empty bottles over the back fence, like the rest of us peasants – you're welcome!)

From what she can recall there were two workers trying to get her settled (although Darcy was seeing four people, after they'd kindly stopped spinning, that is). Rhianna was apologising for Darcy's antics, trying to calm her down. She wasn't doing any harm, but she was mortifyingly drunk. "I'm sorry about this," Rhianna said. It was one of those times where it's funny but not funny at the same time. You can't help yourself but laugh. David, one of the workers, assured her they'd seen a lot worse coming through their doors. If you think about it, they meet new people at the lowest points of their lives on a daily basis. So, some of the sights they've seen are far worse. David was one of the more weathered workers that Darcy had built a good relationship with during her time there and he didn't appear to be phased in the slightest. In fact, he looked as if he was actually enjoying himself at certain points. He later spoke to her about what she was like on the day of her induction. He recalled how pleasant she was, even though she was sozzled. He told her sheepishly, as if not wanting to cause embarrassment, that she was having her own personal meltdown, crying to Rhianna that she wanted to go to sleep and never wake up.

"Then you stripped down to your 'birthday suit' (naked) and your sister-in-law was following you around the room, trying to get you to put some clothes on," his voice shaking as he spoke, trying not to laugh, "it was quite funny. Then, she was trying to help you put your pyjama bottoms on, while you were being stubborn, and you accidentally farted in her face," he said in a hushed voice, as if by saying it quietly, it would absorb some of the embarrassment. *Oh, my good Jesus!!* Thought Darcy, *the shame.*)

When the induction was over and everyone left, Rhianna and Darcy shared a tearful farewell, "Goodbye for now, not forever. I love you; you got this!" She sat in her room, all alone. No more pretending she was being inducted into a clown club, no more messing around of any kind. She felt stripped of everything. The room contained a chest of drawers, a sink and a bed. She felt more alone than she had ever felt in her entire life. Three months! The thought of it made the room feel like it was closing in on her, it was spinning around faster than her eyes could catch up. The duvet and mattress were covered in a plastic coating, just in case anyone using it made a mess of themselves during the detoxification process. She felt sick. She curled up on the bed, pulled the duvet up to her eyes and cried herself to sleep.

Even with her eyes closed, the world felt like it was spinning. Intrusive thoughts of not wanting to be here anymore was all she could think about. She couldn't help but think she would be better off dead; the evil voices inside her head were shouting at her so loudly, her ears rang with the thoughts. *You're a waste of a life; you deserve everything you get.* Sobbing to herself, she pleaded out loud, "I'm sorry…I'm sorry…please, please, I'm sorry…please make it stop."

To attempt to describe that day is beyond explanation. She kept waking up and not knowing where she was. Hallucinating that she had a bottle of wine, but when she reached out her arm to grasp it, to stem the uncontrollable shaking and fear, the bottle disappeared before her eyes (wounded). Then she'd remember where she was. She sobbed silently into her pillow, only soaking it even more with her salty tears (standard – 'just shit on biscuits!' A saying that she used regularly, to describe one bad thing after another type scenario. She used it to try and diminish the power it had over her, so it doesn't seem all that bad, when in reality it's…well… 'shit on biscuits.') The painful realisation was hitting her over and over again. *Look at what you've done to yourself, you stupid cow!! Look at what you've done to everybody!* She felt like a complete failure and felt nothing but total despair. *Where do I go from here? How am I going to do this?* She asked herself, not knowing where to start, to fix things. The knot in her stomach tightened its grip, leaving her breathless. Every movement, every thought, was so painful; to add to the mix, she was retching but nothing was coming out. Every time she moved, even slightly, the cold sweat she was covered in, felt like icy water on her skin, she was freezing cold. Her teeth chattered uncontrollably, as she tried desperately to will it all away. Swaying backwards and forwards. In pain. Unable to keep still and writhing her feet together, almost rubbing off the skin. She honestly felt like she was going to die. All this was followed by hot flushes, skin burning and feeling itchy. There had been times in the past, where she had scratched big patches of her skin, revealing the glistening plasma, that eventually morphed into massive scabs, all over her body. At some points, she had to have her arms bandaged, right up to her elbows, to hide the huge 'chicken scratches' she had inflicted upon herself. (Yeah, but you can't blame those scratches on just the itching though, can you? No, it was also out of frustration, when Thwaite was blaming you for everything and trying to convince you that you were solely responsible for all that had gone wrong in the relationship.) It was as if spiders were crawling all over her.

The hours rolled on as the day faded. The staff kept popping their heads around the door, to ask if she wanted anything to eat or drink, or to bring in her medication, usually, when she had only just managed to nod off. She couldn't face the thought of food. She craved real sleep; to wake up and for it all to have been a dream. She knew the staff were just doing their jobs, but she wanted to lock herself away from the world and never speak to another soul, as long as she lived, although the way she was feeling, she wouldn't be alive much longer. It was so scary. Being that poorly and away from home. There were times she really believed she wasn't going to make it. It was very frightening.

I just want to take a second and hop out of the story, the characters and personalities, to say this: Please... if you feel yourself relating to any of Darcy's experiences, know that there is help out there. It may not seem like a big thing, asking for help, but admitting that you can't bear the burden on your own, is the first step to taking control of your own life. And NO, it doesn't make you weak or any less of a person. In fact, admitting your own weaknesses makes you the strongest you've ever been. Trust me. I believe in you. Anyway... let's get back to Darcy's story. It's not all about you... (joking).

She spent the next couple of days in a haze of cold sweats. Slowly but surely, with each turn of the clock, she began to feel better. For the first time, in what felt like forever, she felt closer to being herself (whatever that even meant.) It was as if she had awoken from a nightmare, with the gift of new beginnings, however, now she had to embark on the long road of self-discovery. She still had to make it through the dark woods to recovery, tackling the next part of her journey, with her past traumas in tow, like a lead weight in her shoes. Each step felt exhausting, without her usual crutch of a 'drink' to boost her self-confidence. She was so fragile, not just physically, but mentally. She felt as though even the gentlest of breezes could have knocked her down. It was time to face the mess she'd caused. She couldn't keep doing this to herself. Stripped down to nothing but a broken, shaking shell of her former self, it was time to rebuild. This time, with stronger foundations. The worst part of the detox was over. The alcohol was out of her system physically, but mentally, all she craved was a drink. She was no longer unable to move for fear of falling off of the edge of the world, it had come to a standstill and there was nothing else. It felt eerily quiet, but the silence was deafening. *Come on*, she told herself, *get up you scruff.* For some reason, the pep talks she gave herself always seemed to be filled with negative affirmations.

Why? Why do people always do that? I don't know if anyone can relate to this? But instead of being kind to yourself, you talk to yourself like a piece of shit. People tend to say things to themselves they wouldn't dream of saying to others, constantly putting themselves down, like: "Come on, Fatty, get a move on," or "Wow, look at you, you rough bitch, get a grip of ya life." It's not nice, is it? It's no wonder so many people develop mental health problems. If you can talk to yourself like that, then you wind up accepting all kinds of negativity into your life and then, they add fuel to the fire, for yet more self-hatred, as if you've not already got enough to deal with. People need to be kinder to themselves. In other words, next time you feel like screaming at yourself for being useless, try to find a better way or kinder words; try to find three things you like about yourself, to balance it out a bit, at least. You never know, it could change your outlook on life. I don't know. Darcy doesn't know either! It's just a thought.

She dragged herself to the shower room. She peeled off the sweat-drenched clothes of the last few days, from her body and stood shakily under the shower of cleansing water. A stupid thought crossed her mind, as she stood under the warm water. For some reason, she never seemed to smell of BO (body odour) no, she would smell a bit foisty instead, as though she'd been left in a damp cupboard for too long. It got her thinking. *Which is the lesser of the two evils?* (I've got an idea, instead of festering away, feeling sorry for yourself, in your pit (bed) for the rest of all time, it might be a good idea to get your ass up and be the 'bad-ass bitch' you know you can be! Move about a bit, then you can smell of nice things, like soap and all things beautiful. Not like a stale bit of cheese.) The water cascaded down her body, washing away the evil. She instantly felt lighter. It symbolised the next step for her. (It was like levelling up – for any gamers reading this, she was on a winner.) At least she had moved today, and honestly, that felt to her like an achievement in itself. She finished her shower and her bizarre wonderings of whether or not she would rather smell funky or foisty and dried herself off. She applied a little light makeup to her face, mainly drawing her eyebrows on, enough to give her face some expression (she's a secret ginger, you know? Well…, strawberry blonde, so without her eyebrows, she's expressionless).

Now, it was a test of mental endurance. She had to wrap her head around the knowledge that she was an addict. She would never be able to touch a drop again. Not even now that she felt ok. She had to accept that she had to abstain from alcohol COMPLETELY. Never again, would she be able to have the odd cheeky glass of wine. NOOOO…, the fun police had come down hard and well and truly arrested her ideas of how to spend her free time in the future. She knew it would only lead back to the chaotic life she had just fled from. But she couldn't help feeling slightly resentful. It was 'shit on biscuits'. She wanted to go home. Everything there felt so unfamiliar, but even returning home was a scary prospect now. What was there to go home for, really? There was no loving husband waiting for her (you don't know this yet love, but he's too busy shagging your best mate, the same best mate who had an affair with Elon, your daughter's dad!) She no longer felt that anyone at home would understand her or what she'd just gone through. She didn't know how to communicate any of it to anyone, especially him! It felt different somehow. It was as if the glass had shattered and she could see him for who he truly was. A horrible piece of shit. Her journey with Thwaite was over. That ship had sailed off, hit a rock, and was now at the bottom of the sea of resentment and contempt, swimming with the fish. He kept in sporadic contact, but she would avoid his calls. She couldn't face the monotony of the same conversations over and over again about the cats. The love they once shared had dwindled down to forced conversation. Their relationship had run its course, although a little bit of both of them were still going through certain motions. For example, saying, "I love you," at the end of each call (I wonder if he was telling HER that as well?) A lot had happened throughout the years. There was fault on both sides. Darcy had been battered in more ways than one and always felt unheard. She had endured broken bones, complete contempt and a lack of empathy; she in turn, had lied and cheated. They became toxic for each other. The story of Darcy and Thwaite is for another time. It is certainly an interesting one. However, right now, she had bigger fish to fry. This is the story of another twat (joking, well not joking, but you know what I mean).

It felt like the first time in forever, she was free to concentrate on nothing but herself. To build herself up from the ashes. Like a phoenix reborn. She set her sights on world domination and started mentally preparing herself to become the first queen of the world. Just kidding, all she longed for was to feel comfortable in her own skin. She wanted what everyone wants, to be happy (it sounds so cheesy but it's true and is that really something so wrong to want?) She needed to break free from her own shackles and embrace the programme. *You're the only one holding yourself back*, she told herself.

She started venturing out into the outside communal area to have cigarettes. Only making small talk with other residents (inmates) for the length of time it took to smoke them, before retreating back to her room, to sit alone and contemplate life. As a means of coping, she took to writing a diary but would regularly run out of words to express how she felt, or she would lie, even to herself, about how she really felt. She'd suppressed everything for so long, it hit her all at once, overwhelming and confusing her; frustration would kick in, taking on all the guilt and shame. She felt rubbish about how she had left things with her mum, but she resented her at the same time. When Angela tried calling her, she would hang up, not knowing what to say. Without her home comforts or a drink in her hand, it was hard to process what was happening to her. Her emotions were heightened to the brink of breaking point. One minute she was ok, the next she was in floods of tears. She'd slam her diary shut and turn her attention to her crossword puzzles, or attempt to draw, to pass the time and to get through the withdrawal symptoms. She would purposely sit in her own misery, welcoming in the pain, as a means of self-punishment. It was sadistic, but pain was the only thing she really understood. It was sad but true. Pain was inevitable, so *why not just sit in it and dwell like the little 'billy no mates' I am*? (Oh dear, maybe at this point we might need to get the tiny violins out, or the full orchestra!) She felt like the world hated her, when in reality, people couldn't get enough (#smileywinkyface). She was the one that was so full of hate for herself, not other people; she hated herself so much and didn't know where to start in all the wreckage.

Darcy sat on her bed overthinking, like always. She showered and put makeup on. Today was the day she was going to attempt to venture into the communal kitchen area, to make herself a cup of tea. She had to try and be a bit more sociable. She couldn't expect to grow as a person if she didn't at least try to embrace a positive mindset. She hadn't had the confidence to make a drink in front of anyone else yet, in case the tremors shook the cup out of her hand. Her shakes were still bad but became worse in front of other people, but today, she had the mindset of, *Just do it dickhead!* It was time to try opening up and interacting with the people she was going to be living with for the next three months. Otherwise, it was going to be a very long and lonely journey.

When she removed her head from her backside, she actually discovered she had a lot in common with the most unexpected of souls. It put her at ease to know that everyone was in the same boat as her. They were all just as dysfunctional and messed up as she was, just in different ways and to different degrees. (It's the similarities and not the differences that bring people together). Everyone had their own story and each one in turn, was just as interesting and traumatic as the next (not that she found interest in trauma, but they had so much substance, sadness and bad luck, if you know what I mean?) Not everyone's story came from a place where you could ever say, "Well, it's your own fault," or "You brought all this on yourself." They were very much like her. Very quickly she became comfortably uncomfortable in her new surroundings. There were people in there from all walks of life. It wasn't just your stereotypic alcoholics. There were some people in there that she would never have guessed were battling addiction.

There was one lady in particular, who looked as if she didn't belong in a place like this. She looked so normal. Like she should have her shit together, if you know what I mean? The kind of woman, that if you were arrested for committing a crime, she would be the one to represent you. (A bit like Anne Robinson from The Weakest Link TV programme.) Darcy was so shocked when she came out as an alcoholic and told the world she'd been so bad at one point, she was given only six weeks to live. Darcy was sure she had heard, somewhere, that Anne Robinson had once drunk perfume for the alcohol content! But it's not true. I've just checked Google. Good job really, isn't it, because if it was true, that would have been some mighty expensive drink, don't you think? So, when she saw this particular woman, she just thought, *How could this be? Wow!* It really got her thinking…, *you never truly know what people are going through behind closed doors.* Alcoholism or other addictions can creep their way into anyone's life. It takes over without prejudice. It doesn't matter where you come from, what you look like or how much money you have in your bank account. If anything, the more money you have, only means your hiding champagne bottles in your Christian Louboutin boots and crying on your private yacht, instead of supping a £3 bottle of White Lightning (cider) and using the empty bottle as a makeshift pillow, while crying underneath a bridge in the rain. It's all relative and it got Darcy to thinking. *Never judge someone before you get to know them.* Also, money doesn't buy you class, it just buys you better class A's (drugs!) Plus, the more money you have, the faster you can speed down the rabbit hole. Nobody should ever become complacent. If you're not careful, it will wrap itself around you; it will get you, good and proper.

Her name was Claire. She was an amazing lady. She and Darcy became so close, as if they had known each other forever. She became like a surrogate mum of sorts. Her story was so sad. She had been diagnosed with breast cancer, right in the midst of an abusive relationship. She had taken to drinking in the evenings, in an attempt to numb the fear of dying and leaving her daughter without a mother. She was told that the only way to remove the cancer was to have her breast removed completely, which led to body dysmorphia. After being given the 'all clear', things had started to look up, only to then be told that her cancer had returned with a vengeance. To cope with the pain and fear of what she believed was going to be a slow and painful death, she had almost drunk herself to death. By the time she realised it, she was gripped by the addiction. She almost lost her job, been copped (arrested) for drink driving and lost her licence. This is to name just a few of the things she'd been through. She and Darcy later joked that Claire had only beaten the cancer by pickling it with alcohol, which is not really something you should joke about – it's 'gallows humour' (quick Google, for anyone who is unaware of the term 'gallows humour'. It's a style of comedy that makes light of a subject that is normally considered serious or painful to discuss). By talking about it openly and light heartedly the way they did, it helped her process a lot of her trauma, in a way that felt manageable. She was a very inspirational woman.

It just goes to show, thought Darcy, *you never truly know somebody until you've walked a mile in their shoes and don't ever judge a book by its cover.* People can surprise you. You don't know what other people have been through to get where they have ended up, at that particular moment in their life. They may have been through a series of bad mistakes and misfortune, landing somewhere in 'Shitsville'. Some may just be visiting, and others may have lived there a while, however, people can grow and people can change, BUT, people can also stumble and fall over what might seem like the smallest of things to you, which could be the final straw to someone else, so why just sit there and judge? It's nobody's place to tell someone else what is right and wrong (well, apart from the obvious, like don't murder, rape or maim – that's just common sense). It really opened up Darcy's eyes. For the first time in a long time, she felt understood. Very quickly, the fear was replaced with a sliver of hope that it might not be such a bad place after all. She felt slightly optimistic that there could be a future out there for her, that wasn't so bleak. Ha-ha, Darcy, you poor deluded fool. Stay away from bright shiny things and remember, that includes turds (shit, poo, faeces…) as they too can be polished to look attractive! It's been proven on MythBusters (an American TV show) and in the form of Finn James Fibberington, who she was just about to meet.

The detox part of her stay was nearing its end. It was almost time to start the rehabilitation process. The first week went by in a haze. It was all a bit blurry. One minute she felt sure of what she wanted, the next, she had no idea how she was going to cope with all of these new-found emotions, for the rest of her life. They'd tried to tell her what the process was a few times, when they'd come to talk to her in her room, to discuss the transition, but she was still feeling very fragile and was suffering from 'brain fog'. Her hands still violently shook at times, and she felt like her body was in a constant low-vibration mode, as if she had forgotten to take her 'love eggs' out (I'm joking, Darcy has never used that particular love toy. I just thought it was funny).

Everyone attending the rehabilitation programme was given morning tasks to complete. The day started at 7.30am, with the first job of making their beds. They tried to drill it into you, that if you started your day with a neatly made bed, then you'd always feel better for it. *Yeah? What do you know?* She thought, with a raised eyebrow and a top lip sneer on her face, which did absolutely nothing for her wrinkles. At the time it seemed pointless and tedious. It was a stupid rule they'd put there as a means of control. (Ladies and gentlemen, she was wrong to have this 'negative nelly' attitude. I can confirm that they do in fact know what they are talking about. It does make you feel better. I know, I tried it. And so does Darcy, although she now only admits it begrudgingly).

She was given light duties, as she was still so unsteady on her feet. Even though she felt a lot better, she was still very fragile. So, she was assigned the task of cleaning the handrails. It was quick and easy, and it doubled up as giving her something to hold on to, while she was doing her part and getting involved. Everyone helped each other out. It quickly became like a mini family. It felt as if they were all in it together, united by moaning and groaning about their symptoms of the detox and withdrawal. She was so grateful for how supportive and nice everyone seemed to be. After the work was over, she made herself a cup of tea and sat herself in the armchair in the pool room, where everyone generally congregated, and started chatting away to Claire about how rough she felt. She was still feeling slightly itchy and sick, from the last bit of the alcohol working its way out of her system. She was still very wary of spending too much time outside of her room. There was only so much she could take from the overwhelming presence of other people, although she was getting better, she preferred to retreat back to her room when she felt stressed out by it all. She was just thinking about making her excuses to retreat back to her safe place, where she could do what she did best – dwell. It was, after all, only her fourth day there. It was all still very new. She remained severely shaky and felt utterly drained. Then out of the corner of her eye, she saw him….

3. PHWOAR FINN

Have you ever looked at someone, where the huge red flag, the exact shade of red that'd match your lipstick perfectly, is blatantly waving away at you, enticing you into naughty thoughts and bad decisions? Yeah? Darcy too. Tut, tut, tut, why? Oh, why do we do it? Between you and I, and Darcy, of course, what is it that is so deeply seated in our DNA, that we ignore all the signals and think it's a good idea getting involved with a 'bad boy'? (There are other names for them, such as: 'dicks', 'fuck-knuckles' and 'doo-lally-tappers'.) Seriously though?! I'm asking you because she and I are at a loss as to why? When you know it's not a good idea, but you still do it anyway? You may be taken for the ride of your life, but your heart and sanity will be shattered in the process. It's laughable, but you know the kind I mean. Cheeky and charming, with a twinkle of mischief and magic behind the eyes? No? Well lucky you, however, I've a sneaking suspicion that at one point or another in their lives, everyone has met a Finn… or two. It's just that some of us have the common sense to steer clear of the inevitable car crash it would be. However, Darcy was drawn to him (and sorry to be flippant here but…well…) like a crackhead is to a crack pipe (this is after all, a book about addiction. It may not be the PC (politically correct) thing to say, however… it's true.) He came across as cocky and confident, yet behind those mischievous eyes and cocksure laughter, she knew he was just as broken as her. He played it off extremely well, or he thought he did. He was intriguing somehow; in a way she couldn't explain. She thought he was bloody beautifully broken, just like her. There was an air about him, but she could see he was 'bricking it' (shitting himself with fear) yet with those bricks, he was building his own defences against a world that felt alien. (Or, maybe, Darcy, my love, you were reading far too much into it? There's broken and then there's BROKEN, if you catch my drift?) She instantly felt connected to him somehow. Stupid right? She couldn't quite place it. Maybe it was because he gave her hope in a hopeless place. She wanted to get to know him; she knew there was more to him than the lovable idiot he portrayed. It's hard to explain, however, let's not get too ahead of ourselves, shall we, and let's get on with the 'story'.

Phwoar! Oh my God! She had just seen Finn for the first time and was yet to be introduced but, *Oh my God! Who is he?* She thought, feeling a rush of nervous energy that made her heart skip a beat but at the same time, beating at what felt like it was three times its normal speed. Suddenly, she was very aware that she looked and felt like crap. Feeling her cheeks beginning to flush, she instantly set about trying to fix her 'bed head', without making it look completely obvious that she fancied him. He was with a woman called Kelsie. She was loud and brash and had set herself up as 'queen bee'. Darcy's initial instincts told her that the two of them were the troublemakers, but in a good way. They looked like a lot of fun; however, she was a bit wary of her, she didn't seem like the kind of person you'd want to get on the wrong side of, but Finn, *phwoar!* She couldn't explain it. He wasn't the most attractive man in the world (you know, like Johnny Depp, or what's his face from the TV programme, The Tudors? Ah yes, Jonathan Rhys Meyers; he didn't look quite like them, but he was a very unique match in her eyes.) Nor did he hold himself with much elegance and grace; she thought he was fit, but it was his presence she instantly found attractive. What she meant by that is not exactly clear, however, just by being in the same room as him, was like all her troubles felt lighter somehow. The room felt brighter, and the world didn't seem so scary anymore. If anything, the raw way he presented himself, was enviable. To her, it felt like nothing phased him; he was so likeable. She watched the two of them laughing and joking away, as she silently cursed herself to hell, for not taking more care in her appearance that morning. The butterflies in her stomach burst out of her and started singing Disney songs about love and lust. She should've metaphorically shot them down, but in all seriousness, something inside her knew he was going to be a big part of her journey, blissfully unaware of the other avenues of hell he was going to take her down. I'm just going to say it: he gave her the 'fanny-flutters'! *Oh Darcy, what are you doing? Just chill out! Act natural, you idiot!*

She had instantly started talking herself out of something that hadn't even happened yet. *Concentrate on yourself, silly woman, you've not even moved the last knobhead out yet*, she told herself. She was determined not to get distracted. Ha-ha! Yeah, whatever! Darcy, you poor deluded fool. Common sense kicked in. You will see a running theme throughout her journey, where common sense kicks in. It is a fleeting sensation that disappears just as quickly, leaving her to her own devices, to make the most shocking decisions.

She wasn't looking for anything new, she just wanted to be around his bubbly presence, nothing more. She was kidding herself really – logic and lust were in a battle. He was so friendly. When he smiled, his eyes shone with mischief, lighting up the room. Clearly, she wasn't the only one who felt this way, as he seemed to have a knack of engaging even the quietest residents into conversation, as he walked around casually introducing himself.

"Easy mate, how are you doing? I'm Finn." Everyone took an instant liking to his straight-talking, inquisitive charm. He was far from graceful, and he looked and sounded like your stereotypical, council estate chav, with a twist. Now I know what you're thinking, the word 'chav' isn't usually used to describe a thirty-odd year-old bloke, however, this is Finn we are talking about; he was like a big kid. Yes, I suppose he was from a council estate and a bit of a troublemaker, and yes, you'd never see him without some sort of tracksuit on, but he was just him; so likeable! She loved it. He looked like the kind of trouble that's thrilling not killing, if you know what I mean? Harmless and fun. The way he kept glancing over at her, while he talked to the others, let her know that he either thought, *bloody hell, she looks rough*, or maybe, he fancied her a bit too?

She tried acting nonchalant, as she carried on her conversation with Claire, as if she'd barely noticed he was there. In reality, she was completely knocked sideways by him. She could hear the laughter and upbeat chatter that bloomed as he talked, creating a new energy in the room.

Concentrate Darcy, it's not the time or the place, she told herself, as she walked back to her room to get ready for the day ahead. Her original plan, to lay on her bed and wait until it was time to hand her phone in, ready to begin the first day of learning sessions, was replaced by YouTubing feel good music, while applying her makeup, taking a lot more care to add that extra hint of sexy to her eyes, just in case she bumped into HIM again.

Detox was over. Now it was time for the hardest part. The drugs and alcohol may have been out of her system physically, but mentally… well, that was a whole different mind-fuckingly annoying little side effect of all this sobriety. Why though? Why, after all the hurt it had caused, did she miss it? Well not miss it, but yeah, miss it? She hated admitting it. After all, it had almost destroyed her life, and if she had kept going the way she did, it could've killed her. So why was her brain tricking her into thoughts of carrying it on? Did she have a death wish? It was like she was going through a bad breakup. She knew it was no good for her in every way imaginable. She had drunk herself to the point where her body had almost turned on her (liver cirrhosis). She didn't have liver cirrhosis, but she had skated dangerously close to it, and she had lumps on her pancreas, but some of the good times she'd shared with her toxic friend were exhilarating. It gave her a confidence she didn't think herself capable of having without it. It gave the impression she could say whatever was on her mind at the time. However, it heightened her emotions and lowered her inhibitions, which gave an overdramatic and unfiltered version of how she really felt. That in turn caused all kinds of chaos (as you can imagine) when she'd start picking up her phone and calling people all kinds of cunts. They might have deserved it, however, calling your boss, "A jumped up old fuckwit, who doesn't know how to do her job properly," was probably not the way to go, when trying to get the day off work! Or, of course, let's not forget, the good old fashioned beer goggles. Everyone's got a bit of sexy in them then, haven't they?

Arghhh! She shook her head in disbelief. Why was her brain trying to trick her into belittling the 'comedown' and mocking it, as if it wasn't really that bad? Bamboozling her brain into the idea that she and alcohol belonged together. She shook her head again, as if to jiggle the common sense back into herself. She knew her brain was lying; it just wanted a quick release from all of the new feelings (and no, she didn't mean how she was feeling about her 'fanny-flutters'; his magical charm didn't work that quick.) It was just everything, absolutely everything. It ranged from next door's cat (she didn't even know if they had a cat, but if they did, then it was included) the kitchen sink and the colour of the leaves.

The booze and cocaine had helped her with her sadness occasionally but would then trick her into hurting herself (as already mentioned with the chicken scratching episodes.) But she had also taken kitchen knives and slashed gashes in her arms and wrists in the past, so that she could see physical evidence, in the form of all the blood, as a visual aid for the pain she felt inside. At her lowest, there were also suicide attempts. She gave suicide up as a bad job in the end, when one night, after a depression session on the booze and cocaine, she'd talked herself into feeling like there was no other way out. She had 'necked' a load of tablets, not really caring what they were; she just wanted to go to sleep and never wake up! However, the next day she awoke, feeling slightly perplexed as to why she felt ok. When she looked at what she'd taken, she saw that she had, in fact, 'necked' a load of multivitamins! Oh dear, Darcy, you can't even do that right, can you? (It's not funny really, it's sad that she felt that ending her life was her only option. There is always another way, even if you don't feel it at the time.) *This is why I need to concentrate on getting better, not boys,* thought Darcy.

I'm taking a second here, to step out of the story, with all its bravado and the false humour surrounding the characters. Because, in all seriousness, suicide is well…, a killer. It's awful when you feel so low, that you think there is no other way out except death. If anyone has been through it, or attempted it before, they will know how despondent you have to feel to get to that point in your life. Words can't describe it.

Everyone's experiences differ, but that does not diminish how it feels to be at your rock bottom. The Samaritans are excellent listeners, even though they can't help with the practical sides of getting help, they listen without prejudice and have talked Darcy down from the edge more than once. Do not suffer alone, even when you don't feel like talking, that's when you really do need to talk. Sometimes it's easier to talk to a stranger than it is to talk to friends and family. It's just a thought.

It was as if the idea of having another drink again was always at the back of her mind, tricking her into thinking that she was nothing without it. She couldn't help it, especially now she had all these new people around her, one of them being HIM. She was going to have to be her sober self in front of all of these new faces and share her deepest thoughts with them all; the prospect filled her with dread. No, it was more than that. She wanted to run away. It was the same feeling she had when she'd first arrived at the rehab facility; that flight response when she had every intention of fleeing, only to turn and run back towards the building. She was torn between accepting her fate and letting her addiction swallow her whole or trying to fight for the right to find herself. He was going to think she was a freak! She wanted the fake confidence that the alcohol gave her, so she could be funny, witty and charming (ha-ha, Darcy, come on now, when you were 'pissed up', you were repetitive, boggle eyed and slurry!) It was all she had known. It was still ingrained, like a cancer in her brain. Every fibre of her being, for the last seven years, had been intermingled with drinking or drugs. She had relied on them for everything.

At the start of her addiction, it all seemed so very sophisticated, only drinking now and again on weekends – it wasn't, as she never knew when to stop. (Aww, bless her, look at her trying to justify it – weekends? Now and again?

Yeah, right!) She'd get thoroughly sozzled and would have to spend the next day with a bucket by the bed and paracetamol by the dozen, nursing the dreaded hangover. But she didn't have a problem because she wasn't doing it every day, right? Then it escalated to having a drink most evenings, (more justification coming…) but she was cooking as she was drinking, so she was just chilling out and relaxing. She didn't have a problem. That's what most people do to relax on an evening, surely? Then it started during work breaks; she was only having one, or two, if she downed it quick enough. It was only a quick drink, during lunch. *What's the issue with that?* her brain would tell her. Then it became first thing in the morning, while she was getting ready for work. *What's the fucking issue? And who cares if I take a flask to work with me? People just need to mind their own business; it isn't their life!* Then it stepped up even further to drinking through the night, to stop the mental torture of thinking about drink when it wasn't near her (she felt lost without it). The more she drank, the more she needed it, until 'POP went the fecking weasel' (it certainly wasn't a champagne cork, she couldn't afford any of that) and she was gripped. It sounds silly, but can you see the slow justification and the increasing denial? Yeah? Well, there's help at the back of the book if you need it, that's all I'm gonna say….

Now, she had to learn how to live without it, by spending the next three months following a strict routine of learning sessions, including meditation, music therapy, arts and crafts, planning for the future, learning a better way of life and understanding more about where her addiction had stemmed from. That was all part of the CBT (cognitive behavioural therapy). She was very sceptical, but at this point, she thought, *What have I got to lose?*

In total, there were twenty-something people sharing the house. They were arranged into small groups, all moving through their journeys at different stages, so some had been there longer and were farther into the programme than her, so she could see the positive effects the programme had. All of them would comment on how far they had come through the process, so she knew it could work. She could see physical, living proof in her peers. Firstly, there was the detox, which lasted for six days, although it was coming to an end for Darcy. It was the hellish stage, as she called it, where she saw the gates of hell and that dodgy, three-headed dog called Cerberus. He wasn't as scary as he seemed, in fact, she fed him the scraps from her plate, and they had a cuddle on the single bed, while she sweated out the poison. For those who can't tell, I'm obviously joking – he tried to bite her. Then after that, it was eight weeks of intensive learning sessions and a strict regime, then the final three-week stretch, where the rules were more relaxed. Sessions started at 10am and the day finished at 5pm. During that time, they had to hand their phones in at the office.

Many of the residents, new to the programme, were slightly shell shocked at how many rules there were, such as the no swearing policy. Darcy thought it was ridiculous. *Fair enough, if someone is using it in a way that is nasty and offensive, then I can understand it but, in this day and age, everyone let's a "fuck" or a "shit" out, every now and then, don't they?* She thought indignantly. *There are people from all walks of life coming through those doors; it's probably more a base level of respect. Offensive language is something that everyone should be aware of anyway. But some people aren't built with any filter… erm, yeah, so maybe having a blanket rule of no swearing, with the exception of the occasional accidental fuckups is probably for the best.* She had talked herself into understanding the rule! However, she wanted things to moan about (why wouldn't she?) Like the bedtime being at 11pm! *Why is it that everyone has to be in their rooms for 11pm? It's stupid. What if they want to talk to each other and socialise? Yeah, but 11pm is kind of late anyway,* she thought begrudgingly, *and some people might think it's ok to be loud, which could keep the rest of the house up. Erm, yeah, maybe that rule is valid as well?* She conceded. However, some of the rules seemed superficial and pointless, like what, she couldn't put her finger on right now, but anyway, that's beside the point. Being told what to do all the time felt like a foreign concept to a lot of the 'newbies', Darcy included. *It isn't just me*, she thought, as she overheard some of the other residents voice what she was thinking. "I'm a grown adult…." or "Why should I have to be told what to do?" She felt uncomfortable, but never expressed herself, regardless of how unbearable it made her feel. This was one of those times when her thoughts were valid. However, she had the same awful knot in her stomach, as if she was being coerced against her will, just like she had experienced countless times before. Ranging from: 'no biggie', right through to the absolutely horrendous. (As time goes on, Darcy may share some of her other stories but for now, let's see which way the wind blows. You're still strangers, and she's still fragile.) It felt as though someone was taking away her liberty. She was never able to stand up for herself in the past, even when she knew it was wrong. The ability to say, "NO," without it all coming out the wrong way, was one of her biggest weaknesses. Being sober heightened the emotions she'd suppressed, and they all jumbled up into one hot mess. So, the idea of someone taking her phone, was as if someone had pissed on her cat. *Why can't I just keep my phone in my room? This is fucking stupid! What the hell am I doing here?* she thought, working herself up to boiling point. She stayed, of course. She also handed in her phone into the office, begrudgingly, without a word, but it put her in an obviously foul mood (that was before the Botox, so the mood was clearly visible on her face). When she was asked what was wrong, all that she managed to say was, "Oh, it's nothing, I'm ok," trying to don a fake smile, so no one would know what she was really thinking.

She walked to her first session, not knowing what to

expect, however, at this point, the phone situation had pissed her off too much to care. She knew she was being pointlessly moody, and it was stinking out her attitude, but she couldn't give two fucks (she only swore in her head, so that bad language would go unnoticed) *Or can these bastards read my mind as well now? Taking my phone off me. Tut. I don't know who they think they are,* she thought grumpily. She enjoyed her self-sabotage; she knew it was only going to be a hinderance, *but they can just fuck off! What's this shit gonna teach me anyway?* Tutting to herself, she internalised it all, subconsciously stewing on it, on purpose, so she could justify the voices of doubt, telling her that she couldn't do this. She was being a petulant child, but nobody would have known it. Maybe, it was all the other emotions she had been feeling that morning as well? She just didn't know. She hadn't felt anything without being under the influence for all this time, so it was hard to process them sensibly. All of these feelings were bubbling away, and she didn't know what to do with them.

Quick pitstop. Does anyone else do this? It's so silly, isn't it? The only person you're hurting is yourself, even when something isn't a big deal, you tend to blow it out of all proportion, to mask the real emotions of what's really bothering you. It's easier to exaggerate the situation, rather than deal with the bigger, underlying issues. Small inconsequential stuff, is like the final straw kinda thing? The human brain and why we do what we do, has always baffled me and Darcy – it's not just you… anyway back to the story.

Her phone was completely forgotten about when she entered the room and saw Finn sitting there. His body language was relaxed and inviting (she just wanted to go and sit on his lap, sink into him and find out everything about him) as if he was comfortable in his surroundings (*why can't I be more like that?*) But again, she could see behind the façade; she couldn't help herself. It was as if they were two lost souls, matching each other, and he was calling out to be understood. (Silly woman!) She couldn't quite gauge him. Was he trouble or just misunderstood? (ERM, HELLO! HE'S TROUBLE, WITH A CAPITAL 'T'!) My take is that it's very rarely the latter! Misunderstood? Nope! So, save yourself the time and tears and just RUN! (Only half kidding). She found a seat near him (sitting next to him would have to suffice – for now) and joined in the conversations he was having with the rest of the group, who were all apprehensively waiting for the session to begin. His energy matched hers in a chaotic way. He was the yang to her yin and vice versa. They immediately began to vibe off each other, as they all discussed their thoughts so far, about being in this 'prison', the rules, and how they were coping with their withdrawals.

There were seven of them in this particular group. There was Claire, with her beautifully kept hair and posture, which gave her the air of being ready to learn and absorb everything, as if she was going to have to take her findings to court. (She wasn't like that really, she was just like everyone else, but she had a style and grace about her that Darcy couldn't explain.) She had already become acquainted with her.

Then there was a big 'Neanderthalian meathead' of a bloke called Arnold, who used to be a body builder and was very much into his fitness. (Yes, you've guessed right, the inspiration for this character's name, came from good old 'Arnie', Arnold Schwartzenegger!) He looked as though he had the ability to be quite formidable if he wanted to be, however, although she was still withdrawn at this point, and if he gave off a scary vibe, there would be no way on God's green earth, she would ever let him know that she was a little intimidated by him. He came across as arrogant and gave off a 'knobhead' vibe, which annoyed her immensely for some reason. Maybe it was the stick she had up her arse that morning, she wasn't sure. (Nope, at that point, he really was being dick!) She didn't like to judge a book for its cover, however, looking back on it, she did! In her defence, he didn't make it easy to think otherwise. He also had a very distinct smell of shit from his arse, as he was always farting, like it was going out of fashion! Straight away, Darcy took an instant dislike to him, especially when he started bragging that he'd already thought about how to escape. He was telling Finn exactly how he would do it.

"There's CCTV there, there and there," he said, pointing at thin air, as if he was pointing at different corners of the building, "and my room is there," he continued, pointing at a different part of the air. The way he was telling Finn, was like he thought he was about to pull off the next big bank heist, and it looked like Finn was lapping it up. It was as if he thought he was a genius. She hoped to God that Finn wasn't stupid enough to get any ideas from him, as she could already tell that Finn was very naïve in some respects. *What a twat*, thought Darcy, rolling her eyes discretely. "So, if I climbed out of my window, and went that way," he pointed, "then I could climb the fence, go to the shop, get a bottle of vodka, come back and they wouldn't have a clue," he finished, looking smug. (And he talked about alcohol, as though it was the only topic in the world for discussion.) *Idiot! Do it then, if you wanna leave, then leave, it's not as if they make you stay. TWAT! Just fuck off then!* she thought angrily. *Why would you wanna go out, get a drink and then come back to the programme? Idiot man*, she thought, as she was listening to his bravado. His attitude stank; his negative aura felt catching. It was hard not to think of ways to trip him up in the hallway, without him pounding her into the ground (joking, but it did piss her off and only added to her original mood.)

Moss (inspired by the English TV series, The IT Crowd, about a group of geeks) was very quiet and came across like a bit of an 'odd bod'. He wore headphones and carried his laptop wherever he went throughout his time there, mostly keeping to himself. His story was so sad, he was a complex character and his age evaded her completely. However, if she was to hazard a guess, then she would say he was in his forties. His problem started when he was in his teens. He would go to all the music festivals with his parents. Even though he didn't have the look of it, his old lifestyle sounded quite 'hippyish', with a lot of peace and love, drinking, taking pills, acid and having party times with his mum, who was also his best friend. His life was turned upside down with grief, when he went to look for her one day and found her body, lying dead in a lake near his house. When he was drinking, he was that bad that he wouldn't even go to the toilet. Instead, he would do his business in old pop bottles. He was so kind in nature and an absolute genius with technology. Wherever he is now, she hopes he's doing ok. Straight away, Finn homed in on the fact that Moss had his earphones in and started to question him as to why? Why was he allowed his gadgets with him, when everyone else had had their phones taken from them?

"Here mate! How does that work? Nah, mate! How come I get me phone took off me, and you're allowed all your shit?" he exclaimed loudly, as if talking to the room, highlighting the fact it was a rule violation. (It's hard to express the manner in which Finn spoke because on paper, it comes across as rude, direct and confrontational, which is, in fact, the way Finn speaks, but he still managed to be likeable with it. How? Only God knows! His mouth did get him into trouble on a regular basis, but he never meant any malice. His inquisitive and outright nosiness, was ironically a breath of fresh air, as he was just saying what everyone else was thinking, it was just his delivery that needed work!)

"FINN!" shouted Claire, shooting daggers at him. She didn't look happy; she wasn't one for putting up with rudeness, however, the way in which she spoke, wasn't confrontational; it was more like a parental nudge, to make him realise how he was coming across.

He automatically changed his tone, as if realising that he was being rude and said, "Nah, sorry mate, I'm just asking, how come you're allowed all ya shit when we're not?" looking at Moss inquisitively, rather than his original confrontational one, as Moss explained it was because he was autistic. His brain worked a million times a minute, so he needed the headphones to play certain calming frequencies. The details eluded her, but he seemed like a very interesting character.

She was too caught up in her first, real group interaction; everyone was talking all at once. There was no chance to make her excuses and retreat back to her hidey-hole, where it was calmer and less overwhelming. She had to force herself to sit in her uncomfortableness. She gave her head a metaphorical shake and pep-talked herself into relaxing, and guess what? She started to feel less disjointed and more interactive. It was strange how connected she felt. It was so hard to put into any comprehensive thought, but she felt understood, without explanation and took comfort in knowing that they were all just as mentally messed up as she was. I think she, like all of us, forgets that no one is perfect. No matter how much some people like to think they are. I'm here to burst their bubble. They're not, and if you're reading this, then let me tell you that it's ok. Every single one of us has flaws that they try to hide from the world as best they can, it's whether or not you're prepared to work on the inner flaws. You know the ones I mean? It's the ones that affect others negatively that make the difference. Simply put, Darcy means the ones that make you a dick. It's when you're not prepared to work on the bigger stuff that makes your insides ugly and that's the worst kind of ugly there is. In here (rehab) maybe she could finally find the freedom to embrace some of her own flaws as quirky character traits instead of putting herself down constantly for being a waste of space. The bigger ones, she was fully aware of (that's why she was here after all). She was finally being herself, which was a foreign concept, *but who better to learn it with, than this dysfunctional bunch*, she thought.

There was another bloke called Buzz (name inspired by the film, Home Alone) Why? I have no idea; however, he was always chasing a 'buzz' and would source pregabalin from somewhere! Then he would sit in later group sessions 'off his tits'. He wasn't someone she associated herself with regularly. He was all 'puffy', and she could see that he was clearly very poorly. It transpired that he'd drunk himself to near complete liver failure; he looked awful, and she could see that he was struggling more than the rest. She kept glancing over at him. Wondering if he was ok, but she was also too withdrawn into herself to ask.

Last but not least, a woman called Cindy (like Barbie, but not quite). She was chatty and friendly, but she was *'up herself'*, thought Darcy. It was as though Cindy thought she was better than everyone else. She had completed her detox three weeks previously and had stayed sober but returned for rehabilitation. She was quite pretty but she looked like one of those girls who used her looks to get what she wanted; you know the kind? Flirty and always wanting to be the centre of attention. *The jury is out on her, for the time being,* thought Darcy, as she looked Cindy up and down, in what she thought was a subtle way. She later found out from Finn, that she wasn't so subtle after all. She looked like she was 'shooting daggers' at her – oops!

D'accord was the member of staff running this particular group (Darcy gave him that name as a personal inside joke. It means 'ok' in French, as he would say, "ok," more times in one sentence, than anyone on the entire planet!) In a later session, she actually counted the number of times he said, "ok," and realised he'd used it over two hundred times in the space of around twenty minutes. He was so lovely though; his passion for the job was second to none. It was inspiring. She later joked with him about his use of the word and asked him, "Do you need rehab for your 'ok' problem? I only ask 'ok', as the number of times, 'ok', you use the word 'ok', makes me wonder, 'ok', whether you have a deep-seated issue with the word 'ok', ok? And I'm just checking, 'ok', if you're 'ok', ok?" Her sarcastic sense of humour was wicked when she came out of her shell; he thought she was hilarious (as all God's creatures do, just joking) but that really wasn't an exaggeration (well, maybe slightly).

D'accord introduced himself, beaming at the group, who all looked back at him as if they thought he was in the wrong place. Surely, no one could be that upbeat all the time? His can-do attitude was irritatingly warm and strangely infectious. He was open and inviting, chatting happily away, as he handed each of them a folder, which only contained a few sheets of information about the programme, a weekly planner and rotas. He told them all, that by the end of their stay, it would be full of personal plans for the future, coping mechanisms and all sorts of other things they may find useful. Everyone seemed to take this information as a positive, however, Arnold (the twat) commented, "Yeah, we know where mine will be going after this don't we? …In the bin!" as if daring D'accord to challenge his attitude, or for the others to laugh and agree. (Attention seeking some may call it). All Darcy could think was, *It'll be getting wrapped around your head if you don't STFU,* (STFU means shut the fuck up in case anyone didn't know).

D'accord simply looked up from what he was doing and said, "Ok, moving swiftly on, ok?" treating the attitude with the contempt it deserved. Darcy, quite quickly, had a newfound respect for some of the staff, especially D'accord, and she gave him an imaginary high five for the way he dealt with Arnold; his approach worked, as Arnold didn't chirp up much more after that. She assumed that he must've realised he was being a tit.

They must have to put up with some right 'knobheads', Darcy thought to herself. It must've been hard for them to deal with twats like that, being disruptive, rude, abrasive and sometimes abusive, and still find a way of dealing with them in a compassionate, yet professional manner. How they resisted the urge sometimes, to poke them in the eye, was a skill that couldn't be taught. Compassion and empathy aren't something we are all blessed with. It usually manifests from traumatic experiences and life; it shapes you as a person. Some people become indifferent to other people's plights and only want to get themselves to the finish line, not caring who they step on, along the way. (Darcy could've named a few of those people quite easily, but she won't because she's not about all that nonsense, she's above those twats.) Then there are the rare few, who want to help and uplift others. They have the ability to put themselves in others' shoes (not pinch them) and give people the confidence and skills to grow on their own.

She sat and wondered how many of the workers had actually gone through their own kind of addiction and were now working in the addiction services as a result? It's always easier to respect how difficult it really is to pull, or sometimes, drag your life back together. Knowing from experience, gains an empathy that can't be taught. She had come to know the majority of the workers in passing and could immediately pick out the ones who seemed to genuinely care. In general, she felt that if she needed to talk to any of them, then she could, but there were a couple who stood out above the rest.

She shook her head slightly, as if to bring herself back

into the room. Her mind had been wandering, daydreaming if you will. That's not to say that the session wasn't interesting but there was so much to think about. It felt great at times, to be able to have clear thoughts, however mismatched and off on tangents they went, they were her own; without the blurred vision she had become accustomed to due to the drink. For the first time in years, she could think with a clear head, remember what she was thinking or what had happened (most of the time anyway.) But in actual fact, Darcy had swapped her beer goggles for the rose-tinted spectacles, that made everything look light and breezy, whenever Finn was around. So, when she says, she thought she was thinking clearly, well, we all know it was probably a 'Pinocchio' moment (meaning a lie) don't we?

Now, D'accord was explaining that each of them was also to be assigned a key worker. They would be the person with whom they'd be having their weekly catch ups; to see how everything was going, and who'd review their progress and help with organising their life outside of rehab. The big stuff, such as housing, benefits and debt advice. All of the staff were there to talk to if needed but the key worker was to be the general port of call for any grievances.

This group was now who she would be with for all future sessions. Her 'rehab family' if you will. D'accord made it clear that whatever was said within the session, stayed between them, so they had to learn to trust each other, so they could grow together. Quite frankly, she wasn't convinced. Finn and Claire were the only people she could see herself as coming to trust, but Arnold? No – she couldn't imagine them ever having any kind of common ground. Cindy seemed to be all about herself, Buzz didn't look as if he would be alive long enough to make it past, "Hello," and Moss was so quiet, she couldn't envision him ever really getting involved. But how wrong she was. The bonds it creates are nothing like you would experience 'in real life'. Rehab was a bubble, creating a surreal experience of what life would be like, without the pressures of work or outside influences, such as 'bat shit crazy exes!' D'accord explained that everyone was there to help each other rebuild and grow. The only struggle they had to deal with while there, was getting better and when the outside world did get in, everyone rallied around each other for support. It was a place to focus on getting better. It was easier for people to become the best versions of themselves for that reason. Not having to worry about money or how to spend the day, with learning sessions keeping them occupied, and meals provided for them, meant people were free to be whoever they wanted to be. There were times, yet to come, of organic laughter and pure elation, which no drug or drink could ever provide.

Outside of group sessions and during downtime hours, the whole house was free to interact with each other in the television room, the dining room or in the pool room (which was generally where everyone congregated). The first week, they were only allowed to leave the premises for an hour in the evening. After the first week was over, then they were allowed out after dinner (which was at 5pm) until 9pm. Or they could simply go to their rooms. She didn't know it yet, but this group of people, including the ones she was unsure of at first, or with whom she didn't have much in common, were to become a massive part of her. Even when some lost touch completely, after returning to 'life', the memories they shared would never leave, and in the case of Finn, she meant that quite literally. For better or worse, she would never be able to shake him without a divorce lawyer. (Anyway, that's for later, for now at least!) He was just some boy, and she was just some girl, who were united by the battle of addiction and recovery, and so were the rest of them, let's not forget about them.

4. ADMISSIONS

Before we resume the storytelling, I'd firstly like to apologise for Darcy. She was becoming a fool in love. There are some romantic gushes and cheesy metaphors, which are enough to make even the most romantic of souls avert their gaze from the flirting, which was obvious to everyone else witnessing it, but them! They thought they were being so subtle that no one would notice it, but subtlety was not Finn's forte. It was as if the pair of them may as well have been walking around with shoes that squeaked and honked loudly, every time they gave each other a bashful gaze, a cheeky smile or a little wiggle. They were smitten with each other. (It was sickening. However, I'd like to point out at this stage, above everything else and regardless of how funny Darcy thought it was to playfully make eyes at each other, they were just friends, nothing more.) She was still in the process of admitting to herself, that her marriage to Thwaite was absolutely over and Finn had his own dramas with the mother of his children (yup – The Bitch) making his life a misery, by putting him down for being a waste of space, for what looked like no good reason. At this point, she didn't know for sure what his relationship status actually was, she had not delved that far into it because she was meant to be concentrating on finding herself. Yeah, she was concentrating on herself, or was she? Or wasn't she? Or was she? Erm... she just didn't know. (Darcy, my darling, you don't imagine your friends naked, nor do you imagine them dressed up like a sexy red Power Ranger (joke) but whatever keeps your dingy afloat I suppose. You also don't imagine your friends riding up to you on a multi-coloured unicorn, reciting cheesy limericks, like:

'Roses are red,
'I'd take you to bed,
'Sugar is sweet,
'Smell my feet,
'And Violets are blue,
'I'd fart on you!
'Lots of Love, Finn xxx'

Plus, seriously!? I'm saying no more. Having to listen to her 'rabbit on', is a bit like when your mates tell you, "Oh, and then we did this, and then he did that," gush, gush, gush. Bless her. "Oh, did you know that Finn was qualified in the Arts?" (Which 'Arts' she means is unclear, however, I have a sneaking suspicion that if he was qualified in anything, it would be the 'Art' of 'chatting shit'! Just a guess). The word deluded springs to mind. But who am I to judge? For I am just a mere figment of someone's imagination, gifted with hindsight and sarcasm. Plus, nobody bloody listens to me anyway! So, I'm unable to tell her to run for the hills, or to be aware of the great big meteor, that'll soon come crashing down to earth, to destroy all her hopes and dreams. No, I can only retell Darcy's story, with as much enthusiasm and feeling as when she first experienced it. Her feelings were all over the place, but she was hooked by him. She felt like she was flying high in his presence. She didn't feel 'the crave' for drugs when she was around him – Finn was the only high she needed. All the events happened within a ten-week period. There was a lot more to it, however, there's only so much I can expose you to in one sitting. You may end up with the 'love bug' and that, in itself, is dangerous, as it gets into your brain and causes all sorts of stupid decisions and pain. For Darcy, it was a hopelessly hopeful time, and it's hard for me to catch up with the timeline or to stop myself being caught in her journey of genuine hope and love. It's sometimes one story after the next, but I'm doing my best. (Plus, I know how this shit ends!) I'm kidding. One thing I will say though, is that this was as true a love story, which was intensified by the setting they were in, as can ever be. Anyway, I'll shut up. Here goes….

The journey of recovery and self-discovery was in full swing. Her first learning sessions were going well, and she found herself regularly thinking, *Come on, Darcy, you're gonna smash this!* (In case anyone is unfamiliar with the phrase 'smash this', it's a positive affirmation she used to pump herself up, ready to learn.) Don't panic, she didn't physically go around smashing things up. Not yet anyway. It was her way of trying to reinforce her own belief and keep the nasty goblins in her head at bay. Plus, she was feeling particularly playful these days. *I am capable of change*, she'd tell herself regularly. Being nice to herself was still a challenge that took some getting used to. Rome wasn't built in a day, and neither was a life size Lego model of a spaceship. However, with a wink and a click of her cheek, she would jokingly say to herself, *you're looking good girl and your life's on track*, whenever she could feel herself falling into self-doubt, but there was no doubt about it, her life WAS worth living. She was doing this for herself, not because she HAD to, but because she WANTED to, and that made all the difference in the world. She was starting to truly love life. She looked forward to getting up in the mornings, even though she would sometimes be late for her cleaning duties, because she was too busy writing in her diary, about what she was looking forward to for the rest of the day. She also wrote about how colours seemed brighter, the birds were singing her favourite tunes and Finn, oh Finn… (see what I mean? She was completely bonkers). Whatever it was, she felt alive and like she was actually living her best life, taking each moment as it came, not simply existing.

She was learning a new way, the 'rehab way' with structure and routine becoming ingrained into her soul. Even handing her phone into the office each morning, had become a 'no biggie' kinda thing, with only the slightest internal grumble. She saw this in itself as personal growth. Ladies and gentlemen, I don't know if you can feel it, but there is a BUT! She was never truly happy. Being positive about sobriety, didn't stop her deep-seated insecurities. Her self-image was shattered, leaving her very self-conscious about her looks. Although she felt a lot better, so much so, that she'd stopped looking over her shoulder for the Grim Reaper, it had been replaced by Finn, following her around, like a lost puppy, all gooey-eyed and adoring. Some may say he was worse than that! (Joking… or am I?) She was enjoying every single moment. She was taking a lot more pride in her appearance. She told herself that she was doing it for her own self-esteem, which it was, but we all know there was another big reason, don't we? Yes, ladies and gentlemen, she was also trying to impress Fuckknuckleby Finn Fibberington. (Silly girl). However, the more she tried to look good, the uglier she felt.

She couldn't do anything with her hair, to make it look nice. Each morning, she would frustrate herself by trying to carefully position the hair she did have, over the noticeable bald patches. Her hair was already very fine naturally, but it was made ten times worse when, years earlier, her daughter's father, Elon, 'Mr Two Can Van Damme' (that was a nickname he'd adopted by not being able to hold his liquor.

It would turn him into a dick and make him believe he was ten men!) He had come home, after a night out on the town, blind drunk, and pulled her out of bed by her hair while she was sleeping and dragged her down the stairs, then beat the living daylights out of her. He sat her on the living room chair and laid into her with his fists, over and over again; knocking her back down, every time she struggled to get up, trying to get away from him, or attempting to calm him down. She recalled seeing stars with every blow of his fist that made contact with her face. His last words to her, before he walked into the kitchen to find a knife were, "We are both going to die tonight." She remembers pleading with him, to think about what he was saying. About what it would mean for the kids if he'd left them parentless, through a drunken mistake? That dreadful night, there was no reasoning with him. Her pleas fell upon deaf ears. Elon was adamant that she was going to die, then he was going to turn the knife on himself. At that moment, she believed him. Whether or not he would have actually done it, we will never know. She says that she had never seen him that way before, but that would be a lie. However, we aren't going to go into that any further for now). As he was searching for a clean knife (they were all soaking in the sink) she managed to escape through the front door, which would usually jam whenever anyone tried to open it, but someone or something must have been looking out for her that night, because it opened properly for the first time ever, and she ran. All she could think to do, was to run to the neighbour's house. She banged on the door so hard that it smashed the first layer of the oval-shaped pane of the double-glazed window in the door, but no one was home. Thank God she hadn't done the washing up that day, was all she could think, as she kept desperately looking for someone to help her, or to find somewhere to hide. Equally thankful that Elon's drunken brain had told him that when he intended to stab her, it needed to be a 'clean' cut, as that had at least given her the few precious seconds it had taken her to get away from him.

I'm sorry if that sounded insensitive. I'm not cold-hearted or uncaring and neither is Darcy. Talking about these kinds of awful situations is uncomfortable, as I'm sure it is for anyone who has suffered a similar fate, so if she makes silly remarks, please know, it is not coming from a place of malice or ignorance; it's from a place of trying to see that by the grace of God, she survived. Who knows what could have happened. She dreads to even let the severity of the situation sink in. If she thought about what could have been, even for a second, it overwhelms her to the point of wanting to curl up into a ball, cry and never stop. Now, let's face it, she had already spent far too much time in bed. To you lovely readers, if you've ever been in an abusive relationship, please know, there is help out there. If you can relate, then please seek the help, before it is too late.

He found her! He grabbed her by the hair again and dragged her, half naked, up the street. To stop him getting any real purchase, she sat, as heavily as she could, body limp in as dead a weight as she could muster, on the pavement, willing herself to be the heaviest she could be, while he tried dragging her back to the house. Her only thought being, *if he gets me back in that house, I'm gonna die!* In that moment, she didn't care about her hair; he could have every last strand of it, if it meant she would live another day. Just when she thought there was no hope; when she realised people had been driving past and could see what was happening but did nothing to help (the absolute bastards) he just let go of her hair, walked back into the house and called the police on himself!

We will definitely leave it there now as it was too hard for Darcy to fully digest it; to retell it all in one sitting. She was starting to realise that half of the reason she was so messed up, had been due to the way she had been treated by the men she had loved. It wasn't just Elon, although he certainly did a number on her. The death of her father was a huge reason she had drunk herself into this gigantic mess of a life. Then Thwaite swooped in with Baby Guinness shots and Jack Daniels, with his loose fists, causing broken bones and constant bruises, only adding to the overloaded 'knobhead' pile Darcy seemed to be collecting. One day, she may share those stories with you, however, for now, let's try to stay on some sort of track. One 'knobhead' at a time please!

The events of that night not only left her battered, bruised and mentally scarred; she was also left with bald spots. She tried her best to disguise them, but it usually just made her lose her temper with herself and she'd throw her hair up into a messy bun. Still, her self-image was utterly shattered, well, not quite, that comes later, but it was certainly close! So, in her attempt to make life easier, she bought a hairpiece to make her hair appear thicker. It helped the voices go from, *Look at you, ugly bitch, nobody's going to accept you for who you are. Ha-ha-ha, why would he look at you? You're a fat, horrible, bald, mess,* to a quieter, *you still look shit, but you'll do for now.* Later on, Helga, ever so kindly, took over that role of fucktard nastiness (you know, because she's ever so kind like that and Finn, ever so kindly gave her the fucking ammunition to do so, by telling the bitch that the reason Darcy wore a hairpiece, was because she was bald!) However, we'll deal with her and him in that capacity later. For now, we are loved up with him and haven't got a clue who Helga really is yet.

Body dysmorphia is such a serious issue. It didn't matter how many times people said her hair looked nice or, "It doesn't look that bad." She absolutely hated it.

Her mum, Angela, would exclaim, "Oh Darcy! Don't be so silly," when she would rant about all the things she hated about herself.

"She's my mum, she's got to be nice," Darcy would joke. However, if she was allowed one wish, it would've been for thicker hair. There were a lot of things she would have also changed, like her stretch marks, or to have boobs that she didn't have to tuck into her socks (joking) but her hair was a big issue that she often stewed on and still does.

It may be hard for some people to understand, but don't you think people's self-image, as a general consensus, is getting worse every day? With the help of social media and filters on phones, making everyone look so blended and perfect, it only adds to the feeling of not being good enough? Seeing an unfiltered version of yourself feels like you've just offended your phone, especially when your phone starts giving you filter options! (It takes the piss). Then there's horrible little witches and online gremlins, who take peoples' insecurities and use them as weapons. Please…, to anyone in general…, please think carefully. The next time you say something nasty to someone, understand that your words have the ability to cut deeper than knives. Do you really want to be that person who has to knock others down to feel good about yourself; to mask your own insecurities? Think before you take the piss – words can kill. It's just something to think about. Anyway, moving on… As a general rule, Darcy was feeling good. She was trying this new thing, by trying to push the negativity away, and let the positive Finn (Ha-ha, see what I did there? I changed 'in' to 'Finn'.) I told you Darcy was clever and hilarious.

The hate and self-loathing were weakened; it was becoming powerfully overshadowed by real life people. The same people, who, at first appeared so scary (like Kelsie) but now, after a couple of cigarettes together in the smoking area outside and a heart to heart even – Kelsie's security wall had been infiltrated; she was defenceless against the 'Darcy charm' (mwah-ha-ha-ha!) and she quickly became one of the people Darcy could talk to, most in the world. Even her initial loathing for Arnold had dulled down to a general dislike. Now that he had relinquished his grip on the 'knobhead badge', he was so intent on showing off when he had first arrived. She had warmed to him enough to see behind the bravado. Don't get it twisted, he was still grumpy and generally uncouth but after he struck up a friendship with Claire, he had softened enough, to a near teddy bear like status, which made him almost tolerable. (Only kidding, he still had the ability to pound you into the ground, but he now looked as if he would have to think twice about it.) He and Claire were like an old married couple, squabbling with each other, in an almost comedic fashion. Especially about Claire's driving licence. It wasn't funny really and maybe you had to be there, however, the two of them were very entertaining. Claire had lost her licence through drinking; her ban was now up, and she needed to renew it. However, she was procrastinating. Why? Darcy wasn't sure.

Arnold would wind her up by telling her, "You might as well do it now, while you're in here, then you've got it for when you get out," whenever she brought the subject up. For one reason or another she kept putting it off. One day, she mentioned something about it to Darcy in passing, when they were sitting having their usual chats during break time. Arnold began chuntering in the background, "Yeah, that's if you ever apply for a new licence," he said, with a side eye, which, Darcy saw, was filled with mischief. She tried keeping a straight face, as she knew what was coming.

Claire didn't avert her gaze from Darcy, as she said loudly, "I will get my fucking licence," as she pursed her lips, trying not to smile.

"Yeah, in about ten years," he said sarcastically. "By the time you get round to it, you'll have to renew your photo as well, coz they won't bloody recognise you," he said jokingly.

She repeated, very matter of factly, still pursing her lips, with a smile that had migrated to her eyes, "I will get my fucking licence." The rest of the memory is a blur, however, the reminiscence of how light-hearted and fun the room felt, while they were squabbling jovially with each other, is a cherished memory. As the oldest of their group (mid 50s) they naturally, unconsciously, adopted a sort of mother and fatherly role, especially to her and Finn.

Arnold was the new 'tea boy' and welcomed in the new residents who were there for detox. Everybody cared for each other with empathy and understanding. Of course, there were people who stood out for being lovely, more so than people who stood out for being absolute knobs, however, there was one man, whose name Darcy cannot recollect, who came in for detox but got thrown out, for stealing 750g jars of coffee from the communal kitchen (I know! Thieving git! She wouldn't have minded so much, but the coffee was decaf, so it's not even like he was trying to get a buzz out of it. Anyway… I digress). The four of them in particular, had the strongest bond out of the group of seven, but throughout her journey, she got to know each of them as individuals. She trusted them, they understood her in a way she had never felt before, nurturing her, in the way a family should. Her actual family was so supportive (minus Thwaite) but this felt different. These people and this place took her back to a feeling of safety she hadn't really felt since she was a child. Darcy could start telling you stories, however, this book isn't long enough. Also, if I let her have her way she would start going off down little side roads, until we are all lost and don't know where we are, so I will pull us back onto the right path for now, also let's just take a moment.

Are you ok? I hope her story isn't making you feel uncomfortable in any way because that really isn't the narrative. If anything does resonate though, then just look in the back of the book. There are numbers and websites of all kinds, to guide you to someone who can help. Please, you do not have to do this alone. Ok? Are we good? Alright, yeah so anyway....

Nobody was there to knock her down or tell her she wasn't good enough. There were boundaries and rules that felt like they had been put there by the loving arm of a parent. There were consequences for breaking the rules, don't get me wrong, but no one seemed to want to break them (lying little monkey, they did. They swapped numbers and told each other personal information about themselves like where they actually lived (outside of rehab). They weren't huge rule violations but still, they were rule breaks. Let's just say that for arguments sake, they all chose to stick to the rules for themselves, because they **wanted** to be there. No one called her a disgrace or dismissed her feelings. She felt validated. She had been so battered down by life, when she first entered through the doors of rehab, carrying so much guilt with her, that she was only now starting to realise wasn't all her fault. She was fully aware of what she should be accountable for. For that, there was no one else to blame but herself, but she'd been abused and spat out so many times and made to believe it was because of her. That she wasn't good enough. *Yeah well, fuck 'em!* she told herself. *Seriously! Fuck 'em!* She had taken on so much guilt throughout the years, some of which was beyond her control. She was learning to let it go.

Peace and love were her new mantras these days. This had nothing to do with the daily meditation sessions, which she often found tedious and hard to take seriously. The sessions always happened right before dinner time, so now her appetite was back, all she could think about was her stomach growling. There were also times she found it hard to concentrate and relax, when the only 'zone' she could imagine being in, was a silent war zone of mini paper balls, flying at her from Finn and Arnold. They'd use her head and the hood of her jacket, as target practice in their mini games, behaving like big kids, in silent fits of laughter, while some of the others would take the meditation so seriously, they would doze off and start snoring merrily away, completely oblivious to the not so silent chaos that was unfolding. She would chuckle away at them, with a bemused look on her face, secretly thanking God in wonder, that her life had come to this! She couldn't imagine a stronger group of people to get better with. It was organic fun, laughter, love and support, something in which she was thriving.

She came out of her shell so much during her stay, and pushed herself to new heights of sheer brilliance, it's a wonder that can't be described. Only kidding, she wasn't changed all of a sudden. Nobody waved a magic wand and made it happen. The magic was all of her own creation. She still struggled with the cravings (she is only human after all). They scared her and made her feel weak minded. But in group sessions, she was quickly learning that sometimes it's ok to not be ok! Raw, unfiltered emotions, without her usual beer goggles, were hard to process. Her brain had been pickled for so many years; she had become familiarly unfamiliar with them. Only now did she feel mentally strong enough to attempt to make some sense of her thoughts and found herself increasingly expressing herself through songwriting and poetry. Even she had to admit they were good, *Give yourself a pat on the back, Darcy. Who knew you had such talents?* she would think to herself jokingly, but the pride in herself was shining above the usual abusive voices.

It really made her think. Before she'd entangled herself in so much grief due to the death of her father, the abuse from Thwaite and the medicine of alcohol, she acknowledged that she was actually really creative. She remembered back to when she used to throw herself into her kids' school projects: creating Easter bonnets (they won their competitions at school) and dressing them up for their Halloween discos (best dressed, of course!) And creating special cakes for them on their birthdays. She'd made a princess cake for Brie and a Minion cake for Jaxon (she won a self-made award, for sheer brilliance!) She'd spend hours drawing Disney characters and photocopying the pictures for her kids to colour in. She kept the original copies, although Brie and Jaxon sometimes got hold of them and created new ways of making her curse real pen and paper; there is no undo button in the real world. She couldn't erase their creative scribbles on the originals, so she would have to attempt to draw them again, then file them away in her secret lockup, that children couldn't get in to (sounds posh, doesn't it? In reality, it was just a black expanding filing case, that she could carry around. I know. Check her out. It held all their schoolwork, star charts and drawings). Darcy smiled to herself. She remembered back to the time she'd begun a new hobby for creative makeup. She and Brie would spend hours together, painting each other's faces. She chuckled at the memory of creating Lego characters with Jaxon. It would start off with the two of them building a model together. Then Jaxon would wander off and play with something else, leaving Darcy engrossed in it, on her own, like a little 'billy no mates'. She remembered the time she'd bought Jaxon a Lego spaceship for Christmas and how it took hours to build. Then, one day, Jaxon lost his temper, for one reason or another (ya know like kids do) and he smashed it to smithereens. To say Darcy wasn't happy, was an understatement. He was told off big time (looking back, Jaxon's tantrums stemmed from a whole lot of other reasons than just being naughty; he always felt like Brie was more important.) We will have to delve into that another time. It's not for now; there is only so much guilt, self-loathing and bitter regret she could deal with before it all got too much. It was like life. When she looked back at the memories, she saw a whole different perspective and so many things she would have changed. It was mind-fuckingly shit.

She refused to fix the spaceship until she felt he had learnt his lesson. (She wanted Jaxon to know that he couldn't simply break things and expect someone to fix or replace them, the instant the tantrum was over.) However, the memory was a bittersweet one. Looking back, she could've dealt with the whole 'Hulk Smash' situation better; she shouldn't have screamed at him (don't worry she wasn't one of those mothers who battered her children, although if she remembered rightly, she did smack him). It left a wistful feeling in the pit of her stomach, as she acknowledged, sadly, that she hadn't tried harder for them, when she should have stayed level-headed and strong for Jaxon especially, instead of falling into a drunken mess that made her no good to anybody. However, let's go back to a lighter note and the memory in point. This time, when she came to fix the spaceship, she made Jaxon find all of the pieces that had been scattered in his bedroom during the blow. She came fully prepared and armed with something, that meant those Lego pieces weren't going anywhere, if by any chance, it was faced with a tantrum attack. Yes, you've guessed it, SUPER GLUE! Let's just say, that spaceship will forevermore stay intact. As the memories flooded her mind, she thought to herself sadly, *I WAS a good mum… but I could've been better!* She was angry with herself. Addiction had taken so much from her but…, *I can be again. This time with no cunt of a man treating my kids anything other than the same as each other,* and more importantly, *because they fucking are. They're my kids. They deserve the world,* she would think, *NO, I WILL be a good mum again, better than before!*

With her new-found empowerment, her past creative abilities were mixing with the present ones, and it was all turning into something you could equate to an extra 'Wonder of the World' (for her anyway). Mwah-ha-ha-ha! The power! Finding that side of herself again, made her happy. I know! HAPPY?! (Darcy calm down mate. Corr, I almost got the fags out. What that phrase really means, God only knows, it is just a saying she always uses in situations of overexcitement. Don't panic, she wasn't being vulgar or derogatory in any way, 'fags' is British slang for cigarettes, so everyone can just calm down with the LGBTQ+ connotations. Let's just try something and see if it works. How about we see people for people and not their sexuality, race, culture, religion, etc. See people for the soul within. At the end of the day, a cunt is a cunt, no matter who they boink, what idol(s) they worship and no matter what colour skin they have, anyway I'm nattering on, trying to preach peace, love and acceptance, when it should be something everyone practices, and I'm meant to be telling Darcy's story…).

It felt as if she had a purpose in life, but what purpose? She didn't quite know yet (except world domination of course, just kidding, that was on the back burner, but she had purpose.) Yay, at last! It meant finally discovering what she wanted from life. She knew it was time to rebuild: *No*, thought Darcy. The term rebuilding meant using the reminiscence of her old life. Even before Thwaite, there was nothing that she wanted from that either, except her kids, however, they had taken some of the broken bricks she left them with and had started to build a life of their own. Never again were things with them going to be the same, but that wasn't to say that she couldn't build better foundations for them, to take a peek and decide for themselves whether or not they would want to visit every now and again, and maybe, come back happier than before. She had the power in her to try again. However, what did she want? A townhouse, a mud hut, a tent, a castle? *Do you catch my drift?* She was obviously thinking in metaphors. What did she want to build? Where did she want to build it and realistically, what resources did she have to do it and, how the hell did she go about making a start to any of it? She was no builder nor was she an architect, but she was the project manager of her life. *Do you see where I'm going with this?* She was all over the place, being pulled from what she thought she knew, to a whole new world of excitement. It was like when Pinocchio was lured to 'Pleasure Island' by 'Honest John' and he was conned into being turned into a donkey, due to his own bad decisions. Darcy didn't want to be a donkey however, whenever she laughed at any of Finn's jokes, she could hear a braying noise that sounded a lot like a "hee-haw". See where I'm going with this?

Finn would look at her in awe. In fact, the more time she spent with him, the more she felt like a rockstar. At times, she even felt like he revered her; she'd catch him glancing over at her, out of the corner of her eye, clinging to every word whenever she talked, his big eyes transfixed in wonder. He was so nosey though, and oh so beautifully manic, so that may have had something to do with it. He was always in the thick of it with her, loving life, loving the feeling of being free to choose a new path, and walking through ideas of living in this happy feeling forever. The feeling was very mutual; she absolutely loved spending time with him. He made her feel heard (the butterflies and unicorns in her stomach were getting ready to break free and start chanting a wedding march, or was it the funeral march? Hmm? She always mixed them up (but Darcy, calm down mate, don't start shopping for wedding dresses, not yet anyway. Also, you've already got a load in the cupboard – you may as well use one of them, coz it ain't gonna last long.) They were best friends. It was so nice. Their connection was becoming an unbreakable one. They clung onto each other, as if they were each other's life raft in rocky seas. He gave her the ability to smile without prejudice, to take risks and believe in herself, and to push her hobby of drawing to new heights. He was always so impressed with everything she did, he would keep on saying, "I bet you can't draw me?" as if trying to challenge her. (Tut, tut, challenge accepted). One thing you should never say to Darcy is: "I bet you can't...." She now had no time for the word 'can't' in her life. Now she'd at least try (in other words, the psychological warfare had already begun). He'd use negative affirmations and bets to stir her to better herself and naturally, she'd prove him wrong (in a nice way of course? Hmm? For now, anyway). However, as much as Finn was a new level of idiot, I will say one thing – through all the shit, he made her who she is today. Well, he didn't, she has done that herself, however, he gave her a new tolerance for 'cockwombling willywankers', which in turn, has developed a fire that burns brighter than a quasar (the brightest thing in the universe).

I feel now is a good time to introduce you to the word 'cockwomble' and how Darcy thought she had in fact made up the word herself. However, it is not the case, so I am going to give you two versions, and you can use the phrase however you so choose. Firstly, the dictionary definition is: 'a foolish or irritating person; someone who behaves inappropriately or makes outrageously stupid statements while having a very high opinion of their own wisdom.' (Now fuck my life, if that is not the most accurate dictionary definition of Finn at times, Darcy cannot recall what is). Secondly, her version of the term is: 'a person who is a massive 'bell end', who wombles about like a dick; being a complete and utter bastard.' Either way, she thinks the word is funny. When she uses it, although it sounds harsh, it was still meant in the play-fullest way. Finn was not a bad man; he had just done some very questionable things.

One day, in the pool room, during downtime, Darcy was relaxing in her usual comfy chair. She had her art book on her lap and a pencil in her hand, sketching away merrily, when Finn casually entered the room. He spotted her and smiled cheekily, before walking over with a swagger, "What's 'appnin' me lady?" he said, as he sat next to her, leaning over to get a closer look, "What you doin'?" he asked inquisitively.

She smiled at him comfortably, as she showed him what she'd been working on. It was a drawing of a photo of the two of them, that had been snapped while they were in town at the weekend. "Nah mate! you didn't do that!" He exclaimed, looking impressed. "Can I have it? …I'm having that," he said. He looked at her, shaking his head at her in pleasant disbelief…, "Is there anything you can't do?"

"Yeah, pee standing up," she joked, "although I'd give it a damn good go," and winked at him. Whenever she received a compliment, she would mask herself with humour; it shielded her shyness. Every time she created anything new, it was instantly claimed by Finn. "Yes, this is for you," she laughed. "Of course it's for you. You nick everything I do anyway," she said smiling. She felt a rush of pleasant pride that her face couldn't hide. She really didn't want to admit it to herself, but his opinion mattered; he mattered to her. This friendship was growing by the day, from a simple 'rehab' friendship, to one that she knew would last beyond the walls….

The flirting continued; the glances became longer and with more meaning. The talks became increasingly profound and pivotal. They were getting to know each other properly. The man/boy and the woman/girl, behind the addiction. They were falling for each other in a way that couldn't be described. She was getting to know his little quirks, and he drew feelings out of her that she had suppressed.

Darcy, Kelsie and Claire were sitting happily, chatting away to each other in the pool room one day, when Finn entered the room with his usual swank, trying his best to make himself look as innocent and helpless as possible, holding what appeared to be a jacket in both hands. The hood was in one hand and the rest in the other, clearly displaying that it'd been torn at the seam. The two pieces clung to each other for dear life, by a small amount of stitching at the end. "Look at me jacket mate!" He exclaimed, to the room in general. *Ah, here goes*, she thought, chuckling to herself. She knew where this was going, and she had a sneaking feeling that it would somehow involve her in some way or another. He looked at her, as if silently hoping that she'd offer to fix it for him, but she enjoyed watching him putting on the, 'Oh no, I'm so helpless,' performance. It was very entertaining to watch him play acting the male equivalent of a 'damsel in distress'. His eyes darted around the room, as if looking for someone to show some interest in what was clearly, an almost '999 emergency situation'. (Can you tell I'm being overdramatic? Yes well, that was Finn all over. Cute, charming and completely bloody helpless!) She also had a sneaking suspicion that the other reason behind all this melodrama, was just an excuse, so they could do something together. However, she sat back and waited. "Look, it's almost off mate!" He said, as he came over to them (again) with his usual bluster, pointing the jacket at them. "Look," he said, looking lost (his puppy dog eyes could've gotten him away with murder).

"I can see that," she said, looking at him with a bemused smile. She waited a moment, before answering his not so silent pleas. "What are you trying to ask me, Finn? If I can sew? Because the answer is yes…, I can do anything," fluttering her eyelashes playfully as she said it.

"Nah," he backtracked, as if he had been caught out, acting helpless, "nah, I'll do it, but just show me how." Slowly, over time, she was noticing a change in his behaviour. He was (for want of a better word) starting to become shy around her. His usual cocksure, 'I don't care what anyone thinks,' attitude, was melting. (The flirting though, was being ramped up noticeably).

"Alright, come on then," she said, nodding towards the dining room, which was a quieter space and less crowded. They sourced a needle and thread from the craft cupboard and as she sewed the hood back onto his jacket (she did the sewing, while he held the pieces of fabric together) they talked.

The topics of conversation were changing from 'normal chitchat', to deeper, more meaningful ones. They included life after rehab; 'the outside land'; their narrative changed from: 'I' and 'me', to 'us' and 'we'. She'd already met Finn's mum, nana and friend, the same weekend they'd taken the photograph together (just as friends) so this wasn't just some run of the mill friendship. He'd obviously thought enough about her, to introduce her so quickly, to two of the most important people in his life. He was asking about her family, as if genuinely interested and hoping to meet them as well one day. Without knowing it, they were planning a future, as if they were already in a relationship, but at this point they'd not even kissed.

As she sewed, the usual jovial conversation turned into something deep. They were talking about life, fucking life! And how badly they'd messed it up, in one way or another. Her protective armour of humour, sarcasm and sheer wit, ebbed away, until all that was left was her naked soul. There were so many parts to her story that had the potential to make him wince away, a bit like a snail's head does when salt is poured on it. Some of her baggage had the ability to change the way he looked at her, but she trusted him. (Yeah, well, ya know where being too trusting has gotten you in the past, don't ya Darcy? For fuck's sake, you silly girl, just be careful.) She took a deep breath and revealed that her kids didn't live with her and the reasons why. (It's a long, long, story which is for another time; however, I am going to summarise it for you. And, as the narrator, I have the power. It may also help you to understand a little more about the woman crying out for acceptance).

It wasn't all clear cut. She hadn't just abandoned them or

had them taken away (an assumption people tend to make when children don't live at home with their mothers). Going back to what Darcy has already mentioned, don't judge someone before you get to know them, and if you're not prepared to get to know them, or the real story, then keep your big fat nose out of people's business. (Helga). It was a slow, drawn-out process, at a time she was most vulnerable. When her father passed away, her whole world changed. It made her realise her own mortality. She had been unhappy with her life, with Elon, for a long time, fed up with him using her as a money tree. Even after Elon hit her that night, she took him back, she even visited him in prison while he was on remand. He was looking at a ten-year stretch; however, he got away with it because... yup, you've guessed it..., she retracted her statement to the police. She did whatever she could to keep her already broken family together, even blaming herself; that she should've seen that he was struggling with his mental health, only for him to continue doing nothing about getting a job. He repaid her by meeting up with her best mate on the sly, and yes, she forgave him for that as well. Her father's death empowered her to break free, so to speak. 'YOLO' became her attitude ('you only live once' in case anyone's unfamiliar with the phrase). So, she ended the nine-year relationship and broke her four-year sobriety streak, a streak she'd self-imposed, on that dreadful night that Elon had hit her. He used the excuse that 'drink' was the reason, so she stopped, to save the relationship, although at that point in time, her drinking was more recreational. Later, she pursued a romantic connection with Thwaite, who she'd been friends with for years (there's a story behind that as well, that she's not entirely proud of, however, she did not cheat on Elon... that's a story for later, however...). There'd always been a spark between Darcy and Thwaite, but she'd never acted on it until now, as she'd always been in a relationship with 'that twat'. Elon was extremely clever; he knew how to pull strings from behind the scenes, to make Darcy look like she was slowly losing the plot, making a bad situation ten times worse.

A breakup is never easy, especially as Elon was a bitter, twisted and self-entitled man, who thought he could do and say whatever he wanted, when he wanted. He continued to make Darcy's life hell, even after he'd left (she was that paranoid, she even checked the house for any hidden cameras or bugs just in case he was watching. His mind games were next level). It's extremely hard to express the gravity of the situation when you're not living in it. The continued taunts from afar and his self-entitled nature infuriated Darcy, who could do nothing but stand back helplessly, as he emptied her bank account, claiming it was 'his cut' (as he'd controlled all her finances when they were together.) She did go to the police, but they were pretty useless, despite all the evidence she had (would you like to hazard a guess as to why he got away with it? Yup, because like a complete fool, she gave him full control of the finances.) He would always say to her, "You look after me, and I'll look after everything else," then he'd spend stupid amounts of money on ridiculous things like clown porn. He spent £1,200, in just six weeks (it wasn't really clown porn, she is just taking the piss, Darcy has changed little details, to make it even harder for him to try to sue her. It was some stupid online gaming thing, online poker, I think, but clown porn sounded funny, didn't it? Ha-ha see what I did there?) The refusal to give back thousands of pounds worth of property, including her brother's car, and more importantly, the abandonment of her son Jaxon; she couldn't understand how he could be so callous. Elon wasn't his biological father but had 'raised' him from the age of sixteen months old. He was his 'dad', although Jaxon was aware he had his own father. (Don't even get her started on him!) Elon came to pick the kids up for the weekend. He put Brie in the car, looked at Jaxon and said, "Sorry mate, there's not enough room," and drove away. (CUNT! Sorry to drop the 'C bomb' but who does something like that?) All of this contributed to her selfishly spiralling even further into depression and anxiety. This only spurred Elon to greater heights. He wasn't happy with the custody arrangements they'd both amicably agreed to before he left. There was no need for all the animosity and refusal to speak to her. (She had to communicate through Brie, not something a seven-year-old should have to deal with) but he wanted to see Darcy broken beyond repair. He took her to court, 'all in the best interests of the kids'. The reality was, he couldn't care less about how all of this was affecting them. He had proved that when he drove away, leaving Jaxon in pieces at the side of the road; he was trying to prove he had the power; he wanted to win. He lost; he was laughed out of court, as they could see there was no foundation of truth to his absurd accusations. But he won the war. Brie wanted a trial period of living with her dad (which Darcy was prepared to trial, even before he pointlessly dragged her to court.) She was trying to make the best out of a terrible situation and failing miserably. In the end he got what he wanted; her nerves had been shot, he had turned Brie's head and poor Jaxon, who clearly wasn't receiving the emotional support from his mother, started spending more and more time at his grandma Angela's house, who only lived a few doors away. It was a time that Darcy gave up trying. She selfishly chose her own grief and anger over theirs. She needed to find a strength for them from somewhere, but everything snowballed into one big, giant, moth ball of complete shit. She sought solace in Thwaite, who she believed was supportive of her and the kids' best interests, but he was more interested in keeping Darcy's 'spirits' up (see what I did there?) The drinking got worse. Thwaite let the drink flow copiously, and unbeknown to Darcy, he was turning siblings against each other. He came across as caring. He was an excellent cook, the kids loved the food he made to begin with, and he would get them involved in making fresh meals from scratch (don't get it twisted, Darcy already did all of this on occasion, even making cakes and homemade chicken nuggets together, before she began to spiral. She tried her best to get the kids eating healthily anyway; however, it felt nice to have someone who appeared to want to spend time together as a family, ya know what I mean?) Thwaite took the reins with the cooking, to the point she felt like she had forgotten how to do it without his guidance. It felt to her, as if this was how a family should be. To the outside it looked as if Thwaite was showing a positive interest. The kids loved it at first, trying different foods. It was new and exciting. The whole ceremony of cooking together, felt like she had found what it truly meant to be a family. Thwaite gave the impression that he was doing it for all the right reasons. Darcy recently learned from Brie, that he would overload their plates (enough to make his intentions unnoticeable) so that they couldn't finish their food and then guilt them into eating it. Darcy only recently found out that Brie and Jaxon were too scared to ask to be excused from the table, for fear they would hurt Thwaite's feelings. He then retaliated (again feigning understanding and kindness) by giving them smaller portions, so it wasn't enough, but they would be too frightened to ask for more, because he would then overload the plate again and be upset if they didn't eat it all. She had no idea of the severity of the mind games. At the time, it looked like the kids were being awkward. He slowly started making foods he knew the kids wouldn't like. It breaks her heart to truly grasp the effect all of this had on them. She felt so shitty, feeling like she should've known what was really happening, instead of being so naive to think she had found someone so perfect, when she should've known it was too good to be true. How could she expect someone to love her properly when she was just a broken waste? Whenever she looked back, it filled her with a gut-wrenching sadness, that her children felt they couldn't tell her what was happening. Had she really become someone they could no longer rely on? Had she really become that person who was too fragile to protect them? There was once a time, when Brie could tell her anything, but with Elon twisting the knife from afar and Thwaite bending her to his will, she had no idea what to think or how to feel anymore. Thwaite was in her ear, manipulating things, to a point where everything became too uncomfortable for the kids to want to be in their own home anymore. He fuelled a lot of resentment towards Elon, which in turn affected how they all behaved as a family. He made life so difficult at home for both Brie and Jaxon, that before she knew it, they hardly stayed at home anymore. Ultimately, it was her fault; she let it happen. She felt like the worst person in the world, for choosing what she thought was best at the time. When really, she chose the easy option.

Her drinking was bad but not to the level that Elon accused her of – not at the start anyway. At the time, he just twisted the knife. It was bad enough that he sat back for the most part of their relationship, happily encouraging her into prostitution and secretly filming it. She did this for six years, while he watched, as it slowly ate away at her sense of self. She begged him to get a job; however, he insisted he was better off at home, making sure she was 'safe'. She felt so used. Before they broke up and she turned into an 'alcoholic monster Gremlin', she did most things with the kids on her own, or with her mother, while Elon made himself important, play-acting in charity work with the local busybody, getting involved in local affairs. He never really moved from his computer desk, where he controlled all the finances. She stopped prostituting herself as soon as she left the relationship, but he still found the absolute, piss-taking nerve to even bring that up in court! She was armed with one thing that he was defenceless against. The truth, although she nearly gave up on everything before she was vindicated. In reality, she should have taken the kids and run a mile, but they would never have forgiven her. It was a double-edged sword and the good old, 'shit on biscuits!'

Finn listened to her story raptly, without interruption (which was unusual.) Half the time, Finn was so overstimulated by his own brain, he barely processed real human emotion, but he sat with her in the moment and held her, without physical contact, in a way that was beyond description. It was a feeling that Darcy can only explain as breathlessness. He cared, NO, he more than cared. As he listened to her, his eyes looked as if they were fighting not to shed a tear of angry protectiveness. She felt heard, unjudged and vindicated. He made her shame feel less heavy, like he was bearing some of the load for her. At that moment in time, it felt like he would never judge or use it against her. (Yeah, well, your judgment has never been the best, has it, Darcy?) He looked at her, at a loss as to what to say. She could see indignation on his face on her behalf. "No man should treat you like that. That's no man is that," he said, shaking his head, looking flushed.

"Yeah well, shit happens, I guess." She said, matter-of-factly, trying to put back on some of the armour she had been wearing before; it was like getting dressed again after really good sex, do you know what I mean? Like when you put on their T-shirt and cuddle. The mood was weirdly relaxed. It felt strange to feel like that after everything she had told him. She felt no awkwardness, as he looked at her, and somehow, everything changed back to light and breezy without any awkwardness. She felt understood, unjudged, even loved. It was like their energy connected somehow and it felt like that's what she had been missing her entire life. He threw her completely. One minute she thought he would be the last person she could bare her entire soul to, the next, he did and said the most surprising things that made her feel like he would protect her to the ends of the earth. He looked around the room silently. She could see him looking at a flower on the windowsill. It was beautiful.

He looked at her and said, "You see that flower over there, yeah? Well, that wa'nt there yesterday, it was just a bud. That's you. You're like that," he said, looking at her, "you've grown into a beautiful flower. You have mate, I've watched you grow. You're worth so much more. You don't deserve to be treated like that."

5. EVERY TIME WE TOUCH, I GET THIS FEELING AND EVERY TIME WE KISS...

So..., as we can all gather, Darcy was having a great time. She thought her recovery was going better than she could've ever hoped for. But was this recovery or a distraction?

There was the 'old toad', Karen, the boss, whose opinion on the matter is expressed explicitly a little later on, however, as Darcy tells her story, she can't help but have the words echoing loudly at her in the background (or was that croaking, trilling or chirping, depending on the breed of toad, of course) as she thinks about it now in hindsight. We can't tell you what 'the toad' said, or what Darcy is thinking though can we? Not yet anyway, if I did it would be a big fat spoiler alert. I'm sure you could hazard a guess though, however, keep your own thoughts on the matter on the backburner for now, as we are going to have our own little Q&A session at the end.

Darcy's underlying issues still lingered in the background,

growing mouldy, like fresh washing left unaired to fester. There was a niggling, pain in the arse of a voice, shouting what she didn't want to hear. (It wasn't 'the toad's'; it was someone or something else entirely.) *Really Darcy?! What are you doing? Kissing some 'Jack the lad'? He never takes anything seriously! What are you expecting to happen? That the two of you will go running off into the sunset and it's going to be all shits, giggles and moonbeam mocktails, hmm? Div!* Her 'voice of reason' was a bit sarcastic for her liking, and in all honesty, a bit of a 'Debbie downer' (let's face it, nobody likes a Debbie downer, do they?) No, they are far too sensible for the likes of Darcy who was floating on clouds ten, eleven and twelve, all places people should visit from time to time because it can be fun and a great getaway from whatever reality you're in; a release if you will, just don't stay up there too long, as it turns your brain into a strawberry slushy) but it was common sense! *Do you really think you're gonna go running off into the sunset together? You're living in 'cloud-cuckoo land' woman!* But she and Finn had stepped it up a notch (and no, for you dirty-minded readers, it wasn't on the bedpost… that comes later – wink, wink!) They'd kissed the night before. I KNOW, KISSED! (For fuck's sake! Oh no, common sense was holding its head in its hands, at a loss as to how to, well…, shake some wisdom back into her). But kissed! It was the next level of 'lurvve'; she was falling for him, big time. You may be thinking, *don't be so bloody stupid woman, you don't even know him properly! How can this be 'lurvve'?* Well, I'm here to tell you that you're probably right.

There were big parts of Finn's character that weren't demonstrated during his time in rehab, BUT she saw the side of him that showed her who he could be, if he was given half the chance. Without the pressure of the outside world getting in and without old habits and influences turning his head. Darcy wants to make it clear that 'maybe' she was blind to his flaws. She wasn't but she chose to ignore them because she truly believed in the raw, real and innocence that he portrayed. She believed in the person he told her he wanted to become (I know! Fucking idiot) and that felt very much like love to her. She didn't fall in love with him because he was perfect, she fell in love with him, for him, and his imperfections. She had no time for negativity; all she felt was warm and fuzzy, as she caressed her lips gently with her finger, reliving the moment they'd kissed, again and again. She couldn't wait to see him.

It all happened the previous night in the pool room. Everyone else had taken themselves off to their rooms for the evening. It was too early to sleep. She didn't much fancy going to her room to sit alone. She and Finn had become, what some may say, the 'social butterflies' of the house. So, they stayed downstairs, left alone, to continue their never-ending pool tournament. More often than not, they were the last ones standing anyway, but this felt different. That night, her mood felt very playful and free. Normally, she was very careful to not make it too obvious that she was falling for him, because the thought of vocalising her growing feelings, for them not to be reciprocated, filled her with terror and embarrassment. But for some reason, at this moment in time, she didn't care. It was as if her armour had slipped; her inhibitions had been weakened by the feeling of acceptance (he now knew about some of the worst parts of her and still looked at her the same, if not fonder than before) and she felt unshackled from her own constraints. As they played, they laughed and joked, mainly at how badly he was losing, "Ha-ha maybe I'm distracting you with my beauty and grace?" she said confidently, as he took a shockingly bad shot.

He looked at her as his nostrils flared slightly, with a cheeky smile he was clearly trying to suppress. "It's this pool cue, it's shit," he replied jovially. They were both behaving so playfully toward each other it felt all fluttery and beautifully relaxed yet erm… What's the word? The only way she can try to explain, is something called the jitterbugs. Do ya know what I mean? Nah, neither does she, however that's how she felt (simples). He looked her up and down, as she danced about playfully. As he chalked his cue, they began to reminisce about their recovery journey so far. "Ya take piss, mate," laughed Finn, shaking his head, looking impressed, as she potted the black ball, winning what must've been the tenth game that evening. "Ya getting too good now," he said, as he watched her little victory wiggle. "I remember when ya first came here, you were like 'Shakin Stevens'. You wu'nt even play; ya just sat and watched me and Kelsie. Ya di'nt even hardly talk. Now look at ya," he said lovingly, as he watched her set the table up for another game. He looked besotted. "Ya take the piss mate," he said again, as he looked away, as if trying to hide the big, imaginary, neon sign that was flashing above his head, saying 'I love Darcy'.

"I know," she said laughing, "don't hate the player, hate the game. It's your fault. You wouldn't leave me alone until I did, would ya? "D'ya wanna play pool, d'ya wanna play pool?" she said, in a frolicsome imitation of Finn, mimicking him in a teasing fashion. "So basically…, you irritated me into beating 'Yo ass' and created a monster." She paused for a moment, before saying, "Seriously, you're the reason I came out of my room." She winked and handed him the pool cue, playfully brushing past him. As they made contact, she felt a rush of the 'ooh la la's'. He grabbed the cue and her hand at the same time and wowzers, their eyes locked onto each other for a few seconds before he loosened his tender grip (wounded). She passed him the cue, averting her gaze and returned to the usual pretence that they were 'just friends.' (Double wounded) "You still can't keep the ball on the table though, can ya?" she teased, as she fell about in fits of laughter. He'd just gone to break, and the white ball went flying off the table, yet again, landing somewhere under the coffee table, in the corner of the room. "Anyway, you only asked me to play with you, coz you can't get enough of me," she said, as she bent down to look under the table to retrieve the ball. As he did the same thing, she was very aware of how close they were to each other, her body tingled all over, making the hairs on her arms and the back of her neck stand up to attention, as if they also knew he was there.

"Yeah well, giz a kiss then," he said, as their faces came close enough for her to see the dark grey edge of his irises. She hesitated for a moment; there was a wild internal war going on in her head. There was a fight to the death going on between love and lust, logic and sense. Love and lust reigned victorious as she thought, *Fuck it*, before pecking him on the lips. His lips were soft and moreish and slightly parted, so that when her lips touched his, she nearly melted into him. It wasn't just any old peck, this was a peck with a purpose, they were sharing their first ever, physically intimate, moment. It was like time had stopped as their eyes sunk into each other further, and she didn't care about anything else. The next thing she knew, they kissed again. This time a serious one that melted her. It only lasted a few seconds, but it was a kiss that spoke a thousand words. It felt tender and loving. There was no awkwardness. It felt so naturally organic. It told her everything she needed to know. This was real. They had to be careful not to fall deeper into another kiss; she needed to try and revive the smallest amount of sense at least. If she didn't then this book could've ended up very 'blue', to say the least (a bit of 'blue', like when Peter Kay said it basically means risqué, indecent or sexual innuendo – just thought you ought to know). She wanted to kiss him again and never stop, but, just as they broke apart, D'accord came around the corner smiling. He must've missed the tender moment they had just shared.

"Right, you two, it's 11 o'clock, ok, it's time for bed, ok?" They tried to muster enough sensibility to look as innocent as possible, as they set about clearing the table, looking at each other and smiling sheepishly. Darcy felt like she was on top of the world. He obviously felt the same way she did....

She shook herself out of her daydream and was back in her bedroom, getting herself ready for the day ahead. She felt truly amazing; however, she had the rest of the day to get through. One of today's sessions was 'diaries'. Once a week, they had to read their diaries out loud to the group and the session leader. Each day, they were asked to score their days on a scale of 1–10, for moods and cravings. *It's a no brainer*, was her automatic thought. Today felt like it was going to be a ten. She had noticed a definite change from when she'd first arrived. The scales were flipping. At first her moods were near to zero and cravings near the 10-mark. Now, her moods were 8 or 9 most days and cravings, around the 1–2 scale. It felt great to look back and physically see with her own eyes, how far she had come. When it came to the diary session she smiled, almost knowing already how the session was going to go.

Finn, Arnold and Buzz, were men of very few words. Their diaries would take around ten minutes to get through combined, but Darcy, Claire, Cindy and Moss took a lot more time, care and detail, in writing out the events of their week, so they would take longer to read out. Moss in particular, was always very descriptive, his intelligent use of words, humour and rationality, would have the group as a whole, on tenterhooks, listening intensely, laughing along. "You should do an audiobook of your life mate, honestly," Finn would say on every session. Even Arnold would stop acting his usual uninterested self. He would sit up and pay attention. It was a sight to behold, and a bit of peace and quiet from the usual sarcastic commentary. He was still a twat, but their ever-growing tolerance for each other, for the sake of Claire, meant that she now had more patience with him. Now, when he wound her up, it was taken in a jovial fashion. Her internal plots to deck him in the hallway, had been scrapped or at least put in her back pocket (ya know, just in case. She'd spent too long plotting, for them to be simply thrown away). He was alright really, you just needed to take him with a pinch of salt, and she would give as good as she got. Arnold and Finn (the little troublemakers of the group) would rarely take anything too seriously. They'd take the piss out of her lengthy diary entries (to be fair they were long. Sometimes you don't ever STFU) jokingly, timing how long it took for her to read them out loud. So naturally, she took the piss right back, by retelling her week with meticulous detail. Her diary entries would go something along the lines of...:

So, I woke up this morning and I yawned deeply. I was feeling tired, as I couldn't sleep properly last night. Hmm, I wonder what that was all about? Maybe it's because I'd eaten some cheese? I don't know..., well anyway, I kicked back the duvet and, even though I was feeling tired, there was a slight spring in my step. I was feeling positive about what this day might bring. However, as I came to get dressed, I noticed I had a missing sock! This caused some concern for me, and I am wondering where it has gone. It's a black sock, of the trainer kind. So anyway, I have written a note for the notice board, offering a reward for its return. I have pinned the left sock along with the note on the board, so people know what it looks like.... And so on....

This week, she had loads written down, maybe too much? Now that she came to think of it, the majority of it involved Finn in some shape or form, but last night's events had to go into her own personal diary (which was even longer than her rehab diary). There was no way she could read out loud what happened last night (I'll spare you the pages of gushing, it's quite embarrassing. Plus, you get the pleasure of reading some of her inner thoughts a bit later). She wanted to shout it from the roof tops, but they'd both run the risk of being chucked out for breaching the rules, if they got caught. Which meant they now had to keep their ever-growing feelings for each other on the QT (means quiet). Is that why it felt so exciting? Because it was forbidden? Or was this relationship authentic? Hmm? Right from the beginning, they'd all been warned not to get too entangled in friendships and romantic relationships. Swapping telephone numbers or saliva, was prohibited between two recovering addicts, as it almost always ends in utter failure. The staff even told them horror stories to scare them into compliance. *But who's not to say we can't be the exception to the rule?* she thought. But really, she should have been using this time to discover herself, not getting wrapped up in romance. She knew, deep down, the 'voice of reason' was right, but the kiss felt so right too. She was so confused. She should be concentrating on how she ended up here in the first place, not him.

HE was a huge red flag, but there was so much more to him than this 'big front' he donned for the others. She'd catch him in the moments he let his guard down. She knew HIM, not the joker he pretended to be for everyone else, but the man who struggled behind the mask. He wanted to change his life around so much, and in that respect, they had so much in common. In other aspects not so much. They were so different in personality. He was 'fly by the seat of your pants' and think about the consequences afterwards type, whereas Darcy was more methodical in nature. They balanced each other out. He put her on the spot (embarrassingly so at times) which forced her out of her shell, displaying her brilliance, and she called him out when he was being a dick, teaching him to think before he spoke, which mainly fell on deaf ears. She could feel herself doing it more often, but guess what? Yup, she looked past it. But she made sure he knew that she saw the brilliance in him too. They came from completely different backgrounds and in reality, lived on completely different planets. In the real world, it was improbable that their paths would have ever crossed. (She lived in 'Just-a-fool-in-lovesville' and he was somewhere near, 'I-hide-my-shittiness-wellington'). But had something brought them together at this exact moment? (Yeah Darcy! Addiction and troubled waters, ya dick). Obviously, she ignored all common sense, as she always does, poking at the metaphorical bear and hoping not to get hurt. It felt like it was meant to be.

He was unfiltered, rough around the edges, and was always in the thick of mischief, keeping himself entertained, raiding the arts and craft cupboards and finding the next fun distraction. During an arts and crafts raid one day, he came across a tie dye kit, so naturally, he roped her into making everyone tie-dye T-shirts. They had so much fun with the different designs. She ended up with multi-coloured socks, knickers and vest tops (basically all her white clothes became Finn's art canvases). She loved watching his eyes light up at his creations, it was only small stuff, but she was so proud that she knew him. She made him a T-shirt, tying the elastic bands in a disorganised fashion, as she didn't have a clue what she was doing, she just knew it was fun. When she washed out the dye the next day, she discovered that she'd inadvertently designed a heart shape, which when worn, would sit right where his heart was (if he'd had one, that is! Sorry I'm joking. I was just being a bitch and spoiling a tender moment). It was like it was written in the stars, or the T-shirt. Basically, anything they could tie-dye became tie-dyed. Even Arnold got involved, by bringing down one of his gym hoodies, to turn into a multi-coloured workout jacket. She remembered that she had been poorly the next day and was given the ok from the staff to stay in bed, however, Finn had other ideas. He wanted to wash the dye out of the hoodie NOW, he couldn't wait. Nor could the lazy bastard do it himself? Nooo, instead, he banged on her bedroom door, to get her to come out and do it for him. It was like he wanted her there all the time, so she could watch and join in whenever he wanted. (At this point, I ain't even gonna say anything, what's the bloody point?) Even though it pissed her off that he didn't seem to care that she was ill, instead insisting she was, "A lazy bitch," who simply wanted to stay in bed all day. Did she say anything? Nope, she rolled up her sleeves, feeling slightly resentful, and washed the hoodie for him, while he wandered off to go play with something else. She followed along with his adventure time, soon forgetting about being annoyed or poorly, when she saw his eyes light up at the finished product. There were no sick days with Finn, it was simply unheard of. Surprisingly but pleasingly, some of the staff brought along white T-shirts to be transformed into random, organic pieces of colourful art. The whole house looked as if they were at some hippie convention, where peace, love and artistic expression was the new mantra (minus the drugs, OBVS, meaning obviously).

He taught her different ways of looking at the world and her problems, with such simplistic, yet absolutely mind-bogglingly genius moments, *Oh yeah..., he's right ya know!* Darcy can't articulate just how much he changed her. Within all the shittiness, even now (although he has done some absolutely shocking and terrible things) if you took the 'knobhead' out of him, then she would still class him as her best friend. It was just a shame there is so much else to get past. He was the kind of man who would surprise her daily. It's hard to explain, but he would spot little loopholes in things, that even the staff couldn't argue against. There was one particular moment, during a learning session, where he spotted a flaw in the wording of some of the session's paperwork. It may have seemed inconsequential to most, and yes, Finn was maybe being pedantic, however, he picked up on it straight away and wouldn't drop it. After a lengthy discussion with Henry, the session leader, Finn refused to drop the subject until he was well and truly heard. When Finn knew he was right, he would keep arguing, even when people were agreeing with him. Henry had to admit that Finn was right (if only to shut him up. Just kidding, he was in fact right, however, exactly what he was right about we will never know, she'd stopped caring halfway through because he was going around in circles with the same point, so she chose to whisper to Claire about how wonderfully fascinating she thought he was instead.)

When Finn got too overexcited, to the point where he was going to get into trouble, Darcy grounded him. She was a naturally calming influence on him. They were both so happy. Their personalities slotted into each other perfectly (nah, you just had the patience of a saint love). They'd sit together for hours doing jigsaw puzzles. It was occasionally nice, to do something calming for a change, as normally, he would get himself into trouble, if left to his own ADHD brain and devices. He hadn't been officially diagnosed; however, he was definitely on the scale. If anything, he tipped it, in fact Finn's dial spun round like a Catherine wheel. His brain fired a million times a minute. He certainly had a raw, unfiltered view of the world, making some highly inappropriate remarks, not really thinking, before the words flooded out of his mouth or about how it came across to other people during the delivery. His remarks and responses (basically some of the shit he would come out with) would get him into trouble. For example: saying to Claire, "You're quite sexy, for an old lady," made Darcy think, *Fuck my life Finn, think before you speak*, with head in hands, in silent fits of giggles at Claire's face, who couldn't help but think it funny as well, but still trying to don a look of indignancy. Finn was so charming with his personality and crude antics, he could quite literally get away with murder if he attempted it. He'd probably say, "Oh shit… sorry… I just had ta."

A quick pitstop, to clarify what Darcy means when she says 'ADHD'. I want to make it clear; she is not adept in qualifying any actual diagnosis in mental health, nor does she think she is any sort of doctor. She knows ADHD means attention deficit hyperactivity disorder, however, what that means in general, or how the ins and outs of it affect any specific individual, she wouldn't even dare to be so arrogant as to pretend to understand. She could always try to fob you off with a jokey Google check, pretending to look like she knows what she's talking about, however, Darcy is very much of the opinion that everyone deals with their mental health in their own way. Some may have a formal diagnosis of their mental health, or like so many of us, they are yet to be diagnosed. Some are content with not knowing or maybe even caring why their brain works the way it does and are at peace with themselves as individuals, which she finds so fucking enviable. There are some of us that are fighting for a diagnosis, feeling like they're alone, just another number and unheard. Like she says, everyone is different, right? And that is ok. She has experience of ADHD, bipolar, anxiety and depression, in her personal life, although she is still fighting for a formal diagnosis, so just know there is not a malicious bone in her body (not when she is sober anyway) whenever she comes across as flippant, please understand, it doesn't come from a bad place of hatred or malice. This book is meant to feel like a safe space for anyone reading, although the topics can be very uncomfortable at times, so the last thing she wants to do is make anyone feel like they can't be here, with her, in her journey. So, let's all buckle up bitches and get on with the fecking show.

One day, they were finishing up this particular jigsaw; it was 500 pieces. It took around four days, only to find that there were two missing pieces. They jokingly said that they were the two pieces missing from each other's lives; missing parts of their puzzle. In reality, they'd spent four days just to be 'wounded' (a phrase that Finn would use all the time, which would make Darcy fall about in fits of laughter at the way he said it. Naturally, over time, they both adopted little phrases they would each use as their own. This is one in particular that Darcy nicked.) Ha-ha, 'wounded' that they couldn't complete the bigger picture, because some dickhead hadn't put all the pieces back in its box when they'd finished with it. The puzzle was a picture of the sea, with sea turtles and fish. What did that mean? Death by drowning? Come on Darcy mate. Really!? They were trying to find cute, hidden meanings and messages in everything they did; almost reaffirming and reassuring each other, how much they wanted to be together. If only to distract themselves from the fear of eventually leaving this place, and maybe, each other behind, and going back to the cold reality of their own lives. It wasn't that far away now. There was only about four weeks left to go. (This is Darcy's guess-timation, don't take the timeline as gospel. You've got to remember that this story is being told from a place almost three years after they happened and although the memories are as vivid as if they happened yesterday, the real time eludes her.) It was about four weeks. Anyway, give her a break; she was too busy having fun!

What did she really expect to happen between them? She knew it may not have been her best decision in the world, to get involved so quickly with someone else, when really, she needed to heal, however, *YOLO*, she thought, as she bound and gagged the voice of reason and shut it in a darkened room. After all, when was she ever going to meet anyone like him again? All logic and reasoning went out the window (well into the darkened room, but you catch my drift.) He made her happy. She was happy for the first time in a long time. She didn't want to come back down to earth where dreams were shattered. She wasn't going to let common sense stand in the way... no... 'cloud-cuckoo land' felt all too safe and welcoming to leave.

Jesus! Thought Darcy, as she shook her head. (It was almost as if she was trying to shake some clarity into her mind.) There was so much to think about. She was still married for one, although he was moving out. She and Thwaite had been distant for weeks. Apart from receiving a text, asking her for their landlord's number, to ask for a reference, they'd not spoken. She'd only seen him twice since entering rehab. She remembered the first time he took her to a pub, ordered himself a Guinness, and tried making awkward conversation, by asking if she thought she'd ever be able to just have the one? She didn't say it at the time, as she just felt like recoiling back into herself, at his callous attitude. The awful feeling of not being good enough came rushing back. The feeling was all too familiar. It was the same feeling she'd have when he used to shame her into going to the gym, or when he'd make her practice the same songs she'd been performing for years, over and over again, because he hated the fact she had the ability to perform flawlessly, without warming up her voice before she'd go on stage. She was a singer in a country band, which broke apart just before she entered rehab. He played the kazoo. Before her addiction hit its peak, she would perform at festivals and write music for the band, but it all went sour through drinking. Her last gig filled her with arse-sweating, gut-wrenching embarrassment. She was kicked out halfway through the set because she was that drunk, she fell off the stage. She called the bouncers a bunch of bastards, as she was escorted off the premises and made a complete doughnut of herself (means absolute idiot). She flushed furiously, as she recalled the memory. *Don't think about that now Darcy, you're meant to be remembering what a complete bastard Thwaite is. Plus, you're meant to be getting ready, woman!* she thought, as she continued, happily putting on her makeup and making all kinds of faces, as the memories and thoughts whizzed around her brain.

Thwaite knows everything I've been through, she thought to herself, as she frowned, which did nothing for her wrinkles. He'd been there from the beginning to watch her spiral. She flitted from blaming herself one minute, to blaming him entirely the next. She laughed at herself, as she had the absurd imagery of putting extra salt on his dinner, to slowly kill him off! She tutted at her stupid brain for not thinking of 'death by salt' sooner. However, she was never going to cook for him again, and in fairness to him, he did most of the cooking when they were together anyway. As her daughter would say, "He might be a dick, but the man can cook." She kicked herself for not asking for the recipe for his arancini (deep fried risotto balls) when she'd had the chance. If she asked him now, it would just feel like she was taking the piss. Or would it? Hmm? (*Maybe I should?... Nah, it'll be in one of Jamie Oliver's many cookbooks somewhere. It's not like the man is original, is it?* She thought to herself. He followed recipes to the letter.

But how could he even ask that question if he actually cared? At the time, she felt like she'd been kicked in the teeth and now she was reliving the memory, she felt a pang of what could've happened. Had she not had rehab to go back to, where she felt safe and accepted, she probably would have craved his acceptance and been like, "Erm…, I dunno, maybe?" It was so stupid. Was it all her fault that he could no longer consider her normal? And why did she need to crave acceptance from a man who was a big part of her losing everything anyway? She lost herself, her kids and her sanity. At the time he just sat back, and looked at her, as if she was more broken than before. This took her on another little thought train into…. It's easy for non-addicts to question complete abstinence (especially him, who only seemed to care about himself) as it is hard to understand the full force of the gravitational pull it had on her.

Drinking is such a social thing and alcohol is everywhere – every time she went to the shop, it was there on the aisle, or near the front doors, on special offers, and on shelves behind the counter. It was like she had to face a 'battle of wills' every time she stepped out to the shop, for God's sake. Her mouth would go dry, then salivate at the idea that maybe, just maybe, one day, she may be able to live a normal life without the stigma of alcoholism. If she was honest with herself, that's what bothered her most. It felt like she had an 'ick' on her, that she felt she was going to have to hide, but why should she? The 'ick' was a part of who she was. Should she embrace it instead of shying away from it? Maybe she should wear her abstinence with honour? Although, it raised so many questions for people, like 'that idiot', who felt she should have to explain herself to their armchair expert opinions. "What? You don't drink? What, like not at all? Surely you can just have the one? It's all in the mind." It's all bullshit. She knew they were uneducated idiots but what if they were right? Could she just have one? NO, but would she be able to continuously resist the temptation, or would she end up hiding away from the world? There would be no more Christmases with a bottle of Baileys, while wrapping presents and listening to cheesy Christmas music. No more Port and Stilton while watching comedy on TV. Would Armstrong and Miller still be funny without her Courvoisier? (Yes, they would, but she knew what she meant). Anyway, she couldn't imagine Finn sitting sophisticatedly, eating Stilton, never mind drinking Port. Even if they weren't alcoholics and had to abstain. If she could imagine anything, it would be a can of lager or a bottle of Sourz). He was her rough and ready, happy chappy, not some pompous prick who thought he was better than everyone else and she preferred it that way. (Not that Port and Stilton is pompous, well, it is but it isn't.) *But Thwaite is a pompous dick.* Put it this way, when Thwaite first introduced her to all the different ways to drink alcohol, pretending it was cultured and refined, nine times out of ten, they would drink themselves into a blackout anyway, plus, it all tasted nasty regardless, in fact, for her, the stronger and posher the alcohol, the dirtier it tasted. Thwaite would say, "It's a sip and savour…," *fuck that,* she would think, as she tasted it and felt it burn out her insides. *It's a… don't overthink it and downer. What's the point in spending a fortune on posh booze when the cheap shit has the same effect? Did Thwaite justify his own issues with alcohol; by pretending it was part of an occasion, rather than 'being on the sesh'? NO Darcy, stop thinking about it. It'll be hot chocolate, with marshmallows and being happy instead. That's all that matters. I can do this,* she thought to herself furiously. She had done it before, but when she thought about it, when she had been teetotal for the four years prior to Thwaite, she hadn't been physically or emotionally dependent on the booze. She never used to drink in the house, nor did she ever drink alone. No, before alcoholism, Darcy was bulimic. (I know, come follow me down this little side road of realisation.)

It was so painful. She was emotionally dependent on putting her fingers down her throat and the release and 'power' it gave her to control her weight, because when she was with Elon, she felt like she had no control of anything. The only thing that was hers was her bulimia. That was the only thing he couldn't have, and she took comfort in it. That all started because he made her feel as if he had no belief in her going on and sticking to a diet. It stayed with her for years after, dipping its toe in and out of her life. She still needed it, but the alcoholism took over, and she no longer needed to put her fingers down her throat, the sickness would come naturally. *Wow,* thought Darcy. She was a little shocked with herself, at how her thoughts were forcing her to bring up new realisations. She was well and truly an addict of sorts. All she had done her whole life was find unhealthy ways of coping – with absolute cunts. Her head was spinning with her thoughts. (Are you getting dizzy too?)

Let's just take a moment to take stock. Are you ok? If you're not, then pull yourself together, this is just the tip of the iceberg. I'm just kidding, as I've said before, if you are struggling, please know there is help. Look in the back of the book, there are numbers to call and websites to refer to. If you need five minutes, then go put the book in the freezer and chill out (see what I did there?) Again, only kidding, I was just making a reference to the TV series, Friends, when Joey puts the book, Little Women, in the freezer, after he was emotionally overwhelmed. As you can see with the joking and daft references, I myself am feeling a little overwhelmed at the sadness of her story. She has had so much pain, but if it makes you feel any better then please know, she is a strong person with the resilience of the CrCoNi alloy (a high-entropy alloy of chromium, cobalt, and nickel, which is considered to be the toughest material known, with its strength actually increasing at extremely low temperatures.) She will be ok, I promise, it's just gonna take a while, but she will get there. Anyway, let's jump back on the train and get back to her original thoughts.

She remembered how grateful she was, that she was able to go back and talk to David that day (the one she did her induction with). He helped her process it all. (Plus of course, Finn gave her a cuddle, which helped distract her from Thwaite's 'knobheaddery'). When she was at rehab (home) she could cope with all these feelings because everyone else was like her. But she went cold at the thought of what could've happened otherwise. She didn't even want to imagine what it was going to be like in everyday life, when she eventually left. Even though it was her choice to stay, rehab put measures in place to ensure nobody was sneaking alcohol into the building, by way of bag searches, and staff would perform random breathalysers, whenever anyone went out, so it was easier not to get tempted into sneakiness.

She felt stronger, but even now, she still had trouble understanding her relationship with alcohol, or anything else for that matter. But, NO – Thwaite's attitude was beyond comprehension. He told her how much of a mess and disgrace she was, and now that she appeared to be fixed, he was trying to mess her head up, by calling her back to the party times, as and when he wanted them! It only reaffirmed her belief, that he only wanted her as nothing more than a drinking buddy, until she realised, he'd broken her beyond use. She refused to allow herself to slip back into that toxic relationship, and that meant both with alcohol and with Thwaite. It was still very early days, but NO. Every day had so many highs and lows. She would go from thinking, *Yeah, I've got this in the bag mate; I've cracked the code; I have solved the secret of life.* Right through to, *Oh my God! I can't do this anymore, it's too hard. Maybe I should just go back home and say hello to Jack, Jim and that bastard. He didn't seem so bad when she was drunk.* (P.S. Jack and Jim were Darcy's old mates, they came in bottle form that were 40% proof). Right now, she felt strong enough to say that she wasn't even going to tempt the mindset of: 'I'll just have the one'. It only ran the risk of slipping straight back into old habits. She needed to kill it from the roots. There was no denying it, even though she was trying this new thing nowadays, called: 'owning one's own shit' – Thwaite WAS the root cause. It was undeniable; however she tried to look at it. He was definitely a massive player in encouraging it… until it went too far.

You know the saying: 'One's too many, a thousand's never enough'? *It's such a true statement if ever there was one.* It's a bit like they say in the Pringles advert, "Once you pop, you just can't stop." Yeah well, next thing you know, your stood barefoot in a pile of nettles, with knickers round your ankles, having a wee, completely oblivious to the thousands of nettle stings your receiving on your 'wobbly-knobbly-bits-and-bobs' (it means…, well you know what it means!) That is, until you wake up the next morning to pee, and you think you've been eaten alive by a cactus! (There was a filthier analogy in there, but let's just slide past it. It's not that type of book, people!)

The second time she saw Thwaite, he'd picked her up and brought her back home for a couple of hours, to get some bits, which included her keyboard, fancy dress wigs, amplifier and microphone, to name a few things (you know, the bare essentials). She felt like she was stood before a stranger. Like she'd never known him in the first place. All she felt, when she stood in front of him, in her own home, was the feeling of utter panic, of wanting to get back to rehab, and to Finn. Now she came to think of it, Thwaite was acting peculiar that day as well. Hmm? But sod it. She didn't care. It didn't really matter anyway. She was one hundred percent ok; that part of her life had reached its conclusion, and it had nothing to do with Finn, although she would've been telling herself porky pies (means lies) if she'd said that he hadn't strengthened her resolve. She wanted Thwaite out of her life and her house, regardless. He had stolen her prime years. Everything was buzzing around her brain. It was a mixture of resentment and her own accountability. The 'kiss' and Finn's messages afterwards, telling her how much she'd changed his life, and that he was falling in love with her, had completely thrown everything out of whack. She felt like a 'wonky donkey'. What she meant by that, she wasn't quite sure. Hmm? Maybe a slightly off-balanced ass, perhaps?

Darcy had been adamant that she was going to use this time to build a solid foundation for herself and her kids. The original plan was to find herself first. Then, and only then, would she be able to give herself fully to 'Mr Right', whenever that may be. Getting clean had given her a second chance at life. Meeting Finn wasn't supposed to be part of the plan, but the bouncing bean, who had more sparkle than a smashed mirror, (I say that because it glimmers and shimmers in the light but still cuts like fucking glass and, gives you multiple years of bad luck) had well and truly stolen her heart away from any kind of path. She was now 'flying by the seat of her pants' right alongside him. It felt exhilarating, exciting and full to the brim of hopefulness, about a bright future, with mystery and spontaneity added to the mix. Something she hadn't had in a long time.

She couldn't help herself. Her imagination took over completely, and she flew away, with a one-way express ticket, to the far-off land of 'I-loves-him-lots-ly'. When she got there, she was greeted by a dancing unicorn, who filled her brain with cotton wool. (Obviously, I'm taking the piss). She wasn't thinking straight. She walked straight past all the danger signs, and right into this filtered, fluffy, pretend world, of wondering what life could be like as Finn's girlfriend? It felt very unnerving, but nice. Finn had six kids, five biologicals, and a stepdaughter. He talked about them constantly and Darcy loved hearing it. Especially how passionate he was when it came to Elle (his stepdaughter). It didn't matter to him that they didn't share the same blood. He had raised her from a baby, so as far as he was concerned, just because he wasn't with Helga (the mother of his children and the woman who was to become the bane of Darcy's life) it didn't change a thing. He didn't abandon Elle, like Elon had dropped Jaxon, and that to Darcy, was so commendable. Just because he and Helga were no longer together, he still wanted to be a part of Elle's life. It was refreshing and something that was missing from her relationship with Thwaite. That 'fucktard' had almost succeeded in completely ostracising Darcy from most of her family connections. Finn seemed to be the complete polar opposite and maybe the breath of fresh air that she had been missing her whole life?

She felt like she could really learn from him. She admired him for trying his best. He had such a fight and passion in his voice when he would say, "I just wanna be a good dad to me kids." The kind of fight that she'd been missing until now. He may have messed his life up and let them down through addiction, but he portrayed himself as a caring, loving, beautiful soul, who was just trying for a fresh start, especially when it came to his kids. It was such an attractive trait. She wasn't stupid. (Yes, she was). She knew if they got serious, then it was going to be hard work. Let's face it, six kids are a lot. She wondered stupidly if Helga owned a TV or had any other aspirations than being a baby making machine? (By the way, just to make it clear, Darcy has no problem with anyone who has a large family, she was simply being a bitch, which was a low blow. Sorry Helga (not sorry). For some reason, the thought of such a large family didn't scare her off at all. Plus, she wasn't expecting to meet them straight away or start playing stepmum. She was simply looking forward to seeing where things went and taking things at a pace that was comfortable for everyone involved, however, this WAS Finn! She wanted 'the good, the bad and the ugly', with 'warts and all', riding the carefree adventures together, taking it one day at a time. (Be careful what ya wish for, I say!) P.S. – when Darcy said, 'warts and all', that, by no means, meant she was referring to his kids as warts. She was, in fact, referring to the big wart on his chest, which was almost like a third nipple. Plus, she never signed up for the huge giant wart Helga was to become. Let's face it, that wart needed to be excised off Finn's arse and treated with respect, for the time she had given him, and the children she bore him, but kept in a glass jar and kept at arm's length, so it couldn't re-attach itself and cause any more trouble! From what Finn had told Darcy,

Helga needed to leave him alone and let him be a father, without any further involvement, except what is considered acceptable for two co-parents.

He seemed to be such a family man and when they'd had their talks, he gave the definite vibe that he wanted more kids, with the right person. He'd made it clear he could, one hundred percent, see Darcy as his next victim (I'm so sorry, I meant: 'love of his life'). The thought of such a large family scared her a little bit because she had missed so much of her own children's lives, through this shitty addiction. Plus, she hadn't even thought about a potential future with more children of her own. Did she even want any more?

All of this was far too much overthinking for one morning, *for fuck's sake, Darcy mate, you've only kissed love. Chill out….* "Whoosah," she said, as she massaged her ear lobes (a technique she had learnt, from the film Bad Boys, to calm herself down.) She'd not even stepped out of her bedroom yet, and she'd already talked herself into acquiring a full-blown family, with thoughts of maybe having more kids; she seriously needed to 'chill her beans'. She still had a full day ahead of her, so she needed to stop the daydreaming. She checked her hairpiece was on firmly and did her last little checks in the mirror, to ensure she was wearing the right amount of sexy and cute, before finally leaving her room. As she made her way downstairs, there was the voice of hope in the back of her head that said, *Why question everything Darcy? Go with the flow…. Yeah…,* she thought, *why question it?* This was a man who she thought was just as misunderstood as her and by discovering Finn, she'd discovered more about herself than she ever thought possible.

6. THE WHIRLWIND ROMANCE

Everything felt so awkward and intense when she next saw him. She was in the television room, ready for the morning, when he came bounding in. God knows why it was referred to as that because aside from the obvious reason (that it housed a big TV) the room was essentially used for anything but watching TV! He barely made eye contact with her, as he walked to the other side of the room and took a seat near the window. He looked far too wrapped up in conversation with Arnold, laughing and joking, to say anything other than, "Morning," from across the room, before resuming his conversation, as if she was a stranger to him. She thought it was odd. His behaviour wasn't right. She wondered why. (But I'll tell ya why, people! Because he was a goddamn player! Darcy, open your eyes love, and take those rose-tinted spectacles off, that you bought from the pink pound shop. You look like a twat!)

The TV room was no bigger than your typical, old-fashioned front room (living room, lounge). At the back of the room was a large bay window with seating, which looked a lot more inviting than it was in reality. It lured its victims into a false sense of thinking, *Hmm, that looks comfortable, maybe I'll sit there.* Tut, yet, before you knew it, you were sandwiched in like sardines in a tin; your left arse cheek fast asleep, while the right cheek tingled back to life. Then, when you'd try to readjust, to get into a little more of a comfortable seating position, the wood underneath the paper-thin cushion, would creak and groan loudly, letting out noises that would make it sound as if you'd just accidently let out a huge bottom burp. (Yes, I do mean a fart in case anyone was confused?)

She now knew, from cold, hard experience, to avoid sitting there for the morning meetings, if she could help it. She'd learnt the hard way during a previous meeting. Very early on in her journey, she had sat at that seat, awkwardly squished between two other people (at that point, she barely even knew anyone's name) and the seat creaked so loudly, making everyone turn their heads to look directly at her. She was so embarrassed but embraced her new-found rosy-red cheeks as extra blusher. With as much bravado as she could muster, she tried to furiously brush it off by stupidly saying, "Oops, that came out louder than I wanted it to," which in turn made everyone (naturally) fall about in fits of laughter. (For some reason, farting noises almost always turn adults from all walks of life, into big kids. Or was it just her?)

Along the right side of the room, as you entered through the door (which was technically a fire door but was always propped open with a doorstop) were more windows. They had an externally facing door between them, which led to the outside of the building. Around the edges of the room, were small, individual, well-used armchairs, with busy looking patterns on the fabric. The walls were a horrible olive-green colour and in dire need of a re-vamp. (The walls, ironically, were the only shade of green that she didn't like.) The room had an electronic keyboard in the corner, which she clocked immediately, making a mental note that when she felt better, she would maybe think about trying to learn how to play it. (That had been put on the back burner for now, as she had no time, what with learning sessions taking up her day and Finn and the gang filling her evenings with laughter, and, in the case of last night... kisses).

Anyway, she'd opted to sit on the left side today, so she could look out at the warm sunshine. She was trying to watch the birds flying past the window and landing on the bird feeder in the small garden outside, but she was too preoccupied with worry that he regretted his decision to kiss her. Finn barely looked over in her direction, as he continued to laugh loudly at something he and Arnold had obviously found highly hilarious. She silently tried to catch his attention with her gaze, to ask him without words, if he was ok, but the morning meeting had just started. All sorts of doom and gloom thoughts flooded her mind about last night. It was as if the voices of doubt, she had taken such great strides in sending packing, had all come flooding back with a vengeance, after taking their mini break from 'fuck-off-a-too-ey'. They seemed intent on unpacking all the baggage she'd tried to give to charity (ya know, coz she's good like that) and she started overthinking, *Oh no, oh no, does he wish last night never happened?*

She sat next to Claire, who sat up straight, as if ready to listen intently to David. He kicked the morning's meeting off with the usual, "Good morning." Usually, she would smile to herself at the way Claire, the little nerd, made herself look super attentive. She did it with the grace of a swan. Her posture always gave the impression that she was a lot more invested in what someone was saying, than she really was. She had a way about her that made her look a lot posher than she was in reality; she was simply very elegant, with her long white hair, fastened up neatly in a bun, at the back of her neck. She was very pretty for an older lady and Darcy could see that she was probably mind-bogglingly stunning in her prime. She had an unmistakable fragrance of either fruitiness or mint, as she was always sucking on a boiled sweet.

Today, Darcy was trying her best to whisper to her that she wanted to talk to her after the meeting but couldn't without drawing too much attention to herself. *For fuck's sake,* why had she waited until now, to decide it was a good time to start a mini counselling session, in the hope that Claire would shed some light as to why Finn appeared to be acting like a dick and ignoring her? She sat uncomfortably in her chair, unable to engage in her surroundings, as there was too much commotion going on in her head. All she could manage to do was mumble, "Good morning," as she stared at her hands, which were starting to feel all clammy and cold.

David was an older looking dude, with a face and voice that looked and sounded as if he was bored stiff all the time. His looks were very deceiving, as he was actually one of the nicest and easiest workers to talk to in there. He never seemed to know his arse from his elbow though. If you ever asked him anything, he never seemed to know the answers, but he was very likable and one of the more 'chilled out' members of staff, who you could have a laugh with, and ultimately, get away with bending the rules more. She and Finn always liked it when David was on the late shift because he would leave them to their own devices – within reason.

This morning, he was reeling off the usual announcements, trying his best to ignore the low hum of commotion Finn and Arnold were causing from their corner of the room. She wondered what was so funny. Usually Darcy, Finn, Claire and Arnold sat together, so it all felt a bit off balance today. For some reason, her irrational brain was making up all sorts of reasons as to why those idiots were laughing. *Maybe he's saying you kiss like a frog?* said one of her fears. *Yeah well, he's a fucking toad*, chimed in another. *Bastards! What's so fucking funny anyway?* she wondered. Her brain was going into hyperdrive, and she was starting to feel very uncomfortable and stupid, about spending that morning fantasising about love. It was probably because they'd not really had much chance to talk during the usual morning chores, but she felt slightly insecure. He'd told her, by text last night, how he felt, and again this morning, but they'd not had a chance to talk face to face yet. *You're overthinking it, chill the fuck out*, she kept saying to herself, willing it to be true, but she couldn't help feeling hurt. Surely, he could have at least given her just that little bit of reassurance. (Yeah, he could've done mate, however you try justifying it, or overthinking it, to the point of making excuses for him – instead of him fucking about like a child and acting the idiot, he could've taken a split second.) It may sound like such a little thing, but it breeds insecurity. *Does he know what he's doing, or is he simply that careless and if he is that careless, then should I tell him, or should I make out it's no big deal? Will he call me stupid for feeling like this? Is it stupid? Arghhh! What the fuck? Why does my brain work this way?*

For morning chores, she had now upgraded to cleaning the kitchen. The term 'kitchen' was a bit too strong and used very loosely. Really it was just somewhere to make a drink. It consisted of a few kitchen units, which housed all the different types of coffee and teas, a few plates, glasses and coffee cups, and a drawer with cutlery, that held a thousand teaspoons, a couple of forks and a knife. People would take things up to their rooms and forget to bring them down again, so it was very difficult to keep track of where anything was and very haphazard. Cleaning the 'kitchen' was an easy enough job. Or it was, in theory anyway. If it wasn't for people coming in and out every five bloody seconds, to put yet more coffee cups in the sink, as they passed through the pool room, which doubled up as a sort of walkway, the job would've been done and dusted in about thirty seconds. All it really consisted of was washing the pots leftover in the sink (because there was always some lazy twat who never washed their cup after using it) wiping the sides down and mopping the floor. Oh, and emptying the bin….

There had been some drama that unfolded near the downstairs toilet, while the morning chores were being done. She had heard Finn shouting overdramatically. His voice rang through rehab, "Errr! Dirty bastard! I've got shit on me finger!"

This was quickly followed by David's quieter voice, which said, "Finn! Swearing…,"

"Aww shit! I'm sorry for swearing but I don't care mate, I got shit on me finger," she heard him exclaim again, which was then followed by laughter and other voices she couldn't identify. She giggled to herself happily at the sound of his voice, *Bloody idiot, how the hell has he managed that?* she wondered quizzically.

At the time, it didn't raise any alarm bells for her. He was always being overdramatic and loud, for one reason or another, and was almost always, constantly being told off for swearing. His voice had become an integral part of the building. Everyone became tuned out to the noise he created, especially the 'old timers' (people who had finished their detox) they were simply just used to it. It became almost like the low hum your kitchen fridge makes; you don't really know it's there anymore, but you always know somethings off, when the noise stops. The only difference really, was there was no quiet filter on Finn. He was loud, proud and lovably unapologetic. In fact, if ever she wanted to find him, all she needed to do was to stand still for a second and listen out for which direction his voice was coming from, follow the sound of laughter and there he would be…, causing chaos. (The cute little dickhead).

Until now, she had thought nothing of the shouting, but David, who looked as if he was under pressure to be as diplomatic as possible, looked over at the boys to say, "Just give me a minute. Alright Finn, just calm down, I'm getting to it," he said, rolling his eyes at Finn's blatant insubordination.

He mumbled quietly, "I got shit on my finger, mate," showing Arnold his finger. Arnold was trying so hard not to laugh. He looked extremely smug with himself. As usual, it looked like whatever David was about to announce, involved Finn… and this time, the drama obviously involved his shitty finger. However, from what she could make out, this time, it looked like he had been on the receiving end of a prank that Arnold had played on him that morning. David was now shedding some light on the commotion. Apparently, some dirty tramp had been causing…well… shit. (David didn't exactly use those words, however it was implied).

"Right, as you can all gather, there's been a bit of an incident this morning," he said, as if trying to take the matter seriously. "There's been somebody using very unhygienic toilet practices in the downstairs bathroom," he continued, his voice rising slightly, as if he was trying to drown out Finn, who was itching to tell his version, however, he caught David's eye and he shut up, although he looked as if he was going to pop at the pressure of holding it all in. "…And they've been putting lumps of pooey tissue in the toilet bin," he said, looking at the room at large. There was a low hum of general chatter from everyone expressing their disgust and shaking their heads. Everyone in the room tried to make themselves look as disgusted as possible, in the hope that by looking repulsed, it would show their innocence.

Claire, who looked scandalised, raised her hand, and waited for the chatter to dull down before speaking. "Erm, yeah, I mentioned something to D'accord the other day. I went to use the bathroom, and somebody had pissed all over the floor and there were shit stains down the back of the toilet as well." She put her hand back down, folded her arms and looked around the room, with her lips pursed, as if to scope out the guilty party, by staring at each and every one of them, to see who looked as guilty as sin. Everyone was looking at everyone else as if to say, "Was it you?" but the culprit, whoever it was (cough, cough... Buzz) wasn't owning up.

Finn chirped up again, "Arnold, the dirty bastard, seen there was shit in't bin, and told me to put me hand in to change it, and I got shit on me finger," he said to the room, as if he was telling everyone a survival tale, where he almost died. Everyone, including Darcy, laughed at him and at the absurdity of it. There were times like this, when it felt like the environment they were in, enabled the most grown of grown-ups to revert back to childishness. Also, Finn had a way with words, there was no doubt about that, "It looked like a Curly Wurly mate, d'ya know that poo emoji? It looked like that mate," he proclaimed, as David, who'd been sat down during the general discussion of, 'who everyone thought the dirty tramp was' (cough, cough... Buzz) stood up to stop Finn from elaborating any further.

"Whoever it was, and to everyone in general, can we be mindful that other people have to use these toilets please? So, can people please leave the toilets how you would expect to find them? And...," he said as an afterthought, "when people clean the toilets or bathrooms in the morning, can you please make sure we all wear gloves?" he suggested, as he looked over at Finn, who was still looking at the finger that had the poo on it, showing it off, like a kid would at school 'show and tell'. Darcy couldn't help but smile at the buffoonery. Firstly, at Finn, whose face looked like a stupidly, comically, beautiful, 'divvy' (foolish) picture. And secondly, at how a group of fully grown adults, had spent most of the morning meeting (which lasted half an hour) talking about shit!

As the narrator, I am going to stop the shit talk here. We all know it was Buzz. Buzz was a scruff. He always looked slimy. As if he had something to hide? Maybe that was an unfair statement, as in reality, he was very shy, but there was always an underlying element of 'ick' (disgust) about him. He would sit in class looking bored, never contributing anything to the group, then he would retreat to his room during downtime, only to pop up here and there. It felt like your creepy uncle was in the room when he was around. She wasn't keen on him at all (if you can't tell?). His personality rubbed her up the wrong way, with some of the utter shite that would come out of his mouth (and apparently his arse). Whenever she heard him talking to any of the lads, it always seemed to be about whose knickers he wanted to get into. He was creepy and was looking for anyone to shag. What made Darcy chuckle more than anything, was that from what she could gather, the way he talked about the girls, it gave her the impression he thought he actually stood a chance! When he stood none (although, that's not strictly true. She had heard through the grapevine (cough, cough, Finn) that Buzz had struck up a sexual relationship with a woman who had entered rehab earlier than her. (For some reason, Buzz stayed in rehab after his own group had 'been released'. Why? She had no idea). The way he talked to Finn about this woman, was absolutely vile (I'll leave that there).

After the morning meeting she tried catching Finn's attention, "Ey up shitty finger, are you coming for a cig?" she asked him, trying to act nonchalant, as she laughed at his facial expressions of disgust and disbelief, at what had happened to him. It was obviously a life altering event! She was trying her best to act casual and breezy, hoping he would say something comforting, to let her know what was on his mind.

"I know mate, it was a Curly Wurly," he said, as he showed her the finger again, laughing as he did so. "It was disgusting mate," he said, looking too caught up in the drama of the morning, to give her even a sliver of his mind. He started to say something else but just as he started to speak, he was distracted by the sound of his name being called from someone in the crowded hallway. Obviously, that was more important, as he abandoned whatever he was about to say to her and wandered off, without a second thought, to go tell the Curly Wurly story to someone else, leaving HER feeling stupid. She stood in the narrow hallway for a few moments, wondering if he was coming back to go for that cigarette together, feeling like a complete plum (her way of saying doughnut, idiot, prat, fool, looser – just go on Google and search different synonyms for absolute 'prick stick'. There's loads more words for it, however, I think you know what I'm trying to say). *Fuck it, I'm going for a fag*, she thought, hoping to God, that the tears which had started to well in her eyes, would quell, before anyone noticed and asked her if she was ok?

He gave her no signs of reassurance at all. She was left wondering throughout the day. She was so unnerved by his apparent cold shoulder. The rest of the day's learning sessions went by in a haze of uncertainty. If you'd have asked her to recall what she had learnt that day (apart from her belief that all men are wankers) she wouldn't have been able to tell you if she tried. The day felt like it wasn't even happening in real time. It was all a big blobby blur. If she had to rate her mood that day, it would've been somewhere in the fiery pits of hell, where her heart was being slowly tortured by…her…; It was her face staring back. She was torturing herself, over what appeared to be yet another dick! (When she looked at her tormentor, she could see herself standing there in full 'domme' gear, squeezing her heart sadistically. She looked quite sexy, which pissed her off all the more. Even when she was feeling like shit, her good old imagination was there to introduce new levels of taking the proverbial. Even her imaginary self, looked better than her. However, she made a mental note to remind herself to ask, when she stopped torturing herself, of course, where she got that outfit from? (I wonder if it was Temu?) But why? Why was she torturing herself? (Alright, maybe, just maybe, that was a slightly overdramatic interpretation. However, she felt at her all time low, or at least the lowest she'd been during her time there to date, and it was all her own stupid fault).

When it came to lunchtime, she walked into the dining room, not in the mood to take in too much of her surroundings, but she knew from memory of eating in there every single day, that there were six round tables, cramped into a small space, with wooden chairs set around them, in groups of four. Finn, who would've normally saved her seat, was already seated around a table at the far corner of the room. He was sitting, laughing and joking away cheerfully, with Cindy and Arnold. He looked as though he had no care in the world. Cindy was giggling away, batting her stupid eyelashes at him as she spoke. (Bitch). What the actual fuck, Darcy, do you want me to chin him for ya? He is taking the piss out of you, love. Please see, this is not something that you deserve. Here's me, the narrator, trying to argue with a memory and Darcy, well, don't get me started. We will just have to ride the wave, because like everything else that has gone into the past, we cannot change it. Neither can we talk sense into someone who doesn't want to see what is right in front of them.

She tried sitting down and acting normal, but the whole mood shift had thrown her chakra off-piste. She hardly touched her food, unable to swallow her chicken curry, which contained peas! *Fucking peas, again! Is there a special offer on these little green balls of death?* she thought moodily, as she tried her best to chew a few mouthfuls of chicken; it tasted like dried up pieces of bark, creating a lump in her throat, as she tried to swallow it down, before finally giving up, scraping the remains into the bin and discarding her plate. (Darcy may have been moody, but she wasn't messy). She couldn't pull her head out of her arse. As much as she tried, she couldn't pretend everything was ok. Her mask was slipping off. She needed to readjust it, before it came off completely, and everyone saw the vulnerable side of her, that she had always tried to hide. She had to get away from the hustle and bustle of the house. Instead, she chose to go to her room, to sit on her bed, write in her diary and wallow in self-pity. (Oh, dear God! Is this the second time we've got to get the tiny violins out? Tut! I'm kidding.) She was in a bit of a mess and didn't know how to resolve it. Her armour was firmly fixed back on, and she was ordering new parts from Amazon. She wasn't going to let him see how much he had hurt her.

They weren't technically allowed to retreat to their rooms during the day, as it encouraged bad habits to sneak back into their routine. However, she didn't care, the world could seriously piss off. She felt safer from the chill in the air that she now felt when she was around him. She wanted to curl up in a ball on her bed and cry. *Why is this happening?* She thought, as she sat down on the bed and stared out of the open window. The sun was shining on her face, which calmed her a little, but the inability to think rationally was still ingrained deeply into her thoughts. She was beginning to feel slightly angry with him now. *What is he playing at? Completely swapping up his mood like that? He could at least have given me a heads-up, instead of saying one thing, then acting in complete contrast? And, to add insult to injury, why is he being so flirtatious with Cindy? Does he want me to put him on my hitlist? Arghhh! This is so frustrating,* she thought. It was agitation at its peak. It felt nasty and icky, as she could feel her addictive personality whispering for her to give into her temptation, just for a moment, so she could forget this horrible feeling of not being good enough. She didn't like this colour on herself at all. She was not a jealous person, yet this felt like jealousy. *Is he doing this on purpose, to see my reaction? So that he has power over me? Is he just another one of them?*

At the bottom of her bed was a small chest of drawers, upon it sat her TV and a couple of picture frames. One of the frames housed the snap of her and Finn from the photobooth. She picked it up and stared at it, as if willing him to talk to her through the glass. (She got no joy out of it, except looking at his beautiful little head.) His eyes shone and smiled before the smile itself. His unshaved face looked rugged and manly, with the hint of 'Peter Pan syndrome' (the boy who never wanted to grow up). To anyone else he was just the boy next door. To her, he was her Prince Charming. Whatever was wrong with him, she just hoped with all her might, that it wasn't going to affect his recovery. Aside from feeling hurt by his behaviour today, she only wanted what was best for him. He had his journey to travel, and if that meant he had to leave any feelings he had for her aside, to grow, then as much as it hurt to think about, she wouldn't blame him for it.

(Aww, Darcy. I nearly got the tissues out.) P.S., I'm sorry for always ruining the sentimental moments. I will try my best to knock it on the head. It's upsetting to see a woman so broken. She had been put to the test to prove herself so many times, to find out they didn't think she was good enough, or that people only wanted her for their own chew toy, wanting more and more until she had nothing left. She truly deserved to find her peace. But so did he. For now, anyway. Later on, the bastard can go and stub his toe, barefoot, on dodgy furniture, at least twice a day for the rest of his life).

She looked away from the picture and picked up her folder (the one they were given on their first session). It held all her paperwork, from all her sessions so far. She flicked through, as if hoping something in there would give her some guidance. And there it was. It was as if it glowed in the sunlight; like it was meant to speak to her at that precise moment. It was her anxiety management. Right in front of her eyes, were the notes she had written down about breathing techniques. As she read, she started to put into practice what she had learnt so far, and her breathing soothed, giving her a sense of calm that washed over her. A wise man once said: 'Negative thoughts need to be treated like birds passing overhead. Thoughts fly past. They come and go whenever they please, without prejudice. Don't let them nest.' Of course, her wicked sense of humour returned, like a superpower returning to the 'chosen one'. She imagined the birds flying past. "Knowing my luck, they'd fly past and shit on my head!" She said out loud. *Hey ho!* Her brain would only allow a certain amount of seriousness before returning to sarcasm. But shit happens. Just quickly wipe it away and get on with your day. She wasn't sure if it was the breathing techniques, the words on the page or the delightful little edits she inserted into the original quote, but she felt slightly better than before.

Even though she had to fight hard to overcome her initial instincts to hit the 'FUCK IT' button – it looks a lot like those self-destruct buttons you see on bombs in action films, where there's only a few minutes before total annihilation. The urge to immediately need to pick up a drink, felt as though it had been weakened; the situation was pulling her into wanting to give up, but she was dealing with her feelings head on, like a little recovery warrior. She would be lying if she said it didn't feel absolutely shit but Jack and Jim (her 40% proof friends) who were beckoning her in the distance, would have to stay away, at least for another day. To try to begin to explain how proud she was of herself, for using the coping tools that rehab was teaching her, on her own, felt more empowering than she thought possible. *Maybe this recovery shit actually makes a bit of sense*, she thought happily.

Her room felt a lot more like her own private sanctuary now, rather than the cold, lonely, cell-like feeling she had when she'd first arrived. However, she still felt locked in, within the same cell-like state in her head. In all honesty, her own mood was pissing herself right off. Yeah, it was true, she felt better than before but she was in her bedroom. Her safe space, away from having to talk to people. Up here, she could remove her mask and let the pretence that she was holding it together, out of the window. It was a bit like the feeling she'd get when she took off her bra at the end of a long day and sit contentedly, while her boobies warmed her bellybutton. (To any of you ladies reading this, you'll know exactly what a relief that is? Although most of you'll probably have boobies that stay where they're supposed to at the moment, but don't get too comfortable, there will come a time in your life when you'll know exactly what I mean).

This room had been hers since the second week into the programme, and it was to remain hers until it was time to move downstairs, into the self-contained apartment, for the last three weeks (the final stretch). After the first week, the rehab centre moved all new clients who had detoxed, into different rooms upstairs, to make way for new 'detoxers'. The detoxification process is treated as high risk, which needs 24-hour monitoring. Although withdrawals themselves are not the cause of death in the detox process, seizures and delirium tremens, more commonly known as DTs, CAN, so when Darcy first arrived, she was given her temporary room outside the office, so staff could easily monitor her. In hindsight they should've bloody kept her there, the naughty little bed hopper!) The room was very much like the room she had downstairs. The only real difference was that she had added her Darcy charm, with her home comforts. Slowly but surely, over time, she'd brought in her own stuff from home (she even brought her old wedding dress in, to show the girls how pretty it was, coz she was a hopeless 'geek-a-tooie'). She learnt very early on, that if she was going to survive the nights here, then she needed her own duvet and pillows because the bedding she had detoxed in, was enough to give anyone nightmares. Yes, they were practical to wipe down, in case of any little accidents, but now she had graduated detox, surely that meant she could be trusted a bit more not to have any little accidents, by giving her something that didn't have plastic wrapping, that crinkled like crepe paper at the slightest movement…? Kelsie, whose room it was before she moved into the apartment downstairs, gave Darcy a proper duvet (from the outside land, where people slept crinkle free). She also told her early on, when Darcy was still a newbie to the programme, that they could bring their own bedding from home if they wanted to. At the time she thanked the lord. She didn't know how she would cope without home comforts and the familiar objects she could call upon at times of need. She didn't want to bring her quilt from home; she couldn't bring herself to sleep under anything that she and Thwaite had shared. So, she had new stuff imported from: 'Mums-are-the-best'. Her bed was now as comfy as could be. It was only a single bed, so she couldn't sprawl or starfish, but Kelsie's duvet on the bottom, like a mattress topper and the new bedding, now meant that she didn't have to deal with waking up in a swimming pool of her own sweat. Her bed was fit for a queen.

She made the space her own, with all her art supplies and artbooks next to her bed, along with her writing pad, which contained a whole range of poetry. She picked it up and looked at one of the poems she'd written recently. One read:

He's always fooling around,
But he never gets you down,
He Effs and Jeffs and calls you a cunt,
And at times, he can be ever so blunt,
He never engages brain before mouth,
And does divvy things, when you're out and about,
One of the funniest people you ever did see,
He makes you laugh so much, you nearly pee,
You get tears of laughter in your eyes,
With streaks of tears, you can't disguise,
He farts all the time,
He even farts right in your face,
One day, he is going to cause himself a disgrace,
One of these days, he is going to poo right in his pants,
Then he will have to do…
The 'I shit myself' dance.

She read it over and over again, smiling to herself as she did so. It was only a crappy poem that she had written quite soon into their friendship. At the time, she'd written it quickly, as an impatient Finn watched over her shoulder. Reading it back to herself, even she had to admit that she captured him perfectly, even if she said so herself. (It was a pat on the back moment, if ever there was one). They had been on such an amazing journey together so far. It felt heart wrenching to think that it could've all been potentially spoilt over a kiss. "You're overthinking it, Darcy. Please, please? You're just overthinking it," she whispered out loud, as she stared at her ceiling. Her eyes scanned the room, looking for a focal point to concentrate on. Her eyes met the pictures she had on a cork noticeboard, which was already in the room when she moved upstairs. They were pictures of her family, that she'd brought with her the first day she had moved in (to rehab). It helped her remember exactly why she was doing this in the first place. It calmed her panic. Yeah, if her relationship with him had been ruined (friendship or otherwise) then it was going to make things a lot harder for her to stay and embrace her recovery journey, but the picture of her kids smiling at her, solidified her resolve. She had to stay and finish what she'd started, no matter what. She wanted to call and talk to them, to hear their voices, however, she wasn't allowed her goddamn phone back until 5pm. *Fucking rules,* she thought scathingly. *Bag of shit, balls and bastards!*

She sat for a moment before she stood up and took a final look at her room. Feeling very grateful that she had allowed herself time away, to sort out her muddled mind. All she cared about was what he was thinking, but he was unreadable. *What a difference a day makes, eh?* She thought wildly, as she walked downstairs. There HE was, alone, walking down the narrow hallway, which had two fire doors at each end. He spotted her and made a beeline for her. The atmosphere had changed again, back to the way it was last night "What you sayin', me sexy lady? I've been looking for you." His smile and warmth firmly fixed back on his face, like it had never been absent. He reached out and touched her waist.

"I was upstairs in my room, writing some poetry," she said, sounding confused but pleased everything seemed to be fine. Wearing a fake smile on her face, she tried to match his energy, not wanting to make a big deal about it.

"What's up wi' ya?" he said, as he smiled boyishly.

"Nowt," she chimed back, trying her best to match his playful tone.

"Good, coz I've missed ya today, ya know?"

She looked at him puzzled, as he looked at her seriously. "I missed you too, ya divvy," trying to act as cool as a cucumber, resuming a mild friendly flirtation. She hesitated for a moment, unsure whether or not to say what was fighting to come out of her mouth. Before she could stop it, the words left her body. "If I'm honest, I thought there was something wrong. You've barely spoken to me all day," she said, trying to keep her voice playful and unaccusatory. She didn't want to seem like she was needy, but she was begging for some sort of explanation, rather than his chalk and cheese attitude. She had absolutely no idea where she stood. She smiled, as she looked into his eyes. It was as if he was completely oblivious to the personal turmoil he had put her through that day. Had she just been imagining it? The day had been a complete blur. Maybe she'd imagined it to be a lot worse than it was? Had she blown it out of all proportion because she was self-sabotaging?

"I've been trying to make it look as if I'm chilling with other people. I flirted with Cindy a bit, so people don't find out about us," he said, as if it was a genius master plan. She couldn't help but giggle at the logic of it. Some of the greatest plans are the simplest, *Fucking idiot!* She thought to herself fondly. "Whyyy…? Were you jealous?" he asked mockingly.

"Nooo," she replied, her face flushed, as she looked away, purposely embracing the embarrassment.

"Yeah, ya wa'," he said, giggling shyly.

She could see he looked quite pleased that she had been a bit jealous, as if it reaffirmed for him, how much she liked him. "Shut up, ya div. No, I wasn't… well, maybe a little." She admitted.

"Yeah well, I don't want her, I want you."

Finn did really love her after all.

7. MY ABUSER IS ME

I'm taking over this chapter, so just a heads up. I promised you a journey of discovery and when I make a promise, I try my best to keep it. This is like a counselling session, with all kinds of thoughts and questions thrown into the mix. If you manage to take anything away from this – then, "You're welcome," there's no need to thank me. That'll be a fiver…!

How are we all managing to digest it so far? It's shit, isn't it? No one person should have to have so much going on. Although, as much as I hate to admit it, the topics we have talked about, are becoming far more prevalent in a lot of people's lives. Some folk go through some pretty harrowing life events. The thing that disturbs me the most, is that a large number of these traumas are caused by other people, and what's even more disturbing, is that the trauma is usually caused by people you love and trust. (In other words, there are a whole bunch of bastards out there in the world, whose toes are left un-stubbed).

She is now only just coming to realise that her journey –

although we are at the beginning of it, and there is so much left to uncover – is a courageous one, that is full of discovery. She still had a lot to learn about herself. She wasn't blameless. She doesn't want you running away with the idea that she is a survivor, devoid of fault (don't go putting her on any pedestal, not yet anyway, it'll give her a big fat head, plus, she was still a 'wobbler'). She was her own worst enemy at times. However, she didn't want to think about it. Trauma can feel too morbid. Dealing with its effects can feel like you have two choices. Choice number one – just get on with it; don't think about it and shove it in a metaphorical cupboard at the back of your mind and never speak of it again. Like Fight Club, ya know? 'The first rule of Fight Club is that you don't talk about Fight Club'. P.S., don't you think that Brad Pitt is fit as fuck in that movie? Especially in his dressing gown with coffee mugs on it? Hmm, sorry, I was having a moment. Where were we?

Yes, some people, like Darcy, go through life trying to ignore their traumas or use substances or other harmful coping mechanisms, to try and bury the real issues, in the hopes it will all go away. It feels weak to admit that it sometimes gets too much to deal with. Nobody wants to see themselves as a victim. Some, however, seem to take the second route or choice; by using their trauma and letting it define them. They let it consume them and turn it into reasons for their shitty behaviour. However, that may just be the sceptic in me. (#justsayin). Then there are those, like Katy Piper (the woman who had acid thrown in her face by an ex-boyfriend) who eventually used her trauma to make a difference for other survivors and doing charity work.

All Darcy wanted was a fresh start. She felt like she had sat with it for long enough, locked in a constant cycle of drink to forget, wake up, and repeat. Her life and the mental torture she felt when she had sobered up, she wished would kindly piss right off. She wanted to rid herself from the horrible memories, without taking the time to process their value, even though it was dreadful to think about it. It had made her the woman she was today. But was it so wrong to want to feel washed clean? For want of a better description. Was that so wrong?

It may sound like she was learning so much but really, she was processing everything with a blind eye. She could see it clearly, but she refused to absorb it fully; she had become so deadened. "It is what it is," and "ah well, shit happens," were her new mantras as well as, "Ah well I don't want to think about that now." She was trying to paint a pretty picture, that she was ok now she was sober, but the past haunted her menacingly. She wanted to be strong, so she tried to be perfectly imperfect by burying her trauma again, as soon as she uncovered it. In finding Finn, yes, she was exploring the gelatine layer of herself that was all bouncy, gooey, light-hearted and carefree, but too much of a good thing can also be detrimental right? That's what the fun police tell you anyway (boring bastards). It's right though, she was too busy wrapped up in Finn; she was also taking away from herself, the time to heal, plus, she was ignoring big fat warning signs, as if they weren't driving her to yet another cliff edge.

In all honesty, he was doing the same thing. It's hard to think with a clear head when you find someone that you obviously connect with immediately. She didn't want to drag the old into the new. Especially under those circumstances. It threw everything that they were originally there for, into question. Both Darcy and Finn were brand new to recovery (well…, it was Darcy's second time. She did a seven-day detox, the year previously. However, looking back to then, she wasn't ready to make the life changes it took to remain sober. It seemed impossible, when she would be going home to Thwaite, and all the same familiarity, without the release of booze. Her marriage had become a train wreck; a car crash; a joke. There had been cheating on her part – he claimed he had been faithful and she believed him, although whether that was true will remain a mystery, she was far too pickled towards the end to even care, and you may also want to ask her best mate about that too? Maybe that bitch can shed some light as to how her and Thwaite got together?) Thwaite had a way of dumping all kinds of guilt and shame onto her, and Darcy, feeling remorseful for what she had done, shouldered the blame in its entirety, when the fault wasn't hers alone. He used to fabricate the details of her wrong doings and make her feel as if SHE was abusing HIM. She would sit and listen to everything he felt she was doing to him, and she took it on board. She listened (she knew she wasn't easy at times) not wanting to rock the boat further, it felt like they were having long heart to hearts during drug and alcohol fuelled benders. She thought, by accepting and validating his feelings, their relationship would improve. (Now there is absolutely no excuse for cheating. It's a sly and dirty deed. However, it would just sound like she was trying to justify it, if she said she had her reasons.) Thwaite was unsupportive in a lot of ways, and she lashed out in all the wrong ways, seeking validation from a man who took advantage of the fact that she was feeling fragile, unloved and unsupported. This may sound sceptical of me to say, as if I am trying to lessen Darcy's part in her infidelity; the man who she had cheated with, used her drinking and capitalised on it; he was her boss, however, he drank and sniffed cocaine with her during work hours, tempting her to stay out later and later. It was just the once and a huge mistake, however, it was such a confusing time. She thought Thwaite was the man who was going to rescue her, if you will. Instead, she was left with nothing but resentment for the way her life was panning out; a drunken mess, who had pushed her family away, with no idea how to fix it. There was absolutely no doubt about it, her boss took what he knew about Darcy's shitty homelife and used it to his advantage.

I may just be the narrator; however, I'm allowed to stick my oar in, if I so choose. Had Darcy been in her right state of mind, she would never have entertained him in the first place, but she was going to work with bruises all over her, not knowing where they had come from. Half the time, Thwaite would use silent treatment and Darcy, not one for confrontation, would apologise, simply to break the tension (this was before she cheated). She is also not the type of person who would cheat if she was sober. When Thwaite found out, they got into a huge row, which resulted in him breaking her arm, by pushing her so hard into a wall, her wrist snapped. The arsehole she cheated with, then made life at work so hard for her, she had to quit. She sought forgiveness from her husband, as he showed remorse for hurting her (all of this is a quick overview for you, as Darcy has said. One knobhead at a time. It's just a little more insight for you lovely people, so you can see that she is not all sweetness and light!)

Darcy wracked her brains, trying to remember that part of her life and, if she was honest, there were some massive gaps in her memory that had been caused by the alcohol and cocaine. A couple of weeks after she had her pot off, for the first break, he broke her other arm. This time, pushing her into some drawers that fell over and shattered her other hand. (Darcy remembers how much of a pain in the arse it was, trying to put her makeup on. She had to stick the makeup brush down her 'pot' (plaster cast) and use the other arm to manoeuvre the pot like a big, dopey, building site crane) not sure if I have described that vividly enough. To say it was a nightmare, would be an understatement.

The day she got out of detox that time, she called her friend to pick her up. Her emotions were all over the place. As she looks back on that day, the thought of seeing Thwaite again, now that she was sober, scared her. How was she meant to live a 'normal life' with him, after all the negative history was being replayed over and over again in her head. The thought of remaining in such a toxic relationship scared her and the thought of ending her marriage, scared her even more. So, she went to the pub, confused and disappointed that she couldn't find the strength she needed, to make the changes she absolutely craved, so she got drunk instead.

That night she called her auntie on her dad's side of the family, who collected her from the pub. She took Darcy to her house, to try and calm down her panicked state. She wasn't thinking straight. She didn't know where she went from there. While they were talking, outside on the patio, so she could smoke, she talked to her aunt while they waited for Angela to arrive. She was in a bit of a mess. Feeling very much like a failure. She remembers nipping to use the toilet. She saw her uncle on the landing, and he asked her how she was etc., but the more they talked, the more he started looking at her funny, to the point she began to feel slightly uncomfortable. She tried making her excuses to go back outside, when he suddenly and unexpectedly pinned her up against the wall, trying to pull her T-shirt up. He tried putting his hands down her pants. She managed to get herself back outside relatively unscathed, but it blew everything she thought she knew even further into a whirl. Did she just start that? What did she just do to cause that? Should she tell her aunt? Long story short, again, one knobhead at a time. She told her aunt. Her uncle denied it to her face, and she lost all faith in humanity, even more. So, she called Thwaite and he came to pick her up. He wanted to come in and confront her uncle but Darcy, who could see her aunt was clearly in distress, told him to leave it alone. She didn't want to cause any more upset. Although Thwaite was a silent bully, he did protect her from others. If she stayed at home, she was safe.

I know, I know. Don't get me started. It is enough to make you scream. So many people feel trapped; so many people feel like they can't find the right way out. Darcy hopes that by sharing her story, it will help people get the help they need, to make changes in their life or, if they have come from trauma and emerged out the other side, then maybe, they can read her story and realise that they themselves, have come a long way. Please know that life can get better. Please reach out. See the many resources and organisations provided in the back of the book.

Anyhow – Whoosah – sorry, I was just composing myself, before I get back to the original point. They, Finn and Darcy, were both in the baby stages of starting new lives, with the opportunity of a fresh start and new beginnings. However, the baggage that they both brought to the table was messy, and some parts had grown deep seated roots, which certainly needed to be dealt with, before anything else beautiful could grow. (Weed killer was always an option, however, murder charges don't necessarily look good on someone's record! And even though Darcy looks fantastic in orange, we are not in America, and let's face it, some weeds just won't fucking die!) Just sayin'.

They had both learnt their own coping mechanisms over the years. Building up their own walls, to keep people at arm's length, for fear of rejection or getting hurt. Finn liked to push people away, living his life in constant contradiction. 'I do, but I don't, I can but I can't'. Darcy would think it was funny to listen to him talking and at times, reading between the lines, that he was confused about the new-found feelings, sobriety gave him. He didn't know how to cope with his feelings for her. He'd only had one proper girlfriend in the past, spending most of his time during their toxic, 'on-again, off-again', relationship, heavily reliant on the drink and drugs. So now he was sober and falling in love, without any substance to hide behind, he was confused. He questioned his whole life, wondering if any of it was real before now. Whether he intentionally or subconsciously played the game of a 'wolf in sheep's clothing', is yet to be discovered. He almost had the schoolyard mentality of: 'treat 'em mean, keep 'em keen', which he had learnt over the years, to guard his heart, making him seemingly unaware just how hurtful he could be at times. Well, that and his broken filter, which allowed all sorts of shite to fall out of his mouth on a daily basis. (Darcy would like to think he didn't do it on purpose because otherwise, that would make him a 'cock-wombling fucktard').

Sorry about that, anyway…, Darcy seemed to want to please others. By craving acceptance and trying to fix other people, she thought she could fix herself (she wanted to be loved). She would change and mould herself into whatever she thought people wanted her to be, for fear of discovering her own identity or to find that it wasn't good enough. Where did that need stem from? She'd had a loving and nurturing childhood. Her mother was her all-time rock, so why? On reflection, she did change for HIM too. Don't get me wrong, it was for the better. He pulled out the adventurous, risk-taking side to her, she never knew she had, and was in dire need of, but she pushed herself to do some of the 'off the wall' stuff, simply to spend time with him, especially in the very beginning.

Darcy and Finn's character traits didn't make them bad or weak people, but it meant they had a lot more to work on individually, instead of wrapping themselves up so firmly in each other. Was it possibly creating more hurdles for themselves and their own individual recoveries? It was either going to be the love story of the century, or it was going to be a thunderstorm in hell. A thunderstorm in hell sounds like a bad analogy, when you think about it, as rain puts out fire, right? So, that sounds like it could be a good idea. However, imagine a big bonfire after the rain, when all the ash and bits of half burnt bits of wood and plastic, have all been turned into a horrible mulchy mess? Can you imagine it? Yeah, it's dirty and messy and… well, shit. But, as we can all see, so far, it looks like Darcy was fully prepared to get her hands dirty, to embrace the adventurous, wild side. Taking a leap into faith for him.

Rehab gives you a second chance at life. It tries to share with you the tools you need to continue to develop and learn. If you're open to and embrace the techniques and coping mechanisms they attempt to instil in you, when put into practice, they do work. That's if you're not too busy going around kissing boys that is. They advise you to get a plant and look after it for a year. If you can keep it alive, then, and only then, should you consider anything romantic. Finn was a 'plant pot'. Did that count? Erm…, I'm not sure but she was up for the challenge of keeping him alive, for a year at least, anyway. Anything after that was up for negotiation.

Some people live their whole lives having negative influences or experiences, which can cause hindrance in how open they are to nurture any form of self-growth. Some unfortunate souls, have nothing and no one, yet still manage to refrain from being 'poor me', self-entitled little twats. However, there are those who are fortunate enough to have people in their lives that they don't necessarily deserve, making far too many excuses for them, and their behaviours, which then gives them the belief they have the God-given right to behave badly! (We won't have time to touch too much upon 'HER' in this book; however, everybody knows a person, who likes to sit on their royal throne of self-righteousness, with nothing to be self-righteous about. We call these people the 'C-word'. Have you ever heard of glass houses and stones? Yeah, well…, I'll leave that bit there).

Everyone has been guilty of taking advantage of someone or something, a bit more than they should've done, at some point or other in their lives; taking advantage of having a 'bad past' or a 'bad relationship' and using that as an excuse for their shitty behaviour (Darcy included). Nobody is perfect. It's human nature and can be easily done sometimes, but most people, when made aware of how their behaviour is affecting others, own it and rectify it. Others, unfortunately, use excuse after excuse for themselves, to the point it's not only disrespectful; it's abusive. Just 'own ya shit' people! We only get one life, so why spend it being a cunt? Just sayin'. Everyone's story is individual. Darcy is a great believer in: 'don't judge, unless you've walked a mile in that person's shoes.' Everyone, even the 'C-words' have a backstory that needs to be peeled back, to see the person behind the mask. Unfortunately, sometimes people can spend far too much time peeling back the mask, just to find there is another more sinister mask. She has always been very forgiving when it comes to people's bad behaviour. Most are just afraid to show the vulnerable side, so find it easier to lash out in the wrong ways. She was also a great believer in seeing past the bravado in people. She always asks herself the question of: What kind of trauma has happened in your life, to make you such a dickhead? However, some people are inexcusable. It's that simple, and a hard lesson she has to learn. 'God-given-rightful-ness' can also make you a 'C-word'. It also makes it far too easy to become closed down to the belief that any form of change needs to come from within. (We like to call those people twats). In other words, some people want everything to be handed to them on a plate, with no real effort from themselves. They want the fairies to come out from their toadstools and sprinkle some sort of magical fairy dust on their lives and not make any mess in the meantime. Well, I'm here to tell you people, magic doesn't work on knobheads, it only gives them dandruff!) Then there are others who are just simply so closed up, from thinking that anyone else can teach them more than they already know.

There is no cure for addiction or at least if they've found one, nobody's informed me about it. However, hold on... I'm gonna do a quick Google search... Nope, apparently there isn't: 'Although there's no cure for drug addiction, treatment options can help you overcome an addiction and stay drug-free. Your treatment depends on the drug used and any related medical or mental health disorders you may have. Long-term follow-up is important to prevent relapse.'

So, you can now see the predicament Darcy and Finn were both in. They were in the recovery stage, with no known cure. Facing a lifelong illness. Now they were sober, they faced contending with the extra baggage they'd pushed away through drinking and drug use, trying at the same time, to grasp the cold hard truth, that 'recovery' would be an ongoing battle for the rest of their lives. It's scary shit! No wonder they clung to each other! They needed each other at that moment in time. There was no one else she would rather be facing this life hurdle with and even knowing what she knows now, she would do it ten times over because through all of it, he shaped her into who she is today. Darcy will never ever regret anything about Finn (even though, maybe she should).

Nobody is gifted with hindsight, and nobody is perfect. Everybody has some form of regret, wishing they could've done things differently and nobody knows (not even the wisest among us) that when anyone embarks on something so life changing, such as trying to get clean and sober, who the person they'll be when they emerge from the other side. Sobriety is a whole new way of life. It's learning new behaviours and techniques of coping with stress, emotions, triggers, peer pressure, confidence and social anxiety etc. The list is endless in a new way.

Darcy didn't become the way she did overnight, although her journey into addiction was quicker than some. She didn't become physically dependent overnight. It was a process, coupled with a number of events that all aligned together (like life does). You know the saying: 'everything comes at once' or 'if it's not one thing, it's the other' and the good old: 'luck (or bad luck) comes in three's'? Well, all of those contributed to Darcy taking a metaphorical bulldozer on her life, oh, and don't forget: 'shit on biscuits'.

Life is ever evolving, as are people. Some evolve quicker than others, firmly set on the path they feel is the best for them. Choosing to take the safest, most sensible of routes, down the rocky road that is life, getting to where they need to be faster. Even then, there is always the off chance that some twat will come along and throw a spanner in the works. Some manage to navigate their journey through pure perseverance, others through sheer luck and some are more fortunate than others, not to be carrying as much unwanted baggage (trauma) with them. Everyone has a story. People's journeys are never ending and unique. It's like a fingerprint; there is no blueprint to life, however hard people strive to find the secret, there is none (although myself and Darcy did say it was still a possibility). I feel we are all on the cusp of an extraordinary discovery anyway, don't you? Hopefully by reading this, it may help you to discover parts of yourself you didn't know you had. If not, you may at least be getting some insight into Darcy. If you can shed some light, then please write in to: No 3223, Decseption Lane, Idlovetoknow, Pleasedotell, DF13 3WH. If not, I hope you're enjoying the read and especially mine and Darcy's witticism?

Anyway… let's get serious again. Except trying to survive as best you can under the circumstances that you've been thrown into, none of us are the same. We are all just a bunch of misfits trying our best. I'm not even really sure what I am trying to say here, although I sound extremely wise. Finn was part of Darcy's journey. Darcy was part of Finn's. From very early on, no matter what anybody thinks, they changed each other's lives. How were they going to come out of this? Was it going to be together or was their love story doomed to echo within the walls of rehab forevermore? How had she managed to spend a day physically seeing and feeling what it would be like to be on the receiving end of a cold shoulder from Finn, and yet all she took from it was, *Oh, he loves me too?*' Hopefully, you can just feel the kind of person Darcy was. She was broken, confused and had so much further to go, before she was ever going to process the full extent of what the men in her life had done to her mental health. Her core was broken. (Well, not broken, because what is so wrong with wanting to be loved? Did it make Darcy a monster or unworthy of love because she craves acceptance?) Anyway, I apologise for chirping up and having my say. I am fully aware we have taken a massive side road from the story. I promise I will reign in my big mouth and only chime in occasionally from now on. But if you think I can talk, then I am going to give you a little taste of listening to Darcy directly. If Arnold and Finn thought her rehab diary entries were long, then their eyebrows would've fallen into the back of their heads, in disbelief, at the length of her private ones.

She was really working on understanding herself. Today had brought a lot of feelings up for her that she was trying to process, and I don't think I would be doing it justice if I was to tell you second hand. So, I'll step aside and let you see for yourself just how much she would internalise everything. This is Darcy's diary entry:

I am my own abuser, it's that simple. I've been reflecting loads, especially being in here. I've had tons of time to think. I think I'm falling in love with him. It sounds so stupid when I say it out loud. Well not out loud coz I'm writing it in here, but ya know what I mean? Tut, don't be pedantic Darcy mate, not to me anyways. Today threw me so much tho. He honestly made me feel like I dint matter. I don't know if I can deal with all these emotions all in one go. Why the fuck am I overcomplicating my life, AGAIN? Arghhh!... And breathe.... It's all good though, coz when we finally got the chance to talk, he told me that he found it really hard to ignore me all day, and that he kept looking over at me when I wasn't looking. He said he didn't want his face to 'give it away'. Little sweetheart, aww, especially how he said it, all shy and gooey. When he told me he couldn't stop thinking about me an us.... eeek! Can't even tell you how fucking happy I was. I'm just glad there was nowt wrong, coz today was shit, shittingly, shit. Now it's all good. We ended up having a right laugh. I need to chill out, go back a tiny step and remember why I fell so hard in the first place. He's my best mate at the end of the day. At first, I didn't even wanna come out my room to face him; I'm really glad I did; flirty, divvy, man child he is. I suppose I have to get used to it, coz that's just him, he shun't have to change coz of my insecurities. I can't help myself. He gives me butterflies. When I asked him why he felt he had to ignore me, it was like he automatically assumed I knew what he was thinking, bloody idiot! How the fuck am I meant to know what's going on in his head, eh? Ha-ha, he don't even know himself half the time. I just thought he'd changed his mind about how he felt. I got a taste of what it would be like to be a stranger to him. It was like I was nothing. He looked genuinely shocked I didn't guess what he was thinking. He said it's coz he didn't want anyone to find out we'd kissed or that he's falling in love with me, the little cutie. I told the big divvy that by ignoring me, it looked more on top than if he'd walked round holding my hand. In fact, it did raise suspicion. Let's face it, we're always together normally, so today looked on top to fuck. Claire asked me if we'd fallen out a few times. She knows bits and pieces. She doesn't know we've both talked about a future together and stuff. She's told me loadsa times how cute we are together and, to be fair to Finn, I've always brushed off the idea of us being anything more than friends in public but I've never brushed him off, if you know what I mean? I wun't do that. She thinks we'd make a great couple. I don't know, I'm having a deep-thinking night tonight. I can't help thinking about it though. Am I really that insecure? It's crazy how my brain works while I'm writing. I'm starting to think, it's the only conclusion in my head that's possible. It's a realisation that's shit to admit, but apparently, that's what I do!!! My main abuser is me. I'm my own worst enemy. Honestly! I just don't know how to love myself. It's not a conscious thing or owt. It's not like I enjoy torturing myself, but everything I do leaves

me hurt again and again, wondering over and over —
why? I've been seriously soul searching and I'm starting
to think my brain's seriously broken. It is. It must be. I
mean, where did all these mad thoughts stem from?
What is the root cause? Haha, who do I think I am? Some
sorta therapist or quack? Look at me, trying to find
reason in the unreasonable (I wonder where the word
'quack' came from? It's such a weird word innit? I've
obviously cared enough to go look on me good old google.
Did you know it's from the Dutch word 'quacksalver'?
Basically, the long and short of it means fake doctor....
Who knew? Look at me, I could be a quizmaster. I'm
actually talking about some deep shit here, so why do I
distract myself, when I feel uncomfortable? I know why,
it's coz then it don't seem so serious. I don't wanna cry
so, yeah, anyway. there's a lot more about it on Google.
I might have a look later when I've stopped chatting shit
to myself. Seriously though, if it's not drug and alcohol
abuse, it's being bashed about by dickheads; it's financial
abuse, although that wan't Thwaite, that was the
wanker before him. I mean, Finn said to me, what man
lets his lady be a prostitute? An it's fucking true. I dunno,
the whole situation's just a load of shit, I don't wanna
even think about it. I mean, Jesus, I've had so much
emotional abuse — the list is fucking endless. I know why
I put up with it. It's coz I wanna be loved. That's the only
conclusion I can think of. I will cling to whatever I can.
Does that make me pathetic? Am I a weak person? Do I

really think I'm that worthless? I must do coz I let myself get treated like shit, by people that claim to love me. Seriously! Anyway, I think I've found someone now who wouldn't do all that. He knows I've been hurt in the past. He knows some of the deepest parts of my soul. Today was shit, but I know why now, in 'Finn land'! It all made sense to him and no one else. Ha-ha, I love it. I accidentally made 'a funny'. Ha-ha. Ah dear.... It's the little things that give me a little chuckle at times. I wonder if I'm the only one that's ever thought of that? Oh god! I chat absolute shit sometimes. Seriously though, do I really need to be needed that much, that I deplete my store of energy to the point I feel completely empty? Give myself so easily to people, who use it to their advantage? They must think I'm too weak minded to stand up for myself and what's right? There's been so many times, I've been subjected to things, where I know it's wrong, and I don't say owt; I've just gone along with it coz I didn't wanna rock the boat. It's like when I've seen my kids being treated unfairly in one way or another and I've not said owt, coz I was worried about further repercussions. Why did I not say, "STOP!"? Fuck sake! Spoken up? Even when I did, all they said was that I was moaning and my reservations are swept under the rug. I let it slide, even when I felt uncomfortable; when I can see it with my own eyes, the behaviour being blatantly displayed! I put up with absolute shameless disrespect. Fuck my life tho, I do. Seriously, though, I do,

I make myself too easily available, when I'm just being used (bastards). I don't know why my brain is thinking all this now. I'm the happiest I have been in a long time. I'm so grateful I'm here with these lot. I know I shouldn't really be letting myself fall in love. It's not the best idea I've had in the world really, is it? Today really got me thinking about when people have made me feel like this, why? Why? When they haven't had a real reason? Finn called me a divvy and I feel like one, for letting my brain doubt him. I was just scared it was happening all over again. I feel so rubbish thinking the worst of him. I should've known he was trying to keep 'us' quiet, because if we get caught, then we could be thrown out. I do sometimes wonder if it's the right thing because I don't like feeling sneaky, but now we've kissed. All I want to do is kiss and touch him, ALL THE TIME. It still feels all... eeek, eekingly exciting... if you know what I mean? We went to the shop tonight, ya know, to get the usual snacks. I was hoping that we'd get to go on our own. That way, we might have been able to sneak a couple more smooches in, but Kelsie came with us. The three of us are like the three musketeers. She doesn't know anything about us yet, although she's not stupid, she sees the way we look at each other. So, I'll have to wait and hope we get a chance to be alone together again. We've got no chance of any sneaky kisses in here, it'd be stupid to risk it, in case anyone comes around the corner, especially coz we are so close to the end. It's madness.

It's exciting but frustrating at the same time. Anyway, it was funny walking to the shop because Finn and Kelsie were fucking around, like big kids as usual. Honestly, they act like brother and sister, always trying to wind each other up and get each other into trouble. Anyway, there was a massive puddle and you'd think we'd have all walked around it, but noooo, not Finn, ha-ha. He walked straight through the centre of it and kicked a load of water at me and Kelsie, soaking us and his shoes, haha, wounded. She went fucking mad with him and chased him all the way down the street. She didn't catch him though; he was too fast. Some of the stuff he does, only he could get away with and make it funny. He didn't realise how deep the puddle was coz as soon as he stepped in it, he regretted it. All he could say was, "Ya dirty bastard," it was hilarious. It might have been one of those, you had to be there, moments, but you weren't, so you'll just have to take my word for it, oh wait... you were derrr!. His face was a picture. It's crazy how three ex-addicts can act like complete kids and have so much fun without drink or drugs. None of us are getting any younger but we all still managed to nearly wet ourselves with laughin. My cheeks were physically hurtin. You'd think we were teenagers, but we're in our late 30s and early 40s. I've realised fun has no age restriction. I can find my adventure. I don't feel so 'over the hill and far away' anymore. I'm still young, fun and ready to play. I haven't had a drink, obvs, and it's not coz they breathalyse you either. I seriously don't feel like I need it when I'm around those two. In fact, I don't really think about it at all when I'm with them. The laughs have already given me the euphoric feeling that I used to get when I had the good times on the beer, but better, coz I remember everything. Ha-ha, oh yeah.... Then on the way back from the shop, Finn spotted a rat near an alleyway and made a beeline for it, chasing it, swinging his shopping bag around, like some crazed old bag lady, shouting, "ratatouille rat!" He looked so comical, running down the alley, shouting insults at this poor thing. What did it ever do to him? Haha, He didn't catch it of course but according to Finn, he was 'this close' (with his thumb and index finger almost touching). It's crazy; the highs and lows I've had today. It's seriously been the bumpiest, rollercoaster ride of a day. The highs have balanced out the lows but now I'm confused. Do I enjoy the feeling of misery? Is it so that I can appreciate it, when the little things come into my life and make me feel like I'm on top of the world, when really I'm just on a mediocre molehill? Am I doing this now? Coz he really hurt me today but the fun I've had knowing he's ok, has made me forget how bad I felt. I've dulled it down because it's so soon into anything. Would Finn think I'm a freak for getting myself so upset over nothing? I don't know mate; it's just so messed up. I can't deal with this. I'm off to brush my teeth for bed. I don't wanna talk to you right now. Sorry to stop mid flow. I get anxious talking about these feelings coz I feel like you're gonna judge me for being stupid. Why do I think you're gonna do that? I don't know? You're just a piece of paper in a diary. But what if someone finds it and everyone will know what a fucking insecure little freak I actually am? Arghhh! I don't know. I'll just tell you this instead. I have just gone to brush my teeth... ya know, ready for bed, like ya do, and the new tube of toothpaste tasted like I just brushed my teeth with rotten fish. God knows where I got this toothpaste from. I bought it just before I came here. It. Is. Disgusting. I'm sorry, when I get uncomfortable, I feel like I have to deflect. All this personal reflection and ownership of feelings blags my head so bad. I know why I started writing today. I know I need to get it out coz I've been thinking about it all day. It's been weaving itself in and out. My brain has been on, like the TV, with what feels like every channel playing at once. I don't know if this applies to Finn. I don't want to put him in the same bracket as everyone else coz it's not fair to base these feelings on him. I just know that today, something has stirred inside of me. It feels like, with the people that have been in my life and hurt me, I know they know they're hurting me and using me, but I let it happen coz that must mean they love me enough to do these things (insane I know!!) I don't even know if this even makes any sense. I could shake myself sometimes at the stupidity of it all. I make too many excuses for people with bad behaviour; I try to understand too much, why people do the things they do, I always seem to have more compassion for them than I do for myself. Why is that? It's madness. I know that some decisions I make are gonna end up with me mopping up my own tears, with their fake-ass apologies or shitty, ingenuine gestures that mean nothing, when it isn't backed up with something substantial like real care, love, but mostly respect. I know what you're thinking! This is some deep shit. This isn't funny, neither am I able to twist it around and make light of it and pretend it's ok. I act like it's not that much of a big deal. It is. It really is. I 'm the one hurting myself, over and over again. I put myself into a constant state of second-guessing what peoples' intentions towards me are, but I don't want to shut the door on something that could be amazing. If I saw someone putting up with, or accepting this as normal behaviour, I'd tell them they were insane! So why? Why do I allow myself to be treated like this? I'm not just talking about how others treat me but how I treat myself. I'm trying so hard to love myself. I want normal love so badly. I want to feel the safe, warm, peaceful love that I hope I deserve. I am the one that isn't allowing myself the chance coz I don't feel worthy. This feeling is so isolating, nobody would believe that this is how I see myself. I am filled with regret and self-loathing at my past, my mistakes, some are small misdemeanours, some are absolute corkers, to say that they are rather large ones, would be putting it mildly. I am not innocent in all this, nor am I some sort of angelic, butter wouldn't melt type. I swear like a sailor, I can argue the toss, and I can hold my own to a certain extent, but I always fold when it's time to stand up for myself and for what's right. In the past, in small intervals in my life, I have been the selfish one. I have been the one to lash out and do hurtful, spiteful things. I have caused hurt, not purposely or out of flagrant malice, but I know I've been in the wrong, sometimes. To put it plain and simple, I've been out of order, just nasty, there is no nice way to try and paint a better picture of the situation, it was simply shit on top of shit. In the past, I've been too selfish to care how my actions have affected others. Especially to my kids. To some degree, I still am. The difference between when I was drinking and now is, now that I'm sober, I try harder than ever to keep everyone happy. Looking at it and really trying to make some sort of sense of it all, I miss the fundamental point that needs addressing. I let men walk all over me. Somehow, even when I don't mean to, they become more of a priority. I just don't know how to mend the past. I overcompensate on the bits that don't matter. I miss the point completely sometimes. It's frustrating but I have to consider them in all of this. (I can only imagine how frustrating it is to have me as a mother). How do they feel about me? I fully understand there is going to be some serious resentment. I don't know where my place is, where and how do I fit back into my kids' lives without disrupting it? I need to try and be selfless, when I want *to be selfish and pretend the past was just a nightmare that I've suddenly woken up from. I don't feel like I have the right to come barging back into their lives, to start to try and be a parent all of a sudden, now that I've miraculously decided I'm well enough!! I should have been there for them in the first place. I know all of this but have no clue what to do about it, just leaves me immobilised mentally. Maybe that's why I don't feel worthy. Maybe I don't feel like I am worth redemption. I feel like I deserve everything I get. I subconsciously, purposefully, seek it as a way of punishing myself for my past. Even the bits that I have been coerced into, I feel like that's all I'm worth. That's all I'm good for while craving love. I normalise it all. I'm not quite sure what I can do about it. I'm so used to being my own worst enemy, my own downfall. My own abuser! How can I begin to accept love, real love? When I don't even know what that means to me? When I don't love myself? And now, on a completely unrelated topic. Why did the chicken cross the road? ...Beak-cause he could. See I can't do it. I sounded for a minute like I knew what I was talking about though? Anyway, I can't deal with all this SHIT in my head. I'm off to bed before I start chatting more SHIT.*

Darcy looked at the words she had written down on the page. She chuckled to herself at the ending joke. She couldn't help it. That was just her way. Her phone bleeped. It was Finn. 'Night Night beautiful. I can't wait to see you tomorrow. I carnt wait till wc get out ov ere then we can be us.'

She smiled at the message, as her stomach fluttered pleasantly and replied with, 'Yeah, there is so much yet to be written to our story. When we get out of here, time will tell. Night night gorgeous, I'll see you in the morning.'

8. THAT'S THE WONDER... THE WONDER OF YOU

I wonder what today will bring? was Darcy's first waking thought. It had nothing to do with wondering how the learning sessions were going to go. She would be lying if she said she wasn't apprehensive about another day, where she would have to watch Finn, pretending he was free, single and ready to mingle. Or listen to Cindy's stupid, giggly voice, thinking that he was genuinely interested in her, "silly bitch," said her scathing voice, before she could stop it. She stretched herself out of bed, as if trying to draw out the jealous thoughts, so it didn't feel so concentrated into one spot. He had told her everything she needed to know, in their late-night talks and text chats. That should be good enough for her, for now at least, anyway. She felt better for allowing herself the time to write her insecurities and thoughts down in her diary. Getting it out on paper helped massively, even if her hand was aching from writing down last night's thoughts. It was as if by getting it out of her head, it cleared some space for the other insecurities in her brain; to start arguing about how they were going to utilise the void as best they could. *Ah, good*, she thought, giggling to herself at her own silliness, *at least they're being organised.*

She decided that it was now time to make a conscious effort and put romance on the back burner, so it was on more of a slow simmer, rather than a quick boil, which could potentially bubble over. It could get really messy. *Let's face it*, she told herself, *if it's meant to be it's meant to be. We can't really start anything until we are out of here anyway.* But she couldn't help feeling a little resentful about the place (rehab). It wasn't their fault. She had complicated her journey by finding love when it was against their policies, but now, she would have to second guess her every action when she was with him in case it raised suspicion. She'd have to be careful about what she said, to avoid anything being read the wrong way (well, the right way but you catch my drift?)

They were very tactile with each other from the start, so now, the natural way they were together, felt unnatural (if that makes sense) and she felt paranoid. Whenever they'd sit in the smoking area, he would find a way of contact, by plucking a hair from her clothes, or picking something out of her eyes or ears (it sounds like Darcy's a bit of a mucky bitch, but I assure you she was always clean; he was just always picking at her, like a big kid). She would let him get on with it, as if it was completely normal, while she continued talking to Claire and Kelsie. Claire would find it highly hilarious that Darcy could carry on talking and smoking, as if she was completely used to being poked and prodded, saving him 'twos' on her cigarette, like they already shared everything together. ('Twos' is where you smoke half the cigarette and pass the remaining half to another person to finish).

"You two are so cute together," she'd say, as the two of them would act like little monkeys in the zoo, grooming each other, as if it was completely normal social behaviour. Now, it felt as if realisation had slapped her awake. Suddenly, she was questioning whether it really was normal?

No, it's not normal, usually, but that's just us! She thought, gooey-eyed and adoringly. *Aww*, she thought stupidly. She was 100% comfortable around him. It really was like she had found her missing piece. (Erm, Darcy mate, we're supposed to be telling everyone about your hobbies and learning sessions and yet still you manage to make it about Finn. Tut, yes, we get the picture you 'love each other lotsly').

She got dressed and went downstairs for a cigarette. Claire was already there, dressed and ready, wearing her usual baggy blue jumper and black leggings. Her hair was down today and swept to one side. She always looked so classy and elegant.

"Morning, gorgeous," said Darcy playfully. She had decided to put all thoughts to one side and just enjoy life; enjoy her friendships, instead of trapping herself so tightly in her head, where the gremlins reigned chaos.

"Morning, lovely, how are you? You ok? You've seemed a bit off lately," smiled Claire. She looked as if she knew something had been bothering her.

She's not stupid, thought Darcy. *Should I just tell her?* "Yeah, I'm good, erm…, me and Finn kissed the other day," she whispered, as she shook her head with bemused, giggly embarrassment. "I know. I know! I just don't know what all this means now…. Claire, I actually like him, like him. It's fucking madness mate. I come in here to sort myself out… and I leave with a bloody present from the gift shop!" she joked. "What do I do now?" she asked, looking Claire straight in the face, as if she was going to give her all the answers. Darcy's face flushed furiously (probably the same shade of red as that fucking flag) as she giggled away, bumping shoulders with Claire, who looked like she'd just been told her daughter was getting married to the love of her life.

"I knew you would," she said, grinning from ear to ear as she spoke. "It's clear by the way he looks at you Darcy, he's besotted, bless him". Claire looked at her reassuringly. They looked at each other, smiling like big girls.

"He told me he's never felt this way about anyone before Claire, what do I do?"

"Fucking enjoy it," she said, with mischief in her eyes. "Just go with it," she continued, looking at her, as if she couldn't be happier.

So, thought Darcy, feeling silly. *Obviously, the mother approves.*

The morning meeting went by, with no talks of shit, or wondering why Finn was being distant. If truth be told, he had firmly cemented himself back to the gorgeous, beautiful, soul, that she knew from the start, if not even more so than before. Maybe there was something in the water? She didn't know. Maybe she was giving off good vibes? Of course she was (she is a beacon of all things positive). Maybe the new carefree, 'chilled out' vibe she was emanating, was infectious, as Finn couldn't get enough. (She was back to the attitude of, *Why wouldn't he? I'm gorgeous!* It was a mask, but it felt better than the self-sabotaging, self-loathing one she wore yesterday). She sat next to him, as the first session of the day was about to start. She caught him looking at her in awe, as she spoke to Claire about a song she was writing.

"What you looking at, ya divvy?" she said to him, as she nudged him playfully.

"Nowt, ya just really clever, the way you talk about music. Like you know what ya talking about mate, it's interesting," he said, as if he was talking to a pro. It was unnervingly nice, and such a contrast from yesterday. However, she wasn't going to engross herself in all things Finn today, although he was still at the top of her list.

"Thanks," she smiled, as they both caught each other's eyes and looked away. Claire nudged her as if to say, "I told you so!" Darcy felt great. She was finding self-discovery hard at times but with his reassurance (in his own ways) and Claire's, who clearly adored her and only wanted good things for her, she decided, *Fuck it, I'm venturing out me shell today, and no fucker's gonna stop me.* If she thought about it, she was reaching new heights, and personal goals of growth and understanding, for what was happening to her. She wasn't, but ignorance really is bliss... until it isn't and that was growth in itself. *I'm growing up*, she thought happily... (like I say, ignorance is bliss!)

Today was music therapy day. *Fuck my life, here we go*, she thought apprehensively, as Jason, the session leader, came into the room, smiling at them, as if to ask if they were all ready to start? He was a short, bald man, who looked to have a very authoritative air about him. Darcy thought Jason had the kindest looking face, although it looked like it had been through a lot. His eyes told stories of conflict and war, without even speaking. Jason was wearing his usual combat-style shorts, with a plain looking T-shirt. He always wore the same kind of thing, as if it was a uniform of sorts, even though there was no set uniform for staff there. Whenever she spotted him talking to anyone, she would notice that he always appeared to talk and listen with interest. Darcy felt heard whenever she spoke to him, even though he kept himself busy all the time, he always had time to stop and say hello and ask about your day. He was very wise and would tell success stories of addicts, with passion in his voice, which gave her hope. She didn't know him as well as D'accord or David. He never really gave anything away about himself, but when he spoke, everybody listened.

She wasn't looking forward to this particular session, for one specific reason. It was definitely going to stir up a shedload of emotions that she wasn't sure she was ready for. She knew it would more than likely end up with her 'bawling like a baby'. (Can you tell she feels uncomfortable with this level of emotion – by creating or using, what she considered as funny words for something, in this case, crying? The method seemed to disconnect her from the emotion itself, if that makes sense.) *I should've picked another song*, she thought, as Jason put the folder and notepad he was carrying, down on the tabletop, which also housed the giant TV. Music therapy was always held in the TV room, so they could watch whatever song they'd picked on YouTube.

"Good morning," he said, looking around the room. "Does everyone want to pull the chairs around closer, so we're all together in a semi-circle?" he suggested purposefully. Music therapy was usually one of Darcy's favourite sessions. Each week they were asked to pick a song that represented a theme. This week, the theme was to pick a song that made you feel sad. The choice of song she opted for communal scrutiny, would knowingly force her to speak openly about the loss of her father, for the first time, without the wall of 'Dutch courage' that alcohol or cocaine provided. Her dad's death was the main catalyst that kicked off her decade long addiction. *Is it really a good idea to do this now? In front of everyone?* She had been thinking about this question on and off, all week. Normally, she wouldn't dare talk about something so personal on such a public platform. For years, she had internalised the pain of missing her dad, as she couldn't stand the agony her heart felt, trying to process the fact she was never going to see him or hear his voice again.

It felt awkward when she talked to her mum about it because she had her own history and memories, and it was difficult for her brothers to be objective, as they'd had such different experiences with him than she had. Darcy was such a 'daddy's girl', even though he was a very absent father to all of his kids, who were scattered about the country, like little 'toddlings'. (He would spread his seed far and wide and never stay around long enough to watch them grow. In other words, he was a massive 'man whore', who dipped his dick into anything that had a hole). Darcy, however, was put on a sort of pedestal above the rest. (Like she said – when he was there).

She was his favourite, and he made it very obvious. He never said it, but he made it painstakingly blatant by the way he behaved. She was his princess. Whenever he was in the mood to 'play dad' to her, that was. When she was a little girl especially, he would show her off like a trophy, taking her down to the 'deaf club', displaying her off with the utmost pride. Her brother, Rocky, who had the same mum and dad, would get the cold shoulder. He wasn't a bad dad (*HE WAS, Darcy!* Said the little voice that piped up in the back of her head.) *Yeah, I know,* she acknowledged furiously, as she sat still, waiting patiently for the session to begin, frantically trying to process all the thoughts that came flooding to her at once, but she didn't want to admit that to herself. She knew, if he'd tried, he could've been so much better. In fact, like all the men that had come and gone in her life, he could've been so much more if only he'd tried. Maybe it was just her that wasn't worth trying for? (No time for that little side road trip, we will come back to that another time mate).

He would still include Rocky, but it was as if he was more of an afterthought. When they were older, Elvis (Darcy's dad) would telephone the house, and whenever Rocky answered the phone, Dad would barely make small talk with him before saying, "Put your sister on," leaving a confused looking Rocky deflated, wondering why his dad appeared to not care. It wasn't nice. She acknowledged it as well. It didn't take away from her memories of him, but she was fully aware he could be a bit of a wanker. That made talking to any of her siblings difficult. It just felt to her like she was just rubbing salt in their wounds.

She'd had her own personal experience of just how thoughtless and uncaring he could be, when she found out through Seamus, her half-brother, that he had somehow discovered she was prostituting herself. Instead of coming to her directly or trying to stop Elon from using her as a cash cow, he preferred to talk about it to people down in his local pub, like she was some piece of gossip that was up for humiliation. Like she was nothing! He didn't call her or demand to know why she had been reduced to doing such a soul sucking job (no pun intended) or play any kind of concerned father role. No, instead, when she called him to ask if what she had heard was true, he lied through his false fucking teeth, acting the 'poor innocent party', who was on the receiving end of someone who was out to cause trouble for HIM!

She knew he could be a nasty bully, but she was fortunate to never see that side of him. Her brothers (with whom she shared HIS DNA, but had different mothers) however, were not so lucky. They didn't have a mother like Angela, who wouldn't tolerate her dad's bullshit. Whenever he would kick off, usually when he'd had a drink, she would set him straight and tell him to leave. She always stood her ground. Darcy had asked her mum the question of whether he had ever hit her. She told Darcy that Elvis was never physically violent towards her, but he would throw his weight around and punch holes in the walls, acting like an antagonist. He never laid a finger on Angela, however, from what Marley (step-brother to another mother, Stella) and Seamus (step-brother to yet another mother, Halia) had touched upon, in rare open conversation, about the darker side of their universal father, it sounded like they were on the receiving end of some pretty horrendous stuff. (I say 'universal' because he could even be your father and yours and yours etc., you get the picture. In fact! If you don't know who your father is, just ask your mother if she has ever met anyone called, Elvis Shaggathon? You may have the same DNA as Darcy as well). For now, though, she would rather concentrate on her dad's good side. She didn't want to think about that now. He wasn't a nasty man, or he wasn't to her anyway. She was fortunate enough not to bear the brunt of his temper and got away lightly, with him only giving her the emotional scars of being picked up and dropped, whenever he was in the mood to display his paternal side.

She could've talked to her friends about it but, her friends? …She didn't really have friends anymore. In the end, all she really had was Thwaite and alcohol. Before she came into rehab, she had become somewhat of a recluse, never really venturing any further than the beer shop over the road, or to her brother Rocky's, who lived next door. She'd never leave her bedroom, sleeping the day away, only to wake for long enough to have a drink of whiskey, to stop the horrible side effects that alcohol caused. The friends she did have, either heavily drank themselves, or had pulled away from the friendship because they couldn't cope to see the damage she was doing to herself. Plus, she felt stupid. She should be over it by now! It had been years since he'd left her all alone; to do her best; to hold it together and support everyone in his absence, not that he was a great support when he was alive. Darcy's mum and dad had split up when she was only young, before she even hit double figures. Her mum had had enough of his drinking and womanising ways, but she never stopped him from having contact. If anything, she was the one that tried her best to pin him down and continue to be involved in their lives, one way or another. Even though they were on good terms when he died, it still felt weird to talk about. It was irrational, as she talked to her mum about anything and everything in the world. Angela was Darcy's 'rock' but dad was off limits (not because of Angela but Darcy, who couldn't articulate just how much she missed him without it all coming out gobbledegooky. Plus, helloooo, you were pissed all the time love).

She concluded that she was as ready as she'd ever be, to talk about such a strange feeling in her stomach. STILL, even after knowing everything he had put her through; feeling everything he had put other people through, in his sixty plus years on this round ball of the weird, the wonderful and the horrendous (she can't just be normal, can she? Nooo…. Why she couldn't simply say earth is beyond me) she STILL wanted to talk about the good in him. She wanted to remember the funny, kind and caring side of him. She wanted to talk more about the huge, gigantic, horrendous hole, he'd left in her life. She needed her dad, and he'd fucked off and left her. Bastard!

The daily sessions with the same group of people, allowed her, and everyone else for that matter, to open up about things she'd never told anyone else in the world. Sharing and learning together, had built relationships of trust that exceeded family. They were detached from the subject matter, but not from each other. Even though they'd formed a bond, she didn't have to worry about upsetting anyone or saying the wrong thing. She just knew that they listened without bias. She felt strangely calm (fuck knows what she was feeling but it was a nice feeling that warmed her heart.) She loved her group so much. Even Cindy (the flirty bitch and Buzz, the little weirdo) somehow, especially today, even those two were endearing and tolerable. Today was the day where there was potential for a number of revelations and breakthroughs. She was nervous, but as ready as she would ever be, to talk about her father and why she was so broken by his parting.

Everyone hobbled their chairs closer together, into a semi-circle, just as Jason had asked. There was a low hum of nervous chatter, as they all sat back down in their seats, shuffling to get themselves as comfortable as they could be, placing their coffee mugs and belongings on the worn carpet by their feet.

"Why does everyone look so nervous?" said Jason, as he looked around the group, smiling reassuringly, "don't be so worried, this is a safe space, remember that," he said, in a way that felt like he had put some 'normal' back into the room (what Darcy means by that is unsure but that was the only way she could explain it to herself, so that's how I am explaining it to you lovely lot). It was as if he could taste the apprehension in the room. Darcy, who had made a point of sitting at the opposite side of the semi-circle from Finn, looked over at him and winked, to try and reassure him that everything was going to be alright. He caught her gaze and nodded ever so slightly in acknowledgment, before looking away. He was sat in the chair, but his posture gave away the fact that he was shitting himself just as much as the rest of them.

In Darcy's opinion, music therapy was the best session by far; she loved it, but... *whoosah..., phew... and breathe.* She was unsettled but she hoped she would feel better afterwards, although all the 'apprehensional fa-la-la-la-la-la-la-la-la' (a new word – because I've Googled all other ways to say 'waiting' but can't find a word strong enough. If you can think of one, then please insert where needed) waiting, was foreboding.

"Who wants to go first?" asked Jason, as if he was trying to entice a brand-new kitten from under a sofa. There was a long pause… nobody looked as if they were going to offer to bare their souls for scrutiny first.

I'm coming out of my shell today, said the voice in her head mockingly. *That's what you said, Darcy. Just get it over and done with, ya dick.* So, she took another deep breath and said, "I'll go."

"Ok," Jason said kindly, with compassion in his tone, "what song have you picked and can you tell us a bit about why you've picked it?" She squirmed in her chair, trying her best to pass it off as a normal readjustment, pretending to get comfortable, so she could have a few more seconds to compose herself before she spoke.

"Erm yeah, I've chosen '0800 Heaven', by Ella Henderson. You know the one? 'If heaven had a phoneline?'" she said, half singing the last bit. "It makes me sad., but it also makes me wishful that I could talk to my dad just one last time and tell him he's a bastard!" She said, as matter of factly as she could. She couldn't help it the 'bastard' bit, it just slipped out. She was, in fact, again, trying to hide her uncomfortableness. However, with each word that she spoke, her voice cracked a little more, into a more sorrowful sound. She smiled, as if to show she was ok, but she could feel the fresh beginnings of hot tears, flooding into her eyes, making them prickle and sparkle, before she quickly tried to blink them away, wiping her cheek where they had unintentionally fallen, betraying her false composure. She kept the smile on her face, as if refusing to acknowledge them yet. She wasn't going to let herself become emotional, for as long as she could, fighting against the urge to 'hit the panic button' and walk out. Suddenly, she felt very aware that she was actually doing this. She was about to embark on a journey down memory lane with this bunch of misfits, and she felt safer than she'd ever felt before. She looked around the room, trying to spot any judgment in their eyes at her vulnerability. Almost wanting it to come, to give her an excuse to shut down and not do this, but none came. They were all silently waiting for Jason, who was busying himself with finding the right version of the song. Claire stood up and walked toward a small table, picked up the box of tissues and brought it over, handing her a couple of tissues from it, as she passed casually, and placed the box on the floor, in the middle of the semi-circle, before sitting back down.

"Ok, let's listen to the song, and then we can talk a little bit about it after," said Jason, nodding at her, as if he was asking for her permission to start, before pressing play. He pumped up the volume, so that it was just the right level to listen comfortably. He wasn't the kind of staff member who had a stick up his arse about volumes; music was therapy and it needed to be listened to properly. He turned his head towards the TV to watch the video, as everyone did the same thing.

Finn looked over at her and mouthed the words, "You ok?" with a look of caring concern on his beautiful face. She nodded her head in confirmation and smiled softly, before looking away.

'If heaven had a phoneline,
'Would I be the first one you would dial?
'If heaven had a phone line,
'Would you call me up from the other side?'

Well, obviously not, you fucktard! she thought adoringly, as she listened to the lyrics fondly. Doing this felt a lot easier than she had anticipated. She embraced what she was feeling, allowing the floodgates to open and the tears to silently fall out, with a calmness that spooked her slightly. (She was allowing herself to feel… to hurt. In that moment, she felt like her dad was in the room with her. It felt like he was right there with her, granting her permission to let go of the pain she was so intent on holding onto, lest she forget him.)

When the music stopped playing, Jason turned to look directly at her tear-streaked face. "How did that feel?" He asked her kindly. Her 'rehab family' looked at her without saying a word. She could feel the love in the room. She felt uplifted somehow. It was as if listening to the song, with everyone else, in this environment, had allowed a massive invisible weighted blanket to lift off her. She opened the door and allowed herself to feel, to understand the 'demons'. She felt lighter. There was a cold, tingling sensation around the back of her head and shoulders, as if her father's spirit had embraced her before saying goodbye. Of course, she didn't voice this or articulate herself in this way. (Nooo, have you ever met Darcy?)

No, she opted for the more comical side of her brain to take over and replied, "If he'd have called, I probably wouldn't be here, in this situation, would I? The bastard." And there it was again. Deflection!

"Do you miss him?" asked Jason, completely ignoring the facade and homing in on the real emotions that were peeping out the side of her invisible mask, itching to get out and have their say. Humour had been suffocating the scared little girl, who just wanted her dad to be the man she needed him to be; the man she knew he could've been. She wanted him back. To slap him, to cuddle him. Fuck! She would've even listened to his famous, "Poor me. I'm so hard done to," rants, about how he had ended up in hospital, yet again through no fault of his own (of course).

"Yeah," she said, as the emotions came spilling out of every orifice, "A LOT, and the bastard's gone! Sorry for swearing," she interjected, "and I'll never get to speak to him again. He just fucked off and left me to deal with everything. He waited until everyone else was out of the room before he took his last breaths in front of me. It's not fucking fair. I hate that I miss him so much," she said, sniffling back the tears. "He just left me to deal with it; to look after my brother, Marley, and to sort the funeral. When everyone was saying they had no money, I thought he was going to end up in a pauper's grave. So, I organised the funeral and paid for it, because, as much of a cunt as he was, he didn't deserve to not have his dying wish. I laid on my back for that man," she said angrily. "And did what I had to, to get it done. All so he could be cremated and scattered in the garden of Shell Cottage, near Tinworth, in Cornwall." *Oh no*, thought Darcy... yup! Snot, and the fact she had just inadvertently said out loud, albeit ambiguously, that she used to be a fucking prostitute. She hoped to God that no one would ask her to elaborate on that little snip bit. It was a day of revelations, and it was all apparently going to come spilling out, whether she wanted it to or not. Snot was now snail trailing it down each side of her philtrum. (The philtrum is the vertical groove between the nose and top lip. It has no purpose in humans now, other than to aid facial expression, but for other mammals it brings saliva to the nose, enhancing the sense of smell). "He'd promise you the world and deliver disappointment and heartbreak". She said with her voice quivering.

Now that Jason felt like he had got his foot inside the door of her soul, he changed his tact and tone, from a serious, emotive one, to a more jovial, playful questioning. (This dude was good!) He was opening her up carefully, asking all the right questions, and letting her talk. It was as if she had verbal diarrhoea.

"Was he a bit like you then?" He said smiling, nodding his head toward her as if to say, "YOU? Always making people laugh? I bet he was a right old giggle, wasn't he?"

"Yeah, but I'm not a bastard," Darcy joked. He sat back looking relaxed, his body language inviting her to speak what she needed to, to get it all out. "He was in and out of my life and left me feeling hurt all the time. I'm angry with him. I always felt abandoned." She spoke to the group as a whole, but somehow her out of focus eyes zoomed in on Finn, why, she didn't know. "You know when you say to yourself. 'Right, that's it. This time they can fuck off.' Then, as soon as they see or call you again, all is forgiven and forgotten in your mind. You're just so happy that they've come back. That they have been thinking about you; that they love you? Yeah, well, that was my dad all over." She went quiet, and Jason didn't fill the silence, encouraging her to continue. "Oh!" She said, chuckling to herself. One minute she was happy, then sad, then mad, then blah. She couldn't even keep up but she had remembered something. "He was in the hospital once, with another one of his angina attacks and he called me. He was telling me all about getting poked and prodded by the nurses. It was honestly like listening to an old war hero, who'd fought the whole battle on his own. It wasn't so much what he said, it was the way he said it. His big, bushy, grandad eyebrows usually told the story for him. I could just imagine his facial expressions, while I was on the phone. I couldn't help but just love him," she continued on. "But there was always a sob story. He would never admit it had anything to do with the fact he was sniffing coke to bring him up, then smoking weed to come down off the coke and boost his appetite…" She trailed off slowly….

"Was he a big drinker?" asked Jason curiously.

"Yeah," said Darcy, "he drank like a fish, except for the last few years of his life, when he got too ill. He could drink the best under the table. There was always a reason for the misery in his life, and he wouldn't ever accept it was of his own making. His lifestyle, to him, had nothing to do with why he ended up ill all the time. Oh noooo," she said, changing her voice to one that was clearly taking the piss, "it must have been the fairies!" Or there must have been someone always hiding around the corner, just to find him and only him, to kick him while he was down. (Sorry, that was me, Lady Jane, being the sarcastic little cherub that I am.) Darcy changed her voice back to her normal, non-singsongy, light and airy one. "His life was a sob story. That was just my dad. Yeah, he was so funny," she said, as if remembering the question Jason had originally asked. "When he was in his prime, he was such a boyo. He used to spray paint his shoes, so they'd match the colour of his cars," she said, laughing through the tears.

"His cars!" laughed Jason, "Oh my God, I bet he was a right old character, wasn't he?" Still giggling to himself, as if envisioning it in his mind.

"Yup he was an absolute idiot," she replied, as Finn sat forward, listening intently, drinking it all in. He looked as if he was thoroughly enjoying learning more about the girl he loved and the man who was responsible for her creation. "He was so cheeky and charming," she said, smiling. "Everyone got along with him. You remind me of him a lot," she said, looking lovingly over at Finn, before she could stop herself.

She flushed, as everyone saw the moment fleetingly, before she quickly diverted herself back to talking about her dad. "Yeah, erm…. It's so hard to express, because on one hand he was a selfish, cowardly bastard, who hated any kind of confrontation. So, he would lie through his false teeth to avoid it, but all he succeeded in doing each time, was to make his problems the size of atomic bombs. BUT…," she said, now in full flow, injecting some comedy back into the seriousness. This time it felt organic, like she was joining in the celebration of his life, rather than miserably mourning the man who was her father. "To be fair to him, there was always an element of truth to the story. You know, you get those films or TV series, which say, 'based on a true story'? When in reality, half of it never happened, it's just put in for dramatic effect? Well, that's what his stories were like," said Darcy, laughing as the whole gang were joining in, enjoying listening to her tell them stories of her dad. "It's a bit like in the TV series, The Tudors. I don't know if you've ever seen it? Yeah, well, there's a bit where Henry VIII's sister marries the king of Portugal. Well…, spoiler alert – she didn't. That bit is factually incorrect. In fact, she married the king of France, then she went on to marry Charles Brandon, played by Henry Cavell," she said, pretending to swoon, "I know!!! So yeah, that's the kind of stories he'd tell. Full of dramatic flair and plot twists, when in fact, the truth of the matter is, he could be a shitty person and the things that happened to him were usually as a result of his own bad behaviour." She finished off, matter of factly. She'd stopped crying now and felt so free.

The hurt never truly leaves you; it's like toxic gas that creeps under the gaps of the 'doors' you try to keep closed and poisons your thoughts and decisions. "When a parent passes away, it doesn't matter how absent they've been in your life, it hits you and it changes something." Said Claire, "It never leaves you babe; it just gets easier to accept over time. You are allowed to feel how you feel. There's no right or wrong way when it comes to something like that. We've got your back. Love you darling," she said, as if trying to hug her with her words.

"Nawww, thanks chicken, loves you too," said Darcy. "This 'therapy' session's going great," she smiled at them, as if to thank them all for simply being themselves. "I was only mid-20s when he died, it felt unfair, he just went! I was angry… but I didn't show it. I had too much shit to sort out. I had to be strong for my brothers. Rocky didn't know how to feel about it, to be fair, I understood… but I hated him a little, for not feeling what I was feeling. The other two were pretty useless when it came to sorting stuff out, you know what I mean?"

"How did he die?" asked Cindy, in her sweet girly voice. Darcy wanted to be petulant and ignore her. She still felt a bit bruised by Finn flirting with her and of course, instead of blaming him, she resented her slightly. She waited for a moment before answering her question as if somebody else had asked it.

"One day, my Auntie Alexia (my dad's sister) called me, which was unusual. I hadn't really had much contact with his side of the family, when my Mum moved us here, when I was only young. Before that, I used to see them all the time, so it felt so strange to hear her voice after all those years. She told me that my dad was in the hospital. My instant reaction, and I regret it now, because I said scathingly, 'what's new!!! Is he gonna die?' she sounded upset and said, 'yeah, quite possibly'".

Darcy took a few deep breaths, as if trying to control her breathing, so she wouldn't fully break down into a sobbing mess. "When she told me, I just froze. I didn't know what to do?" she said, shaking her head in disbelief. Tears were once again falling down her face, thick and fast. Finn jumped up from his seat and came bumbling over to her, looking like he was going to cry as well, and passed her the whole box of tissues. He touched her shoulder as if to say, "it's alright," before sitting back down and wiping his eyes with the sleeve of his jacket. "I'd never have been able to forgive myself if it turned out he did die, and I didn't say goodbye out of stubbornness." She persisted, "I had to think fast. It wasn't like there was a long time to think about my decision because from what she said, it didn't sound like he had that long to live." She said, shaking her head. Everything was screaming at her to stop talking, as she didn't know how much more of these intense feelings she could take, but she willed herself on, *you can do this, you can do this Darcy.* "Anyway…, hella long story short, I went down to see him. He was lying there on the hospital bed; he looked like a little old lady. It was horrible… and when he saw me, he had a heart attack." She said, over sounds of shock from the group. "They came running down with the crash trolley, as I got pushed to the side. All I could think was, 'Oh my God! I've killed him….'" There was silence in the room. Claire got up and put her arms around her from behind, and hugged her tightly, nearly strangling her. Darcy grasped onto Claire's arm, returning the backwards hug. "The nurses took ages to work on him." She looked around the room at everyone; they clung onto every word she was saying. Even Arnold looked like he had forgotten to tell his face he was meant to be chewing a wasp. He forgot to don his usual grumpy pretence that nothing could phase him. He looked like he was struggling with whatever emotions her story had stirred up for him. "Anyway," she said sadly, "he made it out the other side, long enough to say he was sorry. He looked me in the eyes and said, 'Sorry'. He was rushed to ICU and put into an induced coma. He made it through another six months after that, and when he did finally die, he took his last breaths, while I held his hand," she finished off quickly. She wasn't ready to carry on with the full story. It wasn't the time. *Maybe another time*, she thought? For now, delving into more of that part, was too much.

"Our Marley came to live with me for a bit afterwards, as he'd been the one living with dad, looking after him, in the year he had been poorly. Even though I tried to help, we lived in different countries, so I could only get there every other week or so. Plus, I had the kids, and I was doing that God awful job," she said, as she could feel the level of her voice rising in indignant, angry upset. She lowered her voice back down to a normal level as she said, deflated, "It just felt like it was all left down to me. It felt so final, you know?" She paused for a moment, looking at Jason, who nodded in consoling confirmation – he could feel what she was saying. The others were listening with looks of genuine care and compassion on their faces, *maybe I'm talking too much?* She thought, wondering if she should shut up and let someone else have a turn. But she couldn't help it, her mouth was gaining momentum, saying all the things that she had stewed on for years. "Dad had split from Stella ten-plus years beforehand, but they'd never got divorced. That's a story in itself," she said, as an afterthought, "so there was a load of shit with trying to get the ashes and stuff. I knew he wanted to be scattered at Shell Cottage, but it was so far away. Me and my brothers all wanted to go together to do it, but the crematorium wouldn't give us dad's ashes without her permission. It was all messed up mate, just mental stuff, especially as I lived down here," she said, "so, I had to go up and down, backwards and forwards, and felt like I always ended up back where I started. I never felt like I was doing enough! He'd gone! There was more I wanted to do with him, so much more I wanted to say. So many words unspoken and stories to write. It's just so final. It's sad. But I did it, I made sure he got his dying wish. Then…," she said, looking up from her hands, that'd been clasped together tightly, as if trying to hold herself together, "it made me want to jump out of the frying pan, that was my life as I knew it, and into the fire, so to speak. It's just never ending 'shit on biscuits'." She laughed, trying to cover herself back up. "That's when me and Thwaite, who's now my husband, got together and it all turned into a pile of steaming turds." She explained, "And then it all went tits up for real and I ended up in here, with you lot," she said, pretending to turn her nose up at them, in mock disgust. "Nah, I'm only kidding, thank you all so much. I've never really talked so honestly about it all before. I appreciate you all listening to me chatting shit."

9. MY ADDICTION IS YOU

So, I'm just going to tell you where I'm at, because let's face it, I can write what I like. There are no security police for what's right and wrong about how to write someone's story (not yet anyway, however, there's still time).

Some of you may be torn because in trying to provide you with full disclosure, or at least, lifting the veil, to let you peep at what some may call insight, it may not be the kind of story you like to read and it's all a bit convoluted and obscure. This is a story, and yes, there is a timeline, I suppose. However, this is an account of Darcy's time in rehab as she remembers it. I am here to recount the pinnacle moments and help you to understand a complicated girl and a complicated boy, who didn't know their arse from their elbow; they found each other's broken hearts and convinced themselves, and each other, they weren't worlds apart. I say 'girl and boy' because that's sort of what they regressed into. They both had a lot of growing up to do. But for now, they were content with allowing themselves the freedom to feel young again.

Some of you may be thinking, *Just get on with the goddamn story Lady Jane!* I don't know. On the other hand, some of you might be enjoying these little snippets. I prefer to call them, 'The good-old wise words of Lady Jane'. I'm trying my best to give you as much insight as I can, into the ever-complicated machinery of what life is like, for someone who has addictive tendencies, especially someone who can't let go of grief to boot. Darcy's story is so hard to write with justice and all I can hope, is that I am doing a good job so far.

There is no cure for addiction. We have already established that little, unsatisfying nugget of information in a past chapter, however, I am here to tell you again. For any addicts or people in recovery, hoping to seek solace in these words, just know, there is never going to be an easy way. I'm sorry to burst your bubble. It's completely shit. True change is like time, it is never ending and evolving and, evolution needs to come from within. Latching onto things that give you a quick fix; of making you feel better in that moment, may feel preferable to trying to sift through the multiple previous whys, hows and whens of past mistakes. Being in blissful ignorance, can feel good while it lasts, but then reality kicks in, and you realise you're just living a big fat lie. It's all 'hunky dory', 'shits and giggles', until you finally understand that the only person you're hoodwinking and cheating out of life, is yourself.

Have you ever seen The Matrix? Well, yeah, it's a bit like that! Darcy never fully grasped the point of the film either. She'd watched it at least ten times, before she admitted she was still none the wiser! However, it does get you thinking, doesn't it? Understanding the fine machinery of what makes you tick, is the key to staying sober and keeping happy. Either that, or like Darcy, you forever wonder why life keeps throwing you big fat boulders to catch as if they are bouncy balls. I just don't like the idea of trying to throw dust in your eyes or to smuggle anything past you. Nor do I like to feel as if I'm trying to deceive you into thinking that rehab is a cure all. So, what stops us all from beating one thing, only to become addicted to something else, or someone else, without even realising it? People do it all the time, and Darcy WAS addicted to Finn. She became not only emotionally attached to him (because although he could be the most amazing, sweetest, kindest and caring human being, when he wasn't being a selfish, impulsive, unfiltered idiot) but also familiarly attached, because he reminded her of her father. Finn had, ironically, made her feel the way her dad did in the end. Picking her up and dropping her off, whenever he ever so fucking chose to. However, we are not quite there yet. I keep saying that because well, it's true, but Darcy really wants to drill into you, her lovely audience, the full story, because if she doesn't tell this part in particular properly, then it will be harder to understand why she ended up putting up with so much shit from him and HER (Helga) who she'd much rather not be so relevant, in the future. (I was trying to make a reference then to Harry Potter and 'he who must not be named' however' I am now thinking that I failed miserably.)

When she was around Finn, he had such a way of making her feel – like she was the most important person in his world, but at the drop of a hat, and without doing it on purpose, he would leave her questioning if he really was being authentic. (Darcy mate, it's called not knowing what he wants and let's face it, you can't blame the bastard, because to a certain extent, neither did you! Just coz you got clarity on it later!) I don't really want to say this, because I don't want to take away the love you shared. But as your love was ever growing, you were convincing yourself that you wanted the same things he did. Until Finn came into your life, you wanted none of the things he did. You convinced yourself you could give him what he wanted (she could, there was no doubt about it in her mind, that she was the best thing for him. She could make him happy. But, could he be the rock in her life that she needed? Or would he be another 'crank-a-tooie' who would go get a pick and shatter great big crevices into her already fragile heart?) and that felt easier than working on what you wanted. Yet again, without doing it intentionally, you were making yourself far too available, to be used by someone who had no real concept of how his actions affected others. Some people are just born with a bit of 'fuck-knuckle' in them, and what started off as a very two-way relationship, ended with Darcy feeling exasperated at how careless and selfish he was.

For example, their chats became so much more involved about what Finn wanted for them for the future, with no real mention of what she wanted. She was so unsure of herself, when she entered rehab, that the idea of a family, that she'd never really had, since… well, ever, was appealing to say the least! He seemed much surer than her, and made his idea of their future together, far more exciting, than the 'normal', just 'seeing where things go' attitude, that she had. He started talking very early on, making throwaway comments, about how they would eventually integrate each other into their lives. It was still the early stages but there were all these big plans (oh, and I didn't want to make too much of a big deal about it because Darcy doesn't like to kiss and tell…, who am I kidding mate, but I do…. They totally did it! (Ya know, did the whole Netflix and chill, minus the Netflix). They were supposed to wait, but he wasn't the type who waited for anything. Don't get it twisted, it was what they both wanted; however, it was risky and the only one who was taking the risk really, was her.

After the kiss and the thunderstorm of emotions that came after it, they didn't quite know where they were at. They were saying all the right things to each other, to make them believe it was going somewhere, but the restrictions that were placed on their intimate relationship, meant they were in that grey area. They could talk all they wanted, and it felt safe, because even though they both wanted it, it was also as if it was a fantasy land. They were like two teenagers where sex was implied, when they talked about being alone together, but they weren't like two mucky minders, being crude about it. No, it was more like "I can't wait to be with you 'properly'," with a sheepish smile on their faces. "You know what I mean?" said with bashful blushes and fluttery eyelashes. It was sickening (in an awfully romantic fashion). Like 'get a room' kinda shit, although that was the whole point – they had nowhere to seal their relationship. And Darcy wanted to, but she was scared.

Their evening walks to the shop or going to get a coffee at the late-night ice cream parlour around the corner, opened the doorway to frustration. Of course, they both wanted to take their relationship to the next level. If she was honest with herself, even though the thought of taking the next steps physically – ya know – fondling, canoodling, completing the jigsaw puzzle, boinking – was something that shook her nerves, the way she eventually wanted the bedposts shaking. They talked about getting intimate very openly and both came to the realisation that it was going to be a huge step, not just for them as a couple, but also individually. Now she came to think about it, whenever she had been with someone new (except for when she had been 'working'; when she had used the coping strategy of pretending she was someone else entirely, with a whole new persona, name and hairdo; when there was no emotion involved and it was simply robotic) she had always the 'Dutch courage' on her side and to hand, to loosen up the nerves. That was no longer an option; she had to do it dry (and no that is not a euphemism nor a pun intended). It made her arse crack sweat, with the thought of him seeing her naked and all her wobbly bits, and thinking she was ugly, or doing something embarrassing like making weird noises, or farting during the bounce. Don't even get her started on sex faces (it filled her with embarrassment. She couldn't remember the last time she had had sex and truly wanted it for herself, not just because that's what you do when you're married, in a relationship or you know… the other thing). It was huge, and I'm not just talking about his 'you-know-what's-it'!

Of course, she had thought about it. If she said she hadn't imagined him naked, on more than a few occasions now, she would be trying to fool you all. She is only human after all. She certainly didn't fantasise about playing monopoly, if ever she had the chance to spend some real time alone with him, however (maybe naked twister) the thought of, *cleaning the cobwebs with the 'womb broom'*, scared her to death. The thought of them doing the deed and then it turning to nothing, was a prospect that scared her too. What if it all turned out she was just a shag? (Which Helga tried to insinuate later, but guess what? Helga can fuck off). He was just as apprehensive about it, but she felt better knowing he was having the same internal struggle. They couldn't deny that it was a feeling that was becoming ever more overpowering.

They snuck kisses wherever they could. It felt strange transitioning from friends to something more, especially under the circumstances. One minute they had to pretend there was nothing but friendship between them, and the next minute, when they were alone, they'd kiss and hold hands whenever they could. But they were still on constant high alert in case they were seen by someone when they were out and about. Part of it felt very naughty, and the other half exciting and high risk. (I don't know if you can feel what I'm getting at here. She was unintentionally (or intentionally) placing herself in the same (addictive) state of mind; as if chasing the highs and feeling the lows, because Darcy is a 'dick', who somehow likes to complicate her life and hope it all works out for the best. If they could get away with walking to the shop on their own, it would be exciting. When he grabbed for her hand, it felt strangely nice. He would swing their arms to and fro, hand in hand, and then he'd twirl her around, pulling her towards him and embrace her, as if they were the only two people on the planet that mattered; dancing in the street, laughing and cuddling as they went. Then, they would have one final kiss and tell each other, "I love you," before turning the corner to head back towards rehab, and he would let go, as if she was nothing more than an acquaintance, or jokily push her away, "Get off," he would say, smiling and giving her his cute puppy dog smile, but it still hurt. She knew the reasons why. It had to be that way. They had to wait until they were out of eyeshot before they could openly display any PDA (personal displays of affection). And, they had to wait until rehab was over, to come out in public as girlfriend and boyfriend. She was getting fed up living in a state of pretence. It was like she never wanted this part of their friendship and burgeoning relationship to end, but she wanted the life he promised.

His touch and the excitement in his voice, along with the nervous conversation, gave her butterflies, like love-struck teenagers. There was only one more week to go before they moved downstairs into the self-contained apartments and then they would have a lot more freedom to be a couple. (Even that gave her the 'belly wobbles'. It was the next step. Enticing but eekingly nerve-racking).

Nobody knew about them, except Arnold and Claire, and they were the ones who would be moving to the basement with them, when the time came. It would give them an opportunity to maybe even get away with sleeping in the same room as each other, without the fear of getting caught. (That was a dangerous game in itself. One that Finn was fully up for risking, but it was one of those times she knew it wouldn't have been a good idea, but she would've taken the gamble, the fucking idiot! She may as well have walked around baaing (the noise a sheep makes. Yes, I know the spelling looks funny, however that's how it is genuinely spelt). She would never have suggested something so risky. Finn was very much, 'Fuck it and see'. However, that's not what happened.

I'll give you a brief insight of it, because let's face it, this isn't Fifty Shades of rehab, nor is this a kinky novel, with smutty hints and tips of how to 'boink' and get away with it. The tales of how they came to take their relationship to new heights, will remain between Darcy, Finn and room number four, forevermore! However, one night, when the house was sound asleep, she was laid in bed feeling the love. She wanted him to know how much she was falling for him. He was still very unsure of himself and needed constant validation. Underneath the cocky exterior, there was still a man who needed nurturing. He still found it uncomfortable whenever she would tell him how amazing he was, and he was. There was so much good in him, he just needed reminding that he could push people away as much as he liked, but he didn't fool her. He wanted to be loved as much as anyone did. From the impression he had given her about his past relationship, he had never felt like he really mattered, unless he was getting told that he was a shit person, for one thing or another. It just became easier to believe he was a disappointment, that way, he didn't inevitably get hurt. She wrote a love note of sorts and decided on impulse to slip it underneath his bedroom door. It felt like it was the hopelessly romantic thing to do. She wanted him to have something physical to read, something he could hold. Something he could keep that wasn't a text, to let him know how much he meant to her.

She wrote the note and read it over and over, chewing over her decision to make the risky journey down to the other end of the house, before jumping out of bed and throwing on her slippers, all while chuntering to herself, "If ya get caught, ya div, then you're in the shit. Don't be such a baby, Darcy, just do it." *Why does every bastard door have to be a fire door FFS?* (FFS means for fuck's sake) she thought furiously, as she came out of her bedroom door and it slammed loudly. *Eeek! Jesus! Holy moly, mother of the good Lord!* she thought frantically, as she froze to the spot, trying to decide in the moment if she was going to abort the mission and pretend that she was simply getting out of bed to use the toilet? If anyone had been secretly watching, it would've been hard not to laugh at her statue like stance and her facial expressions, as all the thoughts raced through her mind. She waited for what felt like a lifetime, before slowly making the move to embark on the bravest mission of all time (it was a divvy mission, which was silly and risky, but what is life without risk? Bloody idiot!)

She had two long corridors to tackle to get to his door, which was on the other side of the house. To add extra danger and adventure to the little obstacle course of true love, there were another two fire doors to challenge her progress; they made a loud sucking noise, upon opening them, and the closing took a million years and a day. Just as they were on the brink of closure (she was under the impression she was doing a great job at being silent) the door shut at the last minute with another bang, which sounded like a gun being fired, *Oh, fuck, fuckity, fuck!* It was too late to turn back now. Her heart raced, as the adrenaline pumped through her body. She got to his door and slipped the note under it, gently tapping on his door, before rushing back as fast as she could, all the while trying to retain her inner ninja. It was quicker getting back. She didn't care as much about the noise, the closer to 'home' she got, where she could hide under the duvet and pretend she had been there all along. When she got back to her room her heart was in her mouth.

It felt to her as if she may as well have run through the corridors banging a big fuck-off drum, and shouting, "Woohoo! Look what I'm doing. I'm breaking the rules!" She lay on her bed; a few moments passed before her phone rang. It was him, she answered, "Hello?" she whispered.

"Aww, thanks," he said…, "gutted you were at my door and didn't come in… come back," he said quietly. He waited for a second before asking her again "Come to my room, I want to give you a kiss," he said softly.

"I can't love, what if I get caught? Can't you come to me?" She said, her heart was still racing. But she knew what she was about to do already. She was already checking herself in the mirror, to make sure she looked cute. She was about to make another reckless decision, against all her better judgment. (What judgement, Darcy? Erm?)

"Come to me," he said, ignoring her request for him to come to her.

"Ok, but I can't stay long, I don't want to get caught."

She snuck back out of her room and down the corridor. It felt easier this time. She knew where all the creaks were and how to bypass them. She got to the room and laid on the bed with him. It felt so nice to be alone together, but they had to whisper and hardly move, in case the bed creaked. It was awkward as fuck. She had purposefully worn her big lady pants, to try and put preventative measures subconsciously in place, so she wouldn't get tempted into christening their relationship under these extreme circumstances. She imagined a lot more romance, however. Let's just leave it there.

This time, she got back to her room and laid there bemused at what had just happened. *Is that how ninjas do it?* She thought, laughing at the absurdity. It was as if they had just attempted to drill a hole, in silence, without leaving any mess (if ya catch my drift? Wink, wink!) If that achieved anything, it just confirmed that they could find themselves in the most absurd of circumstances and still feel comfortable enough with each other to laugh about it afterwards and find romance in the utterly unromantic. Or was she trying to justify herself? Was she over-thinking it? *This is so fucked! Does he now think I'm easy?* Her mind was buzzing. She wanted what just happened, but she was still so unsure about everything. *I bet he thinks I'm fucking easy. Why did I let that happen? You wasn't even careful you silly bitch!* Then the other voice took over her brain. *Because you wanted it! You love him! Why overthink it? You've done nothing wrong.* As she was going through all her thoughts and emotions in her mind, she picked up the picture of them and looked at it, as if willing him to understand what it all meant to her.

She sat on her bed, wondering how she felt about what had just happened. It was the most unromantic action with the most romantic and loving sentiment. It got her thinking seriously, making everything all the more confusing. What did sex really mean to her now? She wanted the feeling that they portray in the movies. Where it's really passionate and loving. When in reality, all it does, is leave a mess and addle your brain. There are always two extremes when it comes to the portrayal of how the 'boom boom' is boomed. It's either completely loving, in the most romantic setting, where the boy and girl both 'arrive together', or it's in a room full of people, where there are two or three things, all going on at once, and the woman is being passed around like some Olympic baton, where all the mess adds to the value. In other words, it's either a romantic love story or a fucking gangbang. P.S., Sorry for the language, but don't you think it's true? Pornography has ruined the romantic sentiment of sex and now you think you're expected to be some sort of contortionist, whose tits stay where they are and wobble in the right way, when you're getting thrown about, with holes that can be banged, like the privy door when the plague is in town!

The pathway she had gone down in her past, meant that the deed had been thrown into speculation. What is it really that men want from you, except for one thing? It had been so throwaway in the past. Something that hadn't meant anything before (obviously, there had been times in her life that it had felt loving, but the majority of the time, it was just a deed that was done because that's what she felt was just part and parcel of being in a relationship.)

There were only three people in her life that had really meant something to her and every one of them, in their own way, had confused her about what sex was meant to be. Her first husband (Jaxon's dad) had very strange ideas. Possibly from watching far too much porn. What she was trying to say in her head, she didn't know, but everything was more of a chore, rather than a loving deed, although he didn't make her feel dirty. Then there was Elon, who was sixteen years her senior. He had seen and done everything in his time, although he didn't have the first clue about what women really wanted, or he did, but you'd have to ask her best mate about that! (She comes into the story later as well, funnily enough. P.S., the bitch's name is Nickola (because she likes to nick other people's men! Funnily enough Helga fits the same bill however, she was actually spawned from hell and would certainly have something to say about Darcy claiming she nicked men. I can hear her now, "he's me kids' dad." #dontmakeadifference. Elon was Brie's dad, however, that didn't mean Darcy could lay claim to him, whenever she fancied it, did it? (Knobhead). Not that she would want to. Anyway, that's beside the point, for now, Nickola came from, SlytonX2).

ALSO, she thought, becoming indignant, *Elon had an unhealthy relationship with porn as well.* He would watch it for sport. Whenever she checked the history on his computer, there were pages upon pages of the stuff. How was she meant to try and compete with it all? He was too interested in secretly filming what she was doing with other people, to show her any actual 'love making'. She didn't want to diminish what they'd had initially. She must've had something special with him at some point but what? Towards the end, she couldn't think of anything, even though she loved him dearly. But did he ever really love her? All this sober shit had thrown everything into question. *Wow, my brain really is on one tonight,* she thought. Whenever they 'did it', he would have yet more fantasies that involved her screwing other people. She remembered back to the time she regretfully asked the bastard what he wanted for his birthday. Elon's reply threw her into more thoughts of her own inadequacies. His fantasy was to see her have sex with a stranger, without protection! *Why? What's the big issue with simply asking for a birthday card and a blowjob, like normal people, eh?* Not only did she subject herself to being a toy, she sometimes even joined in the dirty talk, to try and make things move faster but he would stop himself on purpose, and now, he wanted even more! Needless to say, that all he got was a card and a coffee.

Then there was Thwaite, who got her out of prostitution, however, their drug fuelled weekends led them to talk about yet more sexual activities that involved other people and porn! What is it that's so exciting about it? She even got into it sometimes, but it was more of her trying to see if she could shock, because, apparently, that's what people do. Her sexual history was more confusing than the existence of the platypus. (And yes, I did Google the most confusing thing in the world, and apparently the platypus is one of life's biggest ponders).

As mentioned earlier, the path that she'd gone down,

meant that sex was such a throwaway thing; it didn't mean anything. However, she never ever thought that that would be her life. She wanted the traditional love but was she giving off the wrong vibe? Was it her? When she was 'working', it was like she was another person; so detached from it, but it was still a part of her, like a tumour that couldn't be removed because it was too close to a vital organ. It was still part of her, and she had to accept it. Like a port wine stain (birthmark) that you could still see beneath the most expensive concealer. Basically, something she couldn't get away from. When people found out what she used to do, they immediately had an impression of her that was completely false. In reality, she was so shy, but she had no right to be, did she? In her eyes, she was a slag, who gave herself away so easily in the past. How could she get away from the stigma? Just how? She didn't want him to see her like that. She wasn't like that; it was just what she became for other people. What did he really think of her? It was confusing her brain; tricking her into thinking this could all just be a joke to him, like a notch on his bedpost. However, he had never given her that impression, so why? *Just stop Darcy*, she said to herself. "You deserve to be happy," she said aloud, as she pulled the picture closer to herself and tried to imagine him with her. Snuggled up with him, keeping her safe from all the terrible memories and the reality, that for the majority of her life, she had simply been used as a piece of meat. She wanted him to kiss her forehead and magically siphon all of it away. It made her quiver at how dirty she felt. She wished so badly it would go away. If only she had said something sooner, instead of covering it up through bulimia, booze and pretending she was the one in control.

With the morals and core values that were instilled in her (she had so many good examples of how love was meant to be) she would have called you a pervert, if you'd have told her that her life was going to go the way it did. Her grandparents were together for over sixty years. They were good enough for each other. It was real love. They were the only people they had ever known, and if she was honest, she wanted a life like that, but it hadn't worked out that way. What did it really mean to her now? Was she really that bad to want those things, after everything she had done? She didn't want to live a life of promiscuity. Shagging about wasn't really her cup of tea; it never had been. From her experience, it was very rare that men had any clue what they were doing anyway. Let's face it, as most women will know from experience, if you want a job doing, nine times out of ten, it's much more satisfying to do it yourself! But that insistent need to be good enough for someone else, meant she had done a lot against her better judgment, always seeking validation from 'knobheads'.

She wanted to find love. She didn't want the old version of herself that allowed her to be used, but how was she meant to pretend she could have those things after all her history? It was a blemish that felt like it would never wash off. It felt very two-faced. How could she say that she hadn't really had experience (which she didn't in one respect)? She was a novice when it came to expressing what she needed, yet she had experienced more than most. On one hand, sex was sacred, on the other hand, it was disposable. Or was it just something that she learnt to expect from men? Where it is meaningless, not meaningful. She couldn't entirely blame the people that she'd been with previously, because, *I'm my own person. I let it happen,* she thought furiously. *I fucking did it. I can't blame anyone else,* she thought. *Don't make out your perfect love, coz you're fucking not,* continued the voice in her head. However, the way she was shaped, meant that she really didn't know any more. Which things were part of her, or which had actually been formed as ideas from someone else? She acquired a lot of bravado over time and tried to laugh it off, but inside her guts, she **just knew** it was wrong. You don't treat people like that if you love them; you shouldn't expect those things from somebody, however, it was expected of her, and she followed along in the blind hope that she would make Elon happy AND be able to provide for her family. She had come from a background of having a mother who did not follow tradition but when she split from her father Elvis, she stayed single for two decades. Her mother made sure she didn't introduce multiple men into her and Rocky's lives. So why? Why did Darcy's life come to this? Why did nobody want her, for her? Was she not worthy? Did she give off an air of being so throw away?

Her mother's side of the family was very traditional, with no broken homes. Marriages were not dissolved; it just simply wasn't the 'done thing'. Even her brother Rocky (and don't get her started on him) had managed to be successful, when it came to keeping his family together. On the other hand, her father didn't care. It sounds so cynical, however, her experience of all men in her life, seemed to be that they were after one thing. Was that just the norm and did she just have to find the best out of a bad bunch? If she was truly honest with herself, she was scared of being alone. She tried to seek validation in whatever she could, in the hope that the men in her life would stay; maybe, one day, she would be good enough. She didn't realise it at the time, but she was doing the same thing with Finn. (I so badly wanted to say something then, as a retaliation to what Darcy just knew from future experience, what Helga would say about all this. However, I am the grown up, so I will in no way tell Helga to fuck off or tell her that just because she's not had this trauma in her past, it still doesn't make her any better than Darcy, because she did the same thing, just in different ways…phew! It's a good job, I'm grown up in all this, isn't it?)

Now, she had complicated things even further; she'd

been a 'dick' and not used any protection. (See! I told you –
she makes a rod for her own bloody back! No wonder her
guardian angels (and shoulder devil, for that matter) are both
in fucking counselling). Her phone pinged. It was Finn,
whose text read, 'I love you so much. I wish you dint ave to
go. Were there loads?' (Ladies and gentlemen, I'll let you fill
in the blanks on that cryptic message yourself. I really am
going to shut up now).

10. ACCEPTING THE UNACCEPTABLE

Talking about her dad so openly in the music therapy sessions had helped her no end. She felt like she had let go of a burden that had been weighing her down. Now, she felt she was ready to celebrate his memory. It was as if when she talked about her dad with the group, all the feelings she had for him, had poured into Finn. Without being conscious of it at the time, Finn seemed to give her so much of a reminder of Elvis; it was as though she got a part of him back. He was with her again and this time she didn't have to let go, because Finn was in love with her. He wanted her, he needed her as much as she needed him. Without sounding weird.

Now, there is so much that rehab can teach you, however, they are not psychologists, nor can they counsel such deep-seated trauma. Darcy thought she had found what she needed. The cure all for happiness, if you will. Plus, she was in denial. She thought she was beating her addiction. All she was doing though, was swapping it for the extreme highs and lows that Finn brought to the table, with his whirlwind personality.

She would get a message from Finn each evening: 'come to my room'. It was so risky; people were starting to ask questions. "Are you together then?" Kelsie asked one day, during a casual conversation outside. It was a small, paved area, with concrete steps, leading down to a poky, sheltered smoking area which housed two benches against either wall. In the middle, was a tiny table. The compact garden area was fenced in, with a few plant pots, sporting some sort of colourful flowers, which swayed in the September breeze. They sat down, simply chilling out (ya know, coz they could) having a rare moment, where they could have a girly chat (ya know, about willies and fannies. Only kidding, they were above all that nonsense.... Who am I trying to kid? They totally weren't, however, today there was a topic for more serious discussion). Finn's rare absence was due to him having a meeting with his key worker, so he was out of earshot.

"Nah, nothing like that. I don't wanna get involved. He's got too much baggage. Plus, we both need to work on ourselves," Darcy replied. Maybe she had overplayed the lie, as Kelsie looked at her, still unconvinced.

"Yeah alright – whatever. Just be careful Darcy. I heard him arguing with his ex-bird, it sounds like nobody should get involved in that! She sounds like a right horrible bitch. I'd love to bray her," she said, with her fists clenched. "After everything he's told me about her, it's not even funny mate. She is a 'sketty' bitch!" (Exactly like 'skanky', but Kelsie chose 'sketty' to emphasise her dislike for Helga, what can I say? When it comes to slagging people off, girlies can reel off a whole plethora of weird and wonderful words, however, the definition of a skank, is an extremely derogatory, offensive term, for a person, particularly a woman, considered to be of low moral character. There are other bits on Google however, those bits don't necessarily apply and if they do, then it's not for Darcy to comment on. She certainly was of low moral character anyway). "But…," she added as an afterthought, "he's not all innocent," she said, with a raised eyebrow. "He was saying he wanted his family back at the start, now all he can talk about is you. I don't think the man knows what he wants. Please, just be careful. You know I love you both. You're both adults, you can do what you want, but please, be careful." She looked at her seriously. Darcy tried to look as pan-faced as possible, but she couldn't deny the uncomfortable feeling in her stomach, upon hearing what he had told Kelsie.

"I will, it don't matter anyway, coz I'm not gettin' involved, but he told me he'd been split from her for years," she said, looking at Kelsie innocently.

"Yeah, he has, but I dunno, she is up his arse daily, having a go, so even though they're not together, she thinks she can say and do whatever she wants mate, and it looks like he goes along with it," Kelsie said, with a raised eyebrow.

Even though it might have been at the start, he wanted his family back. Did that mean he wanted Helga back as well? What was she meant to do? He had told her, without a shadow of a doubt, that he and Helga had been done and dusted for a few years now, so what did all of it mean? Did he just find her and decide to pass the time until it was time to leave? She considered Kelsie one of her closest mates there, so it was highly unlikely that she would be telling her any of this just to cause trouble. Finn and Kelsie were best mates as well, so there was no nastiness in what she was saying. Her tone said it all for her. Darcy could see she sounded genuinely concerned about her two best mates, potentially messing up their futures, simply for a bit of fun. *But it's not a bit of fun though.* Darcy tried to think it with 100% conviction, but she couldn't deny it had thrown a sliver of doubt into the mix, and to top it all off, over the last few days, she hadn't exactly been careful, if you catch my drift? (Ladies and gentlemen, is your head starting to wobble off with all the shit that was going on in her head, heart and the harsh realities she was facing? Yeah? Well, welcome to Darcy's world. Take a number and please wait your turn to speak to a counsellor. However, even the counsellors need counselling, so it may take a while!)

Finn came bumbling out of the door looking slightly annoyed about something. "What's up with you two?" he asked, stopping in his tracks, as if he had forgotten for a moment, about whatever he was going to tell them. Now he was too busy trying to find out their business first, the nosey git!

"Nowt," said Kelsie, "what's up with your face, anyway? You look as if someone's just pissed in your stocking on Christmas day," she added, with giggly concern. "What's up with ya?" she repeated, this time, trying to don a more caring tone. Darcy fell about laughing, she couldn't help it, the look on Finn's face was a picture.

He looked at her slightly confused, as if to say, "WTF you on about?" Kelsie had such a way with words. She did not ever pander to Finn's moods. She was someone who could pull him out of whatever funk he was in at the time, by playfully winding him up, making him inadvertently forget what he was getting worked up for in the first place.

"I've just had a meeting with David and Karen," (because everyone knows a 'Karen!')

"Oh, right," said Darcy, eager to know more, feeling ACTUAL concern now. "What did she want? I thought it was just supposed to be with David?" she said. If Karen was involved, then it immediately sparked her nerves. What did they know? This didn't sound like your regular, weekly key worker meeting. What was SHE doing there? Darcy could feel her face flush, as she began to nervously fidget on the bench.

"They're moving my room to the flat upstairs for the last three weeks," he said, trying to sound like he wasn't that fussed about the news, but she could see he was looking deflated. It now meant that they would effectively be separated from each other. She felt sick, she knew this would not bode well.

Being placed in the upstairs flat, meant that he wouldn't be allowed downstairs in the evenings. There were only four bedrooms available in the apartment, and there were seven of them in their group, so you can see the dilemma. However, Cindy was very much an independent person, she had opted to be moved to a house just down the road from rehab. She would still have to come to the meetings and sessions, like the rest of them, however, Cindy was more than happy to volunteer for the ultimate test of being integrated back into the real world. It would be a lot easier for her to break the rules if she wanted to, but she was a strong, resilient woman, who was definitely taking the programme seriously. It was as if she wanted to be voted 'most improved person of the world'. (Just messing!) She wasn't all that bad, except for her constant need to be the centre of attention. Darcy was still a bit salty, from when Finn was purposely flirting with her. His excuses had been that he wanted to throw the staff off the scent of the two of them, but if she was honest with herself, she'd a feeling, he did it to attempt to get a jealous reaction from her as well (coz he is a cock).

Buzz was allowed to stay in his original room and continue to have his meals prepared for him. Moss was meant to be moving into the flat that Finn would now be inhabiting, so now, it meant that Moss would be moving downstairs with her, Claire and Arnold. It was all a mishmash of disorganised chaos, where now, even though they were still a group, they would be broken apart. Darcy was thinking it over in her head. This would now mean that when it was time for her to move downstairs, she wouldn't be allowed up into the usual communal areas anymore. So, when they moved, she wouldn't be allowed to interact with the other members of the house after 5pm (meaning him). She couldn't help but feel annoyed.

"Why have they done that?" she asked, trying to hide her anger and disappointment. "It makes no sense! What are they thinking – putting you on your own!? You're the most sociable person here Finn! You're gonna be bored stiff, being sat on your own in that flat, knowing we are all downstairs together. Like fuck are you gonna behave yourself up there on your own! Are they bloody stupid or something? What are they try'na do?" she said, looking at him and Kelsie, as if she was acting indignantly on his behalf, however, she was gutted. It wasn't just that though, she thought intensely. All sorts of conspiracy theories swam through her head. *They know about us*, she thought. It was the only conclusion she could make that made any sense. It filled her with a cold feeling of dread as to what was going to happen next.

The staff knew that Finn was someone who would get himself into trouble or break the rules, if left alone with his own company for too long. *Are they waiting for him, or me, for that matter, to make a mistake? The fucking fuck trumpets. I know! Language Darcy!* She thought to herself, as if she was imagining Karen's reaction, if she'd heard her say it out loud (also, that was a bit of a mouthful, wasn't it? You try saying, "fucking fuck trumpets", three times, and see if fucking Karen appears...! The nosey bitch.) She could feel herself wanting to blow, but that would ignite yet more suspicion, around whether or not she and Finn were boinking? *Why is it everyone's bloody business, for God's sake? What was so newsworthy about it anyway? Jesus Christ, why don't people just get on with their own miserable lives?* she thought, wanting to explode. She just wanted this (rehab) to be over, so she didn't have to pretend or lie to anyone anymore. All of this had convinced her that they must want one of them to fuck up, so it could then give them reason to chuck one, the other, or both of them out, for that matter, for breaking the rules. All because they couldn't prove anything, and they hated it. *They are out to get us,* she thought protectively. *If anything happens, I'll just leave. He has a lot more he needs to prove to himself, by completing this programme,* she thought, looking at him with pride. *He has come too far to fall at the last hurdle because of me.*

There was just over three weeks to go. It felt like a lifetime but in reality, it was such an insignificant amount of time. They had the rest of their lives to be together. Completing three more weeks was nothing in the grand scheme of things. He needed this, to prove to himself that he had done it, that he had proven the attitude of: "rehab's for quitters" and he was "ready to quit". To you lovely readers, this may sound contradictory, and it is. However, that is how Finn would say it, when he was trying to be clever, so naturally, it rolled right off Darcy's tongue too... so rehab is for quitters. He went in to quit, and he was ready to quit... do you see the logic? Nope, it took Darcy a few times too, when he would say it but that was Finn and his wonderful brain and there was logic in there somewhere. Without meaning to, she was starting to resent the place. It felt like they were being kept away from each other for no reason. She was almost childlike in the way she was rebelling. She was in the teenage stage of her relationship with rehab, and we all know what teenagers do don't we, ladies and gentlemen? Yes, that's right, they think they know best!

When she looks back now, she can see what was really happening. She was falling for someone who wasn't emotionally available, it's as simple as that. People were commenting on how they shone together, and they had to laugh it off as friendship. It only confirmed to Darcy that she was the right person for him. She would protect him; she could make him happy, if he would let her, for the rest of all time. Her stupid brain was telling her that it was 'them against the world'. Oh, when will she learn? At this point, even I need to sit down and take five minutes, to re-evaluate my own life and life's choices. Let's face it. Yes, she was being naive and stupid, but she clung to hope. She had faith in him, even when he hadn't any faith in himself; she had belief in him, when he told her nobody else did. It wasn't the case but how was she meant to know? (He had his family, even if he tried pushing them away, they did try.) I'm asking you? Life had been so awful for the pair of them. They had so many similarities in the way they had both made the wrong choices in life. Did that really mean they had to be punished for it, for the rest of her life? Plus, she felt that by fixing him (not actually fixing him – Darcy knew what she meant by that, but she couldn't explain it) she was also trying to fix herself. Everybody has done it. Maybe not to this degree because they are not that bloody stupid, but can you really blame her, for trying to find hope, after years of feeling hopeless?

The staff, especially the 'big boss', didn't like it at all; Darcy and Finn were breaking the rules right before their eyes; she was still going to his room at night. It was reckless but she had started not to care. (Like I said she was being a little rebel.) But they couldn't prove it… and it was pissing them off. (P.S., Karen was actually a pretty wonderful woman, who was just doing her job. She could foresee the car crash, but Darcy thought she was exerting her power and just trying to keep them apart).

One night she got the 'come to my room' message, 'ya know you wanna' from Finn. She was now flitting from recklessness, to thinking about ACTUALLY getting thrown out if they got caught. She wanted to go to him. What she really wanted, was to be able to sit with him on a sofa, like a normal couple, with a cold, iced latte (something that had now been adopted as their new favourite drink. It may have been caffeinated (wow wee, I know! The bloody rebels) but it was zero-percent proof.) She wanted to cook for him and for him to cook for her. She wanted off the crazy train every now and again and occasionally, be allowed to bask in the ambiance of normality. But did it really have to be like this? It felt like they were doing something wrong, a quick fumble and a grope, and all for what? Well, they were breaking the rules. Seriously, did she want to risk it?

They only had to wait a few more days before the weekend

set in, and they would be able to have the full day together. (Just to clarify with you lovely readers, that at this point in the 'story', at the weekend, the curfew on Saturday was that everyone was allowed out from 10am until 9pm, if they wanted, which meant they could go out for a whole day. Sunday was 10am until 5pm, so they could all be back in time for the end of weekend meeting, at 5.30pm. I'm simply pointing this out because, my lovely editor has made me aware that Darcy was getting ahead of herself and foolishly assumed you knew all the rules! #thankyou). He only lived a bus ride away from rehab, why couldn't they wait until then? She was having a real dilemma; on the one hand, they ran the risk of being thrown out. Then she would have to explain to her kids and her family the reason. Did she really want to have to explain to them that it was because she'd put a man before herself AGAIN? On the other hand, she didn't want Finn to feel as if she didn't want him, because she did.

It was getting so intense, and he deserved to feel loved. It felt uncomfortable yet again! Not because of the 'you know what' but because of how the 'you know what' was being performed.

Before they had embarked on the bumpy road of silent passion, she'd felt like she could tell Finn anything. Now, it was like she couldn't talk to him about what was going through her mind, because she didn't want him to feel unwanted. She felt trapped by her goddamn brain again. She couldn't even talk to her little shoulder angel and devil, because they'd fucked off, out of exasperation. When she tried talking to them now, all she got was, *don't ask us! You're only going to do what you want to do anyway. We're not getting involved mate!* Not very helpful, but true.

She went to his room, but why was she the one taking the risk every time? She was starting to question why it was, that it was her that seemed to be making all the effort? Even during the day, whenever she would go up to her room, he would come and knock on the door to check she was ok, and he wouldn't even step over the threshold for more than a few seconds, to poke his head around the door, to be nosey and see what her room looked like. However, being apart from him felt like losing a part of herself and she refused to lie about it. In all honesty, she couldn't ignore his behaviour; his neediness was growing, the burden shifting increasingly onto her, while somehow, he seemed to carry less and less. He always managed to talk her round and get his own way because he was a cute and fluffy little Mogwai (you know, from the film Gremlins, which, incidentally, is the transliteration of the mandarin, pinyin: mogui, meaning monster, evil spirit, devil or demon – very fitting in hindsight!) But WARNING! Don't get the bastard wet or feed him after midnight, otherwise chaos reigns and there's slime everywhere! If you don't know what I'm on about, Google it – you'll see what I mean. And no, it's not a porn channel, it's an actual film.

He was utterly charming, in his own unique way. The grip he had on her heart was something that even to this day, she cannot comprehend. Being with him felt so right but did she really want to kick start the relationship like this? Grabbing a 'quickie' whenever they could? The same thing happened each evening, she would go to his room, with the pure intentions of simply wanting to have five minutes, where they could be themselves, but the same thing would inevitably happen. They would have to be silent. (It's not funny and Darcy would kill me if she knew I told you this, but the silent, ninja-style of 'doing the deed' that they had adopted, meant that one night, while he was 'hitting a home run', she turned around to see what he was doing (I know, it sounds so romantic don't it? Tut…tut…) and the bastard was watching football on TV! Instead of Darcy being indignant, she found it hilarious. There were always times when she had to stop, to reset her brain and take in the hilarity of the situation. Having an almost, *did that really just happen?* moment. That was certainly one of them. At least when they scored... so did she, or at least she pretended to. Oops! Remember, keep that to yourselves. Shhhh.... She was starting to get a bit disappointed with his attitude. He seemed to want everything his way. He never once came to hers. But please don't get it twisted, she felt happier than she had in a long time. Or did she? Looking back, was it all a lie?

There was no respect for anything, including what should have been sacred between just them. He didn't seem to grasp the concept of privacy at all; it was a big joke to him, and it hurt her, although she didn't show it. One day, in the smoking area (and God knows how it came about, so don't ask for the details, because she can't remember the exact chain of events) he was talking about her boobs. As if they were up for public discussion: as if they were a fine-art piece on exhibition, which only he had seen, not asked by anybody to critique – but he couldn't help himself. He commented to whoever was there with them (like I said, she can't remember the full details, I think she tried to block it out of her memory) that her boobs looked the same shape as the balloon he was holding. The balloon wasn't completely full of air (and remember, neither were Darcy's boobies, they were heading south for the winter; she was in the latter years of her life after all, and she had breastfed both of her children, so give her a break). He'd moulded the balloon into a teardrop shape (to be fair, when she looked at it with bemused embarrassment on her face, she thought the shape was quite complimentary and he said, "Her titties are amazing, they go like this." He made a swooshing movement and a "me-ow" kind sound, as he ran his finger along the bottom of the balloon, as if to demonstrate the shape with his movement. He laughed excitedly, like a big kid. "She's got beautiful boobies. The best boobies I've ever seen. I love 'em," he said, as he caught her eyes.

She glared at him, as if to say, "Shut the fuck up!" Even though it was an extremely lovely compliment, she felt flushed with embarrassment at how he talked so openly about her body, right in front of her, as if he'd forgotten she was, in fact, an actual person.

"What?" He said, catching himself, he immediately looked sorry, not sorry…. "Sorry love, but I do! I love 'em! I love you, sorry love." He did the swooshing motion again before putting the boobie balloon down and realising he maybe, just maybe, had said too much.

All she could bring herself to do, was laugh, "You're such a dick," she smiled. She couldn't help but glow at how much his eyes shone when he looked at her. (And this, ladies and gentlemen, believe it or not, was one of the 'Finn and Darcy romantic moments!' for the old scrap book, and trust me when I say it only gets better… or worse…hmm? You decide).

However, one minute he wanted to keep things cool, the next, he was saying he wanted to marry her. She was so in love with him, and everyone could see it. Claire kept reaffirming their authenticity by saying, "The way he looks at you, Darcy, you can see that he is a man in love," smiling matter of factly, as she puffed away on one of her posh cigarettes. "He's besotted with you," she would reassure her, whenever she voiced her fears that maybe Finn wasn't what she might need right now? She honestly felt like she had found her missing piece of the puzzle, and she didn't want to let it go, but she couldn't deny that shit was mounting up. Who am I kidding? They wanted to be together. It was true love. She locked it in the cupboard and let it go.

As the leaving date was hurtling towards them faster than the speed of light, he wanted to pretend he didn't have a load of shameless shit to go back to. He pretended he didn't have to deal with Helga slapping her jaw at him, as if somebody had put 50p in the bitch. Instead, he revelled in his new-found happiness with her, and with the group of people who had become the 'new family unit'. Unbreakable and strong. When it came to going home to his far-off land, a bus ride away, to Uttertwat, where he lived, he was trying to bury his head in the sand, convincing himself that the days weren't looming nearer, where he would have to go back home.

Darcy knew he was dreading trying to figure out a way of coming to an amicable agreement with Helga, regarding access to his kids, and telling her that he had a new girlfriend (Darcy was her name you know!) He was dreading what it was going to be like going home, without no one but himself to steer him from temptation. Darcy didn't want to go back to nothing. Let's face it, Thwaite was a wipe out (thank God) she didn't regret that, but what did she have to go home to? Her kids had grown into the older end of their teenage years. She couldn't turn back time. What could she do? She wanted them to come home, but Jaxon and Brie weren't used to being around each other anymore. The events of the past meant that they had been separated from each other. Although they still saw each other and knew each other well, they were no longer the typical, traditional brother and sister. The bond between them had become somewhat broken. It was all Darcy's fault – she tore her family apart. What she had done to them meant they had been raised in two very different ways. There was now a lot of resentment between them. As far as Jaxon was concerned, Brie had got everything she had ever wanted. It's ironic how life pans out isn't it? As soon as Darcy told Elon to sling his hook, he actually got off of his lazy, arrogant backside and got a job! I know! AND he'd done really well for himself, becoming the head of IT, at a large company called, TNUC (can ya see what I did there?) However, that meant that even though Brie got more money than most to play around with, her father was too busy to do any actual raising and lacked having or providing the emotional support any young girl needs. Jaxon was raised by his grandmother who did her absolute best. He got all the love Angela could give (she is an amazing lady) along with a very disconnected and emotionally unavailable mother, who'd given up on everything; it wasn't as if she was far away. She only lived next door, but they barely saw each other. *I've ruined my kids' lives*. She thought about it all the time. All she could do, would be to rebuild when the time came. However, Jaxon had to deal with the reality that he had been abandoned by two father figures (a stepfather Elon, who just fucked him off and his actual father, who was now back in his life occasionally. They had their own relationship now) and finally Thwaite, even though he was a 'prick'. It was all such a mess. And definitely a story for another time. But the gravity of what she had to do now, to try and fix it, if they let her, meant it was a very frightening prospect for her. She didn't know where she fit in. She had missed so much of their lives. She couldn't possibly start demanding that they came home now, because she appeared fixed, could she?

Although – Finn had strong ideas about how she should deal with her tender situation. He'd say, "You're the mum. They need to be at home with you. You need to tell them they need to come home. They're kids, you should just 'ave 'em." (Like they were objects without their own minds.) She didn't think he meant it like that, however, he was never careful of what came out of his mouth, so all he managed to do, would be to make her feel more shit about herself. He would say it, as though it was as simple as blinking. (Unfortunately, she had lost her fairy wand, so when it happened, and *if they do decide to come home, if ever, it has to happen organically*, she thought, as she held her tongue, whenever the subject of her children cropped up. He needed to shut up telling her how to handle a situation he knew nothing about.

She held onto a lot of guilt, because there was that seven-year period where she had been completely useless for them, but there was also a lot of stuff out of her control. She would try to avoid that conversation because his strong ideas threw yet more 'brain eeks' into the mix. (Brain eeks are things that make your brain squeak in the most horrible fashion, making your head spin with "arghhhs". You know what I mean? Or was it just her?) By this point her head was swimming with everything. She agreed with him to a point, but she wanted her kids to have the choice. *I've got no fucking right to do that*, she would think to herself. In her eyes, she had utterly failed them. What right did she have now, to start expecting them to upend their lives, just because SHE had decided it was convenient for HER, that they come home, so she could make the years up to them? They had their own school and colleges that weren't within walking distance of her home and she didn't drive. She would have to think about all of that when she got home. For now, at least, she was glad that they both supported what she was trying to do and that they were talking to her regularly on the phone. Jaxon had even come to see her during her recovery. Brie wasn't allowed, as she was underage, she wanted to, but it was against rehab policy to have minors in the building. It was a safeguarding issue that Darcy was disappointed with, because she missed her daughter, but she fully respected the rule. And they still loved her. That was enough for now. She would have to work her way back up to the honour of them even considering coming home.

So instead of thinking about stuff that was overwhelming, Darcy and Finn clung to their relationship with all their might, throwing themselves further into the fantasy of finding 'the one'.

"I wun't be 'ere if it wan't for you," he would tell her on a regular basis. "You changed my life, honest to God, ya did, mate, I'm not even lying!" She believed him. Could they really be the exception to the rule? She had never felt so understood yet misunderstood. He kept her at a constant level of being in limbo. Even though he would challenge her in ways that nobody else had before, forcing her (in a good way) to become vulnerable around him. He would compliment her, but in a way that was still offensive. It's hard to explain. If he thought she looked nice, he would say, "You're definitely worth 'a squirt'." (I know, how romantic, and Darcy, the silly cow, went weak at the knees, *ooh, he thinks I'm pretty*). Or the classic, "You're not fat, you're my chubba chunks." Oh yeah, and my favourite, "You used to sell ya fanny, but I get it for free. So what? Get over it. I love ya, so you just need to get over it." She heard the back-handed compliments and took what she could. Plus, *that's just the way he talks*, she thought, all gooey eyed, trying to justify it. Really, sometimes, what he said, made him sound like a complete goonie (means idiot, twat, total wanker, in Darcy's way, trying to explain the shit that came out of his mouth).

He wasn't like most people. No filter. No engagement of the brain before the mouth opened and out popped the snide comments, dressed as love and compliments. He would simply say whatever came out of his mouth. He wouldn't be able to understand what he had said that was so wrong or hurtful, because yes, there was some truth in what he was saying. Yes, Darcy was 'worth a squirt', as he would so kindly put it, she is a 'sexy little bitch,' (another one of Finn's tributes) and yes, Darcy did hold a little holiday weight. Let's face it, she had started eating properly again, and now that the alcohol was out of her system, her body craved the sugar she had lost when she had stopped drinking. So, she had started drinking sugary drinks. She craved sweets like Chewits and Skittles, and all sorts of other crap. And yes, the sugar landed on her hips and wouldn't kindly fuck off. However, it apparently gave her boobies that extra bit of swoosh. AND, technically, yes, she did used to 'sell her fanny' but as he said it, she wondered why he would bring that subject up in that way, especially in front of other people. She couldn't recall the exact setting; however, it was the same as the 'boobie situation' in the rehab garden. He taught her quite quickly, that there was no point in being embarrassed or shy, because he just couldn't help himself. She had to just go with whatever flow he was on. That was just him.

When he said it, she did wonder what he really thought of her? That questionable part of her life happened over a decade ago, and yes, she supposed she did have to eventually 'get over it' but injecting a bit of diplomacy and compassion into that statement, wouldn't have gone amiss.

Anyway, there was no talking to Darcy. She would defend his way with words, "That's just him", seeking to justify the often not sometimes, unjustifiable. Accepting the unacceptable.

She'd always found compliments hard to accept. Her brain working overtime as usual with the: They must be after something – Why? What do you want? At least Finn is honest, albeit in an unfiltered way. What did people want from her? They were questions she asked herself all the time when she received praise. However, she masked her shy and scared interior, with a brand-new exterior of comedy gold, wise words and fake self-praise. Darcy!! Wake up! I can't even comfort you with the knowledge that she came to her senses, because she didn't. If she did, it wouldn't really make for a good story now, would it? I hope this gives people insight into a broken woman, hoping to be fixed by a wonky hammer?

11. A B C D E... F U

There was a strange mood that hung in the air during dinner time. The day's sessions of opening up and sharing their fears for the future, had left them all feeling a bit battered emotionally. Finn was clearly out of sorts and struggling to figure himself out. Darcy could see his struggle. Whenever Finn found it hard to process any of his emotions, it was hard to try and stop him from acting out. "I'm craving like mad," he said to her, as he pushed his shepherd's pie around his plate (which had fucking peas in it again! But noooo, the peas didn't end there; they weren't just in the shepherd's pie, as if that wasn't enough, there was a load dumped on the side of the plate as well). She noticed the peas, desperately wanting to mention it to Finn and start an investigation as to why there seemed to be peas in everything. *Were they on special offer or something?* she thought, as if she was entertaining her brain, while maintaining the same outward look of concern. *Had a load of the death bullets fallen off the back of a lorry or summat?* But now was not the time. 'Peagate' would have to wait. She tried making casual conversation, as if that would hopefully coax him out of this unnerving state of mind. He was slouched on the chair. On the outside he looked carefree and relaxed, but she could see the look on his face. It was agitated and detached.

Where is Kelsie when I need her? she thought, as it just occurred to her, she hadn't spotted her dotted about at any point that day? *Where is she?* Maybe together they would have been able to lift his spirits. However, she had just remembered that Kelsie had gone off to the college of 'new tidings'. Rehab would send groups off for the day, in the hope it might inspire any leavers to learn a new skill, to keep them on the right track. *I'll have to tackle this one on my own,* she thought, pondering new ways to make him smile. Just then Finn's phone rang. It was her. Ha-ha! How strange, she thought, marvelling at her new-found super skill she had acquired from where? *My subliminal superpowers are going on my CV,* she thought. He answered the phone in a flat tone.

"Hello, what you sayin'?" he said. He had put her on loudspeaker, so Darcy could join in.

"Hey Kelsie." she chimed in happily.

"I'll tell you what I'm sayin', you little bastard," she said, trying to act angry, however, you could hear a hint of laughter in her voice. "I've just opened me pencil case…" Finn started laughing, as if he had just remembered something. Darcy had no clue what was going on. However, she was so pleased to hear the mischief back in his voice. "Why the fuck is there a knife, a fork and a spoon in there? Ya little dingy," she said loudly, as she burst out laughing…. She couldn't help herself. "Leave my pencil case alone ya twat…. I was just in the middle of the lesson, and I pulled a dinner knife out, as if I wa' about to stab the tutor. He looked at me as if I'd gone wrong!" She said jovially. "Jesus, can you imagine? My street cred ruined if I ended up in the papers. DEATH BY DINNER KNIFE," she finished dramatically.

"Yeah, well, I wanted you to have something you could eat

ya dinner with mate, he-he-he." They all laughed and chatted for a few minutes before Kelsie said she had to go. When he put the phone down, he was chatty for a few minutes, but he seemed to thread off, back into his own head.

Darcy could clearly see that he was agitated and in no mood to be talked down from whatever thought train he was moving on. It was very rare that his moods lasted more than an hour or so, but while he was in them, it felt unnerving. Finn's worst enemy was himself. When he allowed himself to be controlled by his impulses, that was when he would get himself into trouble. She could see that it would take more than the usual 'deep talk', where they usually talked until they felt better. Today she was going to have to get creative.

"Do you want me to get my tits out?" she whispered cheekily at him. (Calm down people, she was obviously joking). He looked up with a twinkle in his eye that was still veiled by his mood. He half smiled, then glanced around furtively, to check the coast was clear. When he was sure no one was watching, he reached over slightly and grasped her hand, as if letting her know he was ok, before retreating back into himself. She could see he was battling with his inner demon child. "You're bound to feel a bit emotional and stuff mate, today's been hard. We've all been talking about triggers and cravings all day," she looked at him. He seemed to be distracted. Only half listening to what she was saying. His mind looked as if it was racing a million times a minute, fighting the urge to hit the 'fuck it' button.

"I just miss me kids," he said, trying to blink the tears from his eyes and avoiding any eye contact. He looked down at the table to his phone. As he clicked the screen to check the time, the front screen flashed up a picture of them.

"Why don't you try to give them a call and talk to them? It'll remind you why you're doing this in the first place?" she suggested, trying to sound as comforting as possible. All she wanted to do was hug him and kiss his forehead (you all know forehead kisses are the best) and tell him he was going to be ok. *But nooo*, she thought, getting wound up with the stupid rules, as if it was their fault. They couldn't be too tactile out in the public areas, so a little shoulder squeeze would have to suffice for now.

"Nah, every time I do, SHE gives me shit. I've had enough of it, mate. I come in here to sort myself out and all she does is give me shit, saying that I'm a shit dad," he said angrily. Darcy didn't know what to do.

"Ok love, just remember, I'm here for you no matter what," she said, firmly looking into his eyes. "Come find me when you feel like talking," she said softly, as she glanced at him, wanting to say more, but knowing at this point in time, all she could do was to let him get on with it, and trust that he would shake himself out of it on his own. She walked out of the dining room, stopping by the door to look back at him playing with his food (she refused to say the word PEAS again). Then she walked away, feeling utterly powerless that she had to watch the man she loved being destroyed by that numpty.

All he would talk about was how much he just wanted to be a dad. His attitude was so refreshing. He was so passionate when he talked about how hard it was to find the strength to deal with the torrent of abuse he was receiving from his children's mother. (Yes Helga, we mean you!) After Darcy had left him alone, to decide whether he should in fact, phone and talk to his children. (He did sometimes listen to her advice. After all, it was very rare that she was wrong).

A while later he came into the pool room. She could see he was visibly upset. She had overheard him arguing on the phone. He was shouting. Most of it was incoherent, however, she caught a few sentences: "I'm tryin' my best, aren't I? Eh? How am I meant to 'ave the kids when I'm in 'ere? Eh? Are you dumb?" There was more chuntering and loud swear words, followed by, "I'm sorry for swearing but fuck me, what am I meant to do?" He shook his head, as if talking to himself, as he stormed into the room. He looked furiously defeated, stopping dead, as if not quite sure what he should do with himself now. Darcy looked up with her eyes, barely moving her head. She didn't want to make matters any worse. This was something he needed to shake out of his system for a few seconds. He needed to be given the chance to quickly process it before anyone started making a fuss. (He was almost like a child, you know, when they fall down and hurt themselves, but they don't cry or make a big deal about it, until you do.)

She was worried. She'd not seen him this irate before. He was looking around, as if wanting to speak but he couldn't seem to find the words. He usually held himself with swagger but right now, his shoulders were slouched, as if he had lost the strings that usually held him up. He had tears in his eyes. She could see he was trying to hide them, but they were falling thick and fast. They were clearly tears of anger and frustration, from whatever had just been said on the other side of that devil phone. His face looked gaunt, as if all the fight had been sucked out of him. She had to fight every fibre in her body, to stop herself jumping up to the rescue. She hated to admit it, because it felt awful seeing him in his internal struggle, but she couldn't save him from his own thoughts, he would have to tackle that to some degree by himself. She felt her protective battle armour kicking in. She was getting herself ready to be there, however she could be. *Who am I gonna have to get Kelsie to chin?* She thought absurdly. (Obviously, that was a joke, before any little idiots she knows, reads this and starts chatting shit. P.S., UP YOURS!) There was an anger that she could feel swelling inside her, as if it was her own.

She looked up from what she was doing. She was sitting in one of the chairs, drawing a picture of a lady in a 'piano dress'. It was supposed to represent herself and her musical passions *but that can wait*, she thought, distracted by wanting to make sure he was ok, without drawing unwanted attention to him. He didn't like to make a fuss (well he did; he did it all the time, but he withdrew when it was serious stuff like this). This needed a unique kind of remedy, yet to be invented. She called over the room signalling discreetly, "You ok?" she asked, trying not to draw any more attention. He was clearly in distress. Everyone rallied around him to see if he was ok, but he was a bloke! So of course, he didn't want to talk about it.

Darcy stayed where she was. He was like a boiling kettle that had been left on the heat for too long. Arnold was talking to him and trying to console him with a blokey pat on his shoulder, "Ey up pal, what's up with ya? You alright pal?" This was Arnold's manly way of showing his attempt at what may have been friendly affection. He was trying to talk him down from the 'edge' but all he got was:

"Nah, nah mate, I'm alright. It's her," (meaning Helga) he said, as he paced around the pool table. Darcy could see him falling apart with all the emotions and thoughts. It was horrible to watch. The more people asked if he was ok, the worse he seemed to get. She was worried. It was as if she could see what he was thinking without the need for words. It was written all over his face. She could see him trying to fight every natural urge to leave and get a drink. She knew him too well (she didn't know him to the full extent, obviously.) However, as much as some may like to bleat that she didn't really know him at all – Darcy knew one thing for a fact, and that was the man who he had presented himself as during the time they had known each other. And... the circumstances meant that, like it or not, she knew him and knew what he needed at that moment. There was no point in her rushing over to make a fuss. She just knew it would only make matters worse. When Finn feels backed into a corner, he runs. However, he was fighting hard against it.

She left him in Arnold's care while looking over every now

and again, to see if she should 'blue light' it over to him. Arnold looked as though he was treating Finn like a new-born baby bird, who had fallen out of its nest and landed on its head. It was clear he was very new to this thing called 'caring'. Men didn't show emotion! At least Arnold didn't think they did anyway. So, he looked uncomfortable. Not in a way that Darcy would've expected him to; he was showing genuine worry for his friend. She had a sneaking suspicion that his and Claire's unshakable bond, had led him to open up more, and now he was displaying this new-found skill called moral support. She watched them both and couldn't help it. She felt a rush of pride at how far everyone had come from the beginning. No way would this have happened a few short weeks ago. It was nice to see, had she not been so concerned about the potential for a disastrous outcome. *Please, please you can do this love*, she thought furiously to herself. She was willing him to hear her thoughts. Hey, you never know, it could've worked, she did display signs of telepathy earlier, *don't let this beat you.*

Finn was saying a lot of things all at once. It was a mixture of upset, anger and rage, that Helga still had the power over him; she was still able to belittle him into thinking that he wasn't good enough. *She sounds like a nasty, horrible, piece of work*, thought Darcy, but she wasn't getting involved too much in the 'slagging off' of the woman she would have to be civil with, if she was to remain in Finn's life, as his girlfriend, and maybe, one day, his wife. *It's so hard though*, she thought, as she sat and watched him hurting. *Why did she have to be so vicious?* Anyway…, she watched Arnold try and say everything and anything to make it better, "She's not worth it. You'll get it sorted pal. She can't keep them from you anymore, you're sober. She's got no excuses now." He patted Finn on the shoulder again in an attempt at consoling him, "I know women like her, she uses the kids to get you to do what she wants pal, just concentrate on yourself for now, your kids'll see your doing well. You'll make them proud." He finished off, looking pleased at how well he had done with his words of wisdom.

If this was any other scenario that didn't involve Finn in such emotional turmoil, she would have found Arnold's looks of sheer panic rather amusing. It was clear he didn't deal with emotions well. He almost looked as if he didn't want to get too close, in case they infected him. Finn just looked lost. Arnold came over with a frantic panic in his voice. "I think he's gonna leave. I don't know what to do. Will you talk to him? He seems to listen to you," he pleaded. If you'd told her at the start, that Arnold would let himself look this vulnerable, displaying what was pure love and concern for another human, she would've thought you'd managed to bypass the breathalyser system and come in sozzled. She got up from her chair without having to be asked twice.

"If he's saying he's gonna leave, I don't know what good it'll do," she said to him, with concern in her voice. She didn't want him to go. She wanted him to make it until the end. *What a BITCH!* she thought, why? *Why do this to him now?* She walked over to Finn and tapped him on the arm, gripping him gently. "What's up with ya?" she asked in a straight-talking fashion.

"Nowt, nowt I'm ok," he said, trying to blink back the tears, looking away, but he couldn't help but keep glancing back. "I don't want anyone to feel sorry for me," he said, pulling his arm away defensively. "Nah, I'm ok." He looked in such a vulnerable state.

"Shut up dickhead," she said softly. She had learnt over time, that Finn didn't respond to nice words. Calling him a dickhead, was like saying, "I love you!" and somehow it seemed to bring him down to earth slightly, like a hot air balloon coming into land. She leaned into him and gave him a hug, which he resisted at first, then briefly leaned into her, before she leant back, looking him in the eye, "I'm not feeling sorry for ya," she said, shaking her head, "I've got no reason to – you're doing enough of that for yourself," she said, winking at him; letting him know she was just ribbing him affectionately.

"Cheer the fuck up, yeah? You know where I am. I'm only over there," she nodded with her head to the spot from where she had just stood up… "P.S.," she said, trying her best to be authoritative, "you're not going nowhere. You're going to stick this thing out to the bitter end. We've all got your back." She looked him dead in the eye, "Ok?" She said, waiting for him to acknowledge the statement. He twitched his head and attempted a smile, while brushing the tears away with his sleeve. She simply nodded at him and walked back over to her chair and carried on with her piano lady without another word. It was as if he knew she was there, without her over facing him with affection, that enabled him to calm down in his own time. She was his calming influence.

A little later, he was ready to talk. They were the last ones to go to bed again. They'd just finished their 'go to' routine for distraction (yup, you've guessed it. They played pool, and yes, she won, again). However, they had exhausted the excitement out of that and were now sitting at the chairs by the pool table. He was word-searching it up, and she continued working on her musical lady. She watched him carefully, as he looked for the words in the puzzle; he looked content and calm. As she watched him, in that moment, she loved him more than she ever thought possible. She couldn't help but feel for his 'shit-tuation' (a situation that's, well… you get the picture) and her stomach twanged with empathy. "I can't help but feel like I'm shit; I let me kids down," he said, looking up, out of nowhere, as if he could feel what she was thinking. He was shaking his head in deflated desperation.

She leant over and looked him straight in the eye, "At least you're still fighting it though," she said with vigour, "come on Finn, please give yourself a break, your fucking trying more than most. Trust me when I say that. I have experience on both ends when it comes to that shit". She sat back and looked at him. He couldn't help but show a little acknowledgment of her point, half nodding in agreement. "Just give yaself a bit of a break, yeah? At least your trying love," she said calmly. Although, she wanted to start on a train of indignancies on his behalf, however, this was his story when it came to Helga and how he was going to move forward with his kids, but she had to remember to bite her tongue and try and remain neutral. At the end of the day, she didn't know this woman; she knew Finn wasn't exactly an easy ride, so for now, at least, it wouldn't be right to make unfair judgments, although it was becoming increasingly difficult.

Learning coping mechanisms and understanding the craving, rather than shying away from it, felt empowering. He looked pleased with himself that he hadn't succumbed to the powers of the 'spirits', as it were. With the staff, and peer support, everyone was growing and becoming the version of themselves they wanted to be. She still couldn't help being awed at how Arnold had stepped up as a rock for support. He had come so far, in fact so far, that he was unrecognisable. Now he was getting bigger, he was a fucking boulder now. He was back on his body building diet, so was growing by the day. *I'll have to try extra hard to trip him over now!* She thought fondly.

Finn had beaten the demons today; the cravings did not defeat him, and he did it mostly on his own. Even though he had moral and emotional support from a few people, he was yet to acknowledge that, ultimately, it was him that had beaten his demons, doing the hard work all by himself, and she couldn't be prouder. "I'm glad ya still here, Numpty," she said fondly, as she outstretched her leg and nudged him playfully.

He pushed her leg back playfully and replied, "Shut up, you beautiful bitch," as he looked at her lovingly. "I'm glad I dint leave, I only stay coz ov you," he added, looking serious.

"No, you stay for yourself, don't take your achievements away from yourself divvy. Celebrate the little stuff. You did good sweetheart." They sat together comfortably doing nothing much at all. They both kept looking up and smiling at each other. It was as if they were connected without words. (Telepathy was also on her CV). These were the moments Darcy cherished. These were the moments she clung onto when he was making her want to put both tea and coffee in his drinks. (Ooh, I know! She's an evil genius).

It was like they had known each other for years, however, the struggle to remain covert was becoming a huge, giant, pain in the arse. She would be lying if she didn't take some of the credit for a few of the great changes in him. Some days she had to work so hard to keep her patience, but it was working. He seemed to cling to her, wanting to develop and grow with her. She was besotted, so, so besotted. She had never known anyone like him (that's a lie Darcy; you just didn't know it yet! It took years of shit and personal therapy sessions, to realise that he reminded you so much of your dad). She was amazed at how his brain seemed to work differently from everyone else's. He would appear so cocky and confident in some ways, usually when he was doing something foolish, that would land him in hot water. Finn was of the mentality, "Well, they're laughing at me anyway, so I might as well give them something to laugh about." It pissed her off that he saw himself as the joke. She didn't want him to simply be content with acting the jester when he had the potential to be the king.

He would remark on how she was much cleverer than he was, but it wasn't true. "I'm thick. I'm not good at owt like what you do," but he was clever in other ways. Darcy knew almost immediately that he had more substance than he was letting on. There was so much more to him, than he even knew himself. He would invent mad ways of setting up boobie traps, which she found highly hilarious and bizarre, but she couldn't deny they worked, were undeniably genius and so simplistic. He would argue points that some of the staff couldn't argue against. Whenever he would find fault in the system, he would point it out, leaving the staff without any words to argue back. It was just his delivery that needed some serious work. He was so used to talking to people and unintentionally belittling them, because he was used to being ready for an argument. He would argue with you even when you were agreeing on the same point. It was learnt behaviour, a defence mechanism. But he was slowly getting better with it. They gave each other the spotlight to shine. But as you can see yourself, everything was all over the place and it was all in a setting that wasn't really real. Would she have walked away before now if she didn't have to live and breathe the same air? Do you see what I'm trying to say? Don't get involved in rehab relationships. In fact, don't get yourself involved in anything that shines like an oasis of hope in a desert. Keep walking until you find civilization.

There are so many good things that the rehab programme can teach you and so much benefit you can gain from it (plus, I am finding it hard not to get too involved with chiming in.) Finn was a firework, who was beautifully coloured and awe inspiring to look at; how he played with life. However, you have to stand well back, in case it goes off in your face! Darcy seriously thought she was winning in life. Without consciously knowing it, she was becoming Finn's emotional crutch. Looking back on the last few years, with the clear unfiltered glasses of hindsight, she was addicted to the chaos. Finn struggled more with his emotions and impulses, so, making sure that he was ok and on the right track, became more important than making sure she wasn't becoming derailed on her own.

She saw what he couldn't. He was such an amazing person in so many different ways, with a brain that was so fascinating, it amazed her. Then he naturally would go and do something fucking stupid. Whenever he would say anything deemed to be 'over the line', she would explain to him how he could be a bit more diplomatic. At first, he took it on board. As time moved on though, he would ignore her more and more, and tell her to,

"Shut up," whenever he found his emotions getting the better of him. He was still very wary of letting it all out and telling her how he felt. He would brush over a big part of his past, as if it was too painful to feel. He would express clearly that he thought she was someone who he wanted to spend the rest of his life with. Well, he did; he told her without a shadow of a doubt, that she had, "Changed his world." He never wanted to do anything on his own. He would quite happily sit with her and watch, as she would sit for hours in the evening, drawing in the dining room, where it was quieter from the hustle and bustle of the house....

...He would sit and watch carefully, as she shaded the lilies she had taken to drawing, as a way of refining her artistic skills. He would observe her lovingly, and she would occasionally look up from what she was doing to catch him watching her. "I love you," he would say, before quickly catching himself, clearly trying to return to remaining indifferent to his feelings. "I mean... I hate you," laughing fondly at her smile.

"Finn...," she would say softly. "I hate you too," before continuing what she was doing. Leaving him flushed with happiness.

Knowing she wasn't the only one struggling, diluted and halved the struggle in itself. Don't get it twisted though, she had internal struggles galore, the difference was she was working through them, in a healthy way, in a hopeless place, which was giving her more than she could have hoped for. Freedom to find herself. The group sessions as a whole, brought out the best in all of them.

12. PEAS, TAKEAWAYS AND FINN'S HOUSE (AND NOT ALL TOGETHER)

One Friday night....

Let's talk about something light-hearted before we delve back into the ever more complicated network of Darcy's soul. Her life had quite literally given her lemons and then squeezed them into her eyes, stinging them, blurring her vision and making her cry. (Coz life's kind like that, int it?) Anyway, what I really want to know is..., has anyone ever heard of tuna pasta with peas? God damn peas! Sweetcorn, yes, but PEAS? It is just outrageously absurd. However, ...

One evening, after the sessions, Darcy was looking forward to eating. She was 'Hank Marvin' (ya know who I mean? The man who's always starvin? Kidding, it's Cockney rhyming slang for 'starving'). Tonight's dinner was tuna pasta, with... peas, AGAIN! She took a deep breath... and started on a rant about,

"Fuckin' peas! Someone's got an obsession with them here, I swear!" she said, as she looked around the room, as if to try and find the culprit? She knew who the culprit was, it was the bloody chef! *Where is he?* She wondered furiously to herself. (Well, I say furiously, it was more of a low hum of annoyance.) If she'd seen him, she would've probably had a laugh and a joke with him about it. (A bit like D'accord with the word 'ok'. It wasn't really that deep. However, …) "They're starting to give me nightmares. Last night I dreamt about a giant pea eating me!" She said with a stupid grin on her face, as Finn looked perplexed. "Seriously mate, what's the deal?" she said, laughing, as she looked up at Finn. Ladies and gentlemen – there he was – her beautiful little weirdo, munching away merrily on the dirty stuff, as if it wasn't something against the laws of nature. She shook her head, with a smile on her face that said it all. She loved him to the moon and stars. *That's my man*, she thought fondly, "Never change," she said to him laughing. He looked back at her with his mouth full, he was happy as a pig in shit.

"What's up with ya," he said, laughing at the look on her face. "I like 'em," he finished off.

"I just love you," she mouthed at him. She had to be careful. There were people around.

"I love you too," he mouthed back. She was tired at having to maintain the pretence that she wasn't head over heels in love with him. Don't get me wrong, as he was getting right on her tits and weighing down her socks, but the wait was going to be worth it. After dinner, Darcy was still starving. She hadn't touched one single bite of her dinner in silent protest, but nobody noticed, so, *Fuck 'em.* Instead, she and Finn decided to get out for a while. That meant she could find some food, without anything green, or round, for that matter. Plus, it served as an excuse to get away from prying eyes.

Finn went to his room to get his jacket. When he came back down, he found her waiting patiently in the pool room. They looked at each other, catching each other's eyes in a loving moment, before reverting back to 'casual'. They made their way through the building towards freedom. In a way, she was really starting to resent the place. It was as if she didn't ever want to leave her bubble of safety it provided, but the bubble was starting to feel overwhelming and suffocating; it was getting smaller and stifling her common sense. (Common sense! Wow, if she really thought she had any at that point, she was sorely mistaken. That had packed its bag and fucked right off, to a little town called 'Here-We-Go-Again'!) She couldn't wait to get started on the life that Finn was forging, to make it sound appealing (Darcy... hellloooo? Forged means being such in appearance only, and made or manufactured, with the intention of committing fraud, WAKE UP). She was getting itchy feet. It was all feeling very overwhelming and claustrophobic. But she had to wait it out. She was determined to achieve something in her life. She needed to finish this programme for so many personal reasons. Thinking about it, it was a big achievement. She wanted to prove to herself, and to him, that when the going got tough, she would stay and tough it out….

And folks, I'm not trying to tell anyone what to do. It's your life, and your story. However, it's true. If you are reading this from wherever you are in the world, and you're feeling like this in any aspect, remember, it's the similarities not the differences. Please stay strong. I mean it. Me and Darcy got your back bro! Keep strong. Keep tough and drive yourself to get to your goal, however far away you feel it is. Believe me when I say, you won't regret it. If your day is overwhelming your senses, break it down into bite-sized chunks. Sometimes you might even have to go as far as breaking it down into five-minute chunks. But YOU WILL get there eventually. That way, the pressure of whatever's going on for you, is easier to digest. Just remember – the only person you are cheating out of life is yourself. I hope, wherever you are, you find the strength that enables you, that gives you the power to help you believe in YOURSELF. If you make the right choices, and when you look back after the tough ride you're on right now, you'll see I was right (I always am…) and hopefully, you'll see just how far you've come. Just a thought. Anyway, enough about you, let's get on with this story, eh? I've got places to be. Oh, and you owe me a fiver, by the way! You've got this!

They were chatting away as usual, using muscle memory to navigate their way through the house to the small porchway at the front door. They had to walk past the office to leave the centre, and as they walked and talked, Darcy informed whoever was in the office, that they were going out, by shouting, "We're off out," as she walked by the office door. She was too engrossed in the conversation, to care who it was she was talking to. She just knew someone would be there, as always. As he opened the door for her, in a very gentlemanly way for once, usually, he was that unaware of his surroundings, that most of the time the door would quite literally bash her on the backside, she noticed he seemed miles away in thought. He stared at the small ornament of a church that was sitting on one of the two windowsills, at either side of the door. It was a quaint, little steepled church, surrounded by a graveyard (do you know the type I mean? You know, the type of ornament your nan would have). It was very pretty. Finn pointed to it, to draw Darcy's attention. She glanced at it, spotting the detail and nodded in recognition that she'd seen it, not really caring, she was thinking of her stomach too much to be arsed.

As they stepped outside into the car park, he said with conviction, "I'm gonna marry you in one of those, one day." He looked at her so seriously, his eyes wide, as if the wider they were, the more resolved he was, it made her smile and look away shyly. She couldn't help feeling that amazing high and felt a bit mean because she had initially thought to herself, *Oh, what now?* when he showed her it. She felt so loved. "I'm gonna marry you, in a church, with steeples and graves and that," he said again lovingly.

Darcy could tell he was being cute; she didn't quite know what to say, so she joked, "That's if I say yes," she said, nudging him gently, as they continued walking.

Wowzers! Everything was moving at lightning speed, but she was riding the rod (and no, mucky pups, I wasn't talking about that, 'wink, wink,' however, she was doing that too! I know! Dirty bitch!) It was all talk at the moment, until they got into the real world. There was no point in planning anything. Plus, there was no marriage proposal, rather than him telling her sweetly but very matter of factly. (Yeah! And you're still married, ya divvy, bigamy is frowned upon ya know. And no, for you lovely fact finders out there, that is not technically correct: bigamy is, in fact, a criminal offense in the UK, so without stating the obvious, it was a joke). It was a dream... for now.

When they got to the takeaway shop, she ordered a great, big, dirty kebab, with all the salad, and chips, with extra grease. Now, SHE was the happiest little piglet in shit. As she ate, he talked (and kept pinching her kebab meat.) She would have pounded him into the ground; however, she was too busy being happy, and she was rather fond of him on flat ground, not in it (for now at least anyway). She had her dirty kebab and her middle-aged, cheeky chav. What more could she ask for? She had everything she needed. #happydays

As they ate, he talked happily about his new house. Last weekend, he had been accepted for a place and was full of ideas for his 'fresh start'. Finn had been on the housing register for ages, trying to be rehomed and had been fortunate enough to be offered a new place, while he was in rehab, so he could break away from the tenements he'd previously lived in; they tended to house all the things, people and temptations, he was trying to steer clear of. The news he would be moving straight into a new home when he left, appeared to give him a boost. He was happy he wouldn't be going back to the bedlam! (Chaos followed Finn around, apparently; it never had fuck all to do with him! Or was he the chaos and simply just an absolute penis?

Finn was a lot more weather worn, with his exposure to class A drugs. He had more than dabbled in all sorts. She was a novice in comparison. Where he came from, drugs and alcoholism were rife. He lived slap bang in the middle, where everybody knew his name. Because he was one of those lads who still flew around the estate in his uncle's car, with fishnet stockings placed over the rear lights. He was with 'his boys'. Being proud of the fact that he was in his mid-thirties and still part of a gang, who called themselves 'The Knob-a-Tooies'. They would get up to all sorts of completely stupid shit. Although, some of the stories may have been quite funny to listen to, they were completely bloody stupid and sometimes dangerous. (You know, the kind of things you get up to when you're teenagers?) Darcy was surprised he had survived for so long.

Moving to a new home was the start of creating positive thresholds. They'd been talking seriously about the possibility of living together when they'd both completed the programme. Thwaite was still living in her house, as he hadn't found somewhere else to kindly disappear to. It was making Darcy uneasy. She certainly didn't want to go back to living with him, until he found somewhere else to kindly fuck off to. Finn had made it clear she was welcome to stay with him for as long as she needed; he almost willed it. She knew it was very quick, but somehow it felt right. Let's face it, they had started off living together, albeit in different rooms and under completely different circumstances, with many other people, but the thought of waking up and not seeing his beautiful little head every day, felt a lot weirder. The weekend before Finn went to view his new home, she went along with him. His mum and dad were there, getting the place ready, so he could move straight in, without much fuss. While they were there, she helped paint and pick out wallpaper for the living room. More and more, everything they did, the choices they made, were becoming joint ones. (Ya know, like a real couple?) *To be fair*, she thought, as she looked around, *it looks as if it's going to be quite nice when it's finished.* The garden was huge; it had a massive tree towards the back and was all overgrown. It needed a lot of work. However, Finn was someone who looked as if he was quite handy with power tools, so she had every faith he would make it a home. A perfect place to start again. Plus, she was always willing to get her hands dirty when it came to anything DIY.

As it transpired, it was about a mile and a half down the road and still slap bang in the thick of his old life, and a bit too close, where Helga was concerned. She lived just down the road, in Skanklington. Finn had told Darcy, in no uncertain terms, how nasty she could be. Plus, she had seen with her own eyes, the effect she had on him, so she was wary and protective of being too close to the chaos. Would Helga turn up kicking off? She didn't even know that he'd moved yet, but she would have to be told at some point, otherwise, eventually, the kids would've said something anyway. However, we're not there yet. It was a tricky one, because she was his kids' mother. Darcy could only hope that when the dust settled, everything would work itself out, and they could be amicable. (Ha-ha, sorry, I couldn't help myself. They both didn't know the meaning of the word. Quite literally! So, if ya ever read this ('amicable' is an adjective that means pleasant and friendly, especially in a difficult situation, where a dispute or disagreement could otherwise arise. It describes a situation, like an agreement or a divorce, which is reached without anger, argument, or hostility, indicating a desire for peace and goodwill between the parties involved.... Now ya know, ya bastards! And we all know they are simply not capable of doing anything without one drama or another.

Or you lovely readers, you will do eventually, for now you'll just have to trust me).

It was so close to temptation. It was on the top of a hill, so it had the potential to quite literally be a slippery slope. Especially if it 'snowed' a certain kind of white powder, if you catch my 'drift'. Oh dear, I do make myself chuckle at my genius at times. However, I in no way, think that drugs or drug abuse is funny, before the PC police come a knockin' at my door #not-in. However, she believed in him so much more than he did in himself and vice versa. (That's why she felt this unconventional relationship worked). He was adamant that this was it for him now. He'd turned a page and was ready to start his happy ending. She was still trying to act cool, calm and collected, even though she could feel herself being swept up in the fantasy land he'd created. Together we are unbreakable, together we are strong; she believed (it was as simple as that).

If she had been told that she was going to meet the absolute love of her life in rehab, she would've shot you down for the absurdity of it. This wasn't the direction she had planned. However, with him, that was a different story. It sounded like it could be wonderful. Starting a new life, albeit a shaky one. (In fact, it was as rickety as fuck.) However, Darcy didn't want to turn back now. She didn't want to fall into the abyss of the unknown, especially when Finn had cleared the pathway for them, and was showing her what her future could be like. He acted so sure that he knew where he was going, and if they got lost, at least he'd be there to help her find the way. Plus, she wanted to follow it through to the end, to see where it led. It was exciting. This is all bullshit. Honestly, her thinking was madness. On the one hand, he had shown her all the red flags (instead of seeing them as warning signs, Darcy, the daft cow, was making fucking bunting out of them) but he had also made her feel something she had never felt before. If you love someone, you take the good with the bad and all the little bits in between, don't you? Yeah, you do. But not shockingly ugly, surely?

Anyway… she finished her kebab with his help. After the long day of sessions and (don't even get her started on the peas again) it was almost 9pm. "We've gotta go back or we will miss curfew," she said, her body language changed, her shoulders dropped and there was an overwhelming sadness in her voice.

"I wish we could stay 'ere all night," he said, looking crestfallen. She touched his face, looking at him, drinking him in, like he was going to disappear.

"I know love. But we've always got tomorrow." She said, smiling and kissing him tenderly. They put the leftover food in the bin and had one final kiss. They embraced each other, not wanting to let go, before making the short journey back home, looking forward to tomorrow.

The next morning. Darcy got herself ready and made her way downstairs. She made herself a drink and went outside for a cigarette. They were allowed out for the day from 10am right through until 9pm. Darcy and Finn were going to his new home again; this time they would be alone. They were off to fit a carpet in his new living room. Oh yeah? Is that what you kids are calling in nowadays? However, they had to wait because it wasn't quite 10am, and the particular member of staff on duty that morning, was well known for being pedantic. (I've just Googled the word pedantic, and yes, if any of you are wondering, I have used it in context). So, there was no point trying to get out now. Even if it was a couple of minutes early, there would be absolutely no point trying to leave until it was 10am on the dot, she simply wouldn't allow it.

Finn was already there. They'd already concocted a plan last night, to hoodwink the staff into thinking they were going off on their own separate journeys. There was an ever-growing suspicion that needed to be quelled. The plan was for Finn to go first. Then she'd meet him around the corner, and they would head off together from there. Claire was sitting in her usual spot on the bench along the back fence. They were chatting about their plans for the day. Now Claire knew everything (ya know? Girly chats!) and she was questioning Finn playfully. Darcy felt happy and chilled, however, *calm down love*, she thought, as Claire was delving deeper, to find out his intentions for her friend. Or maybe she was just a nosey parker, who knows? But Darcy could feel the love and protection from her without a shadow of a doubt.

"Would you ever have any more kids, Finn?" She asked. He was leaning against the wall with his hands in his pockets. He didn't flinch or shy away, he answered straight away.

"Yeah, a hundred percent. I'd definitely want more kids with you," he turned his head to look over at Darcy, who was blushing fiercely. He looked as if he was half joking, trying to gauge Darcy's reaction first, before fully committing into full blown surety. "I'm gonna marry her in a church, the same as the one in the doorway." He said to Claire, then looked at Darcy for confirmation. Her body tingled in a nervous 'Oh fuck' moment. They hadn't been using protection and she was late. Only by a couple of days, however, *careful what you wish for,* she thought.

"Well, it's not like we've been careful," she said, giving Finn the side eye.

Darcy's mind went wild with thoughts. So come join her on this little thought train for two seconds, well maybe a bit longer than two seconds! She was already married, for one. (For the second time, I might add. You will come to learn, as the story later unfolds, that Darcy was to become the woman with Twenty-Seven Dresses and not one single, decent, fucking, husband to her name. However, she knew all the good divorce lawyers in town). She didn't even know if she wanted to ever get remarried. She certainly, before now, had never even contemplated having any more children. But Finn made it feel like a fairytale. Would she have her happy ending? (Pha-ha-ha, I think we all know where this is going. For now though, come join me on Darcy's saccharine fuelled journey; the quixotic feelings of love and adoration, for what the modern-day world would call a (narcissist-a-twat – a mutational form of a narcissist, with a hint of twat. P.S., ya can have that one for your Oxford Dictionary. You're welcome).

She had made such a mess of motherhood and if she did have any more kids, there would be a huge gap in ages. To have another crack of the whip at motherhood, and getting it right this time, felt like she would be doing the children she'd already birthed an injustice. She loved them so much and wished so badly that she could have a do-over with them. She would've even forfeited her one wish for thicker hair. But they were amazing kids. Who was she to turn back time? She loved them the way they were. Who's to say that they would have been better off, if life had gone a different way? Anyway, it was all very much a brain fuck, whichever way she looked at it. It felt like it was too late. In her eyes, she was over the hill and far away, with creaky knees and an onset of diabetes at play, oh, and forgetting what she'd walked in the room for. What made her think it would be any different now? She had wasted her prime years with a man who was two decades her senior, drinking herself into a state of oblivion. To say he wasn't really 'a family man', would be putting it mildly. In fact, she could remember once, when she and Thwaite were on a plane to Rome, there was this kid of about five years old, running up and down the aisles, misbehaving. To be fair, the kid was annoying most of the passengers on the flight, however, what Thwaite did was uncalled for. The tight bastard stuck his leg out and the boy went flying. When she gave him a look of disgust, he simply looked at her with an air of cold detachment, as if it was completely normal for a fully grown man to deck a stranger's kid and then, he nonchalantly called the cabin crew over, to order another drink.

Marriage, and kids with Finn, was something that she would definitely consider, even though in the back of her mind, locked in a box, was a little voice, telling her to be careful. She knew though; she had convinced herself that he was her soul mate. It would all depend on whether she could make him believe it for longer than five minutes at a time; that he was the man he wanted to be, and not the failure of a father, he so often told himself (and her) he was. She flitted from thoughts of seeing small slivers of *Nope… you're pissing me off*, to where a split second later, his loveable side would shine through, which made her sure. (And yeah, I'll say it again. They weren't exactly being careful, so the possibility of having more kids was a probability.)

"I'm going to pick up a test for you Darcy," said Claire, looking excited. Finn started joking about baby names involving rehab.

"Rehaberto," he said, looking very pleased with himself.

To be fair, she thought, as she giggled to herself, *that was very quick-fire wit,* and she laughed as she said to him.

"Don't joke about it, ya divvy," she said. It was all making her nervous.

She checked her watch, and it was now just after ten. "You ready?" she said to Finn, as he stood up straight and looked ready to go. "See you soon then," she said, as he left first. She hung back for about ten minutes before signing herself out of the building, walking down the road and round the corner, where he was waiting impatiently.

"Ya take the piss mate," he said, sounding slightly annoyed.

"What do ya mean?" she responded, wondering what she had done to get that sort of reception. (He did that kind of thing all the time.) He would do or say something to get her on the brink of annoyance, or fear of what she had done now. "What are you moaning about now? She said, feeling slightly deflated.

"I've been waiting ages to do this," he said and smacked a great big kiss on her lips, grabbing her waist, pulling her into him for a few seconds. Before pushing her away playfully and grasping her hand. She looked at him smiling ear to ear.

"Aww, you little cutie. You ready to go then?"

They made their way into town to catch the bus. He had let go of her hand as they walked, just in case anyone saw them, and they talked as they went. The further into town they travelled, the safer they felt being themselves. They messed around, piggy backing each other through the shopping court that doubled up as a shortcut. Right then, just as he was in the middle of telling her something, he stopped dead in his tracks, as if he had seen the most magnificent thing in the world. *Oh no,* she thought adoringly, *what is he up to now?* She turned her head to look around for the culprit. "Oh, fuck me!" she laughed. There in the middle of the shopping court was an old piano. "Why don't you have a go?" She said to him, still giggling at his face, as he walked over to it. "Come on love, show me what you've learnt," she said, encouraging him, and laughing with happiness as she said it. She could see pure elation displayed clearly on his face and it was amazing. He was so easily pleased by the smallest of things and the fun just simply oozed out of him, infecting her with adventure. She took her phone out and recorded him. He took out his fingers, stretched them like an orchestral pianist and pressed down on the keys. The tune rang out loudly, echoing through the whole shopping court, as he played: BAA BAA, BLACK SHEEP... HAVE YOU ANY WOOL? YES SIR, YES SIR, THREE BAGS FULL. ONE FOR THE MASTER AND ONE FOR THE DAME, AND ONE FOR THE LITTLE BOY WHO LIVES DOWN THE LANE.... *Yes!* She thought with glee, as the pride swelled her stomach and burst its seams. That was the first time he had managed to complete the song all the way through; she couldn't be prouder of him if she'd tried. It was as if he'd just completed Beethoven's fifth symphony.

He was clearly just as pleased, as he shouted, "BOOM," and did a victory lap, with his finger running up and down the piano keys, playing each one in turn, making a loud noise. He looked up at Darcy jovially, as she continued to record his antics. "Turn it off," he said playfully. There were people walking past and watching them messing around, carefree, as if there was no one else in the world.

"You did it love," she said to him with sheer joy in her voice. Little did they know that they had been seen laughing, joking and kissing by one of Helga's mates.

All of those 'piano lessons' had paid off. Whenever she would teach herself to play at rehab, he would come over and want to learn. She could only try to teach him so much, as she was a novice herself. However, he would still insist on budging her over, to sit on the small stool next to her and distracting the living life out of her. He was playful and those moments always made her feel like all her troubles had washed away, only to be replaced by the loving frustration of trying to teach the man with the ADHD brain. She would go over the same bit with him again and again, as he got frustrated with himself. He was painstakingly unteachable at times and would get her to the point of wanting to wrap the keyboard around his fucking head! His brain was always on overdrive, and he was always so loud, but it just went to show, he did listen, and he could do it.

After his marvellous performance. They continued on their way to catch the bus. When they got there, Finn checked the timetable to see how long they would have to wait. It wasn't long before the bus pulled up and they got on. It was a double decker. They paid their fare and made their way upstairs to the top deck, where they sat together, simply being Finn and Darcy, boyfriend and girlfriend, in love. "I can get used to this," she said to Finn contentedly, looking up into his eyes. He put his arm around her, and she nestled into him. She could have stayed there for a lifetime, pretending as if it was just the two of them, with nobody else around. She felt so content. They had such a laugh that morning. The piano memory would be one she just knew she was going to savour for all time. He kissed her on the forehead and pushed her away gently. She sat up in her seat, feeling her face going slightly red. *What have I done now? Why has he moved me away?* She tried putting her hand on his leg, but he moved it off, "What's up?" she asked quietly, feeling herself sinking into self-doubt. What had she done? Just as she was about to start falling any further into the land of 'Does-He-Still-Love-Me', he said something that made her laugh with relief and a little bit of pride (she couldn't deny it).

"Nowt love, I've got a boner," he whispered, as his face flushed. She looked at him, then the bulge in his shorts, as he tried pushing it down, willing it to go away. She smiled mischievously, as she felt the lead weight in her stomach lift.

"I thought you looked as if you were pleased to see me," she said, winking at him.

The rest of the bus journey was uneventful. They did what they did best, which was talk. Most of the journey, as they got closer to 'home', consisted of him showing her different places of his childhood. He had more or less lived around the same general area his whole life, never really going further than a couple of miles down the road each time, however he had lived a very colourful life by the sound of it. (You don't know the half of it mate). She enjoyed him retelling stories of his past, however, as she listened, she noticed that they all involved him getting up to one mischief or another. From what she was hearing, it sounded like, what she had on her hands, was a gigantic man-child, full of playful charm and mischief, but she enjoyed getting more insight into what had made him who he was today. Some of the things he told her were vile, in all honesty, but who was she to judge? At the end of the day everyone's got a past, including herself, so what kind of hypocrite would she be to call him out on it? It was in his past. What kind of person would she be to tell him she thought some of the stuff he told her was borderline 'WTF and runners?' She knew who he was now, or she thought she did anyway, so all they could do was go from here. She wasn't going to let it ruin their future.

They arrived at their stop and made the short journey from the bus stop, up the road, to his house. He opened his front door, allowing her to go inside before him. He pinched her bottom playfully, chasing her along the hallway. When they reached the first room, he kissed her deeply before they both rolled up their sleeves, looking around and marvelling at the work that had taken place since the last time they were there. It looked completely different. The bare walls now had wallpaper on them and all the woodwork had been painted. "The wallpaper looks really nice," she said to him, as she slowly spun herself around, looking at the room in a 360-degree angle. "This is going to look lovely, once the carpet and laminates are down and you've got all your furniture in," she said to him smiling. "Aww Finn, I'm so happy for you. You've got this. It's just gonna be ace," she said, jumping into his arms. "I'm so glad I met you. Honestly, I'm so in love with you. Never forget that. I'm just so happy for you," she said, before kissing him. They clung in the moment for a few seconds, before he put her down carefully.

"I'm glad I met you. Honestly mate, I don't think I could've done it without you," he began, as she started to frown. "Well, I could," he said, looking at the frown on her face, as if he knew what she was about to say. "Ya know what I mean?" he said, looking at her, as she nodded, letting him know she knew exactly what he meant. She felt the same way. She knew she could've done it without him, but there's no way she would've wanted to. She wouldn't change him for the world. Well, she would maybe have managed, if it was a little less complicated, however, she loved him in spite of all that. "Right stop," he said smiling, pulling her back towards him and giving her a final kiss. "Let's get this carpet down," he said, putting his serious cap on.

"Right, ok, what do you need me to do?" she asked, clapping her hands together, signalling she was ready to crack on.

They had fun while they worked. Finn had a comedic charm about him. He was always in his element, whenever he was doing something technical like that. She laughed along with him, in absolute contentment. *This is my life now,* she thought fondly. It was chaotic. Anything he did was, but it was so much fun. Even something as simple as laying a bit of old carpet, had her sides splitting painfully with laughter. It was actually harder work than it looked. It was so heavy, when they tried dragging it into place and fucking awkward, because of the size of it. He was effing and jeffing, using phrases such as, "Bag of shit. Ya dirty dog. Oh no," and "Ya 'aving a laugh mate!" Trying to get the piece of carpet to reach the door to the hallway, was a whole new adventure. They had such a laugh trying to force the carpet under the door so that it would reach. He was on one side, and she was on the other, shouting unclear instructions to each other, in vain attempts to get it right. However, they persevered. It was teamwork. But it was nothing short of a comedy sketch in itself, that would never do itself justice, if ever it was attempted to be written or spoken out loud (so I'm going to leave that up to your own imaginations. I can't do everything for you, now can I?)

"Nah, ya tek the piss," he said, standing up with beads of sweat forming on his brow. They'd spent absolutely ages trying to make sure that the carpet would reach all the way around. The room was mostly a simple rectangle, but there was a small added bit, just as you walked into the bedroom, which made it slightly more complicated. After all that effort of cutting around the main area of the room, there was a small sliver of floorboard that was visible and bare. "Bag of shit," he said, laughing slightly, as he looked at it. However, he couldn't deny he was happy with his work.

"It'll be alright," said Darcy, coming over from the other

corner of the room to join him. "All you need to do when you do the laminate in the bedroom, is bring it over the threshold slightly, and then just get one of those silver things, you know?" she said, trying to do the action, to explain what she meant, "You know what I mean?" She finished, looking at him. He looked bemused and had a look that told her that he'd known what she'd meant from the start and had simply just enjoyed watching her in her struggle to find the correct words. "Twat," she said, laughing, as he cuddled her, wrestling her to the floor playfully. He followed her, as she crawled around the carpet on her hands and knees, pretending to escape from him. He grabbed at the waistband of her jeans, which were getting lower and lower, until her bottom was fully exposed. And poof! her trousers seemed to magically fall off! Oops! How they'd managed that you'll never know. I'll leave it there. We don't need to go into how she ended up with carpet burns. Leave them alone. They were in love.

The rest of the day was uneventful. Except her trousers magically fell off – a few times more! It was so strange, so did his, for that matter! Hmm… anyway, they spent the day as a proper girlfriend and boyfriend. When their trousers had finally stopped falling off, Finn's friend came over, and he remarked at how happy and healthy he looked. Forest was a childhood friend, who had been in and out of touch most of his life. He was a true friend, and he was so pleased to see his mate doing so well. Darcy smiled at the two catching up and felt happy. *I'm just happy. We can really do this*, she thought to herself. *We might really be able to do this, you know?* Darcy relaxed into the idea of 'What Will Be, Will Be' (along with the tune – you know the one I mean!)

13. MEMORIES… LIGHT THE CORNER
OF MY MIND

It was looming, drawing nearer. On the one hand, *Thank fuck-a-doodle-dandy*, on the other hand, she felt a great sadness at the thought of saying goodbye to this part of the rehab process. There would soon be the final stretch and the next big test. She was now living her life in complete contradiction, very much like Finn (against all her better judgment of him, she was sure!? Or even if she wasn't, she was certainly willing it to work, if nothing else.) However, she had been provided with the tools and coping mechanisms to manage on her own. Soon, it would be time for her to be given a little more freedom to make her own choices like a 'big girl'. (Oh, if only they knew how much she still had to learn, they would've grounded her for life and put her over their fucking knee.) She couldn't see it, but she still had the emotional age of a toddler. However, every bird has to fly the nest at some point, don't they? And…, I always seem to be bitching about Darcy's choices, so I will say, begrudgingly, that she'd gained hope and perseverance. The programme was working, yet the tools they gave her, were to remain on the back burner until a lot later on.

It was almost time to make the final move to the basement, where the self-contained apartments would expose them to a lot more freedom, to make the right choices for themselves. Wait…, we are not quite there yet. I am here to tell you of a couple of stories that don't quite fit in anywhere else. Like I said, this is Darcy's time and her story. Trying to find a timeline in the mish mash of such loving memories is hard, but she still wants to share them, in the hope that if you are to ever embark on the journey she was going on, it may give you hope. So, let's call them short stories if you will. Let's begin, shall we?

Kitchen Duty With the Tornado Who Could

One morning, she had been tasked with kitchen duty. During the residents' stay, at some point, they would be expected to help out in the kitchen. She did this a few times (how many is a few I hear you ask?) Well, I really couldn't tell you, as Darcy's mind is like a sieve. Ha-ha! See what I did there? I know, it's hilariously cheesy. Also, an item you might find in the kitchen. I could go on with this silliness forever, but we have a story to tell, and I've only so many more words before I hit my word count, so I'll get on with it.

It was at least twice that she can remember. One time was of course with Finn. (How could it not be? They were in lurve) however, he wasn't meant to be on the rota that particular day, although that didn't stop him. He took over the kitchen entirely. She and Kelsie were rushing around, trying to make sure everything was timed right, so the food could all go out all at the same time. There was sausage, bacon, eggs, mushrooms, beans and hash browns, all cooking away. There were all sorts of things going on, and then, there was Finn! Pissing about playfully, and fiddling with the hob settings, moving Darcy out the way to look in the cupboards, because he was a nosey git.

There was a wide array of other circus shit being performed. Then he was chirping in his opinion, "Their burning, turn them down," he said, as he tried taking over completely. It was like trying to cook breakfast for twenty plus people, while trying to deal with a swarm of wasps, a classroom full of toddlers and three radios all tuned into different radio stations at once. To say there was bad language, playful laughter and shouting, would be an understatement. The chaos was utter madness. She couldn't help but cry with laughter, as he and Kelsie, who as mentioned before, argued like brother and sister. Finn wound her up so much they almost ended duelling with spatulas and kitchen towels, which doubled up as makeshift whips, before the breakfast went out perfectly. The rest of the residents who could all hear the commotion, gave them a round of applause when it was all over. Finn, and God only knows how he managed it, did a really good job. *The lovable divvy bastard*, thought Darcy fondly, as she recalled the memory, laughing loudly as she did so.

Making Breakfast with D'accord

Another kitchen activity was with D'accord, under the same sort of circumstances. However, this time, the setting was in the much smaller staff kitchen. The reason for this was that the main kitchen's oven and hob had gone kaput (it means broken) so panic reigned. Darcy quickly saw quite clearly that D'accord had no clue where to start, so naturally she took over. She started, quite literally, telling him what needed to be done. "Right, we can do this. It's no biggie" she said, talking to herself more than anything, but it looked like he needed her words of encouragement more than she did right now. His eyes looked like he was in a sheer panic. "What's up with ya?" she said, laughing. "Have faith, all will be well. We can do this! Well, maybe we can't, but we're gonna give it a bloody good go? Right, those hash browns can fuck off," she said, as she slung them to one side. D'accord, looked at her queryingly, with a raised brow. "I'm sorry for swearing, mate, but we don't have any space to be pissing about with those bloody things," she said. "But desperate times call for desperate measures, and I'm sorry to inform you, that swearing might just have to be a part of the process." She finished off her little pep talk, as D'accord fell about laughing. "What happens in the kitchen, stays in the kitchen," she said, "it's a bit like Fight Club. However, let's just hope we don't resort to fighting. I quite like you mate," she said matter of factly, "but the jury might be out after this shit show!" she exclaimed, looking around at the space. "Look at what we've got to cook with," she said, as she looked at the feeble little cooker. "Come on though, let's do this." She rolled up her sleeves, as they set about putting the rashers of bacon on the grill tray and more on a couple of oven trays. D'accord seemed to be frozen in awe at how she had taken over without faltering, "Erm, sorry to be rude mate, but am I doing this all by myself?" she said, ribbing him into giving himself a boot up the arse.

The long story short is that they chatted, as they rushed about in a disorganised fashion. They talked about a song she had been writing and how much she felt she'd learnt during her stay to date. She was rushed off her feet, trying to turn sausages and flip bacon. She had given Finn the task of using the main kitchen's microwaves, to heat up tinned beans and tomatoes. It served the purpose of making him feel loved and involved, yet kept him out from under their feet, while they dealt with the main chaos. Her brain was on ten things at once, as she turned and passed D'accord the frying pan from the stove, "Here, it's hot. Stick it in there," she said, pointing at the sink.

"OUCH!" came D'accord's voice from behind her. She spun around to look at him in concern, as he grasped his hand, with a pained look on his face that immediately turned to a mischievous grin. "I'm only kidding," he said, as he began to laugh.

She felt a rush of relief, completely forgetting for a split second, who she was talking to, "Don't do that, ya silly bastard." Just then, the pair of them both stopped dead in their tracks. Darcy had a look of complete shock on her face at what she had just blurted out. D'accord's face matched hers. "I'm sorry," she said apologetically, "I'm sorry, I didn't mean for it to come out like that, you scared the bejesus out of me," she said to him, as he looked just as apologetic to her. They simply looked at each other and laughed until they cried. It may have been one of those moments where you had to be there, but you weren't.

Girly Night In

Darcy, Kelsie and Finn were inseparable for most of her time there. The nights that they spent, with the radio belting out (when the staff allowed it) playing pool and dancing (sometimes on the chairs) were times of organic and pure fun, leaving a feeling of elation that no night out on the lash could beat. The good times they shared were countless. However, there's only so much pool that 'one' can play, before 'one' wonders what else there is to do, without simply getting into trouble.

One night, Kelsie decided it was time to have a break from the 'usual' and brought down some facemasks from her room. Of course, Finn wanted to join in. Why wouldn't he? He was a big girl's blouse, who'd spit his dummy out of the pram if, heaven forbid, he thought they were having any kind of fun without him. She and Kelsie applied their own masks to their faces, in the bathrooms downstairs, where there was a mirror. They then both took it in turns to apply the third mask to Finn's face, as he sat on the dining room chair. (Applying it to himself felt far too girly for Finn's liking) so he allowed the two of them to smear gloop on his face. It was one of those peel-off masks, you know the kind? The ones that peel your actual face off along with it. Anyone who knows and has tried the ones I mean, will know full well, not to get it too near the eyebrows, or any kind of facial hair for that matter (and the consequences of doing so!)

The evening was meant to be pampering and relaxing, but don't forget, this is Finn we're talking about. The word relaxing was not in his vocabulary whatsoever. The drama that ensued as a result of him having peach fuzz, was nothing short of comedy gold. When the three of them were together, Darcy would completely forget where she actually was. There was no other place she would rather be at times like these. The simple act of peeling the mask off his face, was like he was being subjected to torturous hell. Darcy had to bribe him with lollipops and sweets to shut him up. It was jovial, fun and completely bat shit crazy.

The next night, she was bored. *Last night was so much fun*, she was thinking of ways to recreate the initial tone, which was meant to be relaxing, without the repetition of the Finn 'drama queen antics'.

Darcy, Kelsie and Finn were in the pool room. The girls were relaxing. She was doing some of her drawing, while Kelsie was on her phone and they chatted about nothing in particular. Darcy looked up every now and again to watch Finn, happily playing pool with the other members of the house. He was busy doing his own thing, and so was she. It was nice, being in the same space but not always in each other's pockets.

Darcy took this as a great opportunity to spend some girly time with Kelsie to talk about boys and 'girly' shit. "Shall I do your make up?" she asked Kelsie, when she looked up from her phone.

"Yeah, deffo mate. I've seen some of the stuff you've done," she replied, looking eager. Kelsie leaned forward in her chair, "When do ya wanna do it?

"Shall we do it now?" Darcy said, looking pensive for a

moment. As if she was thinking the same thing.

"Yeah, shall we do it now? He's busy doing his own thing, so we might get some peace and quiet," she said quietly, as she glanced over at Finn. Darcy looked over to check if it would be safe for her to move, without him realising his two besties were plotting to spend some time without him (how very dare they!) He looked so engrossed in his game, laughing and cracking jokes, while everyone ducked for cover every time he took a shot, in case any of the balls went flying off the table.

Everyone took the piss, "Wow mate, you actually kept the ball on the table that time," said Arnold, as Finn potted a ball.

"Ya tek the piss mate!" said Finn, as he started to celebrate his success before it was cut short, with realisation that he'd potted the wrong colour ball.

"Shame, your colour blind, an all," said Arnold, "two shots, thanks pal."

"Yeah man," said Darcy, as she jumped up to go and put her artwork in her bedroom. "I'll go get my stuff. We'll go to the TV room, it's quieter there." She said to Kelsie, who got up to go and wash her face….

I'll cut a long, drawn-out story, short. They were settled. Darcy was prepping Kelsie's face, ready to apply a foundation to it. It was relaxing away from the distant cheers and laughter of the pool room, a hallway away, and then guess what? …Yup, Finn peeped his little face around the door. *Oh no*, she thought comically. *Here we go.* He walked into the room. It was as if a sixth sense tingled inside him. She could see his brain ticking away menacingly, as if she could hear his brain say, "What can I touch?" spotting the bag of makeup and immediately rooting through it.

"What are you doing?" he asked, as he rummaged through her bag, as if it was his own.

She stopped what she was doing and stared at him stupidly. "I'm crocheting a hat," she said sarcastically. He looked disbelieving and confused for a split second, as if his brain couldn't compute the sarcasm. "I'm taking the piss, ya divvy. What's it look like? I'm trying to do her makeup…. Leave that alone. Put that down and step away from the bag," she added, as she laughed lovingly at his curiosity.

It was painfully frustrating to try to keep a handle on his impulses at times, but she wouldn't have him any other way. He was who he was, unapologetically. It wasn't even as if he was arrogant with it. Whatever he did, there was always an underlying mischief.

"I want mine doing," he said, jokingly, "make me beautiful," he said, batting his eyelashes and laughing.

Kelsie simply burst out laughing. "You just can't keep away, can ya? Aww, yeah, do his after you've done mine, ha-ha-ha. I dare you to get yours done Finn," she said, unable to contain the excitement in her voice. It was as if she was playing dress up with her little brother. "Oh mate, you've got those wigs too, ha-ha-ha!" She looked as if all her Christmases had come at once.

"I'll do yours after Finn, just put that fucking makeup brush down and behave," she said, pushing his hand out the way, as he attempted to put eyeshadow on Kelsie. Darcy could feel the change in atmosphere. The room went from calm and tranquil, to one that was full of fun laughter and chaos. She loved this place so much.

She finished Kelsie's makeup, with a nervousness about her. She hadn't done makeup on someone else in a long time. It was nice to see she still had the magic touch. Kelsie went to have a look in the mirror in the bathroom.

"Right, ya little div, sit down then," she said laughing. Trying to act normal, she began to put make up on him. "Sit fucking still then," she said sternly. "How am I meant to put makeup on you if you don't keep still? Divvy," she laughed at him, as he sat up straight and gave her a look, as if he'd just been told off by his mum. Darcy was waiting, hoping Kelsie liked what she'd done.

"Ok me lady," he said, flirting, "don't be making me look stupid," he said, as he looked up at her.

"Finn, I'm putting makeup on you. You're going to see what you'd look like if you were a girl," just as Kelsie came into the room looking both shocked and pleased.

"Oh my God, Darcy, I love it, I really love it. You're doing my makeup every day from now on." she said, "seriously, I'm gonna sneak in ya room. I love it!"

Once Darcy had finished with Finn, it took them a while to stop laughing. It was silliness and fun. He chose a red wig and put on Darcy's dress, which she had run upstairs to get. She stood back and marvelled at the finished article. He looked like a complete doughnut. There was no way Finn could ever pass as a woman. There was not one single feminine bone in his body. She was having the best laugh. She nearly peed herself with laughter. He decided everyone had to see him dressed as a girl, so Darcy and Kelsie followed him around the whole house, knocking on everyone's doors, pretending there was a new girl in town!

Kelsie Leaving

It was now Kelsie's time to leave; she was further along in the programme. She was having an existential crisis of her own. On the one hand, she had rebuilt her life so much; she was confident in her sobriety and herself, to a certain extent, yet on the other hand, she was scared she was going to falter without the bubble. She worked hard to set things in place for when she got out and was now attending the 'New Tidings' college, to become an alcohol support worker. She wanted to give back. Like most people who cross this threshold in their life, they find their 'calling'. They know how hard it is and gain a passion to help others. Darcy noticed that for Kelsie, leaving rehab was very much like it was for her when she entered. Kelsie was now worried that they were going to forget all about her, like she was 'that' throw away.

"Ya best not forget about me," she said the night before she left.

"Yeah, like anyone's gonna forget you, ya dickhead, are you off your head? We'll be coming to see ya, as soon as we get the opportunity," said Darcy seriously.

"I'll forget ya," said Finn. "I think you're a cunt," he said, but his face didn't lie. There was a definite tear in his eye as he said it, the big softie.

The Stone Angel

Darcy and Finn's attempts to get away from prying eyes, meant that they walked round the towns and the local park, far too many times to recount. Their only chance to be 'themselves', was to go for walks. On the bright side, it was exercise. *Let's face it*, she would think, trying to justify herself for breaking the rules. *At least I'm getting my steps in.*

In the middle of the park that they frequented, there was a big statue of some famous (unknown to them) person. Darcy wasn't really paying attention, neither did she care who the statue was of. She was far too busy living in the moment, as the sky gave up its light for the day and she could gaze at Finn adoringly, as the streetlights shone on his face, making him look dark and mysterious, as they walked hand in hand or chased each other around. He picked her up and she wrapped her legs around him in a loving embrace, as they walked, not much caring where they were going.

Around the statue was a big square of gravel, so naturally,

like any two sane people would do, they laid down, side by side and watched the stars as they made 'gravel angels' (very much like snow angels, except a lot more painful, as the stone scraped her bare skin.) People must've thought that they had nipped off into the bushes for a 'quickie', with all the scratch marks that little game caused, however, I can confirm that there were no 'bush fucker trials'. They kept it PG. It was completely random. It felt light and freeing, not caring what people thought, Darcy just felt adventure. She marvelled at how the smallest of things felt like a fairy tale. (She may just be a cheap date, and ever so easily pleased…. Darcy, you need to up your game mate. Anyone watching the pair of you could see it for what it was, which was two tits, laid on the floor, where tramps piss and dogs shit (and I don't mean homeless people, I'm talking pissed up scruffs) flapping about like an idiot. People who saw it would probably have thought they were pissed! Oh, the irony!

14. AND NOW, THE END IS NEAR…

"Heigh-ho…. Heigh-ho, Heigh-ho. It's off to…' the basement 'we go. With a shovel, and a pick, and a…'. Erm? No. Sorry, that's the wrong story, isn't it? This isn't Snow White. There was no poisoned apple (fermented fruit wasn't allowed on the premises) or any magical kiss, which could wake the living dead (because, let's face it, that's technically what Snow White was when the prince kissed her, and Finn certainly wasn't any Prince Charming. Unless, you were saying, 'Charming' ironically, erm…Anyway…).

Even though there were seven of them in their group, none of them were dwarfs. Plus, there was only four rooms in the self-contained apartment downstairs (in the basement). So, the whole group was split up for the last three-week stretch. There was no shovel, pick or 'heigh-ho, hic' either. Did you know there never has been a 'heigh-ho, hic' in that song? I've just Googled the words to that particular tune, and I'll be blessed if I know what version Darcy listened to her whole life, because it certainly wasn't any version I can find on Google! Also, thinking about it, she did take a shovel and a garden hoe with her, when she could bring things in from home, during an earlier time, before she became too caught up in Finn. She had originally planned to use them to spruce up the garden. Ya know, just in case, however, she should've been using them to dig a hole, a big one…to put HIM in! The garden tools were Angela's husband's. Come to think of it, he did look a bit like Doc! (one of the dwarfs) Hmm? Anyway… instead, there was a wedding dress, keyboard, amplifier, microphone, four huge canvases and God knows how many bags of clothes, amongst the pile of crap that she'd brought from home. When the time came to drag her stuff to her new room downstairs, she had to employ Arnold and Finn's muscles to help her make the three or four trips to move it all. They were really sporting and helped without moaning once (and if you believe that, you'll believe owt). No, they moaned like fuck, the whole fucking time!

Finn moved into his new room a few days before the others and loved it (at first). He now had his own kitchen. It was as if he was the lord of the manor. Darcy laughed at him with a feeling of relief. *Maybe he'll be ok after all?* She thought hopefully, but there was no denying it, she couldn't shake that feeling in her gut. Ya know the one I mean? When you can just feel something is going to go 'BOOM, BANG, OH SHIT?' Yeah, that one! He thought it was fucking great until the realisation hit him, that now he'd have to cook for himself. To be independent and isolated from the hustle of the main house. He reverted straight back to his pre-rehab diet of noodles and other shit. Although, *to be fair,* she thought, *he did buy other things with his shopping budget, such as sausages and broccoli. That didn't mean he was going to cook it,* she thought sceptically, but the good intent was there. *Darcy, ya dick,* she thought angrily, as she berated herself quickly, *give the poor bastard the benefit of the doubt.*

The evening Finn moved into his flat, she snuck down

the hallway to see him (yet again). And once more, she had to use her best ninja moves, and silent tippy toes, to get to the 'love of her life'. He proudly showed her his new surroundings and food purchases, as she sat at his kitchen table with a cup of coffee, from 'his kettle'. He was so excited and kept giving her kisses, "I love you," he said. The flat was on the same floor she was, for now, so it wasn't as dangerous as it was about to become.

"I love you too," she said, smiling coyly. Everything else that mattered, melted away when he smiled this particular smile; it's inexplicable (so I'm not gonna try to explain it. Just trust me). "But we're playing a dangerous game, ya know, love?" she said to Finn nervously, as she drank the last dregs of her coffee. "It's so close to the end. I just don't wanna fuck it up for you or for me," she said, willing him to understand the danger in what they were doing. "I won't be able to come see you anymore. We'll have to wait 'til the weekends. Don't forget we get home visits now," she said. She was getting worried. Every time she embarked on her dangerous visits to see him, they'd got longer and longer. She wanted to be there all night, to wake up next to him, and to have him hold her all night, but there was always a knot of nervousness in her stomach, and head. *You're gonna get caught, you bloody idiot! Is it really worth getting thrown out for? For God's sake!* (He wasn't even worth getting out of bed for, in the end. However, hindsight was a superpower she had yet to acquire. I guess that is where the saying, 'you live and learn,' comes in handy).

"Yeah, I know, but I like it when you come and see me," he said (fucking selfishly, the selfish twat…. Oh, I'm sorry, I apologise. I just caught myself in a moment of indignation. What I meant to say, ladies and gentlemen, is that I will cut it short there, because that's all he could ever really say).

The staff had split Darcy and Finn up. She couldn't prove it, nor could she protest too much, for fear of further arousing their mounting suspicions, but she knew why they'd done it. *They bloody know.* She thought angrily. They could see behind the ruse that she and Finn were bullshitting. In other words, they (the staff) knew they'd (D&F) been shagging, and they (D&F) knew that they (the staff) knew they (D&F) knew. (I know what a head fuck! Try reading that straight away and understanding it, because I couldn't, and I'm writing the bloody thing! Plus, it's a blatant reference to 'Friends', when Rachel, Phoebe and Joey all find out that they know about Monica and Chandler boinking) but no one said anything. It was a very unnerving time. (As if they didn't have enough to contend with). The staff knew Darcy and Finn were flouting the rules, they just had no proof. Anyway, there was nothing either of them could do about it now, they just had to sit it out and wait, almost like a standoff, without words. *It's only three weeks*, she thought to herself, but that didn't stop Darcy stewing on why the staff had done what they did. It wasn't in the best interest of Finn's recovery, and that's all she cared about.

He should have been downstairs with his group. Keeping him away from his support network like that, didn't make any sense to her whatsoever. All she could do, was to keep strong and maintain her resolve. *If we can get past this together,* she thought, with determination on her side, *then that is when our life, as a couple, can truly start.* She longed for a life of sobriety and for them both to achieve, and complete something they could take pride in. It hadn't been easy for more reasons than most. Not only because it was one of the hardest personal journeys anyone should have to endure in their lifetime, but because they'd complicated it by falling in love. (Sounds cute when you say it like that doesn't it? But they were just naughty. Oh, and they were also 'numpties'!)

He was upstairs now, and she was down in the apartment with Claire, Moss and Arnold. At first, the staff didn't appear to make too much fuss about Finn coming downstairs. *Maybe this isn't going to be too bad after all?* she thought, as they all settled themselves in. It was lovely and spacious, and the kitchen was huge. Darcy shut what would be the front door behind her (if it was a real apartment). From entering, there was a long corridor, twice the width of the ones upstairs and no creaky floorboards or fire doors in sight. It stretched as far as the eye could see. At the end, she could see what looked to be a large living area.

She stood at the doorway for a few minutes, leaning back against the door, with her head pressed against it, drinking in the place that was to be her home for the next three weeks. Her whole being was worlds apart from when she had first entered. She felt fixed and empowered. But…, her thoughts took her back to her new surroundings once more. She couldn't help it. *Are you taking the piss?* she thought, laughing out loud to herself. Her laugh echoed through the long hallway, as she was filled with an overwhelming sense of freedom. Chuckling to herself at the irony, she thought stupidly, *Why couldn't this have been the hallway I had to sneak along, instead of that stupid one I've been creeping down, like something out of a comedy sketch?* She shook her head in bemusement. *I've been creeping through that fucker upstairs, like I've been auditioning for a Laurel and Hardy sketch.* She laughed freely, as she looked around. Immediately to her left, were three other doors. She looked through each one in turn and saw they all housed communal bathrooms; one had a gigantic wet room with a bath. She sized it up in her mind's eye. It looked bigger than the one upstairs somehow. It felt luxurious and spacious. She couldn't help it. She felt excited to be here, but the pang of guilt she felt in her stomach at Finn being upstairs and alone, began to take over. *No!* she thought to herself, *NO, Darcy! Embrace it. This is your time too.*

There were four other doors along either side of the long

hallway, which led to the bedrooms; she made her way down to the end. The large living area was warm and inviting, with a dining table against the back wall, which could comfortably seat four people around it. *And,* she remarked to herself as an automatic reflex, *we can always plonk Finn on the end if he ever comes for tea.* He was never far from her thoughts. *Maybe they'll let him come down for dinner?* However, it was improbable. She couldn't wait to get started on making the house a home and immediately began to nest, looking through the cupboards and making a shopping list of what they might need for the week ahead. Even though Claire was 'the mother' of the group, she was quite content to let Darcy take over the role and display her domestic skills. Claire had become rather complacent and happy to remain idle (in the nicest possible way of course). In other words, when Darcy 'started at it', on her mad mission to clean the place, Claire didn't bicker, neither did she protest, and Darcy was grateful for the opportunity to prove her worth, and usefulness. (She isn't just a pretty face after all).

She couldn't wait to get started on trying to show how independent she was. She was more than ready to manage her own home and look after the people in it. There were still a lot of things that had been left over from the group before her. However, *The dirty bastards,* she thought, as she noticed that even though the kitchen was clean on the surface, it hadn't had a proper clean in a long time. Naturally, everything had to be emptied out, cleaned from top to bottom and put back again; organised!

Darcy was sitting on the kitchen floor, knife in hand, stabbing away fiercely at (Finn… nah, I'm only kidding) the ice mountain that had accumulated in the freezer. The thought of leaving it in that state was giving her nightmares. It was like, if she left it, then she was going to open it and see Jack Nicholson's face, like in The Shining, popping out at her, with his maniacal grin. As she hacked away at the ice, she remarked out loud how anyone had managed to use it for its original purpose, "How the fuck have they managed to get it in this state, fucking thing!" Just as she was mid stab, she heard a familiar voice coming from down the hallway. She felt a tingle she couldn't explain. It was Finn! For a moment, she was lost in the idea that he was home from a long day at work. She felt a peace and comfort in her heart, she wished would stay forever. Claire and Arnold were in the living area, chatting away as he entered.

"What you sayin', me lady?" he said, as she tilted her head back to look up at him and he leaned down to kiss her lips, just like the original Spiderman did with Mary-Jane Watson, in their famous upside-down kiss). She had been with Claire to the local supermarket, put the shopping away and added an extra sparkle to the place.

"Get a room," said Arnold, in a bored voice. Finn squeezed her shoulder tenderly before he went and said hello to the others.

While she was defrosting the fridge, they all chatted. About what? She was only half listening. Finn began talking to Arnold about a girl from his old estate. She turned her head to listen, as he announced proudly, that 'this girl' had been in touch. It was as if he wanted a reaction, and a reaction he got.

"Oh right," said Darcy, "what did she say?" she asked, as if she knew he was waiting for her to ask.

"She just said, hi and that I'm looking well and that," he said, but the way he said it, was as though there was more to it. Everyone could feel the mood in the air change slightly. Claire and Arnold were half listening to what was being said, while they attempted to continue their conversation, but too nosey to fully commit.

"Oh right, well that's nice then," she said smiling, feeling relieved that that was all it was. "You are looking good love. You've put weight on, and you do… you're looking amazing. It's nice that people can see that you're doing it! I'm proud of ya," she added, as if reconfirming to him how gorgeous he was, and she continued hacking away at the ice. However, Finn seemed insistent on carrying it on with Arnold. Now Darcy didn't quite know what was said. But, during the confused chat, she distinctly overheard Finn say something about 'Dirty Debbie'. Straight away, Darcy looked over and asked, "Why call her dirty?"

Frowning, Finn replied, "Coz she's a proper dirty bird," half laughing, again, as if there was something more to it. She could feel herself getting pissed off; she knew he was trying to wind her up in front of an audience, almost as if to show her up. *For what gain?* She thought furiously

"So? How do you know that she's dirty? Have you slept with her?" She questioned him. *Why has he suddenly started talking like this?* she thought, her cheeks flushing; feeling angry and confused, as to why he seemed intent on taunting her with only half the information.

"Yeah, I wa' seein' her for a bit. Why?" he said, smiling in twisted satisfaction, as if he was saying, "yeah so!" obviously loving the look of confusion and jealousy on her face.

"Right ok then, can you please take her off your contacts then?" she asked him nicely, feeling slightly uncomfortable, as Finn was laughing again.

She was trying her best not to rise to the baiting. He was having a laugh with Arnold and looking over at Darcy's face, full of cold-hearted bravado, at the way he was disrespecting her in public. It didn't suit him one bit. She knew Finn was unfiltered and he said things 'as they were'. (It's not 'as it is' though, Darcy, is it? He was taking the full-on piss. When are you gonna stand up for yourself? Look at him, he knows he can walk all over you). His attitude was cold and disrespectful. She was processing her thoughts in her mind.

It wasn't so much that a woman had been in contact, it was the way he seemed to revel in telling her.

"Why would I do that?" he challenged, as he laughed at her face, which was becoming angrier. "What's up wi' ya?" he said making his cute face; however, it wasn't cute this time, there was an ugly side to it that she was seeing coming through. He was enjoying winding her up. Claire and Arnold were now protesting his attitude, trying to explain human emotions and how they work. Finn just seemed to fight against every word they were saying, jumping to the defensive. "I hardly know her really. I only smashed her once," he said, laughing at Darcy's utter frustration. He then proceeded to do the actions! But nobody was laughing, not even Arnold (who was what some may call an MCP (a male, chauvinist, pig).

"Come on pal, that's not good," said Arnold, shaking his head, as if to recoil in embarrassment, not knowing where to look. Everyone could see the obvious hole Finn was digging for himself; he didn't just have a shovel; it was more like a crawler excavator; he was digging his way to fucking China. Darcy was just aghast at his callousness; nobody was backing up his protests. It all got to the point where Finn realised he had gone too far, but instead of saying sorry, he looked over at Darcy.

"I'm not even bothered about talking to her. I love you, idiot! Why should I have to tek her off, eh? I told her I met someone. YOU!" He said, jumping to his own defence. He was too stubborn to admit he had taken whatever sick joke he was playing, too far. He walked out shouting down the hallway, "How am I in the wrong 'ere? I di'nt even contact her, did I? I wunt dare mate. How am I getting shit for this? It's wrong, you're all off ya heads!"

Darcy shouted down the hallway, "Because you're a fucking dick. Why tell me in that way, eh? What the fuck did you expect? Get fucked, you big baby!"

Whoopsie daisy, ladies and gentlemen. All I will say about that little shit show that unfolded, is that they'd had their first row. She felt publicly embarrassed and then shamed for her reaction. And do ya wanna know what the silly bitch did? I think you've guessed it. She was the one to apologise to him. (Wanker!)

Now things were at a point where she felt as if she'd set up a constant validation station, simply for Finn, where he'd take a ticket and she'd then suck the life out of herself, by becoming indignant on his behalf. (The argument they had about 'Dirty Debbie', was swept under the rug but Darcy never ever forgot it). He would take a small thing that should have been relatively drama free and turn it into a situation that was worthy of its own TV show. She'd stick up for him and his ever-growing disregard for the rules, as if he wasn't blatantly flouting them, or taking the piss. (Nooo! He was just a 'hard done by' angel and not some idiot man, who did whatever the fuck he wanted and then cry about it whenever things didn't quite go according to his plan). But like the annoying little contradiction that HE was, SHE couldn't help but laugh. That was the problem. On the one hand, he was being a complete cock-a-doodle-do (that's not a swear word, it's just what cock-erals do!) but on the other hand, she couldn't help wanting to protect him, for the sheer innocence of him and his thinking process, plus, he made her sides split and her cheeks sore with the amount of fun and laughter he gave her. He had managed to laugh her into his bed and heart with it. Well, that and, "Do ya wanna play pool?". It was so simplistic but in the most genius of ways.

Alas, he was his own worst enemy. Some of the things he did, from an outside perspective, came across as though he lacked empathy, and let's not get her started on his gauge of human emotions (let's just say, it was well and truly broken, she'd ordered him a new one from Amazon, but it was yet to arrive). Darcy was drained but she loved him no matter what.

It was hard to argue with him too much. She could see his frustration; completely understood it, to a certain degree, "Why split you up from YOUR group?" She said scornfully when it came time to console him. "They know you don't cope well with isolation. They know you hate the idea of being left out," she said to him, one night, after a slightly heated argument with a member of staff. Finn actually did himself no favours, with his swearing and typically unfiltered responses, to their insistence that he had to leave what he was doing and go to his room.

"I wouldn't mind, but you were being quiet for a change," she said, jesting, making light of the shitty situation, in a poor attempt to make him smile. But he was in no mood. He simply looked utterly deflated.

"I wouldn't dare," he said angrily. "I don't see why you lot get to be down here, and I have to go back up there, on my own," he said furiously. He leaned forward and planted a kiss on her forehead, more forcefully than usual. "I'm gonna get in shit for that now," he said moodily, realising that there was bound to be repercussions for his tantrum. (Well idiot, try learning to talk to people properly ya dick). However, that's not what she said, nor what she thought at the time. She validated him, when really, she should have pointed out he was making everyone feel uncomfortable. None of them wanted Finn to get into trouble, everyone had a lot of time for him, but he was becoming unmanageable with his dickhead antics.

Some may call him rude (he was) but he didn't mean to be (see there she is, doing it again). He couldn't control himself when he felt backed into a corner and he would lash out by talking over people, until he defeated them. It was as though he tired and wore people down, until they agreed with him, just to shut him up. He would not stop; he was getting so pushy. He was also too used to getting away with doing what he wanted.

"Why? You weren't doing owt wrong then," she said angrily, only focusing on his side of it, getting herself worked up, the more she thought about it, trying to hold her frustration intact. She wanted to blow. "You weren't doing fuck all wrong," she added, feeling herself about to pop.

"I love you, can't wait till we're out of this shit," he said, as he walked away down the long hallway, to the door leading upstairs to his room. He took one look at her for a moment, wanting to say bye or something, at least, but his mood wouldn't manage it. She could see his crestfallen face before he walked away and disappeared off to his room.

She was so annoyed on his behalf, that even after he left, she was still stewing it over in her head. *Why isolate him so close to the end?* She was fearful he was just going to give up and leave. She knew he would instantly regret it if he did. It certainly wasn't doing anything for his mental health. It was all getting on top of her, but their stance strengthened her resolve even further. *Yeah!* Darcy thought to herself, whenever she could feel herself about to blow her top with him and nick his hat. *Just be patient, he's worth the wait. Of course he's lashing out. He's bound to be going through emotional shit.*

She wanted him to win at life and complete what he'd started. Not for her but for himself and his kids. The one thing he never stopped talking about while he was there. He was lashing out at the rules and the staff but really, all he was doing was giving them the mounting evidence and ammunition, to justify their decision to oust him back into society and the real world, before it was his time. She thought about it all with venom. The place that felt so loving and warm, now felt cold. She resented the place. She resented them. When he was allowed down with his group, he would sit quietly and engage in normal conversation with the 'fabulous four' downstairs. When he wasn't chatting to Arnold about the gym and fitness, he would sit with Darcy at the dining room table and draw on a spare canvas she had. She remembers fondly that he drew a lion that he had copied from her pencil tin. She was amazed at how well he had managed to capture the essence of it. Well, not amazed, because she knew he had talent, but she didn't know that it extended to drawing as well, and by the look of pride on his face when he had finished it, neither did he. It wasn't fair. Why couldn't they just let them be? (Erm, Darcy, they did tell you mate, they gave you horror stories about it and they did tell you that relationships were prohibited… so, wounded! All you did was take it to mean that you belonged together. So…?)

Just as she was talking to Claire about all the drama, Finn rang. She answered the phone.

"Hey, you ok love?" she said in a soft voice, hoping he had calmed down.

"Nah mate, I'm not having it. I'm gonna smoke 'em all out," he said mischievously. "If I can't come down there, then we're all going to sit in the car park," he finished. She could hear the chaos of pots and pans being flung around and could hear something sizzling over the phone. Darcy panicked. She knew he didn't plan to burn the place down, Finn wasn't that malicious, but set the fire alarms off? Abso-fuckin-lutely, he would. He was signing his own death warrant, but he had tipped his own scale of 'fuck it'.

"Ya what?!" she shouted, jumping up. "What you doing now, you idiot? Don't do shit like that love. We have less than three weeks. In fact, it's almost two now." She looked at Claire, as if she didn't know what to do. "Why the fuck does that stupid man have to make it so hard sometimes?" she said frantically. Claire and Arnold were sitting in the lounge area, listening in, watching Darcy panic. Arnold gestured to Darcy to give him the phone so he could say something. She put the phone on speaker at Arnold's silent request. Finn got what he wanted; they all jumped in, talking at once. Trying to get him to calm down. (He was an attention whore, big time).

"Yeah, I know your angry, pal," said Arnold, "but don't do… don't… daft… that's what they want you to do," he finished wisely.

"Nah mate, I don't care, I wunt dare," he laughed stupidly, as if hoping they would all laugh along with him. He was always trying to get people laughing but this was complete absurdity. No laughter came, so he continued… "Can you fry sausage and broccoli in water?" He said, ignoring their pleas….

I'm just gonna brush past the stupidity of that question, as it doesn't deserve an answer. It was almost as stupid as when he'd asked her if she could get pregnant from swallowing 'you know what'?

"I'm gonna have to go up there," she said defeated. "Fuck! Why can't he control his impulses? Big fucking baby, throwing his toys out of the pram." She chuntered angrily. More and more, it felt as if she was becoming his babysitter. (She should've just left him to his own devices, but how could she? Part of this was her fault. If they hadn't flouted the rules, then this wouldn't be happening.) She'd have to make the dangerous journey upstairs to calm him down. Claire and Arnold looked at her, as she was having a meltdown about the dilemma she faced.

"Just be careful Darcy," they said to her, as she made her way upstairs.

It was the hairiest journey of all time. How she didn't get caught, is a wonder that still, to this day, she had no clue. It was utterly inane (means fucking silly (Darcy added the fucking). If she got caught, they would've both been thrown out, however, I *can't just do nothing*, she thought to herself. It was a whole different version of The Titanic moment, when Jack tells Rose, "'You jump, I jump, right?'" Awww, Darcy, look at you justifying it as a romantic moment, ya dick. You do realise, all you were really doing was rescuing a man from ultimately making something extremely shite for dinner. She wasn't, it was a lot deeper than that. He was in his head and didn't know how to get out but it was risky. He calmed as soon as he saw her, but she could clearly see that he was struggling. However, the only way to deal with him, when he was having these types of moments, was to be there for him. She turned his tactics back at him and turned the heat up (it wouldn't have done anything, except perhaps open up their pores, with all the steam). His face changed slightly, as if he was expecting her to come and either have a go at him or start panicking. Instead, she sat calmly at the dining table, waiting for him to let his mood fizzle out. He eventually turned the hob off himself.

Over the next few days, it was hard. It was as though she was on an emotional rollercoaster. Trying to carry on her journey but still on constant high alert in case his mood changed. He was getting more argumentative by the day (not with her but with others and himself.) It was as though he was trying to push everyone to breaking point, to see if they would inevitably walk away, but everyone (the residents) were really patient and supportive. Plus, to top it all off, Helga was now asking by text and shouting in the background during phone calls with his kids, with all the diplomacy of a steaming pile of turds, who the 'slag' was (meaning Darcy) that her mate had spotted him in town with. When Finn relayed the conversation back, Darcy got the feeling he'd only told her half the story. He wasn't in the mood to go into detail and Darcy knew his spirit had already fucked off to 'my-dim-coconut' (it's an almost anagram of 'I'm a moody cunt'. I know what you're thinking and yes, she is a cleverly sarcastic little dolly – maybe she needed to work on that a little bit?). So now Helga knew about Darcy and was less than happy that he appeared to have met someone in rehab, adding the caveat that, "Don't think she's ever coming anywhere near my kids," and "you're not havin' 'em if ya with her. I'm not having 'some druggie bitch near my kids." Darcy didn't know what to do or say. She didn't want to cause any trouble, and she certainly didn't want to get in the middle of something. However, Finn reassured her again, that she was the 'love of his life' and that he 'wanted to spend the rest of his life with her'. It was reassuring. He also made it clear that even though Darcy was an integral part of his life now, his kids needed to come first, in the respect of waiting until the time was right for her to meet them. It only made her love him more. The strain it added, only powered up his knobheaddery. He wasn't coping with all the pressure that was coming from all angles. He seemed to adopt the air of 'I don't care'; he was no longer embracing the programme and was treating everything with scepticism. "It's all a load of bollocks," was his new favourite saying. She was willing for the end.

However, he was still content in flouting the rules, as if testing the staffs' resolve. The next day, during the session, he was called into the office, which only made matters worse. When he came out, he revealed that he had received a written warning, for kicking off with the staff. They had no idea that he had tried smoking everyone out of the building. If they did, then he would've been out on his ear. She had to admit, although begrudgingly (because Finn could do no wrong in her eyes) that he had flouted the rules constantly throughout. It was never anything serious. However, he'd explore parts of the house he wasn't allowed in and insisted on trying to help do things, like taking over kitchen duties, and he was becoming moodier and needier. He wanted the spotlight, so he could act the fool and shine like a 'polished turd', instead of the diamond, she knew was hiding underneath all that homemade bravado. It was funny but it saddened Darcy, as she knew he could be a top-notch fucking legend, if only he gave himself half a chance. He seemed happy to seek being the centre of attention in negative ways. He was like the lovable naughty kid in class. Even when he was in the wrong, she would convince herself he was well within his rights. He'd disappear to his room during breaks and some of the session time, such as art therapy, because he saw no benefit in it. Instead, he pissed about designing a clock for Arnold, with the word CUNT on it! He was petulant when he was asked to do what was expected of him. (*Blabbity, blobbity, arghhh! Finn, just fucking behave!* Is how she felt in the moments he would express his dickheadery.) Darcy felt like she was constantly having to walk on eggshells. Trying to be the calming influence was getting harder, but the thrill of the ride was something she couldn't deny she craved. He was becoming stubborn and yielded to the pressure, as though separating him from the group, had stirred something up inside him, making him revert to some of his old behaviours, especially the one of 'cutting his nose off, to spite his face'!

Darcy's attempts at talking him out of his own stubbornness, seemed to be her new role in their relationship. Now, he was also becoming weird about her being married. He was mentioning it more and more, through throwaway comments. "You're cheating on your husband wi' me," he would joke. The joke wasn't funny, and clearly untrue. She and Thwaite had been over, long before she had met him and he knew it, however, he would still say things that made her feel like she was being dirty and cheating. So, like she always did, seeking to prove her love and commitment to him, she applied for a divorce. It was going to cost money that she simply didn't have but she justified it to herself by thinking, *it needs to be done at some point. Why not now?*

I'd just like to take a moment here, to regroup and check in with you guys reading this. It was a crazy time, in which she was trying to embrace the change and get her head around the ever-looming end herself. Trying to process everything that had happened in such a short space of time, but she couldn't take her mind off of HIS struggle. How he felt, became more important. She could see he wasn't coping and she tried understanding him. Not wanting to give up on the man who had changed her entire life. Even through her struggles with him, she learnt more about herself than she'd ever done before and had so much fun learning how to be silly, how to let go and how to find the daft hidden meanings and loopholes in things, that only he could find. He was becoming erratic. However, the deep understanding they shared, meant all she could think was, *he needs me* (which he did) so she made herself too available to be his emotional sounding board, confidante and… just say it Darcy, go on you can admit it. You were his emotional punching bag, whether he intended it or not. He may have been making you happy, but he was draining your resources, love. He was depending on Darcy subconsciously, to soothe him, rather than learning how to be himself. She didn't truly know him at this point. How could she, really? The setting was such a confined one, with so many pressures. She just knew that she wanted to believe in them – in him – and she ignored all the warning signs. She saw in him, what he could never see in himself. She didn't want him to just give up. At times he looked as though he was faltering; when it felt like he was giving up the fight, she would drag him back on track. She saw the potential. He had the ability to be a great man. The only person who didn't believe in him, was himself. Darcy's resilience and resolve had always held fast when she had fallen in love. Easy to fall into, hard to get out of. Which meant she excused the inexcusable, accepted the unacceptable and gave people more than enough chances to be the best versions of themselves. In the end, she just got used and hurt. He knew all of this. She knew all of this. She knew he knew all of this too. It's maddening. Remember that diamond Darcy could perceive within him? Yeah, well, Darcy would do well to remember that diamonds are multi-faceted, and in this case, she'd only been looking at the forward-facing sparkly bits, and although she'd seen some of the darker bits, she chose to ignore the flaws in the jewel!

Today, they were all venturing into town, to go to a meeting. Now they were on their new timetable, they were going to a lot of resources from outside the comfort of the house. *What good's this gonna do anyway?* she thought. It was all well and good finding local resources to fall back on, for when she was back home, but she didn't live around there. She didn't drive, and the way she was feeling, she didn't know how any of this was going to help anyway. *What's the point in continuing to talk about it; highlighting the fact that I am damaged? I'm not craving as much now, so why do I need to keep going on about it?* I think the technical term is complacency. The most dangerous place she could be. Her mindset had her kidding herself that she could do it all herself. Fighting against support. She didn't want to feel like she was different to the world. When she left, she and Finn would work it out from there.

I'm going to do a quick stop here, as Darcy now freely admits in hindsight, that her attitude was the absolute wrong one to have. Never kid yourself into thinking you know it all. Never become one of those dicks, who think they are above falling through their own cracks. People helping people, brings about so many benefits. If you're going through the same mindset – that help is for the weak or there's nothing more you can be taught – think about it like this: your input and your presence may also be a source of comfort to someone else. If you think you know it all, don't keep it to yourself. Share your knowledge with others who have been in the same boat as you. Help your fellow kin. If, like Darcy, you're not the type of person who likes to go to meetings religiously, then don't do it religiously, do it for you. However, make recovery a priority. Let's face it, you spent enough of your life making your habit a priority, why can't you save a little time each week, to give back? Just a thought. Anyway, enough about you and all this self-reflective bollocks, lets jump back to the mindset Darcy was in, the 'moody Margaret'....

As they walked into town, Arnold, Finn and Claire all chatted and laughed as they went. Claire seemed to be looking forward to what the meeting was going to be about, and Arnold was too busy moaning that it was cutting short his gym time. Finn was content with messing about, as he piggybacked her through town laughing.

The meeting itself went by in a haze. What it was really about was unclear. She had stopped listening. She had stopped caring. (Darcy was doing what so many people tend to do in rehab. Falling into the trap of thinking the code was cracked. Nose-diving into the mentality of thinking that asking for help and admitting you are powerless over your addiction, makes you weak, when really, it makes you stronger. She was already thinking dangerously. She was too wrapped up in him.) She was leaving the meeting early today because she was meeting Jaxon in town. Finn, who was always by her side, came along for the ride.

As they walked through the town to get to the coffee shop meeting place, they chatted about the group session. However, she was far too wrapped up in him, to take in much of what they'd said in the session, as they'd been too busy texting each other, covertly under the table. Even when they were in the same room as each other, they still couldn't get enough. He had the ability to make a mundane afternoon feel exciting and freeing. Everything was brighter when it was just the two of them, but adventure and chaos were never far away. They could relax into each other, instead of all the lying and sneaking around they had to do back at rehab. She was mid conversation when she saw a seagull, its wing clearly broken. It was in the middle of the road, stopping all the traffic (and no it wasn't the local lollypop lady). It looked as if it had given up the fight and had accepted its fate…. She couldn't help but want to help. "Poor thing," she said to Finn, as a bus came round the corner, "Jesus! Look at the poor bastard, it's gonna get splattered. Maybe we should help?" She grasped his arm and nestled her head in his chest, unable to watch the poor bird's imminent execution. "Go get it love, we can't leave it there," she said, nudging him. The town was busy and there were people everywhere. He didn't need much encouragement; he was so kind-hearted when it came to anyone or anything in need. He walked straight over to it and put his hand up to stop the bus and other traffic, which was edging closer, and tenderly cupped the bird in both hands. As he walked back over to her, he looked comically panicked.

"What the fuck do I do with it Darcy?" he said, laughing at her laughing.

Well, ladies and gentlemen, oh dear God, what can I say? As soon as Finn looked into that gull's eyes, he fell in love, he was gripped, as if he had found a new best mate. He called it Steven (shall I tell you why, or have you heard it before? He called it Steven, as in Steven Sea-gal – I know! Because he's a funny bastard).

He had now adopted Steven. He was immediately making big plans for the future. All while they were walking, he had Steven cradled in his arms. It did not protest or put up a fight; its wing was too damaged. Finn took that to mean that the bird liked him back. He was so comical.

"I'm gonna look after it, then, when it's better, I'm gonna go fishing with it and it's gonna come back to me, with dinner for both of us," he said happily. Darcy wasn't sure anymore if Finn was being serious or if he was joking, however, the adventure of it all was exciting. Her 'loved up' brain took her imagination…. Finn, her and this fucking seagull – on a boat trip, where the water was calm and they were sipping their iced coffees, totally in love, while Steven was merrily perched at the side of them, as the smell of fresh fish was cooking nicely away on a small disposable barbeque. *Silly woman*, as she belly-laughed through town. While he talked excitedly about Steven, her thoughts switched to Jaxon, she couldn't wait to see him. When they met Jaxon, he looked so pleased to see her. She ran over to him and hugged him tightly; however, he looked as confused as fuck!

"Erm, Mum," he said puzzled, "who's this and why has he got a dirty great seagull with him?" Darcy couldn't help herself. She fell about in stitches of laughter, as Finn passed Jaxon an open hand and introduced himself, as if he had known him for years. Jaxon took to Finn straight away. Granted, he thought Finn was a bloody nutcase. Darcy could see straight away that Jaxon felt at ease, as he laughed and joked along with the absurdity of the situation. She was chuffed to bits that he looked happy to see his mum, as they chatted away, drinking coffee, and Finn sat happily attempting to feed Steven biscuits.

On the journey back to rehab, Finn was still insistent that he was going to keep the gull as his pet, in his room. The closer they got to 'home', the more the realisation hit Darcy, that Finn wasn't joking, and she started to feel unnerved. "It needs to go to a vet or something, or you'll need to put it somewhere quiet, away from people and hopefully it'll be alright, but we can't take it back."

"Nah mate, I'm keeping it," he insisted.

"Finn, seriously, it needs a vet. They won't let you have it in there, come on now! What do you think they're gonna say? Please take this seriously. You can't keep playing games your whole life. You're not a bloody vet," she said softly, as if trying to explain to a toddler, why, just why this was not a good idea. "They are not going to let you keep him. FINN, stop please, stop being so fucking stupid." It made Darcy's head swell and explode with frustration, that he didn't take any notice of her pleas. While her treacherous heart surged, for the fact that he wanted to nurse and love this seagull back to its full health, as she could see his eyes light up and his mind work overtime, thinking about the adventures he and this fucking seagull were going to have together.

How the fuck do you explain to a fully grown man, who is a bloody idiot and acts out like a fucking toddler, why he can't take a fucking seagull back to rehab as a pet? Also, how do you do this without falling about laughing at the absolute absurdity of the situation, encouraging his lunacy, when in reality, it's fucking insane? Furthermore, why didn't this behaviour trigger a 'get me the fuck away from this little weirdo' reaction, from Darcy? And only serve to love him more? DARCY, wake up. You have fallen in love with a MANCHILD.

It's all a bit of light-hearted fun… until it's not. When they got back to rehab and knocked on the doors to be let in, the staff behaved just as she'd expected. However, Finn insisted that he wasn't leaving the gull outside to die (which was fair enough) he kicked up a fuss. So much so, that in the end, they allowed him to take it downstairs to the apartment's garden and wait for a member of staff, to have someone come to take it to the vets, which was also fair enough. However, Finn wouldn't leave the issue alone. He was insisting and arguing, to the point where Darcy seriously thought that they were going to ask him to leave. He went on and on and on. Eventually, someone came to remove

Steven and take him to the vets. It was a tearful goodbye (nah, it wasn't I'm taking the piss.) Finn's a bloke, so he hid his tears under a veil of moaning. He chewed the ear off anyone who stupidly agreed to listen to him and how unfair it was that the staff had taken his poorly seagull away from him to a vet who, may I add, would be able to provide better care for him. Darcy tried her very best to be as empathetic as she could, however, the sarcastic, unfiltered bastard accidentally slipped out in poetry form. Oops....

"I once had a seagull, but it didn't fly away,

"The staff took him from me, and it ruined my whole day.

"When you learn to fly again,

"Please come back to me,

"Then we can go on an adventure, right by the sea.

"I looked right in his little eyes, and I fell in love,

"I rescued my poorly seagull,

"I really found true love.

"Then Jason, the bastard, took him,

"He stole my precious baby,

"Steven, Steven, please,

"I truly love and miss you on my knee.

"I nearly shed a tear and had water in my eyes,

"I miss my poorly seagull,

"I hope you're still alive.

"When I looked at you, my heart just swelled with pride,

"Why did you leave me?

"Why did you have to go?

"I miss you so much, Steven,

"I hope that my love showed,

"Even though you shit on my shorts,

"And shit right in my hand,

"I love you that much, that I completely understand,

"That you are just a seagull,

"And that's what seagulls do,

"Whenever the mood takes them,

"They simply have a poo.

"I know I'm being mushy, and you do not know my name,

"Just call me Daddy, without you, my life won't be the same."

Needless to say, Finn didn't see the funny side. (He did, he simply liked to play act indignance). Fighting the urge to laugh. He looked at Darcy, with his face full of disbelief and awe, "Have you just written that now?" He said, as if he was genuinely impressed, but didn't want to show it.

"Yeah, you've just seen me. I've not moved from this spot. I've been listening to you having your meltdown." (What she really meant, was that she had been dipping in and out of consciousness, while he had been having his ten minutes of whingeing, like a big unfiltered baby, however, she couldn't quite bring herself to say it like that to him.) "I just thought I'd write you a poem to remember Steven by," she said, trying with all her might to make her voice sound as caring as she could. She was taking the mickey, but he knew there was no malice.

He stared into her face for a few moments before saying, "Ya tek piss mate," laughing and shaking his head. "Ya tek piss." Her response to his mood, of writing a funny poem, had the desired effect she had hoped for. It settled him down to a quieter version. He still moaned about it. Alas, she was yet to find a cure for that, however, he seemed, once more, happy and chilled again.

15. UTTER SHAMBLES AND SHIT

Right, ladies and gentlemen. Finn wasn't chucked out that night. However, the moving target that he had on his back, was now steadfast and wide open for the powers that be to make the 'kill shot'. He had been flouting the rules. His behaviour was erratic. His completely unfiltered charm had worn thin. He was still the lovable, charming, squeezable piece of eye candy she fell in love with; however, as previously stated, he was ever more prone to bouts of the 'Gremlins'. It was hard to keep a track of his moods. (In other words, Darcy was on constant high alert, in case anyone got the bastard wet, in any way, shape or form). The staff were becoming wearisome of having to pull him up on the little things, such as swearing, or butting in with childish remarks. She could see he was trying to keep the resolve and spirit he had come into rehab with, alive. It was as if he'd been darkened with a resentment of being kept away from his 'rehab family', and her. He had become so used to getting away with his schoolyard antics that he found it hard to know where the line was anymore, and to which he had danced dangerously close to crossing. (It was hard for him to take anyone's warnings seriously because people couldn't help but laugh, even though they were completely serious, when they warned him that he was taking things too far).

The next morning the high tensions from the night before had left a really bad taste in her mouth, like pine nut syndrome: After eating pine nuts, some people experience a lingering metallic or bitter taste in their mouth for a few days, or even weeks, according to Healthline. (Just in case anyone was unaware. See, it's not all about Finn!)

Darcy was woken up by a gentle tap on her door, as Arnold entered to bring in her usual morning coffee. This morning, she was however, hilariously embarrassed when she heard him put the coffee on the table.

"Morning," he said, with his usual, straight to the point tone, "erm Darcy, sort it out mate, you've got a load of Chewits stuck to your face love," he said, amused, yet confused. And then he left the room before she'd even opened her eyes. *Damn those midnight munchies*, she thought, as she picked them off her face, laughing to herself. Now this could be a long story with intricate detail, however, I am running out of metaphors and similes, and 'he said', 'they said' etc., so I will break it down, because she can go on a bit, I don't know if you've noticed? Plus, it's all starting to hurt my head. I don't know about you?

Today was the day she was having her final review. It was a meeting with the big boss, her key worker and her alcohol support worker, from the 'outside land', where she usually resided. The end was looming; she felt so shaken by the whole experience. There had been so many high points but now, like she said, it was all beginning to leave a bad taste. But she had to admit, she felt she'd come a long way from the shivering, scared little girl, who had lost her way. (Darcy's self-reflection is at the end. That way we don't run the risk of repeating ourselves). She was nervous about what they were going to say, plus, she couldn't concentrate. She could hear a commotion, as the doors to the apartment flung open and Finn was shouting down the hallway, as staff were following along, trying to get him to calm down. "They've been in my room! Nah, I wunt dare! Someone's been in my room," he shouted, ignoring everything they were saying back. Just before she could get to him, to calm him down, David appeared at the apartment doorway. He calmly but authoritatively said:

"Finn, come with me."

This is the very last thing I need, on today, of all days, she thought. The tension in the air of not knowing what was going on, lingered menacingly. No matter what it was, she knew it wasn't going to bode well for Finn. Maybe, just maybe, they were going to take that 'kill shot'? She couldn't think about that now, she had her own shit to deal with, but how could she concentrate on herself now? How? When the man she loved was in obvious distress. (Erm, Darcy, I want to scream at you but there is no point, as I know from the past, you can't hear. No, wait, you can hear but you probably won't listen anyway – but YOU ARE IMPORTANT TOO!) She would have to wait it out and act like any normal resident, who wasn't so emotionally involved.

How she managed to get herself ready and get herself to the meeting, when all she was encumbered with, were thoughts of him, I cannot say. *Is he ok? Fuck my life man. I hope the little bastard's ok,* was all she could think. It was all a very big, hazy blur, but she did (like she always does; she finds the strength from God knows where. Darcy is a survivor who runs off nervous energy and worry for other people. It was easier than worrying about herself. Darcy, take your own advice from time to time, eh? Remember it's ok, not to be ok. Even as I am writing, she is giving me the raised eyebrow look, not too happy that I'm turning her own advice against her. (Wounded). She tried acting as if nothing was wrong. She sat uncomfortably in the swivel chair, in one of the session rooms, listening to her key worker regurgitate all the formalities, as her head swam with the nightmare of the unknown.

She was trying her absolute best to act positively and embrace the meeting ('best foot forward' and 'all that jazz', ya know?) It was an important part of HER recovery after all, but she wasn't in the mood. Especially when she was asked, "How do you feel your recovery is going so far?" She began to answer the room at large, with all of the positive things that she had embraced through the process, when she was cut short by the 'big boss', Karen. She chimed in….

"Erm no, Darcy, I don't think you've come as far as you think you have, have ya, really?" The 'old toad' looked at her, with her head tilted in a way that felt as if she was being mocked. (It probably wasn't the case at all. She was actually a woman who cared deeply for her clients' wellbeing, but her delivery was shocking, and it was just rubbing her up the wrong way. Bitch!! P.S., she didn't really mean that). "You haven't embraced the programme as much as you could've done." She said, matter of factly, with an air that Darcy had convinced herself, was uncaring and cold. She suddenly had the urge to flick shit at her (and no not actual poo, she's not that disgusting. She just meant stuff like…? I don't know… a chair… nah, like pencils and erm …? I dunno, just shit, ok? Use your imagination. They were in a room very much like a classroom. I challenge you – if you were in the same scenario and felt the same frustration, what shit would you imagine throwing at her, without being too nasty? Please do tell. It would be interesting to know. You can send your suggestions via email to: darcywantstoknow13@gmail.com.

Anyway…, back to the story. (Oh dear, and fuck my life and yabba dabba doodle dandy. Ladies, gentleman, as you may have guessed, that statement went down like she was highlighting a complete masterpiece of all Darcy's failures and quite frankly, she wasn't in the fucking mood to admit there was an element of truth to her words.) Right now, she didn't want to admit that 'The Toad' was trying to stop her from making the most regrettable mistake. No, right now, all she could think was, *You fucking CUNT!* (P.S., sorry for the language.) The indignancy of it! She popped her lid. It blew off completely. Every frustration, every resentment spilled out.

"You fucking what? Well seriously, if that's what you think, you old toad, then you can seriously fuck off. I'm sorry for swearing," she added, as an afterthought, "but you can kindly get, absolutely fucked," she said, totally overwhelmed, as she got out of her chair and leaned forward. Tears of anger and injustice flowed freely. She felt inconsolably broken. Everything was too much. It was all becoming such a mess. She was not prepared to listen to someone telling her that she'd not tried, after all the positive changes she'd made (looking back with hindsight, the old goat was completely correct). "If that's what you honestly think, then there's no point in me even being here then, is there?" she said sobbing, as she walked to the door. She could hear them talking, not sure what they were saying, or at that point, even caring, "Nah, I'm done," she said resolutely. "I'm gone. Fuck ya!"

She stormed back to her room, effing and blinding. Arnold and Claire were there. They told her even more devastating news. Finn had been thrown out. She shook her head in disbelief! (I don't know what you were shocked by, ya silly cow, you knew it was coming!) "I'm off." she said, as she went to her room to begin packing her things. "I'M FUCKING GONE!" she shouted, unable to contain her emotions. "I'm not having her, tell me, I ain't tried," she said, as her head went numb. It just wasn't fair. *Why have they done this now? How in God's name is this going to help my recovery, or his, for that matter?* Claire was becoming indignant on her behalf.

"Well, if you're off, then I'm off," said Claire, lost in all the wreckage. "They can't do this," she said, flabbergasted. Arnold again stood there comedically, not knowing what the hell to do, like an amputee who'd not only lost his leg but also his prosthetic one as well. (I'm so sorry, I couldn't find any other words to describe it, and as per usual, it's Darcy's poor attempt at trying to make light of an absolutely shitty situation, by putting her foot in it… oh dear God, Darcy, just STFU. P.S., just another one for the PC police. Please know, in no way, am I or Darcy trying to be horrible towards amputees. We are compassionate and caring people, who have a horrendously dark sense of humour at times. If you can't find the humour in things sometimes, all that there is left to do is to cry and there is no way that's happening. We, and I'm making a blanket statement here; I'm talking to you and anyone else who is having a moment of weakness or disparity – WE, YOU, are stronger than that. Crying is good sometimes, but you know the saying, 'best foot forward and all that'… if you can find it.) It was clear that 'the pack' had been injured significantly by the loss, and it was devastating to see them fold. Or were they trying to stay strong, as if united? What good would all of them leaving do? Nothing, except hurt their recovery.

She was in her room, on the phone with Finn. He was around the corner at the coffee shop, at a loss for what to do, waiting to find out if they were going together, or if he was going to make his way home alone and lost. (What he'd done with his bags or how they expected him to get home at all, she can't recall). The whole thing was a mess that descended into a spiral of thoughts. *What am I doing!? What the actual fuck! Just stick it out… but what about him?* Arnold came into the room. He had a look on his face that she'd never seen before.

He looked almost scared. He looked mournful; he looked…
human? Which smashed her resolve to leave to smithereens.
"Darcy, don't go. Please don't go. You're the glue that's
keeping us all together," he said pleadingly. "Now Finn's
gone as well, Claire's talking about going if you're going. I
can't do this without you lot," he finished sorrowfully.

Wow! she thought, *just wow!* If you'd have told her that
Arnold had ever had the ability to feel that way towards
another human being, she would have told you that you'd
had too much of your nan's sherry. It brought her to her
knees. She didn't know what to say. Did Arnold actually have
a heart? Just the realisation of that made her take stock and
reevaluate everything. She had no idea he held her in such
high esteem. It even felt too big headed to say it to herself.
Just then, 'the toad' came around the corner and knocked on
the open door.

"I'm sorry for swearing at you. I just couldn't believe what
you were saying," she said apologetically. She stopped
packing her bag for a moment and looked up. "I'd like to
stay, if that's possible and finish what I started?" she asked,
smiling slightly in apology. "I'd like to complete the
programme." But nooo, 'the toad' had already sealed her fate.
"No. Sorry Darcy. We've already started your discharge
papers. We can't change it now, you said you wanted to go.
There's nothing I can do."

She couldn't believe it. *WHAT THE ACTUAL FUCK?*
She knew why they were doing it. It was because of her
relationship with Finn, but they couldn't prove it. So why be
so callous and uncaring? Rehab policy stated clearly that they
would always talk people out of leaving where they could.
She was asking to stay, and they were chucking her out, for
what appeared to be no valid or provable reason. It made no
sense. She'd no prior warnings. She'd never even raised her

voice to any of the staff before this, so this seemed like an extreme reaction.

Arnold and Claire were up in arms. It was a mess. Darcy could do nothing but wait for her mum and sister-in-law to arrive. Now anyone who knows Rhianna, will know she is an absolute force to be reckoned with. Ya don't fuck about with her! She was having none of it. She'd already read the policies on the way over and demanded a meeting with the 'big, big boss' for the next day. In the meantime, Darcy said a tearful goodbye to Claire and Arnold, then went to meet Finn, who was still waiting around the corner, looking forlorn. That day she lost complete faith in the system. It was tainted. It only solidified her resolve; she felt even more protective of Finn. They didn't seem to care about what became of him. So, it was down to her to make sure he didn't spiral. That night she stayed with him. "You're going back Darcy. If they let you back, you are going back," he said resolutely. "You've gotta do this for yaself. I love you," he said, kissing her head, making her feel torn. *Absolute BASTARDS, how can they do this to him?* She thought with devotion. *How can they? Yeah, he's an annoying little rule breaker who pushed his luck, but there isn't a bad bone in the man's body.* (Ha-ha, ya think?) She was furious. She was worried. She believed in him, but he felt let down and abandoned, which was basically what had happened. There were so many things that could have been done differently. No aftercare (there was.) He had been given the resources. He could've sought aftercare but there was no transitional process, it was like, "Bye. See ya later. Adios and Adieu." With the door slammed in his face. Could they have dealt with it better? Abso-fucking-lutely!

The next day she kissed him goodbye. She wasn't sure if she would be coming straight back or if rehab were going to let her back in. Rhianna was with Angela, waiting outside to take her back for the meeting. She wasn't sure she wanted to go back now. How was she meant to integrate herself back in, after what they'd done? Finn was all alone, with nothing. They had simply dropped him to the curb, not even making sure he had enough money or resolve to make it through the day, never mind the rest of all time. She thought that they cared, but it was as if it was 'out of sight out of mind'. But he had her. She wasn't giving up so easily. She would see him later, whichever way things worked out.

The meeting went by in a haze. She just sat there numb and let Rihanna do all the talking. Being in the same room as 'the toad', felt like she was being forced to have tea with Hitler. Yes, we know Hitler's dead and yes, the analogy may be a little extreme, however, that's how she felt at the time. It's not how she feels now but then, she fucking hated her. There was no doubt about it; they both acted and reacted in the heat of the moment. That's another thing, ladies and gentlemen, think carefully before you do or say anything, that has the ability to cut deep or cause issues for you or other people, as once you have acted on impulse, it's impossible to take it back. You can only deal with the wreckage it causes. Wounds may heal but they leave scars. I know what I'm trying to say, you know what I'm trying to say. Basically, think before you act. It's just a thought. Anyway, they let her back in. Of course they did. She had technically done nothing wrong. They didn't know about the 'hanky-panky' or the 'smoochie ooh-la-la' happening in room four, after all. They couldn't prove a thing. But nah, she'd given up. She was going to stay and do it for the both of them. However, whatever they said now, felt like it was a load of complete bollocks.

Now I want to take a minute. To anyone who is thinking of seeking help, don't fall into the trap of letting this story taint your view. Just go, embrace the programme and don't fall for a lovable, idiot cockwomble and don't flout the rules, like some idiot baby, who thought he was untouchable. Yes, 'the toad' was wrong to do what she did, but she did it out of love for the group as a whole and for the programme as a collective. Even though Darcy couldn't admit it at the time. There were new people coming for detox every week; it was clear that Darcy and Finn were breaching what the programme stood for. It wasn't setting a good example to any newcomers. Even she had to begrudgingly admit, 'the toad' was actually a pretty amazing woman. However, there is still just the right amount of resentment there, to keep justifying calling her a 'toad'. Rehab is the best experience; you discover so much about yourself there. It's a shame that the aftercare isn't much actual aftercare or follow up. They could deal with that differently, definitely, but alas…Que Sera, Sera. There is only so much resource, funding and staff for such things and these services are working with what they have. They can only do so much, especially when some use the services as a… I can't think of the word or analogy without sounding awful. And I am going to say something anyway. It does not stem from ignorance, nor from a place of being a complete bastard, but it's like when you get some people who use abortion as a means of contraception. Rehab should be used as a last resort. I know what Darcy is trying to say. Maybe she is being too unfiltered when it comes to her analogies, as they are extremely controversial. Just know it's not from a place of judgement. Darcy herself was once in a position where she had to make the heart-wrenching choice regarding abortion, but that is for another story. Maybe she had spent far too much time with Finn, and she too has become an unfiltered idiot? Maybe, aside from the way she presented her views, she does in fact have a point? Some people do stretch the services to breaking point, with no real want for trying to help themselves. It's just a thought.

Moving forward. Things just weren't the same. It was as if the soul had been sucked out of the place. Finn was truly missed. However, life had a funny way of moving on. Darcy, Claire and Arnold became inseparable. Learning sessions were sparse, as they were now expected to fill their own time with outside groups and things that would prepare them for leaving. The staff had been trying to reinforce the notion that planning ahead increased commitments and reduced the risk of relapse. This time was meant to be used as a protective bubble, where they were left to make their own choices, while building their own structure, without relying on staff or peers for support (but with the safety net of knowing they could if they needed to). It was meant to be a transitioning platform, to re-adjust them back into 'normal life'. (Sounds good in theory, doesn't it? If practiced, it works.) However, the bond that the four of them had formed, meant they never did anything alone; they became overly dependent on each other, which did not bode well for when they all finally left.

Finn and Arnold would meet up every day in town, to go to the gym together. Darcy and Claire would chat, or go to groups, and afterwards, they would meet at their usual coffee shop. Finn was so lonely by himself, and Darcy was exhausting herself, running to and fro, going to see him in the evenings for as long as she could, to keep his morale up. She was wearing herself out. Even when she tried telling him, that she was knackered, it didn't occur to him that she was breaking her back to make sure HE was ok. It was wearing thin; he only seemed interested in what he needed, without a thought of what she had to do to get to him each time. She was feeling very displaced and the running about was causing stress and arguments and draining her bank account. The cost in taxis alone, just to go spend an hour with him, were causing the bank managers to sit her down and set up an intervention, that they titled, 'Darcy WTF you doin?' (Just kidding, …if only they did.) She loved the absolute bones of him, but his attitude was starting to make her want to throat punch him, back to the land of 'care-about-someone-else-but-yourself-for-a-change'. In other words, the distance and time was difficult to manage under such stressful circumstances. (Sorry, a bit of Darcy spilled out for a moment. It's not really my place to say Finn was being an absolute baby; selfish idiot; cockwombling, fucking selfish prick. No, HE was just 'struggling').

When they weren't at each other's throats; arguing and talking to each other like shit, seemed to be the way Finn was used to communicating and Darcy was slowly adopting a whole new plethora of language to match his energy; their resolve to be together was strong. She was hoping that he would settle back into the man she knew, when the pressure of her finishing off the programme without him was over, and she blamed the circumstances, for all the niggling she was feeling about them as a couple. She was looking forward to a land of freedom, when they could finally be together, and so was he. He felt trapped in his own bubble, alone at home. So, waiting for her to return back to his side, was like he was waiting for Christmas, with nothing to look forward to at the end, except a life of never drinking again. (Sounds easy, right? But the stuff is absolutely everywhere). It sounded shit. They needed something positive, a celebration to mark the end of an achievement and an era (even though he hadn't completed the programme, he had stayed strong and was determined not to falter, and she was proud of him in spite of his selfishness.)

However resentful Finn felt towards the place, he was determined to be as supportive as his own selfishness would allow. He would tell her he was proud of her, and that he loved her, constantly, he just never backed up any of his words with actions. And you know what 'actions speak', don't ya, ladies and gentlemen? Yes, that's right, 'louder than WORDS'. But anyway, I digress. How the hell does an ex-alcoholic celebrate? With a glass of still water (sparkling if you're feeling a bit cheeky) and a packet of pork scratchings? While ya best mates are disappearing off every five minutes, leaving you alone with some random stranger at the bar, chatting bollocks? To go and have a cheeky line in the toilets. Everyone simply goes about their lives in blissful ignorance of just how hard it is to be like you. She wondered how to mark it, so it felt special? They had come such a long way from the beginning. It had been such a tough slog. What could she do to make it feel lionised?

Then, he said what she was thinking, "I love you," he said, in the coffee shop, in front of Arnold and Claire one day, she could see the giddy mischief swelling inside him. "I wanna do something proper together, after you've finished your rehab. I wanna go on holiday," he said, as his eyes lit up at the genius of his own thoughts. He was bouncing around like all the 'Finn' had rushed back into him all at once, overwhelming her senses and he was full of 'all things bright and beautiful' again.

"Oh, my God, I love you too, that's a fucking great idea," she said, her voice full of excitement again. She'd been nervous about what was going to happen after all this was over. Was he going to feel the same way about her? Did he really mean it when he said he wanted a life together? She second guessed herself constantly. Even though they'd made plans for the future and they hadn't been using protection, on the silly idea of, 'what'll be, will be'. Plus, his conviction that he wanted to be with her forever, still had her thinking, *Is it all going to change in the real world?* (I know! I know. Don't judge me, judge Darcy. Or should we really judge? She was so caught up, so confused and so in love, who are we to judge, really? It's hard not to, isn't it though? You and I can see everything that's wrong in the bigger picture. However, she was too close to it. She wanted to ignore the red flags. (No, again, she was making bunting with them instead – daft cow.) When she had been so unhappy for so long, she had now found someone who challenged her in ways that gave her life purpose. She was taking it. Insecurity and the fear of being left on the shelf to rot, surpassed any kind of common sense.

He'd been so down lately, he was alone and don't forget, folks – time in rehab feels like it is standing still. Nothing had a true timeline to it. Everything felt heightened, emotions and time, were but an illusion. So much could happen in such a short space of time, but it also created a feeling as if no time had passed at all. It was mind-boggling, headfuckingly scary, and now they were apart, and he was sat with his own thoughts, while she was still able to at least share hers with her peers. She felt guilty. He should've been the one to stay for the duration. He needed it more than she did.

"Yeah, I'd definitely go on holiday with you," she said, smiling at his new-found energy.

"I wanna go straight after you've finished here," he said, looking at her, as if to say, 'pleeease?'. "I'm gonna look for a summat now, for the day you leave," he finished, sitting back down, getting his phone out and setting about on his quest, to find the next location for their new adventure.

"I can't do that," she said. He looked as if he was going to start arguing with her. She shook her head at his absolutely beautiful face; looking at the lost, puppy-eyed pleading and disappointed look he gave her. "Finn, what about getting packed and shit? I wanna go but think! Don't forget...," she said, sounding slightly pissed off that he never ever thought anything through. "You've been home and got your shit sorted," she said to him exasperated. She wanted to go but she'd never 'just done' anything like this, on a whim before. It was a massive step. Her face began to flush, as the angel and devil inside her, argued like fuck with each other, before she shook her head in a 'wowzer' moment, of what she was about to say. "Ok, ok, let's do it," she said, feigning excitement. She wanted to match his energy but for all the desire to be able to feel more carefree, he needed to be more methodical. "Look for the day after, then it gives me time."

Well, ladies and gentlemen, they booked it, packed it and in a few short days' time, Darcy and Finn were gonna fuck off. It was against her better judgment. She wanted to go away with him, but Jesus! When he first mentioned it, it sounded like a good idea, but the booking process alone had her wanting to murder him. Holidays are dangerous enough as it is but with two alcoholics, fresh out of rehab? What the hell were they thinking? Hindsight is the biggest bitch you've ever met. (Don't temp fate, Darcy love, you've not met Helga yet.) However, it can give you so much clarity on things (yeah, but that's not always a good thing, when she realises what a muppet she is. Hindsight can, in fact, fuck right off. Give her back those rose-coloured gigs. Let her live in denial for a bit longer.) It was too soon. But that's a story for another time.

Over the next few days, Darcy seemed to be content in her own bubble. Keeping away from the staff as much as she could. She was so bitter. It wasn't supposed to be like this. It simply wasn't the same. She got on with it as best she could, but she cut her nose off to spite her face. It was a dangerous mindset. However, trying to juggle Finn and rehab, felt like choosing a side. It was simple. She chose him (I can hear you screaming at the page about how much of an idiot she was being, but alas, she can't hear you). The way he had been discarded, felt like something she would never come back from. The system failed him. It was as simple as that. There were so many good things that she now refused to admit, such as: it gave her a family; a group of people who understood her more than the world. It taught her coping mechanisms she still uses to this day and still looks back on fondly. It gave her hope, love and understanding. There was so much. Do not despair though. You know one thing for sure – she is still alive (she must be to have gone through the next two and a half years, and let's not forget, she hasn't yet met that hell spawn, we mentioned at the beginning (Helga. For fuck's sake, don't say the name too many times, she might come out from behind her fence and start throwing stones again). So, that's one thing to be grateful for, I suppose? 'Every cloud…' and all that.

Her resolve for finding a life outside of addiction, was stronger than words can say. She wanted it. She now felt as if she had a purpose. Even when she was feeling weak, she had Finn to confide in. When she felt like she would falter, though, she couldn't say anything. There was the fear of being treated like a butterfly, every time she voiced her feelings, holding her back. Sometimes she felt as though people would think she was going to shatter into smithereens and go on a drink and drug-fuelled rampage. Some days she would find strength for herself, even if it was simply to keep him strong. She was not going to admit she was struggling as much as she was, not so much with the idea of falling off the wagon but all the extra thoughts that came with sobriety. *What do I do now? Who am I really? Am I going to be ok?*

It was time to embark on a new journey. One where she was her own master and they could find strength in recovery together. She wanted this to work so badly, it was beyond words. It was time to rebuild her relationships with her children. They had been so supportive. (I know she hasn't gone into too much detail about them. However, they were there and proud of her, plus, she is trying to keep some of it private) but she no longer knew where she fit into their lives. She wanted to nurture and care for them, as if there had been no time passed but she knew she couldn't be selfish with them. She still had Finn. She knew how much he loved her, but he was hard work. She was starting to wonder if it was going to work between them (in other words, he was doing her fucking head in).

The holiday now loomed like a black cloud. However, *where we're going, it will be sunny and warm, so there is always a brighter side,* she thought to herself. Trying to enjoy the last day at rehab, was overwhelming. It was full of tears. Everyone felt out of sorts and muddled up. It was the end of an era. She was going to miss everyone (even 'the toad') but Claire and Arnold? The thought of not seeing them every day, made her brain hurt. She had learnt so much through this process, and as far as she knew, had made life-long friends. She still had the final affirmation (a speech that she had to read out to the entire house and all the friends and families of the leavers. Her mum, son and sister-in-law and her niece, as well as Finn were going to be there.) The powers that be, had allowed him to join his group for the final goodbye. Unfortunately, her daughter wasn't allowed to be there because she was under sixteen. How she was going to make it through, without shedding a few tears, she didn't know. Saying goodbye was going to be one of the hardest things she would do. (Well, it wasn't, but the emotions it stirred, even now, fill her eyes with salty tears). She had loved the discovery and the feeling of such belonging, and she had suffered the pain of seeing first hand, that breaking the rules had painful wrath.

She started to write down what she wanted to say so many times, before scrunching up the paper and throwing it in the bin. It was all just too much. How could she start to write about the place and people who meant so much, especially when it was competing with the very recent memory of being let down so badly at the end? In reality, the resentment she held onto wasn't really her burden to bear, was it? No, it was Finn's. But she was his advocate, and she felt so hurt on his behalf. Most nights, when she had gone to see him, he looked like a lost puppy, knowing she would be going back to the one place that truly felt like home for him, and she felt so protective of him, knowing that he had felt betrayed. In reality it was the dickhead's own fault, but still, she had managed to throw something coherent together.

They all piled into the church next door, for the final affirmation because there were too many people to fit into any of the rooms of rehab. The number of friends and family who came to support the group on the last day, was nice to see. Everyone had support on the outside. She felt content seeing how proud Claire's daughter was of her mother and Arnold's partner, who was a petite woman, looked happy to see the change in him.

Her final affirmation read:

'I want to start by saying thank you, to each and every one of you, for all for the love, support and understanding I have received during my stay.

'When I first entered through these doors, I was lost. Even though I had my family, it felt like I would never find my way. I had fallen down the darkest hole, with no torch to help me see my way out. It felt infinite, like there would never again be a light at the end of the tunnel. Then, as the poison left my body, I felt like I had nothing left to build upon. Where did I go from there?

'Through the rehabilitation process, I slowly started to believe again. In myself, in the kindness and compassion of other people and in the idea that there is life, beyond the hellish and tortuous wreckage that drugs and alcohol have brought to my life. In the Groundhog Day that I had become so content in entrapping myself in. I did all of this to cover up the pain of the past. I abused myself daily, thinking that I wasn't worth anything. I have found there is pleasure and growth in pain. Working through my trauma as best I can. With the help of all you amazing people. The staff, my little rehab family, my real family and let's not forget Finn, the naughty boy, whose journey was cut short through…, well, let's not go into all that, we don't need to go through that little shit show again, do we? (Sorry for swearing). I have learnt that there is a woman worth knowing. I don't want to leave you all with doom and gloom. There has been a lot of shits and giggles (sorry for swearing). The organic laughter of the karaoke night we had, where the staff joined in. And the yoga session with Cindy and Finn, in the TV room, where Moss actually looked up from his laptop and saw us all in the most compromising positions. These are all memories I will cherish forevermore.

I have learnt so much and taken so many positive things from this. I would honestly do it all over again if I had to. Not that I'm tryna poke at the bear with a sharp stick, because, no offense, I will be glad to see the back of that chapter in my life. I only hope to see you all again, under positive circumstances, however, I doubt you'd let me back, as I've not been easy have I? Anyway, *thank you so, so much. You will all be with me forevermore. You've no idea what you've done for me. You've given me my life back. Thank you. Yeah, just thank you.'*

It was the most emotional goodbye. It felt weird when the meeting finished, she was no longer a 'client' if you will. There was nothing more to it, other than to say goodbye. (Obviously, she broke all the rules again, by swapping numbers with everyone before she left. She already had Arnold and Claire's (of course she did). Now, she had to finish her day by going home and facing, not just an empty house (Thwaite had gone. What he had taken in the process; she was yet to discover) but her family as well.

The idea that the end had come and she was now free to make her own choices, with nobody holding the reins, was freaking her out. She was going to leave rehab just as scared, if not more so, than when she entered. Now she had no excuses. Now she had so much to prove. She was scared of what was to be. She'd missed her family and friends so much, but nobody knew who she was anymore, except for her rehab family. It was as if she would have to reintroduce herself to the people she had known a lifetime, and convince them of who she was now, when they knew the person she was before.

She saw Finn briefly, before she said goodbye to him at the coffee shop. She had to go home and face the music and pack for the holiday she was looking forward to but dreading all at once. Seeing her family come and support her felt amazing. Having her son by her side, was everything she needed. She was leaving a whole new person. She didn't know it yet, but she went in as a lost soul and found another in Finn. Had they made three? In other words, the silly cow was pregnant!

TO BE CONTINUED…

ABOUT THE AUTHOR

Ria Tocsin is a new author with a hilariously, colloquial, unique style of writing. What started as a ranting journal, soon morphed into this autofiction, memoir style, offering you see today.

She has experienced a difficult and traumatic life, culminating in over ten years battling an alcohol and drug addiction. There is no cure for addiction, and her writing has helped her face and banish the demons that contributed to her downwards spiral.

Now facing the ever-difficult challenge of sobriety in an environment where temptations are a daily presence, she hopes these fictionalised accounts of her struggles, hopes, dreams and achievements, will help others in similar situations to also find hope in a hopeless place.

She lives in the UK with her Gremlins and is busy writing the follow up books in this debut collection.

USEFUL RESOURCES

Now, here are a few resources, which you may find useful. However, I do not claim to be an expert in any of them. These are mostly based in the UK, however, if you have read this book in a different country, know that there are so many more out there. I'm sure if you did a quick Google search, you would find many more in your local area, however, to get you started, I have done a little research of my own. (Just a quick side note, without sounding condescending.) If you are looking to seek help, then you've got this. Good luck. You can do this. If you are in a serious crisis, then please call 111 or go to your local hospital accident and emergency.

Mind's Support Line – 0300 102 1234
This is a safe space for you to talk about your mental health. Their advisors are trained to listen to you and help to find specialist support if needed. Open from 9am–6pm

Website: **www.mind.org.uk**

The Samaritans – Call 116 123 free from any phone
Open 24 hours a day, 365 days a year. It's a call line for if you're in distress and need someone to talk to. They will listen without prejudice.

Website: **Samaritans | Every life lost to suicide is a tragedy | Here to listen**.

Narcotics Anonymous
Narcotics Anonymous UK – 0300 999 1212
Open 10amMidnight. A drug and alcohol organisation who help recovering addicts from all walks of life, as long as you have the want to get clean, then they will aid you. Just use the links below and you will be able to find a local meeting near you, an online one if you can't get there face to face. They are just for today. They are excellent. However, you need to have the desire to change. They offer sponsorship if you wish to do the twelve

steps. All the information is right there at your fingertips.

Websites: **www.na.org** or **www.ukna.org**

National Domestic Abuse Helpline – 0808 2000 247
Chat hours: Mon-Fri, 10am-10pm

Website: **www.nationaldahelpline.org.uk/**

Other Useful Websites:
www.nhs.uk/live-well/addiction-support/drug-addiction-getting-help/

www.talktofrank.com/get-help/find-support-near-you

www.betterhelp.com
There is no GP referral needed. It's a service where they tailor make a specific therapist for your individual needs.

Printed in Dunstable, United Kingdom